To Mom and Dad.

For all the big, obvious reasons; but mostly for all the small, significant ones that make all the difference.

Also by Teri Harman:

Blood Moon, Book I of The Moonlight Trilogy

THE MOONLIGHT WITCHES

The New Light Covenant

Rowan
*Gift of Earth, Luminary (leader),
married to Wynter*

Wynter
Gift of Earth

Willa
*Gift of Dreams with the Power of
Spirits*

Simon
Gift of Mind and a True Healer

Elliot
Gift of Dreams

Charlotte
Gift of Mind

Darby
Gift of Fire, married to Cal

Cal
Gift of Fire

Rain
Gift of Water

Corbin
Gift of Water

Hazel
Gift of Air

Toby
Gift of Air

The Light Witches of Early Twelve Acres

Ruby Plate
*Gift of Mind, founder of Twelve Acres,
Luminary of the first American Light
Covenant. Married to Charles Plate.*

Amelia Plate
*Gift of Water, granddaughter of Ruby
and Charles. Married to Peter Wilson,
daughter named Lilly. Luminary of
the Covenant after Ruby's death.*

Camille Krance
*Gift of Air, also a founder of Twelve
Acres and member of Ruby's original
Covenant. Married to Ronald Krance,
mother of Solace.*

Solace Krance
*Gift of Mind, member of the Light
Covenant under Amelia's leadership.
Daughter of Camille and Ronald.
Ghost in Twelve Acres Museum.*

THE DARK WITCHES

Archard
Gift of Fire, leader of the Dark covens.

Rachel
Gift of Fire, the only surviving member of the Dark covens.

Holmes
Gift of Mind, the witch who held Wynter hostage. Wynter killed him after she escaped.

Bartholomew the Dark
An infamous Dark witch during medieval times, the only Dark witch to ever form a Covenant. Married to Brigid.

Black Moon

The Moonlight Trilogy

II

TERI HARMAN

JOLLY
FISH
PRESS
Provo, Utah

On the rare occasion that two new moons occur in one calendar month, the second new moon is known to witches as a black moon. It is a time of Darkness, when the evil of magic thrives with the gift of extra power awarded by the obsidian sky.

On this night, Dark witches rise.

CHAPTER 1
WANING GIBBOUS

January 500 A.D.

The bookmaker bent over his worktable, forehead pinched in concentration, eyes straining in the candlelight. In his calloused, ink-stained hand, he held a knife, small and sharp. One by one he lifted the dried goat hides onto the table. With practiced precision, he cut each exactly sixteen inches tall and thirty-two inches long. When folded over, each piece would make two pages. It was delicate work, but the thin, soft hides made the smoothest parchment. And only the best could be used for this book.

He paused for a moment to wipe the sweat from his corrugated brow and rub the exhaustion from his eyes. Through three days of nearly nonstop work, he'd barely dared to sleep or eat, even when the smell of lime wafting off the hides stung his eyes or he grew dizzy from lack of food. If his customer arrived and the book was not finished (and perfect), there would be far worse things to suffer than hunger and watery eyes.

Finally, he cut and stacked the last page.

Carefully, the craftsman mixed his special red ink and sharpened his quill to a deadly point. He pulled the top piece of parchment from the stack and, with his ruler in place, began to line the page. Line after line after line. This task was usually done by an apprentice scribe, but the customer had insisted that no other hands touch it.

Line after line after line after line after . . .

When dawn breathed light into the sky, the craftsman slumped over the last page, half asleep. When the cock crowed, he jerked awake in a moment of panic. A quick look around the room set his heart at ease.

He gathered the lined pages and his binding materials. His stomach twisted with hunger, but with a sigh the craftsman set back to work. He folded the first few pages and nestled them into gatherings, or sections of pages. Once the gatherings were prepared, he skillfully sewed them onto the cords of leather that would support the pages.

Near midday he finally paused for a quick meal of stale bread and hard cheese. With the last bite still in his mouth, he returned to his workbench. When he finished the sewing, the craftsman prepared to form the book. From a high shelf he pulled two thin wooden planks. Carefully, he laced the ends of the leather supports though channels carved into the cover planks.

The bookmaker worked hard to keep his mind on his task, forbidding himself to wonder what this book might be meant for; but it was nearly impossible—considering the man who would own it. He'd heard the rumors, the hushed speculations about the mysterious man known as Bartholomew. Some said he had burned an entire town to the ground with the townspeople trapped inside, unable to escape. Others said he never aged. And some even whispered the word *witch* in fearful tones.

When the tall man with shadows in his face had walked into the shop, the craftsman's bones had turned to ice; and he knew instantly who stood before him. Bartholomew was everything and nothing like what he'd expected. But his voice—like foul whispers from hell spun into silk—had haunted the craftsman every moment since that day.

Another rumor flew around in whispers: Bartholomew was gathering others like him, forming some sort of terrible coven. The bookmaker loved and cherished every book he made; he longed to protect his art, but feared this book would be put to unspeakable uses. He knew, deep inside, that this one book would forever taint his legacy.

Yet refusal was not an option. He'd known that, looking at Bartholomew's intense, otherworldly eyes.

The old craftsman, his back aching, stretched a thick piece of high quality black leather over the cover planks and secured it with several small tacks. Next, he placed the metal corner pieces, meant to protect the soft leather but also to serve as ornamentation. Bartholomew himself had provided these pieces, and the bookmaker tried hard to ignore how each one felt warm to the touch.

He secured two large metal clasps to the back of the book, each with a thick leather strap attached which wrapped around the fore edge and slid into clasps on the cover to keep the book closed. The final detail, a round metal medallion for the center of the front cover, was also warm, almost hot. Several unsettling symbols were etched into the metal. On the outside of the circle, arrayed around the middle, were six odd triangles. In the center were two more symbols: a sun with curved rays spiraling outward, and three ovals stacked on top of each other, progressively larger in size, with a single line running down through the center of them all.

The craftsman let his hands drop.

Finished.

The impressive but sadistic book was complete. As the bookmaker stood up from his chair and stretched, his body felt brittle and hard, like dried wax. Looking down at his work—some of his finest—he felt like crying. A chill moved through him as he ran a stiff hand over the cover. Normally, he would brand his mark on the back to claim his work, but not on this book. He pulled a cloth from a drawer and covered the tome.

The sun had nearly set. The craftsman, exhausted but unable to sleep with the perverse book in his home, collapsed into the chair by the fire. He watched the flames, his eyes blurry and heart heavy.

The door of the shop burst open.

The old man jumped in his chair, but did not turn to see his visitor; he knew. Bartholomew had returned to collect his book.

"Is it finished?" asked a voice like burning velvet.

The craftsman couldn't speak but merely gestured to where the tome sat beneath its cloth, like the dead. The stranger's footfalls were barely audible on the wooden floor, but the craftsman heard every little noise—the whisper of the cloth falling to the floor, the *brush* of Bartholomew's gloves as he lifted the book, and his deep *hum* of pleasure as he stroked the cover.

The craftsman cringed, his heart aching.

Then the tall, shadowy figure stood next to his chair. He dared a glance at Bartholomew's face. The eyes were like small moons, nearly silver and luminous like marsh lights. The skin was pale, almost the same color as the parchment in the book, but flushed with a healthy vigor. Bartholomew's long hair, dark blond, like wheat at harvest time, was pulled back from his face and his neatly-trimmed beard. If not for the air of evil that pulsed from him, Bartholomew might have been handsome.

The craftsman looked back at the flames.

"Fine work, bookmaker," Bartholomew whispered in his velvet voice.

The craftsman didn't respond. All he could think about was sleep; beautiful, restful sleep.

"You deserve to sleep, old man. Your work is finished." Bartholomew removed one of his black gloves and placed his hand on the craftsman's chest.

The old man felt his heart thump once, then stop.

His soul drifted off to sleep.

CHAPTER 2
WAXING HALF MOON

February—Present Day

Normally, Willa woke from dreams in the middle of the night, but tonight it was Simon.

His eyes flashed open, a gargled cry caught in his throat. Instinctively, he reached out for Willa, but the bed was empty. He wished she *were* there. She was the only thing that helped calm the storm inside him; but, of course, she was across town at her parents' house.

With a long sigh, he rolled onto his back. His heart beat furiously, blood pulsing at his temples. *Only a dream.* He stared at the shadows on the ceiling, forcing his mind and body to believe it. *Only a dream.* He turned his head and looked at his phone on the nightstand. He could call her; hearing her voice would help. But what would he say? He'd established a strict rule of not talking about this with anyone—even her. He'd built a thick wall to hide his emotions.

Simon shifted his eyes to the window and the glow of the street lamps outside. Sparsely decorated, the bedroom in his small apartment had only a practical double bed, one night-stand, and a squat lamp. A large closet doubled as storage for both his clothes and hiking and camping gear. One picture hung on the wall: a framed 8 x 10 of him and Willa in the mountains, taken on one of their summer hikes. Simon loved the picture because Willa's eyes were the same color as the sky above them.

She should be here.

Every night, it got harder to send her home to her parents. It felt wrong to watch her walk into another house and sleep in a bed without him. But Willa's parents had reverted to over-protective mode ever since the binding of the Covenant. They hovered over her like she might shatter into a million pieces, or as though she might be brainwashed by the "witches in that cult," as her dad was fond of saying. Willa let it slide and dismissed it as a knee-jerk reaction to nearly losing her in the fight with Archard. But, now, four months later, they hadn't eased up; and it weighed on them all.

However hard it was to let her go each night, however much he longed to be with her all the time, Simon would be patient while Willa and her family worked things out. He wished his own parents cared enough to overprotect him.

Cynthia and Gabe Howard's faces moved through his mind: Cynthia, with her sharply angled face made sharper by her blunt haircut and fake blond hair, and Gabe, with his pinched, judgmental eyes and villainously muscular body.

There were few people more poorly suited to be parents, especially of a boy who heals injuries and illnesses alike with a mere touch.

Simon wondered briefly if he should visit and tell them about his magic and what had happened in the fall. He almost laughed out loud, knowing that it wouldn't make one bit of difference. *By the way, Mom and Dad, I'm a witch.* It would only alienate them more—if that were possible. Simon closed his eyes and tried to banish his parents from his mind.

Rolling his head to the side, Simon looked at the empty space beside him, picturing Willa asleep there. His heart thudded once. *You're my family now, Willa.* The thought made him smile in the dark. The hole inside him was finally filling in, the hole his parents had dug with every dismissal, every disapproving look, and every hateful thought that Simon had sensed. Willa helped him believe there was life beyond that of a pariah.

As his mind wandered, the scene from his dream broke through his thoughts, erasing his smile.

With a sigh Simon eased out of the bed and pulled on jeans, a t-shirt, and a hoodie. He shoved on his black biker boots and left. Out in the cold winter night, he forced himself to go back through the dream and to examine every part of it. If he was going to rid himself of the nightmare that had troubled him for the last four months, he had to face it, understand it, and move past it.

But how? This isn't just a dream; this is . . . something I did.

Simon shuffled down the sidewalk. The biting cold felt good on his face, cleared his mind and pushed away the fear.

Three people. I killed three people.

The words rang with a hollow twang across his brain, discordant and foreign. They didn't fit into the puzzle of things that made him *him*. He still wasn't sure how he'd done it. The moments at the cave were a blur in his head, coming back clearly only in his dreams. As soon as he woke, the details clouded over again as quickly as a coastline in the rainy season.

Several times, after awaking from the dreams, he had walked like this and then stopped to try and summon that power again, to make his body alive with the energy of so much magic; but it never happened. Not even close. It made the whole thing seem even more unreal.

I killed three people.

The justifications always followed: the 'but they were evil Dark witches,' and the 'I was protecting Wynter, Willa, and my coven-mates,' and the 'I *had* to.' But they too were hollow, like twisted echoes of truth.

His stomach knotted uncomfortably as he remembered the Dark witches sailing through the air. He'd never seen them hit the ground—his attention had turned fully to Willa, her startling blue eyes bright in the rainy clearing, like little lighthouses, pulling him away from the rocks. Only later did he realize what he'd done

Willa wanted to talk about it. He felt it from her more often than she intended, but he couldn't bring himself to put his thoughts into words. Spoken words were real, were truth. Thoughts lived somewhere on the edge of truth, and that's where he needed to keep this.

Rowan, leader of the Covenant, had also come to him, wanting to talk, to help. When Simon had answered Rowan's questions with silence and pleading eyes, Rowan had simply laid a hand on his shoulder and said, "When you're ready."

Simon didn't know if he would *ever* be ready. If he just

worked it out in his mind, made sense of it, he'd be fine. It would take time, but eventually . . . maybe . . .

But these dreams . . .

They kept everything fresh, and they twisted his confusion into tighter knots. These dreams might drive him crazy. *How does Willa deal with this all the time?*

Simon walked through the playground behind his apartment complex, through cold gray shadows. He stopped to sit on a bench, suddenly exhausted. A heavy and smothering sense of desperation settled over him, and the knot in his stomach tightened. He would not attempt to summon the power tonight. Just the thought made his arms hang heavy.

The worst part of what he had done was the loss of control. Simon hated not being in control, especially of himself. Despite the inherent craziness of his life and what he could do, he liked order and control. He worked hard to keep things well in hand. But this . . . this was slippery.

What if it happened again? What if, somehow, that explosion of blue power came back? What if someone else got hurt because of it?

What if it's Willa?

A shiver moved through him. He dropped his head into his hands, with his elbows on his knees.

Not that they were likely to battle any Dark witches soon. Archard died at the cave—burned by his own raging fire—and his covens were broken. Simon and Willa only had to worry about school and training for the Elemental Challenge coming up in the summer, a rite of passage, and something all witches in a True Coven must do to prove their abilities. If he and Willa passed, they'd earn the title of True Witch like their coven-mates.

Simon looked forward to the challenge, but even his powers during training were beginning to make him nervous. Everything came so easily, and no skill seemed hard to master. *Something* should be hard or take some concentrated practice, but the only thing hard was trying to hold back, hiding his true capabilities just to avoid the worried glances in his direction.

I can't even be normal when it comes to magic. Wynter, Rowan's wife, had told him that he seemed to have *two* Gifts: his Mind gift and his healing ability, which normally came with the Gift of Water. Having multiple gifts wasn't supposed to be possible, and no one could explain it—not even Rowan and Wynter. Inside him, the convoluted mix of power he didn't understand and couldn't predict worsened by what he'd done that night at the cave, coalesced into fear—fear of himself, lurking in the back of his mind, out of reach but lingering, like a bad taste.

He ran a hand back over his hair, the blond curls bouncing back into place. *Maybe my parents were right. Maybe I am nothing but a freak.*

Cold and tired, he walked slowly back around the complex, his eyes on the ground, hands shoved deep in his pockets. He didn't look up until he started up the front walk to his unit. Sitting on the front steps, he found Willa, a blanket wrapped around her and fuzzy leopard-print slippers on her feet. Her wavy chestnut hair was an attractive mess around her rosy-cheeked face. She smiled as he approached. Suddenly Simon didn't feel cold anymore.

She yawned sleepily. "I had a dream that you were walking."

He half smiled and sat beside her. "I had a dream, too."

"Wanna talk about it?"

Simon put an arm around her and pulled her close, a layer

of comfort. She dropped her head to his shoulder. "Not really, but I'm okay now," he whispered, lying to them both. A wave of disappointment moved from her to him.

"Want me to stay? I can sneak back in my house early, before my parents wake up."

He kissed her hair. "Yes, please."

Willa looked up at his troubled, tired eyes and touched his cheek. "I'm here."

THE NEXT DAY, AFTER HER classes at the university, Willa stopped at the Twelve Acres Museum, which housed a small but impressive collection of town artifacts in the old Town Hall building. She needed to catch up on some filing that the curator, Bill Bentley, had asked her to do. She'd been volunteering at the Museum since eighth grade and knew the collection and history as well as he did. Bill had told her on several occasions that he hoped she'd take his place one day.

After chatting with the receptionist, Bertie, for a minute or two, Willa went to the cramped, stuffy back office. It was freezing, and she flipped on the space heater before dropping her bag and navy blue pea coat to the floor. She grabbed the pile of papers from the desk, plopped them in the seat of the chair, and rolled it over to the filing cabinet.

As she worked, Willa's mind wandered to her night with Simon. Her dream about him had been far more complicated than she'd let on. In the dream, she'd watched Simon walk down an empty sidewalk suspended in a black void. But he wasn't alone. A menacing shadow followed only a few feet behind, its form constantly shifting and morphing so that

Willa could never identify it. She'd woken just as the shadow reached out to grasp Simon's shoulder.

She'd immediately gotten up and snuck out of the house, knowing he needed her—and that he probably wouldn't talk about what was really bothering him. It'd been four months—almost to the day—since the battle at the cave, since Rachel had stabbed Willa, Charlotte, and Elliot, and taken Simon hostage; since Simon and Wynter had been imprisoned in the cave; and since Archard nearly killed Wynter just to see Simon heal her. Four months since Simon summoned a power no one seemed to understand, to free himself and Wynter, killing their captors in the process.

Willa tucked a paper into a file and moved to the next drawer.

She knew it was eating him up inside, his healing nature in upheaval because of what he'd done. Simon fixed things, never broke them; and it didn't matter why he'd done it, or even that he'd *had* to do it—it still hurt him. So then why wouldn't he say anything? Their relationship was based on talking about the strangeness and on being open about how confusing it was to be witches; but something about this was untouchable. And the not-talking left a constant phantom pain in the bottom of Willa's heart.

"Willa the Witch!"

Willa jumped and almost screamed. Lost in her thoughts, hearing the sudden sound of Solace's shrill voice, Willa dropped a file, scattering papers everywhere. "Solace! How many times have I told you *not* to sneak up on me like that?"

The ghost laughed, her round face, framed by chin-length blonde hair, flickering in and out of focus. "But it's just too entertaining!" She leaned against the desk, arms folded. She wore an early 1930's style dress: straight silhouette, dark purple, short sleeves, and playful organza ruffles at the collar. "I *am* sorry about the papers, though."

Willa smiled. "Oh, sure you are."

Solace smiled back, pale blue eyes sparkling. "I like your sweater. Black is a good color on you."

Willa threw the mess of papers on the desk and then pulled the bottom of her black v-neck sweater down over the top of her boot cut jeans. "Changing the subject? Well, thanks, I like it, too. I got it last week when Simon took me to dinner at that great Indian place in Denver."

"Sounds fun. Sure wish there was a way for me to leave this place and come with you on your dates." Solace frowned as she looked around the bleak office. "I get so *sick* of this place. Why do ghosts have to be stuck in one place? Why can't we roam free?"

"Why? So you can go around screaming in people's ears?" Willa teased, but Solace didn't smile.

"It'd just be nice to leave." The ghost averted her eyes, looking down at her black Mary-Janes.

Willa sighed. "I know, Solace. I'm sorry."

After another beat of silence, Solace looked up. "So, what scandalous thought were you lost in when I snuck up on you?" She added a waggle of her eyebrows.

Willa shook her head and turned back to the filing cabinet. "Sorry, nothing scandalous. I'm just worried about Simon."

"Hmm. What is it now? Is he *still* not talking about the whole killing people thing?"

Willa shot her a look. "No, he's not, but he's still having nightmares about it. Last night I snuck out to see him, and he was so . . ." She paused, his face flashing in her mind. "So sad, I guess. I hate to see him like that. And these nightmares are wearing on him. No one understands that better than I do."

"He did what he had to do."

"Yeah, but this is Simon. It's not as simple as that."

"Yes, I know," Solace said quietly. For a moment there was only the sound of Willa moving papers, and then the ghost said, "I'm sure he'll talk to you when he's ready."

Willa frowned. "That's what I keep telling myself. But I don't like it. It doesn't feel right."

Solace frowned, nodding thoughtfully. "Because it *isn't* right. Not for him, for you, or for your relationship. It'll drive a wedge between you."

Willa looked up. Sometimes Solace was more insightful than she expected. A seed of fear grew in Willa's mind, one she'd yet to acknowledge, the fear that this would, in fact, be a problem between her and Simon. She shook her head, turned back to the files. "I don't think anything could ever really drive us apart, but . . ."

"But it will change things." Solace lifted her eyebrows and leaned forward, giving Willa a knowing look. "Because he won't let it out, and you won't let it go."

Turning back to the files, avoiding Solace's gaze, Willa mumbled, more to herself than to her friend, "That's what I'm afraid of." Perhaps mostly that it would change Simon, *permanently.* Her hands froze over the files. *Has it already?*

Solace inhaled loudly and then clicked her tongue, "What about your parents? Any improvement on the home front?"

Willa rolled her eyes, and, as if on cue, her phone buzzed. She picked it up off the desk and read the text from her mom. *Did you go to the museum? When are you coming home?* Willa scoffed and shoved the open file drawer closed. Then she dropped into the old swivel chair and stared at the phone. "It's getting ridiculous, Solace." She typed a quick reply. "They've always been really protective, and we've always been close. I get it—I'm their only kid. But they refuse to let go of how things used to be."

Solace rolled a ballpoint pen back and forth on the desktop. Solace was the only ghost in the museum who could touch things, move things. She read books, hid Willa's phone on occasion, and often moved an artifact to a different display case when she was bored—much to Mr. Bentley's dismay. Willa figured it had something to do with the fact that Solace was also a witch, as Willa had discovered in the fall.

"So what are you going to do?" Solace asked.

Willa dropped her head back and sighed heavily. "I have no idea. Things are rough between me and my mom. She keeps trying to make up for not telling me who I was all my life by being overly nice. And my dad . . . well, he's in total denial. Some days he barely looks at me." She put her phone on the desk, spun it around, fighting a sudden rise of emotion in her throat. "Part of me just wants to storm out, tell them I'm moving in with Simon, and living on my own like a normal adult. But . . ."

"But?" Solace flicked the pen and watched it roll off the edge of the desk.

Willa bent down, picked up the pen, and threw it back among the papers. Quietly, she said, "I don't want to hurt them anymore than I already have. Even if the Covenant feels right to me, I don't want to ruin things with my parents over it." Looking at her hands, she added, "I don't want to end up like Simon."

Solace folded her hands in her lap. "I wonder how my parents and I got along? I can see both their faces in my mind"—she closed her eyes—"and sometimes I almost think I can hear their voices, but then . . ." She opened her eyes, now marked with sadness. "But then it's gone."

Willa's heart ached for her friend. Not only was Solace trapped in the museum for an unknown reason, but she couldn't remember any details of her life, not even her death. "I'm sorry, Solace. I wish I could help you remember."

She shrugged. "At least I have a few of my mother's grimoires, right?"

Willa smiled. Camille Krance's grimoires, given to Wynter and Rowan while visiting her in Italy before her death, had become Solace's new favorite reading material. She'd been through them at least six times. Willa said, "I just wish we could figure out what the Lilly references mean. Maybe we aren't such good mystery solvers after all." Willa had discovered the vague references to a person named Lilly when Wynter gave her Camille's grimoires in the fall. But no one seemed to know anything about this person Camille was supposedly protecting or hiding . . . or both.

Solace pursed her lips, picked up the pen and twiddled it in her hands. "Well, that's because you never read *Sherlock Holmes* like I told you to."

Willa laughed, shook her head. Her eyes caught on the small clock hanging crookedly on the wall. "Holy moon!" She jumped up and grabbed her coat and bag. "Sorry, Solace, I gotta go. Training."

"Oh, of course. Wish I were going." She rolled her eyes and then smiled. "Have fun!"

Willa, half way out the door, pushed her head back into the

room. "You've read *Sherlock* like twenty times. How come *you* can't figure out who Lilly is?" She grinned, lifted an eyebrow in a mocking expression.

Solace huffed, threw the pen at the door, and disappeared.

CHAPTER 3
BLOOD MOON

October 1931

Ripples of Dark magic pulsed through the gloomy pre-dawn air, so repugnant that the stars turned out their lights. Camille Krance ran, pressing a precious and blanket-wrapped bundle to her chest. Tears dripped from her eyes, turning to ice on her cheeks in the cold October air. Terror and grief churned in her stomach and weakened her limbs.

Solace! My sweet, Solace!

The ground was hard beneath her slippered feet, and her long flannel nightgown was a poor hedge against the biting cold. Her face throbbed where a Dark witch had beaten her, with one of her stone-blue eyes already swollen shut and her gut sharply sore where she'd been kicked. Half of her graying blonde hair had pulled out of its braid and was matted to her forehead, cheeks, and neck. But she thought little about her own condition. At least Amelia's baby was warm and content to sleep as Camille bobbed through the trees.

Horrible thoughts raced through her mind as she ran, visions of the night's Dark events choking her.

Why?! Why my Solace?

Camille couldn't help wishing her daughter's terrible fate had fallen on someone else, anyone else. She'd waited so long for Solace, sacrificed so much to be her mother, and now . . . She couldn't bring herself to think the devastating words. If only she had fled Twelve Acres weeks ago, as soon as the trouble began, she might have protected her daughter. The desire to flee had been so strong, especially after Amelia's husband and the others had been killed. *I should have listened to myself.* But she and her husband, Ronald, had a duty to the Covenant, to Ruby's legacy. But this sacrifice . . .

Our daughter, our perfect little girl.

After the Dark witches had left her beaten and sobbing, Camille had taken Amelia's baby to the safety of Town Hall. There, in the dark of the Covenant's chamber, she'd hurried to perform a spell. The kind she hated, dreaded. But she was so desperate to do something—anything—for Solace. If she couldn't save her daughter's life, perhaps she could help her soul find peace.

With trembling hands, Camille lit a single black candle, placed it on top of Solace's favorite book, *Sense and Sensibility* by Jane Austen, and chanted the words she hoped would guide Solace's soul away from wherever the Dark covens had taken her. Murdered souls were forever trapped in the place of their death. The idea that her daughter would spend eternity locked inside the last horrible moments of her life made Camille sick.

She turned and vomited. After wiping her mouth with the back of her hand, she continued her chant.

The room filled with waves of hot and cold magic, churning all around her. Lilly started to cry, but Camille pushed on. *Come, Solace. Come to me, and I will help you rest.*

Ronald burst into the room, interrupting the spell. "What are you doing?!" He looked at the candle, moved his eyes around the room. "Oh, Camille."

"I can't leave her there, Ronald. I can't let her be trapped where they murdered her," she yelled, voice shrill, shaking.

"This kind of magic is dangerous. You know that!" He hurried over, picked up Lilly and pushed the baby into Camille's arms. He kicked over the candle and the flame hissed out.

A rush of wind moved through the room, final and sad. "No! I have to finish the spell!" Camille yelled.

"No!" Ronald grabbed Camille by the shoulders. "Camille, they are coming back. We have to go. Now!"

"But . . . Solace. Our baby . . ."

Ronald's round face and hazel eyes clouded with grief. "I know . . . It's time to save someone else." He looked down at Lilly's tear streaked face. The baby was calm now.

Camille sobbed. Something crashed outside the Town Hall. Ronald pushed her to the door. "Go!"

Now, as she hurried through the forest, cold hatred hardened inside her—hatred for the Covenant, for magic, and for every little decision that led to this night.

Ronald was now busy helping their coven-mates and fellow witches escape—*those that are left*—and removing the Covenant's records from Town Hall. Her heart reached out to him, praying they would all be safe. *I'm so sorry, Ruby, my dear friend!* But there had been enough death, and they couldn't risk the lives of all their neighbors who were not witches and also called Twelve Acres home. Their exodus was a necessary evil

Be safe, Ronald. The Earth knows I can't lose you too.

Exhausted, Camille collapsed against a tree, gasping for air. Gently, she pulled back the blankets to look at the sweet babe in her arms. The little round face was relaxed; the tiny lips parted as she breathed. Camille stroked the golden-red hair, her entire body aching with grief. Memories of her sweet Solace as a baby beat her down in an unbearable barrage: Solace asleep, nestled against her chest; Solace's bright eyes shining with life and looking up at her only moments after she arrived in the world; her first steps and first experiments with magic; her lust for life; her sense of humor.

Then tonight, the memories Camille knew would *never* leave her: Solace's screams as the Dark witches dragged her from Ruby's house; echoing pleas for her mother's help shattering Camille's heart; Camille unable to help, bound by Dark magic and savage beatings.

Sobs rose in her chest, bouncing the little baby. If it were not for this orphaned baby that she'd promised to protect, she would have collapsed to the ground and prayed for death. Instead, compelled by duty, friendship, and a burning desire to save someone from this horrible life, Camille pushed away from the tree and trudged forward.

Soon she came to the forest's edge and a road.

Time for a spell.

Camille reached up and grabbed a handful of aspen leaves, little round coins of yellow-gold. She held them tightly in her grip and closed her eyes. Then, in a strained, raspy voice, she sang the necessary words, *"Swift and effectual power of air, guide my feet and hear my prayer. Lead me to a home of Light, to place this baby out of sight."*

A burst of warm air answered Camille's plea, pulling the cold from her bones. She lifted her hand, opened the palm, and the air took the leaves, pulling them upward, spiraling. Then, in one long stream, the leaves floated through the air, beckoning Camille. She followed, her heart a bit lighter. At least she could save *this* child—Amelia's baby girl—from sharing her mother's fate . . . and Solace's.

Oh, those poor girls! They must have been so scared.

Camille's heart clenched, and her legs nearly gave way, but she kept going. It wasn't long before the trail of wafting leaves descended before one of the doors of a small motel just off the road. One car stood in the parking lot—a yellow Ford model A with Oregon plates. Camille scanned the dark windows of the car, and then the motel. She crossed to the doorstep and tried to look in, but the curtains were drawn. She sniffed at the smell of goodness, of Light, but not magic. These were kind and honest people, people with love to spare—normal people who would never be pursued by Darkness.

Camille clutched the baby tightly, suddenly loath to leave her. *Is this a mistake?* She pulled the blankets back, kissed the smooth forehead. The baby stirred and looked up into Camille's bloody, tear-streaked face. Her bright eyes gazed steadily up at Camille. Camille sobbed and laughed at the same time, felt her resolve steady. She didn't want this child growing up with the threat of Darkness looming over her.

With her left hand supporting the baby, she reached out

her right hand, summoning one of the aspen leaves back to her. It floated through the dying night air and landed in her palm, golden yellow, touched by the hand of autumn.

She pressed the leaf to her lips and kissed it, marking it with a bit of magic. When it grew warm she pressed it to the baby's forehead. "I'll be watching, Lilly."

CHAPTER 4
Waxing Half Moon

February—Present Day

Archard's own gift had finally betrayed him. In one moment of weakness, he'd been overcome; and now he was paying the price—the stinging, throbbing, agonizing price. The mutilated folds of his flesh rippled over him like cooled lava. Every breath was an ordeal; each time his chest moved to draw air, his skin screamed. His muscles were seized and tough, like over-cooked meat. Even a simple task like scratching the remains of his nose was painful and exhausting.

His recovery was glacially slow, even with the aid of magic. If he ever desired to look in the mirror again—*doubtful*—he would see a gruesome stranger. He would never again look like the man inside his head. The fire—*his own fire*—should have killed him, and yet he lived: a twisted, horrific shadow of his former greatness, but alive nonetheless. And if he had survived, there was a reason.

Though doubtful he'd ever get out of his bed again, burning nearly to death had not deadened his desire for power and Dark triumph. The flames hadn't burned away his ambition. No physical deformity or pain could quell *that*. Archard refused to accept defeat, and each day his desire for revenge grew, steady and unrelenting, like a fungus. He wanted nothing more than to rise up again, gather new covens, and *kill* every single one of Rowan's Light witches, breaking their Covenant so he could form his own.

And so he filled the long hours in his bed with schemes and machinations, daydreams of torturing and murdering Rowan's Light witches and drinking in their horror.

I'm still alive, and I'm coming for you!

He'd have to start from nothing. He didn't know how he could do it, but he was determined to find a way. The only thing truly standing in his way was his damned, deformed, *useless* body.

Cursing the pain, Archard stirred in his hospital bed, in the cabin not far from the cave. He'd lasted only a few weeks in a hospital before *demanding* to go home. He had no patience for the arrogant doctors and simpering nurses. He'd take control of his recovery with money and magic.

"Rachel!" he hissed, his fire-ravaged vocal chords rasping horribly. "Raaacheeel!" He winced in pain.

The blonde beauty, resplendent in a red scoop neck sweater, skinny jeans, and tall stiletto boots, rounded the corner of the room and crossed to his bed, unhurried. She still wouldn't look him directly in the face. It didn't matter, as long as she stayed and followed his commands. "Yes, Archard?"

"The book," he wheezed.

Rachel moved to the opposite side of the room and lifted Bartholomew's grimoire from its resting place on a black lacquered table. She ran her hand lovingly over the ancient black leather and its metal adornments as she crossed back to his bedside. Archard watched her curiously. *She stays for the power. She's as obsessed as I am.* If he still had lips, he would have smiled.

Rachel sat in a comfortable leather armchair next to his bed and rested the heavy book in her lap. She released the clasps that held it closed and then lifted the cover. A breath of icy air flowed into the room, and Archard's pulse quickened.

Rachel turned to the marked page and waved her hand over the Latin text. Most of the words morphed into English, while some remained hidden from sight. They planned to decode and read every single word in the grimoire, searching out the secrets of Bartholomew the Dark, the most powerful witch who ever lived.

Archard believed all his answers rested somewhere in those pages, perhaps even the solution to restoring his body. Bartholomew's magic had helped before, but there was so much Archard hadn't had time to study yet. He'd only scratched the surface when he found and attacked the Light covens. Ultimately, his lack of knowledge led to his downfall. But not this time. He'd be patient; he'd study; he'd decode every page, every spell, *everything.*

He'd wait until the right moment.

After a deep breath, Rachel began to read.

"STALL THE CHATTER!" YELLED DARBY, the female Fire in the Covenant. Her vibrant voice cut through the din around the dinner table. Finished with the meal of Thai takeout, everyone remained at the table in the half-renovated kitchen of Ruby Plate's old house, surrounded by exposed pipes, wires, and dust.

After Archard had destroyed Rowan's cottage in the woods, Rowan and Wynter decided to make Twelve Acres their home. The small town had little in the way of available real estate, but when the police had vacated Plate's Place, taken down the yellow tape, and written off Holmes's bizarre murder as unsolved, a FOR SALE sign had been hammered into the dead grass. After eighty years of neglect by the mysterious owner, the old house finally had a chance for a new life.

Wynter had shocked everyone by suggesting they buy it. Rowan fought her, refusing the idea that they live in the house that had been her prison for five months, almost the place of her death. But Wynter insisted, explaining that she needed to right the wrong. Simon had known that Willa had quietly taken Wynter's side, saying that she couldn't think of anyone better suited to take care of Ruby Plate's house.

Finally, Rowan gave in, on one condition: the basement must be erased from existence.

So the basement was filled in, the small window cemented over, and the door removed. Erased.

Besides the basement, renovations had begun on the kitchen and a small laundry room off the back of the house, while one of the smaller upstairs bedrooms was being converted to a third bathroom. With so much space, Rowan and Wynter invited anyone who wanted to move in to pick a room. Rain, the female Water, had already moved in. She'd gotten a job at the local auto repair shop, leaving her home in Boulder.

Charlotte and Elliot had also taken a room, moving all the way from New York to be with the Covenant. Toby, Hazel, and Corbin had decided to stay at their own homes in Denver, making the drive to Twelve Acres often. And Cal and Darby had purchased a small house a few blocks over.

Willa wanted to move in to Ruby's house, too, but decided to wait until she smoothed things over with her parents.

Simon told her that as soon as she was ready, they'd move in together. She'd leave her parents' house, and he his apartment. He didn't love the idea of living with so many members of the Covenant, but the chance to be with Willa outweighed his discomfort.

The two True Covens of the Covenant now sat around the long wooden table. Bound together by the magic of the blood moon, there were twelve witches, six male, six female, a pair of each of the Six Gifts. Simon and Willa, gifts of Mind and Dreams, sat next to their counterparts, Charlotte and Elliot. Char and Elliot were also the same age and now attending the University of Colorado, same as Willa and Simon. Next to them were Wynter and Rowan, the two Earth witches and leaders of the Covenant—Rowan as the head, or Luminary. On the other side of the table sat Cal, Darby's husband and the other Fire; Hazel and Toby, the Air witches; and finally, Rain and Corbin, the Waters.

Everyone turned and quieted at Darby's command, and she tossed back her blonde hair and grinned a toothy grin. "That's better. It's time to train."

Simon exhaled quietly. He both looked forward to and dreaded this time of day. Every night, he and Willa were put through a series of exercises to hone their magical skills in preparation for the Elemental Challenge. He certainly wanted to earn the title of True Witch, but he worried what might happen along the way.

Most witches trained their whole childhood and adolescence before attempting the Challenge; Simon and Willa were trying to do it in less than a year.

Wynter got up from the table. Her strawberry hair glowed in the dim light of a single lamp. She wore a white dress, trimmed in green, with a full skirt and long sleeves. Most of her wardrobe had long sleeves now, to cover the line of scars on her right arm where Holmes had cut her. She retrieved a basket from a box near the side door and passed it over to Darby. From the basket, the Fire witch pulled six different stones, lining them up on the table in front of Willa.

"Okay, girly," Darby said, sitting back, tugging her bright red, pearly snap shirt into place. "Stones and herbs are essential to working spells. Use the wrong ones and the spell will fail—or worse. Six stones, six gifts. Each one has certain magical properties tied to its appropriate gift. Name them."

Willa inhaled, narrowed her eyes at the row of stones. This would be easy for her; she was good with the retention of facts. She pointed to the stone farthest to the left. "Emerald—Gift of Earth. Mica—Gift of Air. This garnet is for Fire. Amethyst is Water. The lapis is Mind; and lastly, the moonstone is mine, Dreams."

Darby grinned again. "Quick draw. Didn't even hesitate. Very nice." Wynter brought over another basket. From this one she took six different plants, placed them in front of Simon. "Okay, Simon, match the plant to the gift."

Simon dropped his eyes to the plants on the wooden table

surface. "Moss goes with Earth; the dill with Air. Coffee beans are used with Fire. Seaweed for Water. Cinnamon can be used for Mind. And the lavender is Dreams."

"Nice work," Darby said with a nod. "I thought we might throw you off with that cinnamon, since peppermint is the preferred." She looked over at Char and Elliot. "Will y'all go grab those candles?"

Char and Elliot jumped up from the table, left the room. "Clear the table," Rowan said, his Scottish brogue drawing out the vowels of the words. The stones, herbs, and remaining dinner plates were whisked away. Simon and Willa moved back, standing near the table. Willa looked up at him with a wonder-what-we-get-to-do-next look. He shrugged. The tests were always a surprise, which made Simon even more uneasy about what might happen with his powers.

Char and Elliot returned with a large box. Elliot proceeded to place glass candlesticks, about six inches in height, along the table in one long row. Char followed behind, placing a red taper in each one. When thirty candles lined the eight-foot farmhouse table from end to end, they stepped back with the other witches hovering behind Willa and Simon.

Simon frowned. Candles probably meant Fire; Fire was the most unpredictable element, the hardest to control.

Rowan cleared his throat, gave his dusty brown beard a stroke, and then said, "You both know how to light a single candle, but this exercise tests your ability to control fire more precisely. Darby will call out instructions and then you must light only the candles she names. Make sense?"

Simon nodded. Willa said, "Yes."

"Okay, Willa, you first." Rowan motioned for her to step

forward. Simon sensed her nervousness; Fire was her weakest skill. Darby nodded to her, and Willa lifted her right hand. Energy sparked on the air as she summoned magic.

"Two!" Darby called out.

Willa snapped her fingers and two candles burst to life.

"Good. That was an easy one." Darby waved her hand and the candles went out. "Now, five."

Willa snapped again; five candles lit in the middle of the row. She smiled and rubbed her hand on her jeans.

"Eight on the left."

Willa did it easily.

"Two on each end."

Another snap, and two lit on one end but only one on the other. Willa's shoulders tensed, and Simon could hear her berating herself in her mind.

Darby waved them out. "No problem. That's a tricky one. Let's try one more. One on each end and one in the middle."

Willa narrowed her eyes and then snapped. Several random candles flared. She dropped her arm with a sigh. Simon wanted to step forward and comfort her.

"Sorry," Willa said quietly.

"Nothing to be sorry for, Willa," Rowan said. "This skill takes a lot of practice. We didn't expect you to be able to do them all."

"Heck, no," Darby added. "Even I messed up a few times on this test. Good job, girl."

Willa nodded somberly, "Thanks."

"Take a break, and let's switch. Simon, you're up," Rowan said.

Simon's heart gave a nervous twitch. He put a hand on

Willa's shoulder as they passed. *Control it. Just take a deep breath, and control it*, he told himself

"Ready?" Darby asked. Simon nodded. "Ten together."

Snap! Heat flowed out of his fingertips, and ten candles on the right end burst to life, just as he'd wanted. He exhaled.

"Three on each end."

Three and three orange flames flickering. Energy stirred in his gut, the magic eager to move out of him. *Calm and control.*

"One in the middle."

Easy. Darby narrowed her eyes slightly, evaluating him, deciding what to ask next.

"Okay, let's go faster. Ready?" she asked. Simon gave an eager nod.

"Five." He lit, and she waved them out quickly. "Two on each end." *Done.* "Half of them." *Easy.* The magic bubbled excitedly inside him, his hand hot.

"One . . . Eight . . . Two . . . Twelve . . ." Each number was easily executed. The room grew quiet except for Darby's voice and Simon's snapping. Darby folded her arms smugly. "All of them."

Simon snapped immediately, his fingers giving off a tiny spark. All the candles on the table flared, flames rising high. Someone behind him gasped. He wanted to smile, but something in the tone of the gasp and the uneasy silence that followed turned his mouth down instead.

Darby's eyes were wide, but she wasn't looking at the table. He followed her gaze. The extra candles in the box Elliot had brought in were floating midair above it, all brightly lit. A few random candles sitting on the kitchen counter also burned. The group moved robotically into the front living room, where several other candles on the mantle and bookshelves were lit.

Simon's heart thudded uncomfortably. Someone whispered, "All the candles in the house!" His hands turned cold, his throat dry. The candles hovering in the air fell to the floor and the rest puffed out. He said, "I didn't mean to."

Collectively, the other witches turned to him, shock and a sliver of fear marking their faces. He'd seen that look before; he *hated* that look. Willa stepped next to him, slipped her hand in his and held on tightly.

WILLA WISHED EVERYONE WOULD STOP looking at Simon like he'd burned down the house instead of lit a few extra candles. His hand was stiff in hers, his eyes looking toward the side door. He'd demonstrated superior abilities in training before, but this was the most shocking . . . since the cave, of course.

Rowan moved toward them.

"I'm sorry," Simon blurted out.

Rowan shook his head, smiling. "Don't be. I'm impressed."

Simon looked around the room. "No, you're all nervous. I can feel it."

"It's just unexpected," Rowan soothed. "But there's nothing to feel worried about. You are learning. Learning includes mistakes and missteps. This is just proof of your exceptional skills."

"Exceptional is just another word for abnormal."

"No, it's not," Wynter said firmly.

Simon plowed a hand through his hair, finally looked at Willa. "I didn't mean to."

That bothered him the most. Simon did everything deliberately. She placed a hand on his arm, held his eyes. "I know. It's okay. It's just a few extra candles."

Rowan added, "Control will come with time, Simon."

"But how do I control something I don't understand? We don't know *why* I'm like this. How do we solve a problem that doesn't have a source?"

Wynter took a step closer. "I'm working on it. I've been reading all the grimoires we have, and asking around. It's slow going, but I promise we will find a way to help you."

Willa gripped Simon's wrist in a reassuring gesture. "We'll find out why."

"But what if we can't? And what do I do until then?"

Rowan answered, "We do our best to help you learn how to handle it. It will take extra effort on your part, especially as we get into more serious magic. Can you do that?"

Simon exhaled, nodded. "Yeah, okay."

Rowan nodded. "Good. I think that is enough for tonight. Go home, get some rest."

Simon nodded again, looked to the door again.

"I'll go get our stuff," Willa offered.

A few minutes later, the couple was parked outside Willa's house, the heater finally warming up the frigid car. Simon had his arm propped on the back of the seat, lazily twirling one of Willa's curls around his finger. She could tell by the creases in his forehead that he was still thinking about the candles.

"I know you hate this question, but are you *sure* you're okay?" she asked.

He gave half a smile. "Yeah, I'll be fine. It wasn't that big a deal."

"You suck at lying," she smiled back.

The half-smile spread. "I know." He tugged gently on her hair. "I just don't want it to get worse, you know?"

"Yeah, I know. But why would it get worse? If anything, you'll get better at controlling it."

"I hope so."

Willa studied the worry on his face. *Do I dare ask?* She wetted her lips. "Anything else you want to talk about?" He'd know exactly what she meant, and she couldn't help feeling that she'd breeched some code of their relationship in asking. She held her breath.

He stared out the windshield for a moment, then said "You better get inside before your mom puts her face through that window."

Willa turned. Her mom stood at the front window, curtain pulled back, watching. Even in the dark, her expression looked worried—not that it ever look differently lately. Willa sighed. "Okay." She opened the door, wincing at the rush of cold air.

Simon came around the Jeep and put his arm around her shoulders. "I'm sorry," he offered.

"I know." And she did, but she was starting to wonder if he'd *ever* talk to her, or if she'd ever be able to stop asking. Solace's words echoed in her mind: *He won't let it out, and you won't let it go.*

On the porch, Willa lifted to her toes to kiss him. "Good night. I'll miss you."

Simon sighed, wrapped his arms around her. "Miss you too!" He kissed the top of her head. "I love you," he whispered.

"Love you, too."

Reluctantly, Willa pulled away and went inside. Later, as she lay alone in bed, she searched her mind for a way to help Simon. When nothing came, she rolled over and closed her eyes. *Maybe an answer will come in a dream*, she thought hopefully.

CHAPTER 5
WANING CRESCENT

March—Present Day

Willa hurried to the Twelve Acres Diner, late for her dinner shift. After changing into her uniform—a white polo shirt and short black skirt—she hustled to the server's station to get her note pad. Two tables were already waiting.

She greeted the first table, an older couple that came in every night at five o'clock sharp. "Hi, Pearl. Hi, Bob. How are you guys tonight?"

Pearl, a wispy-haired woman in her late seventies with a kind face and several strings of fake pearls around her neck, said, "Oh, just fine, Willa. Same as always: old, tired, and hungry."

Willa smiled. "What can I get you tonight?"

Pearl pointed to the menu and started talking, but Willa didn't hear a word. Movement out the front window caught her eye; she looked up. Her gaze snagged on a dark figure across the street.

A woman, huddled in a long black coat, hood pulled low over her face, her white-blonde hair spilling out onto her chest, stood watching the diner. Willa couldn't see her eyes in the shadow of the hood, but she had no doubt the woman was looking at her.

The triangular pendant tucked inside Willa's shirt flared hot. She gasped, pressed a hand to the spot.

"Willa? Willa, honey?" Pearl reached out to put her hand on Willa's arm. Willa jerked away, disoriented and unsettled. Her eyes flashed to Pearl and then back to the window.

The woman was gone.

Order pad gripped in her hand, Willa ran from the table, bolted out into the cold night, ignoring Pearl's and the hostess's calls after her. Only a few weak streetlights lit the street, circles of yellow on the black asphalt. It smelled like snow and . . . smoke. *Is that smoke?* She jerked her head from side to side, scanning for the mysterious figure. Her necklace pulsed hot against her chest.

Nothing.

The hostess, Rosa, appeared at the door, yelling. "Willa! What the heck are you doing? It's freezing, and you got tables. Get back in here."

Willa looked once more up, down, side to side. Her trembling hands were warm with magic, ready to act; but she saw nothing. The pendant of her necklace began to cool.

Nothing.

Reluctantly, she turned back, her heart racing, mind spinning. "Sorry," she said as she stepped past Rosa. "Thought

I saw someone." Rosa shook her head and pulled the door closed.

Willa returned to Pearl and Bob and took their orders, apologizing for her behavior. She looked out the window several times while she scribbled down their regular order of pot roast and fried chicken. They eyed her nervously but said nothing.

After she placed the order with the kitchen, she ducked into the break room and dug her phone out of her purse to text Simon.

I just saw Rachel outside the diner!

SIMON DIDN'T SEE THE TEXT until after his physics night class as he was climbing into his Jeep. At first, he could only stare, wondering if somehow the name was a typo. *There is no way!*

Then the only thing he could think about was how he'd watched Rachel stab Willa in the back, slicing into her lung and heart, nearly killing her; how he'd seen Willa's hot, sticky blood spill out all over the floor of Darby's kitchen, and then *stepped* in her blood to follow Rachel outside.

He sent a quick text back—*I'm coming!*—and slammed the Jeep into gear.

His panic grew with each passing second. Not only had Rachel been the one to sneak up behind Willa, Charlotte, and Elliot, but she'd also cut Wynter's arm so Archard could test Simon's healing ability. The last time anyone had thought about Rachel was when she ran off into the woods during the battle at the cave.

Would she really come after them? Alone?

Maybe she's not alone.

Simon pushed the gas pedal to the floor, his body flushed

with heat, anger, worry . . . and magic. He couldn't let Willa get hurt again.

A flicker of blue power flashed to life in his gut.

Squealing to a stop in front of the diner, Simon jumped out of the car and barreled inside. The simmer of power inside him flared when he saw Willa standing at a table on the other side of the restaurant. Her back was turned, her long wavy hair up in a ponytail. His eyes moved instinctively to the spot on her back where Rachel had stabbed her.

He exhaled, pulling the magic back from his hands. *She's safe. Calm down.* All eyes turned to him as he rushed through the tables to take Willa into his arms. "Are you okay?" he whispered.

Her arms tightened around him before she pulled back. "Yeah, but umm . . ." She looked passed his shoulder to the diner full of staring people. She smiled reassuringly at the customers as she pushed him toward the kitchen doors.

They passed Rosa at the hostess station. Her eyes widened and called out "Simon, you're not on the schedule tonight. What's going on with you two?"

Simon ignored her, continuing toward the break room in the back of the restaurant. When they were alone, he pulled Willa into his arms again. "Are you *sure* it was Rachel?" His body still felt tense, ready to spring at the first sign of trouble. He took a deep breath, trying to calm himself and ease the push of power bubbling inside him. *Calm down. Stay in control.*

Willa trembled slightly in his arms. "Not positive, but I *swear* it was her. She was standing out in the road in this creepy hooded coat and staring right at me. And my necklace—it turned hot when I saw her. Rowan said that means danger is near." She pulled back to look at him. "Do you think she'd really come after us? I thought we were safe!" Her voice pitched near to hysteria on the last word, and he tightened his hold on her.

"Honestly, I don't know." His stomach churned. It *was* supposed to be safe now, the threat was supposed to have died with Archard. Simon had felt comfortable joining the Covenant *because* it was safe.

"What do we do now?" Willa asked, gripping his leather jacket at his chest. "Holy moon! The others. What if she's there now? I was so freaked out I didn't even think to text Charlotte, warn them. What's wrong with me?" Her body shook fiercely. "Oh, no! Simon . . ."

"Let's go." He pulled her with him, out the back door and helped her into the Jeep. "What time did you see her?"

Willa's face twisted with emotions. "Umm, it was a little after six, I think." She moved her eyes to the dashboard. "A half an hour ago!" Her frantic eyes found his.

He slammed the Jeep into gear and peeled out into the street. "If she went after them, she won't stand a chance. Don't worry; I'm sure they're fine." Simon offered her the comforting words, but his own heart beat a worried staccato against his sternum. *Is this really happening? I can't do this again.*

WILLA GRIPPED THE DOOR HANDLE as Simon raced down the road. Her mind was a chaotic jumble of thoughts. When she first saw the hooded figure in the dark street, she was sure it was Rachel, but now . . . now, doubt nagged at her, eroding her confidence. Maybe it had been someone else, or a trick of the shadows, or a twisted reflection in the window. Maybe there hadn't been anyone there in the first place.

But ...

Rachel *was* alive—none of Willa's coven-mates had killed her. She *could* show up in Twelve Acres. Willa's stomach tightened. Leaning forward, she reached around to touch the spot on her back where Rachel's blade had pierced her. Thanks to Simon's healing powers, there was no scar; but the memory of fiery pain lingered, an invisible mark, now throbbing and cold. She closed her eyes and swallowed the bile in her throat.

Not again! Please not again!

Simon screeched to a stop in front of Ruby's house. Everything looked normal: yellow lights illuminating the windows of the two-story Victorian, the old green clapboards stripped for new ones, the wrap-around porch under repair, cars in the driveway, the massive willow tree's branches framing the structure from behind. Simon leaned forward to stare at the house. "They are all in there, safe and undisturbed."

Willa let out a shaky breath. "Oh, thank goodness."

They hurried inside. Most of their coven-mates were sitting in the living room on the sheet-covered couches, the room freshly painted in a steel blue, the built-in bookshelves restained. The air was thick with harsh chemical smells mixed with wood smoke from the fire in the hearth.

"Hey, guys," Char called out, smiling until she saw their faces, sensing their fear. "Whoa! What happened?"

Everyone turned to look at the couple. Rain and Toby came in from the kitchen.

Willa and Simon exchanged a look and then sat near Wynter and Rowan. Willa held her icy fingers out to the flickering fire. "I think I saw Rachel outside the diner tonight."

Wynter and Rowan flinched; a few others gasped. Wynter

reached out, gripping Willa's forearm. "What happened? Tell us everything."

Willa recounted the details quickly.

"Why do you think it was Rachel?" Rowan asked, his face bright with the firelight. "It could have been anyone."

Willa looked around the room at the expectant faces of her friends. "My pendant burned," Willa lifted the necklace out of her shirt and fingered the symbol, "and also the way she looked at me . . . I could *feel* her eyes, but . . ." she looked back at Rowan, "I suppose I could be wrong."

Rowan shook his head thoughtfully. "A witch's instincts are rarely wrong."

A brief silence followed, heavy with menace. Any relief Willa had felt at finding her friends safe evaporated. *I wasn't wrong. I did see her.* She wished she were wrong.

"We were worried she might have come after you guys," Simon said quietly, scooting closer to Willa. "If she's here for revenge, she'll come after all of us. So what do we do?"

Rowan abruptly stood. "Cal and Darby, check the protection spells around the house; reinforce them. Rain and Corbin, do a scrying spell; look for threats. Everyone else, set up watch at the windows and tune your magic outward. If she's coming, we'll be ready."

"Do you think she's alone?" Rain asked. The Water witch, a short, twenty-something Asian woman with spiky black hair, the tips dyed royal blue, rubbed nervously at her tattooed arm.

Wynter and Rowan exchanged a worried look. Rowan sighed and then said, "She may not be, but all her coven-mates and her Luminary are dead. I'd wager she's acting alone—and probably out of desperation."

"But why now?" Darby asked. "It's been months since the cave."

"Who knows?" Rowan said. "We'll worry about details later. Right now, let's make sure we are safe. If she comes . . . well, I'm afraid we will have to do the job that didn't get done last fall. Understood?" Rowan looked around the group, accepting the nods of understanding. His eyes settled on Simon.

Willa's stomach twisted with a new worry. Rowan meant that, if Rachel attacked, they should kill her. It was the only way to stop her from hurting them any further. It was why they had killed the rest of Archard's followers. Death was the only way to end a serious Dark threat.

Simon pursed his lips and looked away. Willa watched him, sensing his sudden tension. She waited for him to answer, wanting desperately for him to say something—anything — about what happened at the cave. The muscles in his jaw and neck tensed and relaxed several times; he said nothing.

Wynter broke the moment. "Willa and Simon, stay close to either Rowan or me. You're not ready to fight a Dark witch on your own."

Willa nodded, partially relieved. "Okay." Simon still said nothing. Charlotte put her hand on Willa's arm and gave her a sympathetic smile which seemed to say, *give him time*. Willa only frowned. He'd had plenty of time.

The group dispersed to their assigned places. Willa and Simon each went to one of the tall living room windows, currently covered in brown paper to protect them from the paint. Willa pulled back a corner of the paper to look out. Wynter and Rowan hovered near the fire, whispering.

Willa scanned the dark street, waiting for Rachel's hooded

figure to appear. Her mind stuck on the question in Rowan's eyes when he'd looked at Simon. Would Simon be able to kill again, if he had to? What would it do to him if he did? Willa shivered. The others had killed Dark witches—Wynter, Rowan, Hazel—but they didn't seem as affected by it as Simon. Why was he still hanging on to so much regret and anger about the cave?

Please, no more Dark witches. We can't do this again.

A car rushed passed. Willa watched its tail lights disappear. She looked over at Simon, tall and brooding next to the other window, the paper on the window casting contorted shadows across his face and darkening his blond curls. The short distance between them felt heavy with unsaid words.

"Simon," she whispered.

He looked over, eyes hidden in a shadow. "Yeah?"

"You okay?"

"Yeah. Why?"

She exhaled and dropped her hand from the window. "Well, with what Rowan said . . ." She hesitated and then, before she lost her nerve, said, "Please talk to me."

Simon stiffened, turned back to the window. Willa waited, holding her breath. He looked at her, opened his mouth, then closed it again, and looked away.

"Simon?" she whispered.

"There's nothing to say. I'll do whatever I have to do to protect you."

Willa turned away, face to the window, and fought to hold back a rush of hot tears. *This isn't about me!*

WHEN RACHEL ARRIVED BACK AT the cabin, she went straight

into Archard's room and was greeted by the hiss and hum of all his medical machines.

Awake and waiting, he stirred, winced at the pain, but ignored it. "Well?" he asked impatiently.

Rachel pulled off her long black coat, threw it over the end of the bed, and dropped into the leather armchair next to him. She crossed her legs, tossed back her hair, but avoided his eyes. Archard wanted to spit at her for making him wait. Finally, she said, "They are there. Wynter and Rowan bought Ruby's place. A few of them are living there; the others spend most of their time there. One big, ridiculous family."

"I knew they'd buy that old dump." He wheezed. "Do they have any idea I'm alive?"

"Not as far as I could tell."

A slow, hideous grin spread on Archard's red, lipless mouth. "Now, we just have to make sure we have all the parts of Bartholomew's healing spell correct. The book is so deviously protected. Bartholomew was nothing short of genius in hiding his best spells."

"We are closer. Only a few more lines to uncover, and then we will be ready." Rachel pushed out of her chair, retrieved the large black tome from its table, and cracked it open. "Shall we work on it now, or do you need rest?"

Archard's heart picked up speed. "No. Let's get to work. The new moon approaches."

CHAPTER 6
WANING CRESCENT

March—Present Day

Three days after Willa's sighting of Rachel, the Covenant gave up their vigil. They'd performed dozens of spells, searched the whole of Twelve Acres, and even some of the surrounding towns. They found no sign—not even a hint—of Rachel's whereabouts.

Exhausted and discouraged, the witches decided it was time to return to normal life. What else could they do? Simon and Willa had both missed a few shifts at the diner and a couple classes. If they didn't get back to things soon, the consequences would be serious. The diner manager, Ron, had already threatened to fire them, and Simon had forgotten to turn in an important assignment in his anatomy class.

"I've got to go talk to this professor," Simon said, standing outside Ruby's house, holding Willa in his arms. The early March sky was brilliant blue and cloudless. He and Willa both wore heavy coats and scarves to hedge out the biting cold. "Maybe I can convince him to let me turn in that paper for half credit. Half is better than none."

"I'm so sorry," Willa said, shaking her head.

"Why? It's not your fault I forgot what day it was."

"Yes, it is. These last three days are *all* my fault. If I hadn't thought I saw Rachel . . ." Willa frowned and looked away. Frustration and embarrassment pulsed out of her.

"Hey, no," he put a finger under her chin, lifted her face. "You *did* see her. Why else would your pendant have burned? But she probably got scared off *because* you saw her. We had to make sure she wasn't still around."

Willa nodded, her eyes still pinched. "Yeah, I know. Okay, you go beg for a grade, and I'll go to work and be extra nice to Ron so we don't get fired."

"Good plan." Simon kissed her. "I'll see you tonight for training."

"Yep. I'll be there." She lifted to her toes and kissed him again. "Good luck."

Simon waved as he drove away. In truth, he was much more upset about messing up on his anatomy paper than he let on. He couldn't let his grades suffer because of the Covenant. Not again. It'd been hard enough keeping things on track last semester. He wanted to be a witch, but he didn't want it to screw up the future he'd spent a lifetime planning.

He merged onto the freeway and turned down the heater.

Becoming a doctor was something he'd fixated on since his youth. He clearly remembered the moment he'd decided to go to medical school so he could carefully, discreetly, use his healing powers to help others.

He'd been ten years old, and his grandmother was dying of cancer.

His mother's mother—Grandma Silvia as he knew her—was nearly as cold and unfeeling as her daughter. She'd barely acknowledged her grandson's existence, and Simon had only seen her a handful of times. But in her final hours, compelled by a rare moment of human tenderness, his mom took him to say goodbye.

He could still smell the bitter scent of decay in her hospital room, the smell of her body being eaten alive by cancerous tumors. To his ten-year-old eyes, no creature had ever looked more hideous than his grandmother on that day. Her skin was ashen, as gray as thunderclouds, her hair gone, exposing a wrinkled, age-spotted scalp that she didn't bother to cover anymore. Her eyebrows were gone as well, which made her face look like a skull.

Simon had wanted to turn from the room and run back to the car, but his mom pushed him forward, gripping his shoulders so tightly her nails left marks in his skin. Thinking back, Simon wondered if she'd been just as appalled and scared to approach the woman as he.

Grandma Silvia blinked her eyes open at the sound of her daughter's greeting. "Silvia, it's Cynthia. Simon is with me."

The old woman grunted. "Did you bring that horrid husband, too?"

Cynthia frowned. "No. It's just me and Simon."

Black pupils ringed in nearly colorless irises, curtained with wrinkled, heavy lids, focused on Simon. Something registered in those eyes, and Simon sensed a shift in the dying woman's emotions. "You've gotten big," she whispered, followed up with a crackling-paper cough.

Simon didn't know what to say, so he only nodded.

"Come closer, please. I can't see you."

The please caught his attention, a word he rarely heard from the adults in his life. Simon swallowed, took a step closer and tried not to gag at the smell. Her shriveled body occupied only a small portion of the hospital bed; her shoulders, hips, and knees made sharp mountains in the blankets covering her. She looked nothing like the picture on his mother's bedroom mantel of a tall, stately woman with cool blue eyes and raven black hair. Even for someone so young, Simon understood the injustice and humiliation of death.

"Did she tell you I'm dying?" Silvia hissed and coughed again.

Simon nodded, "Yes."

"Do you feel sorry for me?"

Simon furrowed his brows. He certainly felt sorry for her current state, but it was hard to feel any genuine remorse for a stranger. "I'm sorry if you're in pain."

She laughed the sound like tree branches snapping in half. "What do you know of pain?"

Simon lifted his chin. "Everything," he said confidently. For every animal, every person he'd ever healed, he had first felt their pain. Only for half a second as his body connected to theirs, and then his magic would take over, pull away the pain. He was intimately familiar with pain.

"Simon!" his mother scolded, eyeing him with anger and contempt.

"Now, shut up, Cynthia. I'm talking to the boy," Silvia cut in. Cynthia looked away, jaw set.

His grandmother looked back at him, her drooping eyes intense despite their withered state. "What do you mean?"

Simon looked at his mother and then back. "Nothing."

Silvia stared hard at him for a few moments. The medical instruments attached to her body beeped and hissed in the silence. "Hmm. I see. Cynthia, I need some water. Go fetch it."

Cynthia turned, looked at the full jug of water on the side table and then huffed out of the room.

"There now, she's gone, Simon. You can tell me what you meant."

Simon couldn't remember his grandma ever speaking his name. He looked at her face, stifling a flinch. *Could I heal her?* he wondered. Could he take away so much damage, so much pain? He'd healed a few animals in terrible condition, but the worst he'd ever fixed on a person was a broken arm. Just the thought had warmth rising in his hands, as if his powers wanted to know too.

"I didn't mean anything," he told her.

"Ah, but you did. I can see something in your face right at this moment. Being close to death has made it quite easy for me to see people for what they truly are. And you, Simon, are not like the rest of us. Why?"

The heart monitor beeped steadily. Part of him wanted to confide in the dying woman. After all, who would she tell? The burden of his secrets could go to the grave with her. But what if his mother came back? Simon would feel the back of his father's hand for sure. He looked at the door.

"Don't worry about my weak-minded daughter," Silvia said. "Tell a dying woman your secret, boy."

Could she read his mind too? His hands were still flushed with heat. He looked down at her pasty, skeletal hand on top of the blankets. *All I have to do is touch her.* Simon's body filled with the desire to test his abilities. He didn't even think about the consequences of explaining such a miraculous recovery. He had to know.

He took a slow step forward and then thrust his hand out and put it on top of her cold, limp skin. A brief flash of her pain, her all-consuming pain, weakened his knees, and then the warmth traveled out of him and into her. Silvia's eyes went wide, with a million questions inside them. "What?" she gasped and then fell into a fit of coughs.

The heart monitor wailed an alarm.

Recovering from her coughing, she looked him in the eyes; and all the bitterness melted away. "Thank you, Simon," she whispered and then closed her eyes. The heart monitor let out a steady, sustained beep.

Nurses and doctors rushed into the room, all in white and blue clothes, shoving him aside. His mom came running in after them, a paper cup of water in her hand. Cynthia looked from her dead mother to her son, blinking quickly. She looked at his hands, and he hurried to put them behind his back. Understanding spread across her face like a shadow. She dropped the cup to the floor; Simon watched the water quickly run across the white tile.

Cynthia grabbed Simon by his arm and hauled him from the hospital.

Now, driving toward the University, Simon could still feel the anger in her grip, the pure hatred. That night as he'd sat in his room, waiting for his body to heal the welts from his father's belt, he thought of his grandmother's last words. She'd *thanked* him, and he didn't know why. Why would she thank him for being unable to heal her, for bringing on her death?

The answer had come a short time later as he crawled into bed, his back healed and ready for sleep. She had thanked him because she *needed* to die, wanted to die. She didn't need to be healed; she needed to be freed from her disgusting body.

He had realized that night that healing wasn't always about fixing.

The next morning, he'd started researching medical schools.

Pulling into the parking lot at the University, Simon took a steadying breath. He rehearsed the words he would say to the professor, prepared to beg if he had to. He had to fix this and, as he walked up to the biology building, vowed not to mess up again, no matter what was going on with the Covenant.

YOU'VE GOT TO BE KIDDING *me!*

Willa stood out on the end of a diving board at the indoor pool of the Twelve Acres Recreation Center, *blindfolded.* This was by far the weirdest thing she'd had to do for training so far.

The board gave and bounced with her slightest movement, so she tried to stay as still as possible. With her eyes covered in the black silk blindfold, it felt like the board was only the width of a balance beam, as high as those Olympic platforms. The smell of chlorine burned her nose.

"All right, Willa," Rowan called out, his voice echoing in the pool area. "We're ready to begin." This meant they had enchanted all the windows and doors to the pool, which kept out unwanted guests and made it look like the group was just enjoying a private pool party to any who might look in the windows.

Willa shifted her feet; and the board bounced slightly,

bringing her heart into her throat. *Some party!* She waited for the board to stop moving. She didn't like the idea of falling from the fifteen-foot board into the water below, blindfolded and fully clothed. Of course, it had to be the highest diving board, not the ones only a few feet off the water. She'd only gone off this board once in her whole life—on a dare by her dad—and it'd scared her to death.

Rowan went on. "This is the first in a series of difficult exercises that will prepare you for the challenge. This exercise tests your psychic awareness, your instincts, and your ability to react to threats you can't see. You must use magic to feel out what comes at you. You may use the power of Water or Air to defend yourself. Three consecutive defenses without falling counts as a completed exercise. If you fall off the board, we start over."

"Sun and moon," Willa mumbled to herself. She felt wholly unprepared and as nervous as she'd ever been in training. This was the first time they'd ventured beyond the back yard of Plate's Place, and, although she'd spent plenty of summer days at this pool, it felt unsettlingly strange and hostile now.

"Are you ready, Willa? Any questions?"

"Can I skip this?" she asked sarcastically. Everyone laughed. She pictured the blue water below. *Why do I always have to go first?* "I'm ready," she said as loud and clear as she could muster.

"Okay, focus your mind and your magic," Rowan instructed.

Willa took a deep breath, slightly bent her knees, and lifted her hands in front of her. Her heart thrummed in her throat, her mouth dry. She exhaled. *Focus. Feel.* Heat stirred around her as the magic answered her call. She thought how easy this would be for Simon, who practically had psychic x-ray vision because of his powerful Mind gift. Her skills only included having crazy dreams and seeing ghosts—neither of which could help her right now. *But I have magic inside me. Come on! Focus. Feel.*

The pool grew quiet except for her ragged breathing and the hum of a filter. She tried to reach out with the magic to feel for the things around her. She knew the spectator stairs were to her left, the other diving boards to her right, and, of course, the very deep water was directly below. Her coven-mates had been standing on the opposite side of the pool. Were they still there?

Willa focused and felt a tremor of response. Someone was moving.

A second later a burst of air hit her, knocking her easily from the board. She fell, tumbling, and splashed into the water. She clawed at the blindfold, kicked her legs. Blinking and sputtering, she struggled to swim to the surface. Finally, lungs painfully tight, she came up. Simon knelt at the side of the pool, hand out. She swam to him, and he lifted her out of the pool, setting her on the deck.

"Are you okay?" He searched her face as she coughed up more water.

"I guess," she muttered. Embarrassed and shaken, Willa got to her feet. Simon held her arm for support. Rowan stepped close.

"Let's try again," he said.

Willa resisted the urge to scowl at him and headed back to the ladder leading up to the springboard. Looking up at the rungs, she almost couldn't talk her legs into moving. *Come on. Up! You can do this.* So, up the ladder and out onto the board she went. She pulled the dripping blindfold into place. Her jeans and long sleeve Henley shirt felt like lead. She wriggled her right toes, realizing for the first time that one of her Tiffany blue Converse shoes was still somewhere in the pool. *Great!*

"Okay, Willa, here we go," Rowan yelled.

Deep inhale, slow exhale. She focused her mind. No way she was falling off the board again. *Let's just get this over with, please!* Pressing her teeth together, she reached out with her magic. Everything was in place, except for two people. *I think. Is it two or just one?*

Another deep breath. *Two, definitely two people moved.* A shift in the energy around her and a rush of heat coming at her from left and right forced her to react and she summoned the water to rise up on both sides. A loud hiss next to each of her ears and the feel of steam on her face followed.

Then the cheers of her coven-mates.

She released the water. *Did I do it?*

"Well done!" Rowan yelled. "You stopped Darby and Cal's fireballs. Fire was one of the easier types of magic to detect. One test completed. Now number two."

Willa smiled, but didn't let herself bask in the triumph for too long. She wondered briefly what would have happened if she hadn't stopped the fire. Would Rowan have let her be burned? Simon could easily heal her, but, still, would her Luminary let her feel the fire? Or would Darby and Cal have pushed the balls away from her? She hoped the latter but was quickly learning that witches didn't go easy when it came to training.

She pulled back her focus, ready for the second test. Inhale, exhale. A tremor in the energy, this time from below her. In her mind, she saw the water churning, rising. *Is that what's really happening?*

She lowered to her haunches and gripped the board with one hand, while extending the other. She pushed a rush of air downward and heard it plow through the rising water. Water sprayed up into her face and she nearly lost her balance, but she had stopped the churning wall of water from rising to the board.

A second round of cheers.

"Test two complete!" Rowan called.

Willa, shaking, managed to get back to her feet, now twice as wet. Cold and shivering, she tried to steady herself and the board, which wobbled beneath her. *One more. Just one more then it's over.*

"Here we go, Willa. Remember, stay on your board no matter what and you're done," Rowan called.

She nodded. "Ready."

Calm and focused, Willa felt outward with the magic. The air grew too still, too thick. There was a flash in her mind; and she flinched, rocking the board. *What was that?!* She shifted her feet to steady things. In her mind, she saw Charlotte fall into the pool, thrash to the surface and call for help. Willa flinched again, nearly sprang from the board.

The splashing and calls echoed in her head, but was she hearing them with her ears? It was impossible to tell the difference. *Willa, please help me!* Willa bit her bottom lip. *Why isn't anyone else helping her?* Charlotte went under and then scrambled back to the surface, coughing and calling out to Willa. *Everyone else left. You've got to help me! I can't swim.* Under she went and this time didn't come back up.

Willa crouched, ready to dive. It was so real in her mind, but yet everything around her felt calm, quiet. Her senses didn't match her thoughts. The conflicting information tore at her ability to decide.

Charlotte had not come back up. Bubbles broke the surface of the pool, and then the water stilled. Willa wanted to cry out in frustration, but then a thought broke through. *It's not real! It's only in your mind!* If it was only in her mind . . . she chanted a quick spell to block her mind from others, "Powerful Earth, accept this mind-lock. A magical door, make it solid as rock."

The image disappeared. Willa ripped the blindfold from her face and scanned the water. Still as glass. Charlotte stood on the edge of the pool, smiling up at her. "Sorry!" she called out.

"Did you break into my mind?" Willa asked, breathless.

"Yeah . . . I totally did. When you reach out with your mind, it makes you vulnerable," Char explained. "Great job sensing the difference between the vision and reality." She gave two thumbs up.

"So I can get down now?" Willa asked weakly to the amusement of the group.

"Yes!" Wynter called out. "Come on down."

WILLA WAS RIGHT. THIS SUCKS!

Simon now stood out on the diving board, the fiberglass flexing severely under his weight. It was hard just to stay on the thing. He took a couple steps back. The height didn't scare him, even with the blindfold, but being knocked from the board was not something he really wanted to experience. *Poor Willa.*

"Simon, you ready?" Rowan called.

"Sure," Simon called back.

"Here we go."

Simon opened his mind and immediately felt the presence of all his coven-mates, plus several people in other parts of the facility. Not only could he tell exactly where they were, but what they were feeling. He realized with a tug of regret that no one would be able to sneak up on him or surprise him with magic. *This is supposed to be hard! Why is nothing hard?*

Rain and Corbin stepped forward, summoning up a huge wave and sent it rolling toward him. He lifted his hands instinctively to send a burst of air in defense. The air plowed into the water, dissipating the wave. Test one done.

"Nice work," Rowan called. "Here comes number two."

Simon frowned, the wet blindfold moving against his forehead. Rowan had pulled him aside before the challenge. "You need to be extra careful tonight. What we are doing will open your mind and expose your powers to stress. Can you keep everything under control?"

Simon had stiffened at the implied meaning under the question. "So you want to know if I will hurt anyone?"

Rowan frowned, touched his beard. "No. But you refuse to talk to me about what's going on, so I do get a little nervous. We are moving into more serious magic here. I want to keep you and everyone safe."

Simon exhaled. He couldn't berate his Luminary for his own shortcomings. "I'll be very careful; I promise."

Now Cal broke off from the group and moved up to the spectator benches. Simon saw it clearly in his head. *What should I do?* He knew Cal was about to throw a stream of fire his way, and he knew he could stop it easily. *Maybe I shouldn't?* The idea shocked him. Fake a failure? The shock gave way to intrigue. If he faked a failure, everyone would stop looking at him like some kind of freak. This challenge was supposed to be hard; he was supposed to fail at least once. So why not give them what they wanted?

Cal's fire came on, and Simon pretended to flinch, duck out of its way, and loose his footing. He crashed into the cold water. He swam to the side where Willa waited. Lifting himself out, dripping, he met the smiles and words of encouragement from his friends. Exactly what he'd been hoping for. No narrowed eyes; no fear.

Darby whooped out a laugh. "Well, who knew? Even the mighty fall." The rest of the Covenant laughed. Simon smiled, a little high on the success of his fake failure. Then he turned back to Willa, who was not laughing or smiling. She lowered her chin and looked at him as if trying to solve a problem.

"You okay?" he asked, stepping closer.

She hurried to clear the look from her face. "Yeah, yeah. You?"

"Yes, but you were right. That fall is awful."

"Yeah, it is."

Rowan stepped between them, blocking Willa. "Okay, okay. Let's keep going. Back up, Simon. We start over."

Simon moved forward, his biker boots squashing loudly as he walked. At the ladder he looked around and caught Willa's eyes. *She knows. I can't fool her.* All happiness he'd felt a moment ago evaporated, replaced by a dull ache behind his heart.

He climbed the ladder to finish his challenge, which he knew would be as easy as it'd been to fall off the board.

CHAPTER 7
WAXING CRESCENT

June 1936

The Tuscan hillside was bathed in sumptuous sunlight. The light embraced the vineyard, highlighting the tops of the vines in their comforting straight lines, pooling in the deep recesses of the curving hills. The sky, a blinding blue, rose up from the earth to set the background for life in its quiet rhythm. The scent of sun-baked grapes and thousand-year-old dirt swam on the breeze.

No matter how many times Camille sat here, the scene still took her breath away. The remnants of her humble lunch—bread topped with arugula, tomato, and olive oil—sat next to her in a small wicker basket. She'd carried it up the hill an hour earlier; and now she sat in quiet contemplation, preparing for what she would do next.

She glanced at the empty grass beside her. Usually, Ronald, her husband and partner in magic, would sit there; but he'd been gone for over a year now—an unexpected heart attack in the night, Camille waking to his cold body beside her. His heart had finally given out under the weight of their grief. She couldn't get used to his absence and to the throbbing emptiness that followed her around. She lived with grief every day, but it never got easier and never got lighter as people often told her it would. Instead it grew, like an untreated tumor, metastasizing through her whole soul. And she knew one day it would stop her heart, too.

Alone.

One small thing brought her an ounce of fleeting joy these days. Although bittersweet, at least it still made her smile.

From her small basket, Camille took a wooden bowl, some herbs, and a thermos of water. She poured the water into the bowl and then dropped in a fresh sprig of dill, a small chunk of mica, the petals of several fragrant flowers, and, lastly, one round aspen leaf.

As the water absorbed the energy of the offerings, she looked out over the picturesque scene. Then, to focus her mind and power, she closed her eyes and listened to all the tiny sounds of nature. A flock of birds passed overhead, their calls faint and illusive on the air. Leaves quivered on trees, small creatures scurried over and under the ground, and grapes grew on their vines.

Finally, with her mind clear and her heart turned to the Earth, she called to the magic, now her rare, seldom-seen friend. The heat was subtle at first, like a warm passing breeze, but then it flared, rushing into her body like a flood. She gasped at the suddenness of it, her head rocking backwards. Part of her called out in joy to have the magic back, but another part of her cringed as memories of all the sadness it had caused filled her head and heart. Camille fought with both parts, trying to calm her emotions enough to perform the spell.

With effort, she quieted the excitement and dammed the memories.

Deep breaths.

Without opening her eyes she held her hands over the bowl and sent a wave of magic into the water and its contents to charge them. Then she sang her spell, a soft and lilting chant, *"Power of the Earth, please accept my humble gift. This day, take my power of Air, carry it sure and swift. Let me see the one I left behind, a sweet, revealing vision, clear in my mind."*

First came a snap in her head, like a camera shutter flicking, and then she opened her eyes. Clear and bright on the surface of the water, the vision took shape. A small girl—five years old, dressed in a striped sundress of pink, green, and orange—flew through the air, back and forth, on a backyard swing. She smiled a glorious smile, her long bronze hair twirling out behind her.

Lilly!

Amelia Plate's sweet baby—no longer a baby, but a bright, beautiful little girl. Camille smiled, inhaling the scent of lilacs from a tall hedge near the swing set.

After a few more minutes, the girl jumped off the swing and skipped over to a large garden. She walked along the edge, singing to herself. At the head of the garden stood a small stone birdbath, a simple open basin with blue and green marbles in the bottom. The girl stopped beside it and looked around.

Hesitantly she dipped her fingers in the warm water, flicking them, throwing little splashes across the surface. She looked up again, moved her eyes back and forth as if to make sure she was alone. Her eyes returned to the rippling water, and then she submerged both her hands up to the wrists and closed her eyes.

Camille leaned forward, her heart skipping.

After a few quiet moments, the girl opened her eyes again. She lifted her arms up; and the water came too, a clear liquid bubble encasing her small hands. A wide grin spread her lips. She clapped her hands together; and the water burst apart, separating into a million tiny diamond droplets. Stirring her hands in front of her, she guided the droplets to dance and swirl around her.

Camille gasped and put a hand over her heart. *Just like her mother.*

The midday sunlight cast colorful rainbow prisms through the drops. Surrounded by sparkles and colors, Lilly giggled, a fairy princess in a sparkling wonderland, weaving the drops into elaborate patterns.

"Chloe!"

The water fell from the air with a sad *swoosh* as Lilly—Chloe to her adoptive parents—lost control. Her clothes and red-brown hair wet with the water, she looked across the yard at her mother's hand covering her mouth and her eyes wide with shock. Her mother was a thin woman, with a kind oval face and short black hair. She marched across the yard to her adopted daughter, knelt down in front of the girl, who stared back with fearful, guilty green eyes.

"What did we talk about, Chloe?" the woman asked quietly.

"I know. I'm sorry," Chloe answered sheepishly, fiddling with the hem of her dress.

"You have to promise not to do these things. It's bad, and

it scares Mommy. Okay?" The woman placed a tender hand on her daughter's head.

"Okay. I promise."

The woman stood, offered a tiny smile. "Okay. Run inside, and get ready for lunch."

Chloe jumped up and ran away, eager to please.

The mother waited until the child went into the house, out of sight, and then she turned to look at the birdbath. She bit her bottom lip, shook her head, and looked suddenly worried, even desperate. She bent down, placed her hands on the lip of the basin. She stood blinking forcefully for a long moment, and then with a grunt she pushed the bath over, the basin breaking off from the stand to roll into the fence with a disappointed thud. The blue and green marbles bounced over the grass and disappeared among the blades.

The vision ended, and the water cleared.

Camille inhaled and exhaled deeply. She looked down at her folded hands. The part of her that still loved the magic wanted to cry, to go retrieve the girl, to teach her what her talent meant and where it came from, and to tell the child her real name and show her pictures of her real parents. The other part of her, the one that hated the magic, that blamed it for Solace's death, sat back in pleased triumph.

The old witch inclined her head and watched the sun climb higher in the Tuscan sky.

CHAPTER 8
NEW MOON

March—Present Day

Willa grabbed her purse and headed for the front door.

"Where are you going?" came her dad's voice from behind. "I thought you were staying for dinner."

Willa clenched her teeth, resisting the urge to sigh. She turned, hand still on the doorknob. "I left my phone at the museum. I'll be right back."

Ethan Fairfield was nearly as tall as Simon, but lean and thin, like a sapling tree. He patted the side of his head, smoothing salt and pepper hair. "Okay, but hurry. It's almost ready."

Willa studied the man for a moment. As a little girl, she and her father had been inseparable. He'd spent every Saturday taking her to parks, museums, and the zoo. He'd listened intently as she talked excitedly about history facts she'd read.

He had bought her books and had recorded TV shows he thought she'd like. She wasn't sure exactly when they'd drifted apart, maybe high school as her life got busier; but with a twang in her heart she realized that she missed him. She longed to throw her arms around him and hug him tightly and have all the tension between them disappear.

Why can't you be happy about this? She wanted to ask him, but said, "Yeah. Right back."

"Okay," Ethan said skeptically, already turning away.

Willa scowled sadly at his back, biting back a few choice words. *I'm not sneaking off to consort with the devil, Dad, just to get my phone.* She yanked open the door, fresh cold air rushing into her face. *I've always been a good daughter. Never gotten into trouble. Done well at school. But suddenly, when I try to follow the true path of who I am, I'm a delinquent to him.*

She looked back over her shoulder at the empty hall and then went out the door. Willa spent the few minutes from her house to the museum trying hard not to think about how things used to be.

"Solace? Hey, where are you?" Willa called as she pulled her set of museum keys from the lock and stepped into the dark, empty foyer. "Solace?"

"Hello, Willa! What are you doing back?" Solace appeared next to her.

"I left my phone. Have you seen it?" Willa dropped her purse to the floor and sat under one of the tall paned windows. The lights from the street poured in, casting a grid-patterned shadow on the tile floor. "Also, I'm hiding from dinner with my parents." Solace sat next to her and held out her phone. "Thanks," Willa said. "Were you reading my text messages again?"

Solace's eyes widened. "I would never!" she said sarcastically. "Next time could you make sure they are a little more exciting?"

Willa laughed. "So sorry."

Solace laughed and then turned to her, eyes shimmering in the gray light. "I'm glad you came back because I just had a weird experience."

"What happened?"

The ghost's eyes moved off, now distant and vague. "This picture appeared in my mind. I was leaning over a young woman in her bed—a very pretty girl, older than me, with red hair and green eyes. Her brow was sweaty, and in her arms she held a little bundle wrapped in blankets. I reached out"—the ghost reached her hand forward, imitating the movement—"pulled back the edge of a blanket and found a little baby. Beautiful baby. A girl, I think." Solace sighed.

"Solace! That sounds like a memory. Do you think it was?" Willa's heart pumped a little faster with the idea.

"I don't dare hope, but . . . maybe." Solace clasped her hands together in her lap.

Willa stared at her friend for a minute, the light cutting through her shadowy figure. "Red hair and green eyes. Sounds like Ruby or Amelia. Probably Amelia. She was about five years older than you, but there's no record of Amelia having a baby."

"I don't know. It was just a brief flash."

"Has that ever happened before?"

Solace studied her hands. "No, not really. A few times I've seen a flash of what I think is forest trees, a full moon." A stiff pause, her figure almost flickering out of sight. "Pain. Sometimes there is a burst of pain, an echo, just here." Her sheer fingers fluttered at her neck.

A chill snaked down Willa's spine, and she remained quiet for a moment. What had happened to her best friend? "Solace, I . . ."

Solace's eyes flashed up to her. "Do you think it means I'm close to crossing over? Having these maybe-memories?"

Willa blinked, surprised. "Maybe. There is no way to know. But either way, memories are good. Right?"

"I suppose." She pursed her lips. "But I'd rather remember my life when I'm *there* and not still stuck here."

Willa watched the ghost closely, studying the permanent sadness on her face. Quietly, she asked, "So you *want* to cross over?"

Solace smiled grimly. "Of course, I do, Willa. As much as I love you, I shouldn't be here. I shouldn't *live* like this." She rolled her eyes at the word. "It's wrong, unnatural." She looked vacantly at the dark space of the foyer. "I can feel it all the time—a whispering tug from the Otherworld. It's stronger lately, but still blocked somehow. I can't answer it, can't move toward it. I *need* to cross over, but I'm stuck. And that connection is a constant mockery."

Solace's eyes shimmered, almost as if blurred by tears. Willa leaned closer. She'd never heard Solace talk like this before. "I wish there was something I could do to help. I am a witch with the Power of Spirits, after all. You'd think there was something more to that than just seeing ghosts. Maybe one day I'll find something that can help you."

"Thank you, Willa. You are sweet." She inhaled, shook her head. "Let's talk about something else. Did you talk to Simon about faking it in training yesterday?"

Willa looked over at the crisscrossing shadows. Simon had obviously and purposely failed the second part of the test at the pool. At least it was obvious to her. To everyone else it seemed a huge relief. Because of that, she couldn't really blame Simon, but something about it bothered her. Was he ashamed of himself? "Not yet, but it's weird, right?"

"It's a little weird. Simon has never struck me as one to pretend just to please others."

"Exactly! I mean, we all pretend a little, hiding our true selves from the world, but that's different." She exhaled, rubbed at her forehead. "I don't know. I guess it's not that big of a deal. I just don't understand why everything has gotten so complicated with his powers. Why he won't talk to me or Rowan, make some effort to understand it."

"I wonder if he'll make it a habit—the faking."

Willa shook her head. "I hope not," she whispered. A rock of concern settled into the bottom of her stomach. "Solace, what's happening? Why can't we talk about this stuff? Soul mates are supposed to be close, to tell each other *everything*. But lately . . . I couldn't even bring myself to ask him if he really had faked it."

The floor under them shook violently. Willa instinctively reached out for Solace, but her hand met the cold floor. The window rattled overhead. Willa scrambled away from it, afraid it might shatter down on her.

"Willa! What's happening?" Solace cried out.

Before Willa could answer, the quake had stopped. Chest heaving, heart pounding, she jumped to her feet, looked out the window. Nothing seemed seriously damaged; the power hadn't even gone out. "An earthquake," she answered in disbelief.

Solace joined her at the window. "I don't think I like earthquakes."

"Me neither." Willa had never felt a quake before, and she hoped she never did again. "That was a really bizarre feeling. The floor should *not* move like that."

"Not ever."

It happened again. The window rattled, and the old building shuddered. Solace screamed as Willa dove to the ground. By the time she looked back at her ghost-friend the quake ended. "Whoa! What's going on?"

Solace hovered, rubbing her hands nervously. "I know it can't hurt me, but it still makes me nervous."

Willa's phone beeped from her purse. She crawled over, dug it out, and suddenly the weight in her stomach felt like a writhing ball of snakes. "It's Charlotte. She says I need to get to the house right now, that the quakes are not natural." Willa squinted at the message. "What does that mean?" Solace squeaked in protest. "Will you be okay, Solace?"

She frowned, eyes wide. "I guess so. But will *you*? If the quakes aren't natural, does that mean Dark magic? Is it Rachel? Maybe she didn't leave after all."

"I don't know." Willa snatched her purse, rose to her feet. She looked at Solace, trembling and flickering in and out of focus. "I'll come back and tell you what I find out. I'm sorry I have to go."

"It's okay. Go." She waved toward the door. "Be safe, Willa!"

"I will." She opened the door. "Bye," she added with a despondent expression.

THE DINER CLOSED AFTER THE fifth quake, and Simon hurried over to Plate's Place.

The windows of the Victorian home glowed. The exterior of the house had been stripped of the peeling, rotting clapboards and prepped for new ones, ordered in the same aspen green Ruby originally had. It'd look amazing when completed, but right now, in the dark, the house looked like the skeleton of some great beast.

"What's going on?" he asked as he stepped inside. The group gathered in the large kitchen, now almost finished. The recycled glass counters, sparkling white and green, and dark walnut cabinets made the house feel like it might actually be livable one day.

Simon crossed the room, fighting off the wave of uncertainty coming from his friends, and took his seat next to Willa at the long table.

Rowan, at the head of the table answered, "We don't know. Something has unsettled the balance of the Powers. The frequent small earthquakes have made the animals and trees very nervous."

"What 'something'?" Simon said. "Do you mean Dark magic, not just a freak natural occurrence? Colorado actually gets a lot of small quakes."

Rowan nodded. "Yes, we are quite certain this is Dark magic. The trees don't whisper when it's natural. Besides, Colorado doesn't get this many quakes at once . . . nowhere does."

Trees whispering? Even after almost six months in the Covenant, things like that still sounded strange.

"Is this Rachel?" Willa asked, her hand growing cold in Simon's.

Rowan shook his head. "I don't know. Rain and Corbin

tried another scrying spell a few minutes ago, and still nothing. I'm starting to wonder if someone or something is blocking us."

"What do you mean? For someone to block us, they would have to *know* about us." Willa asked.

"Exactly." Rowan frowned.

"Another reason to suspect Rachel," Simon said.

Rowan nodded, "Yes."

Rain moved to the window that looked out onto the driveway on the side of the house. She was dressed in ripped black skinny jeans, combat boots, and an obscure punk band t-shirt. She asked, "Are we sure Archard is dead?"

Everyone turned, a weighted silence answering her.

Elliot said quietly, "We all saw him burn." Simon flinched at the memories of Archard's smoking, burning body. He groaned slightly and Willa looked over. He shook his head, gave her an *I'm okay* look.

Rain nodded, still looking out the window between the blind slats. "I know, but . . . it's Archard. And since Rachel was his lackey, I just can't help wondering. Are we *absolutely* sure?"

Rowan cleared his throat. "I checked into it." Eyes moved back to him. Simon held his breath. There could be nothing worse than finding out Archard lived. Just the thought made his skin grow cold and his head ache. Rowan continued, "A group of hikers discovered the body about a week after the battle. It was identified as Archard and is now buried in his family's mausoleum in Denver."

Simon sighed and relaxed his shoulders. Willa squeezed his hand.

Rain stepped away from the window and nodded. "Good to know." She smiled and then frowned, folded her inked arms. "But I guess that means this is a new threat. Or Rachel seeking revenge."

Simon exhaled. "So what now? How do we stop it or fix it? Did the . . . *trees* give you any clue?"

Rowan shook his head. "No, only that there is Darkness nearby."

Willa stiffened next to him.

"So there's nothing we can do?" Simon said.

"No, there is something. There is a spell in Ruby's grimoire that allows us to . . . *check up,* if you will, on the Powers. Wynter and I have prepared everything."

"Form a circle," Wynter instructed as she stood. The kitchen filled with the sound of chairs pushing back from the table and feet shuffling. The covens gathered in a tight circle behind the table.

Wynter held Ruby's large, rust-colored grimoire in her arms. "Rowan . . ." At her word, Rowan pulled over a large clay basin filled with rich, black dirt and set it in the center of the circle. He reached into his pocket and produced a golf ball-sized green-yellow peridot. After pushing the stone halfway into the dirt, he sprinkled a handful of kosher salt over it.

Then the Luminary stood, stepped into his place in the circle. "Join hands," he said quietly.

Simon took Willa and Rain's hands. Whether it was Rachel or a new threat, Simon worried what it would mean for them, for him. *Are we facing another fight?* The memory of the three Dark witches sailing through the air filled his mind. His heart picked up speed. *No. Not again.* When he agreed to join the Covenant, he hadn't considered that other Dark witches might rise against them, that there might be frequent fights. With

Archard dead, the evil seemed at an end. *I was wrong. I should have thought this through more carefully.*

Rowan cleared his throat. "Focus your energy on the stone and draw power from the earth. Repeat the spell after me." He took a breath and closed his eyes.

Simon tried to push his thoughts aside as he squeezed his eyes shut, and called to the magic, focusing his mind. His hands grew hot, energy swirling inside him and on the air. The strength of the Covenant magic still surprised him. Each time they circled, it was like being connected to every plant, tree, rock, creature, and drop of water nearby, the sensations almost overwhelming, tingling along his nerves, threatening to awaken that stranger power inside him.

"*Energy of the Earth, grant us this night, the magic to see, to know, give us the sight.*" Rowan's voiced boomed in the sudden quiet, and when the group joined him Simon felt their voices reverberate in his chest.

A flash of heat pushed out from the center of the circle; Simon opened his eyes. From the surface of the stone, a plant burst upwards, growing rapidly. A trunk formed, branches burst out of it, and green leaves popped open. Within seconds, a tiny tree had grown, a miniature oak slightly larger than most Bonsai trees. Collectively, the witches leaned forward, watching carefully.

The tree burst into vicious red flames.

Willa gasped; Simon pulled her back from the fire. The circle broke apart. Rain acted quickly to summon a spurt of water to put out the growing red flames. An eerie silence followed as they all blinked at the smoking, charred skeleton of the miniature tree.

Simon put his arm around Willa's shoulders and pulled her close. Goose flesh rose on his arms. "So this is bad?" Simon asked, breaking the silence, his voice quiet and thin.

Rowan frowned, exhaled. "Yes, this is bad."

CHAPTER 9
New Moon

March—Present Day

Archard sat in his wheelchair, slumped over like a sack of flour. Shriveled and deformed, he hardly looked human, wrapped in two thick flannel blankets to keep in the warmth that his burned skin could no longer contain. The imperious black sky loomed overhead, stars like shards of glass pressed into the firmament. No moon rose in the sky—it was a new moon. The best time for healing spells.

The cave smirked at him, the place of his shame, the place where his own fire had betrayed him. He stared back with narrowed eyes at the entrance scorched black, fingerprints of flames rimming it. Ashes piled into gray drifts on the ground against the rocks. If Rachel hadn't come back for him and rushed him to the hospital, his remains would be among those ashes. Parts of him *were*.

From these ashes I will be reborn.

Rachel set Bartholomew's book down on another blanket spread out on the frosted dirt next to Archard's chair. It lay open to a very specific spell, one they had been seeking out for months. It'd taken several revealing spells to uncover the words, but Rachel had been diligent.

"Are you ready, Archard?" she asked in a hushed tone, leaning in close to the hole where his ear had been.

"Yes," he mumbled in the voice, no longer his own.

"You remember everything?"

He scoffed. "Don't treat me like a fool!"

She nodded, ignoring his temper. "I'll bring him, then." Rachel slipped away into the trees surrounding the clearing. There was a scuffle of feet, and then pathetic pleas for mercy. Archard rolled his eyes.

Rachel pushed the whimpering man forward. His dark jeans and black parka were dusty, his shoes heavy with mud. His hands were bound behind his back and a burlap sack covered his head. Archard wondered if it was itchy on the man's skin. He'd lost all sensation in his own skin, except for pain, and he often wondered about such things.

Rachel gave the man a powerful shove, and he collapsed at Archard's feet. She gripped the top of the sack and ripped it upward.

Archard met the man's watery, red eyes, and the man recoiled, horrified by the spectacle before him. Archard grinned a lipless smile.

"Please," the man whined between sobs, "please let me go."

Archard said nothing. He needed to gather his strength.

"Please. I'll do anything, give you anything. I'm sure I could get some money. I have a nice car. What if . . ."

"Shut up," Rachel said coolly, her arms folded over her

short, fitted leather coat. She rolled her icy blue eyes, and the man cowered under the venom of her words, dropping his head close to the ground. A fresh fit of sobs shook his thin body.

Archard lifted his hand, a mangled mass of red and white flesh. "The athame."

Rachel set his favorite ritual dagger, wickedly sharp and impressively long, in his hand. The man tried to crawl away, but Rachel grabbed him and pushed him closer. Archard met his victim's watery red eyes again, enjoying the fear and revulsion in them. "Your life for mine," he whispered with irreverent pleasure. Then, gathering all the strength his damaged body could manage, he plunged the knife into the man's gut. It didn't go as far as it should, so Rachel reached around, put her hand on Archard's, and thrust in the blade to the hilt. The man's eyes flashed open wide, a silent scream caught in his throat.

Blood trickled from his mouth, an odd gurgle escaping his throat. The wound was not immediately fatal, a detail vital to Bartholomew's spell.

Rachel pulled the victim's slack body away, and Archard dropped his hand to his lap, huffing painful breaths. Rachel dumped the man into a hole, stepping in after him. She pulled the athame from his body—the man screaming in pain—and set it on the ground, the blade shiny with blood. Then, hopping out of the hole, she stood at its edge and waved her hand. A mound of dirt rose into the air in one big clump. Seeing the dirt, the wounded man's screams pitched louder in protest. His hands clawed at the side of the hole. Rachel dropped the dirt heavily onto the man; it fell in staccato thuds, accompanied by his muffled screams.

Archard's heart pounded uncomfortably in his chest, but he ignored it. Rachel pushed his chair to the edge of the fresh grave. Gently she laid him down on the hard, cold dirt, tucking the blankets around him. Beneath him, Archard heard the weakening struggles of the interred victim.

Rachel placed four blue pillar candles at each corner of the grave and lit them with a quick snap of her fingers. In the dirt above his head she drew a symbol: a strange stick tree with two crooked branches.

Next she took a small glass bowl and filled it with some ashes from the cave. She set the bowl on the dirt above Archard's head. Into the bowl she tossed a handful of eucalyptus and sage. Then, holding her hand over the bowl, she set the contents afire.

"Ready?" she asked, her eyes burning with eagerness, reflecting the small flames in the bowl.

Archard's entire body felt cold as stone and just as stiff. Pain pulsed down his limbs. But he had to stay with it, see it to the end, no matter how much it hurt. "Yes," he hissed.

Rachel darted away and scooped Bartholomew's book into her arms. With the massive black tome balanced on her forearms, she stood over Archard's shivering body. Then she read from the Dark book, her voice like a snake, slithering and cold. *"A life for a life, we offer mighty Earth. One now dead to give the other rebirth. Heal the wounds, make all complete. A body now whole, all weakness retreats."*

Both witches gasped as the force of Bartholomew's spell took over. The burning ash and herbs lifted out of the bowl to cyclone over Archard's face. After a moment, the flames snuffed out; and what remained showered down into his eyes and mouth. He fought the urge to cough. Below him, more yells and moans came through the layers of dirt.

The air in the clearing grew cold, crackling with a bizarre energy.

The earth shook, bucking against the reigns of the Darkness, resistant, angry. The trees bent away, some snapping loudly in the quiet night. A rush of icy energy moved up through the dirt, pulling the dying man's life force up and into Archard's body. Droplets of blood bubbled out of the dirt, the victim's blood. It rose above Archard, hovering over him for a protracted moment before falling hard onto his body. His face and chest and arms were covered in the man's steaming blood, more rising and falling as the spell continued to work.

Archard felt the man's fight, his terrified struggle to cling to life, but his efforts were wasted. The man's energy flowed into Archard, like water into a streambed, pleasant at first, but then morphing into searing pain. The witch screamed out, the action tearing at his throat and vocal chords. Clawing at the ground, he arched his back as the magic in the victim's blood reformed him, repaired him. Below him, the dirt was silent.

The magic continued to torment Archard's body, the energy ripping through his skin, clawing at his wounds. Several minutes passed, an endless barrage. Near the end, he wished to die, the awful pain so overwhelming. Finally, the candles around him flared high, their flames reaching for the moonless sky, and then snuffed out. With them went the twisted pain.

The night fell eerily still.

Rachel held her breath. Archard looked dead, unmoving on the dirt, and covered in blood.

"Archard?" she whispered.

With a deep, rattling breath, he sat bolt upright. Rachel jumped back a step. He lifted his arms and looked down at skin pulled a little tighter, scars a little less harsh. He touched his face. There were lips, although thin and uneven. The skin along his jawline had smoothed a bit; there was half an ear. He gasped. "Rachel!"

"Yes," she breathed, stepping closer, "yes, it worked. You look . . ."

"A little better."

She grinned slowly. "Yes."

Archard tested his feet, stumbling slightly, and stood for the first time in months. His muscles were weak, atrophied. He held his arms out, stretched his fingers. He rolled his neck and took a deep, full breath, pleased when it resulted in only a tiny jab of pain instead of a full punch in the face.

"It worked," he said, his eyes alive and bright. "Get me another sacrifice!"

WILLA HELD ON TO SIMON's arm, worry worming under her skin. The small tree continued to smoke.

The house shook, another quake. No one moved.

Finally, Cal broke the silence. "I think this is more than someone blocking our spells."

All eyes turned to the bear of a man.

"What do you mean, Cal?" Darby asked.

Cal rubbed at his large chin. "Just think about it. Not one of our spells has worked successfully since the Binding. We are supposed to have all this power, the *most* power, and yet we can't even get simple scrying spells to work right. And now this spell," he gestured to the tree. "How the heck do you explain that mess? A spell *made* for the Covenant blowing up like that?" He shook his head, folded his arms. "Either someone is blocking us with some mad-powerful magic we've never heard of, or something is wrong with *us*."

Willa's heart stuttered. *Wrong with us? What could be wrong with us?*

Rowan stroked his beard pensively. "The Binding was successful. I don't see how something could be wrong with the Covenant magic. But you have a point, Cal. Ruby's notes say a message is suppose to appear in the leaves of the tree, words or images. But that . . ."

A branch of the tree fell off, crumbling into the pot of dirt. Willa shivered. She looked up at Simon. He looked back with the same nervous confusion.

Wynter stepped forward. "I think it's time to talk to other witches, see if there are any rumors of a new Dark witch or coven."

Darby clicked her tongue. "That's risky, Wynter. If word gets out, no one will leave us alone."

Willa had read in Ruby's grimoire about the importance of secrecy to protect the powerful Covenant magic. One breath of the Binding would bring dozens, if not hundreds of other witches down on them—Dark witches intent on breaking the bond, and Light witches wanting to be part of the powerful magic.

"I understand that," Wynter said with a nod, "but we don't need to say anything about the Covenant to make a few phone calls and ask a few questions."

Rowan nodded, "I agree. If we can't figure out what's going on the magical way, then we'll do it the old fashioned way. Everyone start calling any contacts you know we can trust. Start with the ones near us, and go from there. Let's see if we can find something—give us a starting point."

Everyone immediately pulled out their cell phones and started dialing. Willa looked at Simon, who shrugged; they didn't have anyone to call. Simon took her hand, led her up the stairs and into their room—or the room that would be theirs when Willa finally managed to break away from her parents.

The room was currently a disaster. The ugly wallpaper with a sad paisley design bubbled and peeled in several places. It might have been green once. The wood floor had warped and cracked, and the small brick fireplace was slowly crumbling. Willa lifted her chin, ran her eyes along a jagged crack in the ceiling. The radiant heater clicked loudly, putting off an inadequate amount of warmth.

At least there was a new queen-sized bed with a barn-wood headboard provided by Wynter. She had told them, "I know you can't move in yet, but I still want this to feel like your home." Something about the antique blue-and-green patchwork quilt and pile of white pillows felt very much like home to Willa, despite the condition of the room.

Another quake rumbled through the house, shaking a chunk of brick off the fireplace. Willa picked it up and held it in her hands. "Poor house. I'm not sure it can take many more of these. The whole thing might collapse on top of us."

Simon lay down on the bed, hands behind his head. He kicked off his boots and crossed his ankles. Willa tossed the chunk of brick into the grate, brushed her hands off and joined him. "So what do you think is going on?"

"I don't know," he answered, face serious. "But the way that tree burst into flames . . . something felt so wrong about that."

"Very wrong." Willa laid her hand on Simon's chest, felt the shape of his triangular gift pendant under his shirt.

Rachel's hooded figured flashed in her mind. "I didn't think it would be like this," she whispered.

"Like what?" Simon placed his hand on top of hers, turned his head to look at her.

"The unknown. These weird things happening, and we don't know why or what to do about it." She scooted closer to him, wanting to feel his solid warmth. "I guess that shows how naïve I was about joining the Covenant. For all we know, it will always be like this."

After a long sigh, Simon said, "I was thinking the same thing. I assumed Archard's death was the end of it. It makes it hard to have a normal life with all this crap going on. I'm lucky my professor let me turn in that paper for half credit. That might not happen next time. I can't mess up my chances at a good med school."

"I know. I'm not doing as well as I should either. I got a C on a test today because I was too busy looking for Rachel and doing the pool test to get any good studying done. A C! I've never gotten less than an A minus before." She rolled her eyes at the memory of how shocked and upset she'd been, seeing that red C. "And it's not like we can plan for these things. It's not like the Dark witches will give us the courtesy of calling in advance before attacking."

Simon smiled, but a shadow passed through his eyes. *Just ask him. Try again. Get him to talk!*

"Simon, can we talk about something?"

He noticeably stiffened, but said, "What is it?"

Willa swallowed, pushed past the urge to drop the subject. "I don't like this . . . this thing where we don't talk. It feels so wrong." Simon opened his mouth, but she cut him off.

"I know you don't want to talk about the cave. So let's start with something small, like why you pretended to fail part of the pool test."

His jaw tensed; he looked away. "I knew you could tell. Did anyone else notice?"

"I don't think so. Why do you think you have to hide from them?"

"You've seen how nervous they get around me, how they've looked at me since the cave. I'm not supposed to be this good at everything. It creeps them out. Hell, it creeps *me* out." A muscle twitched in his jaw; Willa touched his face.

"I know, but pretending isn't going to solve the problem. So what if you are more powerful than any of us? That's nothing to be ashamed of. Wynter, Rowan, and the others killed Dark witches that day, too. You don't need to torture yourself." He sat up abruptly, startling her. The room shook with another quake, and Willa wanted to yell at it for interrupting.

"But they *meant* to do it." He swung his legs off the bed, put his head in his hands, elbows on knees. "I had no idea what I was doing. And that's what scares me . . . and them. My whole life, I've been this freakin' outcast. I thought I'd finally found somewhere I could be myself, somewhere I fit in. But it turns out I'm still the outcast." He took an unstable breath. "Why can't I just have one simple gift like the rest of you? Why do I always have to be the *freak?!*"

Willa's mouth hung open; she had no idea what to say to that. Maybe that was why she'd been avoiding this conversation—she really didn't know how to help him. And that hurt in his eyes . . . how she hated that look! Why *couldn't* he be a normal witch like the rest of them? What had made him so different? Was there a way to find out? *I have to find out.*

Sitting up, she knee-walked over and knelt behind him, arms around his tense neck and shoulders. She kissed the side of his neck. "I want to help you, but I don't know how."

Simon turned to her, eyes tight with frustration. "I don't know either." His hand slipped onto her cheek, and he stretched his neck to kiss her lips. Willa sensed desperation in that one small kiss, so she answered it with a deeper one. Simon sighed, his breath tickling her lips. Swiftly, he shifted, maneuvering her to the bed and under his body. Hands in his hair, Willa met his passion with her own. If she couldn't give him answers, she could give him comfort.

A quake shook the house, but neither of them noticed.

SIMON WOKE FROM HIS CAVE nightmare a little after three in the morning. Immediately he turned to check for Willa. The contented rise-and-fall of her chest immediately eased his anxiety. She wouldn't normally be there, but they'd spent the night at Plate's Place because of the quakes. Rowan and Wynter wanted everyone close—just in case. Hazel, Corbin, and Toby were camped out on couches; and even Cal and Darby, whose house was only a few blocks away, had stayed. It'd taken Willa fifteen minutes on the phone with her parents apologizing for missing dinner and convincing them it was okay for her to spend the night. That it was Covenant business and not some rebellion on her part.

Just a dream, just a dream, Simon told himself. *The same stupid dream you've had for months.* After he managed to slow his heart rate and calm the jittery energy in his core, he turned on the TV, which sat on a small desk in the corner by the fireplace. The television was another gift from Wynter and Rowan.

Simon flipped through several channels, not really paying attention, hoping to distract himself from the fear with some brainless entertainment. A thought nagged at him, an itchy scab he tried to ignore. He'd picked at it before and then let it heal over, but again he wanted to scratch. Willa's comment about this not being what she expected gave him enough reason to reopen the thought.

So he dropped the remote on the bed next to him and picked at the question.

What would happen if we left the Covenant?

It was a small thought, not yet a qualified idea, but one his logical mind couldn't leave alone. Lately, he felt like he and Willa made the decision too quickly, floating on the high of defeating Archard and discovering the source of their supernatural abilities. Now, he wasn't sure he'd make the same decision.

It wasn't that he didn't want to be a witch or to learn magic; instead it was the Covenant, the obligation to be in the line of fire of Dark witches. Without conscious thought, he'd killed three of them already. How many more might he have to kill? The idea made him physically ill. *Did I sign up to be a killer?* The others had killed members of Archard's covens without a second thought, just like Willa had said, but he couldn't seem to move past his own transgressions.

But if they stayed, he knew—as hard as it was to hurt instead of heal—that he would do it to keep Willa safe.

So is it better in the long run to leave? Avoid the whole thing?

Simon rubbed his arm nervously. A chef on the TV expertly flipped the contents of a large skillet.

What would Willa say? The Covenant made her happy.

She wasn't accustomed to being alone like he was. She thrived on the camaraderie of being a part of the covens. She adored her home here in Twelve Acres and her work at the Museum. And although he'd grown to enjoy the company of the witches and a home in a small town, it'd be easy to slip back into the anonymity of independence.

Maybe his lifetime of broken relationships skewed his view. He expected it to fail; there was no previous evidence to support success. Everything good in his life had ended because of what he could do. Why would the Covenant be any different? What if they turned on him too? His exceptional abilities made him an alien even among other witches. Eventually they'd want him gone, or he'd get sick of pretending to fit in.

What would happen if we left the Covenant?

The Covenant bond might be for life, but it couldn't stop him from taking Willa and walking away. If it kept her safe and kept him from killing anyone else . . .

Could I really do it? What would Willa say? Would she come?

Willa stirred in her sleep. "Another nightmare?" she mumbled sleepily.

He brushed the hair from her face. *If I need to leave will you come? I can't go without you.* "Yeah, but I'm okay. Go back to sleep."

"Are you sure?" Her pretty eyes fluttered open for a second and then closed.

He wondered if he should ask her. She'd said earlier that she hated how he kept bottling things up, not talking to her. "Willa, would you come with me if I needed to leave? Would you leave the Covenant?"

"Hmmm?" she said.

Simon exhaled. "Nothing. Go back to sleep." Willa didn't answer, already asleep. Simon turned off the TV, rolled onto his side, and gathered her warm body into his arms.

But sleep eluded him, the question set on repeat.

What would happen if we left the Covenant?

THE NEXT MORNING, NO ONE had answers.

·"Not one thing?" Wynter asked, sitting on the couch in the front room, sipping tea. Willa sat next to her, nursing her own cup of hot mint tea, which helped take the edge off the chill in the morning air.

"Nothing," Darby confirmed. "I called every one of my contacts. No one has heard anything about Dark witches stirring up trouble."

Wynter looked around the room. "Same for all of you?" Everyone nodded and mumbled confirmation. She shook her head. "So strange."

"So, what now?" Simon asked from his perch next to Willa on the arm of the couch.

"Well," Rowan said, spreading his hands in a gesture of defeat, "we keep an eye to the sky and an ear to the ground. If it happens again, we can try repeating the spell. Maybe what happened last night was a fluke."

Elliot, who had been looking at his phone during the conversation, leaned forward. "Holy moon!"

"What is it?" Char asked, leaning over to look at his phone.

Elliot frowned and then read from a news article. "'Thirteen people have been reported missing in the areas within and surrounding Denver. There appears to be no discernible pattern to the disappearances and no evidence left at any of the last known locations. The Denver Police suspect foul play but are unable to point to the source of the disappearances. As of this morning, no bodies have been recovered, and no one has been located.'" He looked up, his brown skin somehow paler. "*Thirteen* people."

Rowan inhaled sharply. "There were exactly thirteen quakes last night."

Willa's skin prickled with cold, the hairs on her arm standing up. "What does it mean?"

Wynter shook her head. "Well, it's hard to imagine, but . . . it may mean that whatever Dark magic was being performed last night required sacrifices."

"Whoa! Like *human sacrifices?*" Simon asked, eyes wide.

Rowan rubbed his beard. "It's an ancient practice—done away with centuries ago. Dark witches once used the blood, or worse, the death of others to control the magic in terrible ways. Sacrifices—human or animal—are dangerous, and unpredictable. And they are the worst kind of affront to the Powers of the Earth, which is why the practice was done away with—even among Dark witches."

"Looks like we got a serious crazy running around," Darby said.

"Rachel had blood on her forehead," Simon said quietly, looking at the floor.

"What?" Wynter breathed.

"She had a red dot," Simon pointed to the middle of his forehead, "right here when she attacked Willa, Char, and Elliot. I'm pretty sure it was blood. It didn't look like a wound or spatter because there was a thumb print in it, as if put there on purpose."

A weighted pause followed. "So maybe Archard used blood

sacrifices," Rowan thought out loud. "That could explain some of the powerful things he was able to do. But, even for him, that seems extreme."

"Well, if he was, then maybe this *is* Rachel, trying to pick up where he left off," Darby added.

"Does it say anything else, Elliot?" Rowan asked, nodding to the phone.

"No, not really. The police are clueless, and there were no witnesses to any of the disappearances."

"Even more reason to suspect magic," Cal offered. "People leave behind clues—witches don't."

The clock on the freshly-polished mantel chimed seven. "We gotta go, Willa," Simon said, standing. "It feels weird to leave right now, but is there anything we can do? Or should we go to class?"

"Go," Wynter said, waving her hand to the door. "We'll monitor the situation and contact you if there is any reason to come back."

Simon nodded and turned to Willa. "Let's go."

"Okay. I just need my bag." She stood. "I'll meet you at the car." Taking the stairs two at a time, Willa rushed into their room, grabbed her purse, and then hurried back downstairs. They'd have to stop at her parent's house for her backpack.

It felt so odd to think of the need to get her backpack and go sit through classes when thirteen people were missing and a Dark witch might be out there.

Her heart thudded uncomfortably as she came back down the stairs, another issue on her mind. Hesitating at the door, she turned to look back in the front room. An idea had come to her late last night, right before she fell asleep. Wynter and Rowan had been looking for an answer to Simon's strange powers, but they weren't trained historians. Willa knew how to research, how to look for small details, connections. She planned to take over, to read through their extensive collection of grimoires. She wanted to do it anyway, but now she had serious motivation. And then she'd also ask how to find other grimoires, other sources of information. She'd go anywhere and talk to anyone she had to. Simon needed answers, and that was something she was good at.

She stopped outside the front room. Her first class started in half an hour. She sighed in disappointment.

Now wasn't the right time to ask, but she'd take the first opportunity she had.

CHAPTER 10
New Moon

April—Present Day

The earthquakes came again on the April new moon. Willa was at home with her parents, sitting in the family room, reading yet another dusty grimoire when the first one hit.

She'd spent the last weeks poring over every grimoire in Wynter and Rowan's collection. Then she'd driven all over the state looking for others. So far her search for the key to Simon's multiple gifts had turned up nothing. She was, however, learning a lot about magic and witchcraft; but none of it immediately helpful, which frustrated her.

Her mom sat next to her on the couch, reading a novel she'd brought home today from the bookstore where she worked; her dad lounged in an arm chair watching the History Channel. Sarah wore yoga pants and a baggy sweatshirt, her brown hair pulled into a messy bun at the base of her skull. Ethan wore black fleece sweats and a t-shirt, his favorite after-work attire, since his job as manager of the local grocery store required a shirt and tie.

Willa, also in yoga pants and a tank top and comfortable under a heavy blanket, looked up from the dull spellbook of an Earth witch to check the clock. Eight-forty-five. Simon had the closing shift tonight, but planned to stop by after—around ten o'clock. She sighed and turned back to the boring passage on growing parsley.

The house shook without warning.

A tremor, strong enough to shift the magazines on the coffee table but not buck the pictures off the walls, rattled the structure. Sarah instinctively reached out to touch Willa's arm, and Willa reached back. The quake lasted only a few seconds, but Willa's heart rate spiked.

When the house quieted, Sarah said breathlessly, "Are you okay? Is everyone okay?"

Willa exhaled, "Yeah, of course."

Sarah huffed and leaned forward to stack the magazines, mumbling about needing to get an emergency storage together. A magazine in each hand, she stopped and turned back to Willa. "Last month—the quakes—you said something about magic."

Willa frowned. Last time, she'd downplayed the seriousness of the situation, telling her parents the quakes were caused by magic, but it was nothing to worry about. Should she tell them about the whispers of the trees and the unbalanced Powers? The missing people? Should she tell them that the Covenant had been searching for a cause for a month and hadn't found anything?

The memory of the tree bursting into flames filled her mind. If the quakes were back, did that mean more people were missing? And what was happening to them? Despite her dad's distrust of Rowan and Wynter, and her mother's certain worry, maybe it was time she let them in on more of what she knew.

Sarah dropped the magazines, narrowing her eyes. "Willa? What's going on?"

At Sarah's tone, Ethan looked over, also waiting for Willa's response. She carefully closed the book and held it against her chest like a shield. After a breath, she said quietly, "It's Dark magic."

Her father's eyes widened, and then he scoffed and turned away. Sarah, however, scooted closer. "What do you mean?"

"It's not normal. We . . ."

"Of course, it's not normal," Ethan interrupted, still turned to the TV. "But it's an earthquake. There's nothing magical about that."

Willa rolled her eyes. "Dad, come on! Why do you still insist on pretending magic doesn't exist? Magic is the energy of everything around us. When the balance of that energy gets thrown off by Dark witches, bad things happen. Like those thirteen people who went missing."

That got his attention. He turned, eyes pinched in anger. "What do you know about *that*?"

"We think a Dark witch or coven took them to work some kind of spell, possibly killing them in the process. *That* spell is causing the quakes."

Sarah gasped. "Oh no! Do you know who?"

"No. We've been looking for a month and can't find anything."

Ethan grunted, switched the channel. "That because it's a load of crap." He scoffed again, turning abruptly. "This whole thing is a big, sadistic joke. I mean, now our daughter is talking about missing people and murders. What kind of a life is that?" He pointed a judgmental finger at Willa. "You better not go around town telling people you know something about thirteen people missing. You're gonna end up in trouble."

Willa's anger flashed hot. "Dad! This isn't some kind of delusion or brainwashing. This is very real. You can't keep—"

Sarah cut her off with a hand on her arm. "You've got to stop this, Ethan. This is our daughter's *life*—it's not a joke. It's very serious. She could be in danger again. I know you don't understand or want to understand the witch world, but if you're not going to try, then keep your mouth *shut!*"

Willa blinked. She'd never heard her mom talk that way to her dad. Certainly not raise her voice. Usually, Ethan took the authoritative stance, doing the managing as he was accustomed to. Willa watched him carefully, her hands balling into nervous fists, arms still locked around the grimoire. His face hardened a bit, but then his shoulders sagged.

"You never gave me a chance to understand, Sarah." He clicked off the TV and stood. Willa blinked, shocked. Sarah's face collapsed. For the first time, Willa realized her mother wasn't only fighting to regain her daughter's trust, but her husband's as well.

"I'm sorry, Willa," Ethan added quietly, not looking at either of them, "but I'll never be okay with this." With that he left the room, his steps sounding up the stairs.

Sarah exhaled slowly, her face pale, her shoulders hunched forward. She turned to Willa. "Sorry, honey. I'm working on him, but he's got that Fairfield stubbornness and naïve practicality. He can't see past his own ideas." She shook her head and glared in the direction of the stairs. "And I hurt him badly," she added, almost too quietly for Willa to hear.

Willa nodded, the back of her throat suddenly tight. "Maybe I should move out." She hadn't intended to say that, but the words spilled out before she could grab onto them.

Sarah blinked like Willa had slapped her. "*What?!* Why would you move out? You're not to blame for what's going on between your dad and me."

"I know that, but Dad hates what I am," she said, looking down at the grimoire, pulling it tighter against her chest.

Her mom touched her leg gently. "Willa, no. He's just worried about his little girl. Yes, it's hard for him, but he doesn't *hate* anything about you. He just doesn't understand it, and that scares him. And he doesn't know how to handle being scared. The whole witch thing is as new to him as it is to you; but he's not a witch, so it's much harder for him to deal with."

Willa looked up into her mom's wide, worried face. "Mom . . . I think I should be on my own. I want to be. Maybe things could get better between all of us if there was a little distance." She bit her bottom lip, pained by the look on her mom's face, but needed to go on. She'd sat on the idea long enough. "There is a room already waiting at Plate's Place. I want to be with the Covenant."

Sarah's eyebrows lifted in a look of shock and hurt. She opened her mouth, but didn't get a chance to say anything. Another tremor shook the house. This time a vase fell over on the kitchen table, the water and flowers spilling out. Her mom swore under her breath as she jumped up to clean the mess.

Willa's phone buzzed from the coffee table, a text from

Wynter: *Come as soon as you can.* She gripped the phone and stood. "Mom, I gotta go." Willa felt she should stay and talk about the bomb she'd just dropped, but the desire to flee from the impending fight was too strong.

Sarah looked up, her face tight with worry. "Can't we talk some more? We need to talk about this."

"Later, okay? I have to meet the Covenant. We have to stop this." Willa moved toward the stairs. "But please think about what I said."

"Okay," her mom said stiffly. She turned back to mopping up the water. With her eyes on the mess, she said, "Be safe, Willa."

Willa blinked at the strong tug of guilt the words caused: guilt that her strangeness had to worry and affect her parents so much and guilt that she wanted to get away from their worry. She watched her mom's lowered head and the tense curve of her shoulders. "I will," she mumbled and then slipped upstairs to change.

WILLA HURRIED THROUGH THE EMPTY streets to Ruby's house. The weather still clung to winter, the air laced with the smell of snow. She pulled her scarf higher on her neck and picked up the pace.

Her coven-mates huddled in the kitchen, now almost completely renovated. She shut the door behind her and turned to the group. Willa felt instantly safer being with them, but their concerned, solemn looks slightly dampened the sensation.

Charlotte walked over to put her arm through Willa's, guiding her to the group. "Where's Simon?"

"His shift ends at ten."

She nodded slowly, bit her bottom lip. "More people are missing."

Willa's breath caught in her chest. "How many?"

"Fourteen that we know of," Char said solemnly. "It hasn't been officially announced, but Cal knows someone at the Denver P.D."

Willa sat at the table, dazed by the news and turned to look at Wynter. "It's new moon again."

"Yes," Wynter said as she rubbed her right forearm where her scars were hidden under the long sleeve of her peasant top. "The power of the new moon can be used for many types of spells: starting a journey, renewal, healing. But it's hard to say what a Dark witch would use it for, especially while employing blood sacrifices."

Elliot came into the room carrying his laptop and sat next to Willa. "Well, this isn't working like I hoped," he announced, his face sour with disappointment.

"What are you doing?" Willa asked, looking at the complicated, scientific graphics on his screen.

"I was trying to pinpoint the location of the quakes. I thought if we found the point of origin, then we could go there and find whoever is responsible. But," he made a few clicks with his mouse, "it's really weird."

"Weird how?" Rowan asked.

"The location seems to . . . float, even disappear at times. It's like the instruments can't really read these tremors. So all I can say is that they are happening somewhere within a one hundred mile radius."

"Well, that's inconvenient," Cal grunted. "Now even the 'good old-fashioned way' is failing us."

The side door opened. Rain came in, shivering in a battered army jacket. She sighed loudly. "I tried the scrying spell again. Even tried to focus only on the quakes and not the magic, but still saw nothing. Only a gray cloud moving just under the surface of the water."

"This is so bizarre," Wynter said, rubbing at her temple. "Has anyone heard from friends? Any updates from other witches?"

No one had anything to offer.

By the time Simon arrived at the house, the air was ripe with tension and frustration. He strolled in just as everyone stood up from the table. Willa hurried over. "What's going on?" he asked.

"More people are missing, none of the spells are helping, and we can't even use science to find out where the quakes are coming from. So we are splitting up the surrounding areas and driving around."

"To do what, exactly?"

"See if we can spot anything suspicious or get closer to where the quakes are coming from." She shrugged as if to say, *It's pointless, but what else can we do?*

Rowan stepped to the side door. "Simon, good, you're here. You and Willa go up the east canyon. Whatever these witches are doing would need privacy. Maybe they're in the mountains."

Simon nodded. "Okay."

"Text if you find anything."

Out the door they went, pouring into the driveway and dispersing into the fleet of cars. Simon and Willa hurried back to the Jeep parked on the road in front of the house. Another quake shook the car as Simon started the engine.

"That's seven," Willa said warily, looking out the windshield.

"How many people this time?"

"Fourteen." She looked at him with worried eyes. "Halfway through."

Simon flipped the Jeep around and headed in the direction of the canyon.

ARCHARD STOOD UP FROM THE frigid, lumpy dirt and flexed his arms. His muscles responded with vigor. The cold night air pricked his perfected skin and moved through the clearing with crackling energy. "It's done!" he hissed. Twenty-seven bodies lay buried in the dirt beneath his feet, the clearing a bloody mess.

Rachel's eyes traveled up and down his body. "It's incredible." She touched a small rippled scar over his right eye—the last remaining trace of his former condition. "This spot right here won't heal, but I think the scar suits you."

He pulled a hand back through his full head of black hair. All the pain, the burning agony, had been worth it. Bartholomew's healing spell had produced results that surprised even Archard. He locked his eyes on hers. "Now, the real work begins."

"WILLA?" A QUIET KNOCK SOUNDED on Willa's bedroom door. She paused in reaching for her bedside lamp and turned. Her mom cracked open the door, putting her head in. "Can I come in?"

The clock read twelve-o-three. She and Simon had driven

around for two hours before the quakes stopped and the Covenant gave up the fruitless search. Willa's parents had been in bed when she came quietly into the house, a flood of relief washing over her, knowing she'd avoided talking to her mom about what she'd said earlier about moving out. Tired and ready to get a few hours of sleep before her early class, the last thing she wanted was a strained conversation with her mom. But, she hadn't escaped as cleanly as she thought.

Willa sat up, pulling her knees to her chest. She sighed and looked at her mom, "Yeah, of course."

Sarah came in and shut the door behind her. She sat on the edge of the bed, nervously wedging her hands between her knees. "How did things go tonight? Did you find the Dark witches?"

"No. Something is still preventing us from discovering what's going on." Willa yawned.

Sarah nodded slowly. "And did more people go missing?"

"Yeah. Fourteen."

"Their poor families."

Willa nodded. "Mom, is this really what you wanted to talk about?"

Sarah shook her head and exhaled. "No, of course not." She looked around the dimly lit room. "Funny thing is, it wasn't the quakes that kept me from going to sleep earlier—it was what you said about moving out."

Willa's chest tightened. "Okay . . ."

"Don't worry. I didn't tell your dad. He's not ready for that." Willa exhaled. "Yeah, probably not."

Sarah looked up and scooted a little closer. "I know I don't have the right to ask you to do anything after . . . after keeping the secret of who you really are. And also since things have been so strained between us all since the fall, but . . ." She pressed her teeth together, grimaced slightly.

"What, Mom?" Willa said gently. Part of her still hated that her mom had kept the truth from her, but she was working on not being mad about it. She hated the way it felt to be mad at her mom.

After a short exhale, Sarah said, "Can you wait until the summer to move out?"

Willa blinked in surprise, not sure whether to be relieved or upset. "Why?"

"So I can work on your dad." She gave a little smile. "Give me the next couple months to convince him that it's okay for you to move out and live with the other witches. If you were to suddenly go now, he might say or do things he'll regret. I don't want him to permanently ruin your relationship with him over this—he's already pushing it." She reached out to put her hand on Willa's knee. "I know that this really isn't fair to you, but do you think you can wait? Can you be patient with us a little longer?"

A dual feeling bloomed in Willa's chest. She understood the reason to wait, but summer seemed so far away. However, nothing in her mom's request was unreasonable. Willa didn't want to make things worse with her dad either. So, she could be smug and pull the guilt card on her mom, using her betrayal as an excuse not to agree, or she could do the kind, respectable thing and stay until summer. She knew Simon would tell her to stay to protect her relationship with her parents.

Sarah studied her face, waiting anxiously. Willa exhaled, "Okay. Until summer. After the semester ends."

Her mom exhaled and released a small bubble of a laugh.

"Oh, good. Thank you, Willa. Really. We are so lucky to have you as our daughter."

Willa nodded, uncomfortable with her mom's thanks. "But, Mom, this is something I really want *and* need to do. It's not just about getting separation from you and Dad. Come summer, no matter what, I'm moving out."

"I know," Sarah said meekly. "And I really do understand. I think you should do it. I moved out of my house at eighteen and never looked back. I learned a lot on my own, and I want you to have those experiences too." She chewed on her lip for a moment and then added, "What about Simon? Will he move in too or stay at his apartment?"

Willa almost lied, thinking it might make things easier, but lies like that never worked. "The room at Plate's Place is for both of us, if we want."

Sarah lifted her eyebrows, tried to hide her shock. She laughed, "Well, that won't make things any easier with your dad. You know how he is—always a little traditional about things." She looked at the bedroom door, her body shifting as if to leave. Then very quietly, she asked, "Will you get married? I know you are young, but . . . being married is a good thing. And I've dreamed about your wedding your whole life."

Willa's heart fell. She and Simon had never discussed the idea of getting married. Their bond was so strong, so complete, that a ceremony to make it official didn't feel necessary. Did she truly want to get married, need to? She reached out to touch her mom's arm. "Mom, we are *already* bound together forever. It's different with us; we're soul mates."

Sarah nodded stiffly, her eyes suddenly wet. "I know. I understand that, really I do." She tried to smile. "I just . . . it'd be so sad not to hang a picture of you in a white dress." She looked over and then gently, hesitantly touched Willa's hair. "With your hair down, no veil. And maybe a vintage dress? I have my Grandma Mabel's dress in a box downstairs. She got married in like 1940, but the dress looks like it's from the twenties. Lace and beads and . . ." Her voice trailed off, stalled by emotion.

Willa had never realized a wedding was that important to her mom. Of course, she'd also fantasized about her wedding, just like every other girl in the world—she'd never wanted a veil either—but a big traditional wedding didn't seem to fit in with who she was now, with the covens and witchcraft. *How do witches get married?* she wondered. She squeezed her mom's arm. "Grandma Mable's dress sounds pretty." She smiled.

Sarah smiled back, and then seriousness returned. "Willa, it's not just about the dress and the pictures and the party." Her face screwed up for a moment, and she bit her lower lip. "It's about being one, being partners. My mom wasn't very good at being a mom; but when I started high school, she sat me down to talk. It's probably the most normal memory I have of her." She shook her head sadly. Willa had never heard Sarah talk about her mom like this. She leaned forward, attentive.

Sarah went on. "She said something that always stuck with me, something I should have told you a long time ago, but it wouldn't have made sense to you before now." Sarah paused to take a breath and perhaps steady herself. "A marriage between soul mates is the most perfect magical circle. Find your soul mate, get married, be happy." She caught Willa's eyes.

Willa nodded, her heart full, and her head busy with thoughts. How could she talk to Simon about getting married now, with everything going on? Maybe by summer, by the time she could move out, things would be calmer, and they could make a decision then.

Sarah added, "Please, think about it. It's your decision—yours and Simon's—but thank you for waiting until summer to move out. That will help your dad and me a lot." She reached forward and pulled Willa into a tight hug. "We love you so much. You're truly amazing."

"I love you, too. Thanks for coming to talk."

Sarah stood with a tired sigh. "Get some sleep. See you in the morning."

"Mom?" Willa said on impulse.

Sarah turned back, her hand on the doorknob. "Yeah?"

"I know you were just trying to give me a good life. I know you didn't tell me about the witch thing because you love me." Emotion pulled at Willa's heart.

Sarah blinked quickly and put a hand on her heart. "Yes," she whispered.

Willa nodded. "I don't want you to feel like you owe me something now or have to work really hard to make up for it. And I don't want you to think I want to move out because of what you did. We're okay."

Sarah half-smiled and nodded, looking relieved. A fresh sheen of tears glistened in her eyes.

"Goodnight, Mom." Willa's chest filled with warmth, and it surprised her how good it felt to say those things. Before she'd said them, she wasn't sure she believed them.

Sarah exhaled. "Goodnight, baby."

CHAPTER 11
WANING GIBBOUS

April—Present Day

When Archard's butler brought the package to his office, he knew immediately what it was. It'd taken Rachel weeks to track down a mirror from the Dark Ages. Finally, an obscure dealer in Prague acquired one small round mirror believed to originate somewhere between 600 and 1000 A.D. She had it rush delivered, despite the small fortune it added to the cost of the mirror itself.

The butler retreated, leaving the office door open. Archard and Rachel had moved back into his home in the foothills of Denver after the success of the healing spell. Officially, the house had been sold after his death, but it still belonged to him. The careful scheming to ensure the validity of his demise had gone smoothly, thanks in large part to Rachel. She'd sold the house and then purchased it under a false name.

She'd planted the body in the cave and switched the results of DNA and dental testing so that it was identified as Archard. She'd written the obituary and even wept over his grave for the funeral officials to witness.

No one but she and his butler knew the truth.

"Rachel!" he called. Soon she came into the office. He held the box out to her with a smile.

Her eyes lit up as she snatched it and sat in the nearest chair. She pulled a thin, sharp knife from inside her boot and sliced open the packing tape. Her hand dove into the foam packing peanuts. She pulled out a small tissue-wrapped object and tossed the box aside, scattering the packing across the floor. After stripping the tissue, she cradled the small mirror in her hands and gasped.

"What is it?" Archard asked, leaning forward in his desk chair.

She looked up, icy blue eyes bright with discovery. "It's known magic."

Archard returned her grin.

The mirror was a slightly convex disk of pure silver, about the size of a dessert plate. The edge was rimmed in bronze, the back etched with a pattern of the moon's cycle. The antique dealer had done his best to polish the ancient metal, but a fractured pattern of golden lace, the mark of tarnish and age, remained. Archard crossed to stand over her shoulder. Despite its age, Rachel's reflection shone clear on the surface.

Archard held out his hand, and she handed him the heavy object. The dealer assumed it had belonged to a noble or royal woman, but Archard felt the heat on the metal, the echo of spells, of magic. This mirror had belonged to a witch. *How fortunate for us.*

After handing the mirror back, he went to his desk and pulled Bartholomew's grimoire into his arms. He laid the book on the black marble hearth of his fireplace, a gigantic black opening in the wall, framed by a white volcanic ash glass mantel, and he flipped to the correct page. To all appearances, the page was blank, marked only with faint red lines; but the Dark witches knew it was enchanted and must contain something extraordinary if Bartholomew had hidden it so well. Several of their attempts to uncover it had already failed. But this mirror . . . *It must be the answer!*

Rachel scooped up three large blue pillar candles and handed them to Archard. He set them along the top of the book, evenly spaced—right, center, left. From the large bookshelves in the corner of the room, she gathered a vial of ocean water, a bowl of seashells, and Archard's black athame. She handed those to him as well and then went back to find a small picture easel. Kneeling next to Archard, she placed the easel at the bottom of the blank page and set the silver mirror into it, her hands hovering to make sure it didn't tip. After it didn't fall, she angled it to reflect the candlelight and blank page.

She nodded to Archard, who snapped the candles to life.

Rachel picked up a pen and pad of paper from the desk and set them next to the book. With the round pommel of his athame, Archard smashed the shells in the bowl into tiny pieces, which he then sprinkled around the perimeter of the blank page. Rachel unstopped the small vial and gently poured the salt water over the surface of the mirror. The water dripped off and formed a puddle underneath the easel.

Everything was prepared.

Eyes alive with anticipation, Archard looked over at Rachel. She smiled broadly, offering the palm of her hand.

He held her eyes for a moment and then pressed the tip of his ritual knife to her skin. She didn't blink as he opened a small cut. He then did the same to his own hand.

Each of them pressed several drops of blood into the bowl, which Archard mixed together with the tip of his knife. Then, carefully, using the knife like a pen, he drew a crescent moon symbol in blood at the top of the page.

Rachel lifted the pad of paper onto her lap, pen poised and ready, and hand trembling slightly with nervous antic-ipation. Archard's heart raced, eager to uncover another of Bartholomew's secrets. After the tremendous success of his healing, Archard was certain Bartholomew would never fail him. He *knew* the answer to exacting his revenge and forging his own Covenant was in this book. He only had to find it.

Archard closed his eyes and said the spell. *"Powers of water and sea, we come to you with a plea. Mirror so clear and bright, reveal things lost with your mystic sight."*

The air stirred with magic, first hot and then quickly turning cold, as the Powers recognized the Dark source of the call. The bloody moon at the top of the page pulsed bright red. Rachel's eyes stayed locked on the mirror.

In his deep and commanding voice, Archard repeated the spell. The temperature of the air plummeted until their breaths plumed out in white puffs. Rachel shivered, but kept her eyes fixed on the mirror, not even daring to blink, afraid of missing something.

"Archard . . ." she whispered.

"Shh," he hissed, his own eyes carefully watching the silver surface.

A flash of light burst out of the mirror. The sound of whispers crept into the room, but neither of the witches looked up. Finally, it appeared: the page, reflected in the mirror, with the hidden words revealed at last, crisp and clear.

"Rachel . . ." Archard gasped. She ignored him, frantically copying down every word, all of it in Latin, but that was easily dealt with later.

Frost rimed the mantel and the marble floor around the book. The candle flames flickered, almost sputtering out. Archard turned his head, listening, trying to pick out words as the whispers grew louder. Rachel flipped to the next page of her pad. She copied down everything for a second time—just to be safe.

The whispers grew louder and louder until Archard wanted to put his hands over his ears. Then, with a rush of wind, the voices were gone and the reflection in the mirror vanished.

"Did you get it?" Archard asked.

She nodded, taking a deep breath. "Every word."

Narrowing his eyes in pleasure, Archard turned to the cold hearth. With one sweep of his hand, an enormous fire burst to life, heat instant and wonderful. "Let's see what Bartholomew was hiding."

Together, Archard and Rachel sat huddled in front of the roaring fire. Rachel waved a hand over the Latin words, which shimmered and morphed into English. Archard hovered over her, looking down at the paper. Anticipation skittered around inside his gut, and he could hear Rachel's heart pounding as loudly as his.

"Read it," Archard commanded in a hushed, eager tone.

Rachel swallowed. Tipping the page toward the fire to catch the light, she read:

Another town rose against us tonight. I grow weary of these ignorant rebellions, but the unenlightened always fight what they do not understand. However, tonight I gave them a display of power they will not soon forget.

I'm pleased with the results of the spell. It took a great deal of preparation, and I had worried about its ability to raise so many, but it worked. With my unique skills and the Covenant's magic, the Otherworld could not resist my command. A whole graveyard of souls raised, and half a town's souls extracted and stored in my carefully crafted iron boxes.

I had full control.

Rumors of this power will spread far and wide. Therefore, I must protect it with a most potent enchantment. Otherworld magic is not for every witch who walks the earth, and any attempt to perform this spell—or any similar—without the abilities I possess, will surely result in death . . . or worse.

The air once again grew cold around them, and Rachel's lips were pale from speaking the Dark words aloud. She paused, put a hand to her mouth, and let her eyes travel down the rest of the page. She looked up at Archard. "He outlines the specifics of the spell here. Every detail. But it takes a Covenant, a black moon, and Bartholomew's 'unique skills.'"

Archard nodded, the fire throwing shadows over his angular face. "What were those skills, I wonder?"

She glanced down at the paper. "It doesn't say here. We know he could control others, and now it appears that he could control the dead, but how . . . ?"

Archard frowned, narrowed his metal-colored eyes in thought. "Just think of the possibilities—controlling the dead, commanding the Otherworld. Let me see the spell." Archard held out his hand, Rachel handed over the paper. "There's a black moon at the end of July," he said absently as he continued to read. After scanning to the bottom of the page, his eyes widened. "This symbol," he pointed to a stack of three ovals, with a line through the middle of all three. "It was on the page?"

"Yes, at the very bottom, in the corner and kind of small. But I don't recognize it. Do you?"

Archard tossed the paper aside as he jumped to his feet. He raced across the room to the bookshelves, scanned quickly until he found what he needed. He brought back a small cloth-bound book, sat next to Rachel again, and flipped pages. She watched him intently.

After a moment he jabbed a finger to the page, a triumphant smile on his thin lips. "There. Look. The key to Bartholomew's powers." His heart raced, heat swirling under his skin.

Rachel leaned over to look at the page. At the top was the same symbol and below it the explanation of what it meant.

"*Holy* mother moon!" she whispered.

"Exactly!" Archard returned. "We know Bartholomew was a Mind witch—there are Mind symbols throughout the whole book—but this . . . *this* explains how he could do all he did." He pointed to the spell that had raised the dead. "How he could do *that*." Archard flipped the grimoire closed and pointed to the worn, indecipherable symbol on the front, below the Luminary sun. "That must be what this symbol is, rubbed out, either by time or purposely." Archard inhaled deeply. "Unbelievable. Bartholomew was a True Healer."

He paused to take another breath, attempting to control the fever of excitement burning inside him. "We can't duplicate his skills, but maybe there is something else. He mentions capturing souls. Those trapped souls would have *tremendous* power. Those souls will be particularly angry and potent."

He rubbed at his goatee, grown back as thick as before, and stared into the fire. Suddenly, he jumped up and went back to his shelves. Several minutes later, he returned with a large, crumbling grimoire made of crusty brown leather. Releasing the clasp, he threw it open. After flipping pages for a moment, he looked up at Rachel, his eyes full of devious plans. The fire flared, responding to his heightened emotions.

"What?" she begged.

"I think the souls may be powerful enough to use *in place* of Bartholomew's unique skills."

"What do you mean? You think they can make you as powerful as Bartholomew, a Mind witch *and* True Healer? Why not just snatch that Light witch boy—the one who's *actually* a True Healer?"

Archard waved his hand dismissively. "Because this is far less messy than trying to force him to do the work for us. No, we must use those imprisoned souls. They are already connected to the Otherworld and ripe with Dark magic."

"And do what?"

The fire flared again as Archard's mind raced toward the possibilities. "We use them to pull ghosts from the Otherworld, just as Bartholomew did. This grimoire," he pointed to the dusty pages, "is the last surviving book of a very powerful Dreamer with the Gift of Spirits. Long ago, Light witches tried to wipe out all the ghost spells to keep people from trying to raise the dead—too many people died or worse in the process. But this book survived. With these spells and Bartholomew's, I can pull any ghost I want back from the arms of the Otherworld."

"And do what with them?" Her brow furrowed as she lagged behind his thoughts.

Archard slowly smiled. "Form a Covenant, of course." He eyed Rachel and watched her face as the idea took root.

"A Covenant of *ghosts*."

"Exactly! One I will control *completely*, one that cannot die, or leave, or fail."

Rachel inhaled sharply, smiled wickedly. "Sun and moon!" she whispered.

Archard snapped the large grimoire shut, dust puffing out in all directions. "We have to find those souls."

CHAPTER 12
Black Moon

May 569 A.D.

Mist crept through the graveyard like an unwanted guest, slithering over the headstones, tasting the names of the dead. A squat stone church slept peacefully near the gate, the mist a blanket around its feet. Bartholomew's boots cut through the dense white fog as easily and determinedly as swords. He strode to the highest hill in the small yard and stopped. A chill breeze licked at his long black cloak, throwing it around his sturdy legs.

His eyes, silver and bright, like the color of the moon behind a cloud, carefully surveyed the marked graves and surrounding area. The smell of the dead perfumed the air all around him: foul, meaningful, encouraging. He shifted his eyes upward to the dark sky—the sky of the black moon—and breathed in its power.

Bartholomew felt the man's presence long before he heard the loud crunching footsteps.

"Luminary," the man whispered roughly, "everything is prepared."

Bartholomew nodded, but said nothing. His energy and attention were elsewhere. With practiced skill, he opened his mind to the energies around him. Immediately he felt the presence of the eleven witches of his Covenant at the base of the hill. He reached past them, found the sleeping graveyard keeper in the crooked shed at the edge of the yard. Farther still was the small town north of the lonely graveyard, and humble church. Each person's presence filled his head, their intentions shockingly clear.

He exhaled his annoyance. Rebellion was such a bother.

The witch standing next to him leaned closer and whispered. "The mob is now armed and coming this way, Luminary."

"Of course," Bartholomew said, his voice like rich, luxurious velvet. "Let us begin then." He held out his hand, and the witch handed him a moonstone with a crude skull and crossbones symbol etched into the surface, blackened with ash. "Tell them to start."

The witch bowed and hurried off down the hill to his counterparts, who were already gathered in a circle around a small wooden altar, heavy with candles, herbs, and blood.

Their quiet chanting rose on the air like steam.

Bartholomew lifted the hood of his cloak and focused his mind on the bodies below the earth, turning away from the ones marching up the road. He pushed his powers to their limit and reached into the Otherworld, an icy blast of cold answering his intrusion. His lips twitched into a half smile.

It took immense concentration to push into the world beyond the living, to abuse the link that existed between the spirits of the dead and their decaying bodies, but Bartholomew's unique powers gave him a keen mind and impeccable concentration.

The stone grew hot in his gloved hand, answering the chant of his Covenant and his own formidable magic. He gripped it tightly, the muscles in his arm and shoulder trembling.

The earth quivered under his boots.

He lifted his other hand and curled the fingers inward, pulling with all his power.

With a mournful cry, like wind over the moors, the Otherworld lost its battle to keep its own. Reluctantly, the ghosts of every body in the graveyard were pulled from the shuddering earth. At first, the wisps of white spirits were indiscernible from the mist, but Bartholomew pulled harder, and they rose above the fog, an army of ghosts hovering over their graves.

His lips pulled into a wide grin.

The ghosts moaned in protest, furious for being ripped from their rest. Lamenting cries flowed from their contorted mouths, staining the air, sending a chill through every person within a hundred miles.

A ways down the road, the mob stopped and lowered their weapons to listen. A whole town in pursuit of evil, blazing torches raised, paused, suddenly harboring fearful doubts. Each heart fluttered with cold dread.

Bartholomew directed the ghosts forward, using his hand to control and direct them. The moonstone in his other hand burned the leather of his glove, reaching for his skin, but he didn't flinch. The spirits collected in a liquid-like mass at his

feet, moaning, shoulders slumped forward, hollow eyes sending daggers at him.

Bartholomew looked into their cavernous faces and felt
only the thrill of his impending conquest.

He turned, marched down the hill, his risen army slithering along behind him. They followed, wailing their pro-
tests, through the iron gates and onto the road. His Covenant
stepped in behind, iron boxes in hand.

They marched until they found the townspeople, huddled
like frightened animals in the middle of the road.

Bartholomew stopped, planted his boots firmly in the
dirt, and let his ghosts collect around him. They rolled their
heads on their feathery shoulders, shrieks rising from their
open mouths as they sensed the intentions of the Dark witch.
Reaching fluttering arms out at him, they begged to be released.
They clawed at his cloak, but, again, he didn't flinch. Instead,
he stared at the pathetic group of men on the road, old and
young, with the full force of his moonlight eyes.

At first the group could only stare in horror at the blas-
phemy before them, but then the panic eroded the shock.
Some screamed, some stumbled backwards, and others dropped
to their knees in prayer. Bartholomew quickly thrust out a
hand and, with a merciless command, froze them all in place,
locked in the chains of his magic. The screaming intensified,
pushing upwards against the gray clouds.

Bartholomew moved closer. A few men cried out for mercy;
he didn't even glance at them. Lifting his hands, one palm
open to the sky, the other gripping the moonstone, he closed
his eyes.

Blinding light burst from the stone in a thick ribbon. The
witch whipped it forward to wrap around the group, a lasso,

a death sentence. His free hand twisted forward, directing the army of ghosts to do their duty.

The ghosts wailed.

The men wept.

Bartholomew opened his eyes and watched.

The cloud of angry spirits—fathers, brothers, grandmothers, wives, and great-grandfathers of those in the mob—moved into the circle. Bartholomew dipped his hand to the earth, and the ghosts followed his command. They plunged their ephemeral limbs into the chests of the men, still frozen by the Dark witch's command. One by one, the ghosts wrapped their hands around the souls of the mob and then, like tugging weeds from the garden, wrenched them out.

The night shivered with tortured cries.

When the souls of all but one of the offenders was extracted, Bartholomew sent the ghosts flying back to his Covenant, ready and waiting with his specially prepared iron boxes. The ghosts dutifully deposited each soul into a box, and then they returned to prostrate and moan at Bartholomew's feet.

The boxes clanged shut, the locks clicked into place.

Nearly a whole town of souls boxed and put away.

On the road lay a mass of bodies, wilted on the cold dirt, faces frozen in horror. One young man stood fixed and alive, a single survivor. Bartholomew stepped around the bodies, stopped in front of the boy, towering over him. The Dark witch fixed his fathomless eyes on the boy's and whispered in his burning voice, "You live to tell the tale. Go back and warn the living of what happens when you cross Bartholomew the Dark." Bartholomew nodded, and the magic holding the young man in place released. The poor boy fell to the earth, cowering. Bartholomew withdrew the circle of light back into the moonstone, now melting the flesh of his hand. He gazed down on the boy, who finally scrambled to his feet and ran back to the town.

Bartholomew turned, walked away, his cloak flapping behind him. He led the ghosts back to the graveyard. At the top of the hill, he directed them out to their individual graves, still partially hidden in the mist. They wailed in sorrow and relief.

The witch raised the moonstone out in front of him and dropped it to the earth, bits of his burned flesh going with it. By the time the stone hit the grass, Bartholomew's hand was fully healed.

The Otherworld took back its borrowed souls with a hiss of freezing air.

Bartholomew turned and made his way out of the graveyard. His silent Covenant, burdened with the boxes, followed.

CHAPTER 13
WANING HALF MOON

May—Present Day

A fickle spring had finally descended on Twelve Acres, casting off the winter chill and bathing the world in warmth. The windows of Willa and Simon's room at Plate's Place were thrown open wide, the new sheer curtains dancing in the breeze. Early evening sun poured into the room as thick and bright as honey. Outside, the massive weeping willow tree laughed in the breeze, its lithe branches swaying in tune with the buzz of new life.

Willa and Charlotte sat on the bed, studying for finals. Willa was dangerously behind, having spent most of her free time searching through grimoires for clues to the mystery of Simon's powers instead of studying. Despite the looming threat of losing her academic standing, her lack of focus was made worse by the echoes of last night's dream.

Shortly after dropping off to sleep in her bed at her parent's house, Willa dreamed she was standing in *this* bedroom, the Plate's Place room, watching herself and Simon asleep in the bed. The room was a pallet of gray, with colors muted by the cold night. Suddenly, Simon woke, eyes wide and frightened as he looked around the room. He immediately woke her and said, "Willa, we have to go. We can't stay with the Covenant. We don't belong here."

His sense of urgency, the plea in his eyes, woke her from the dream. Unsettled, Willa soon realized that what she'd seen was more than a dream—it was a lost memory. The night of the first earthquakes, back in March. Simon had had his nightmare, turned on the TV, and he'd said something to her, but she'd been too sleepy to remember his words. Until now.

Simon's words came back to her with startling clarity. *Willa, would you come with me if I needed to leave? Would you leave the Covenant?*

Simon was thinking about leaving.

The idea rocked her off center. That night she'd been able to get him to open up and talk about his powers. Since then, he'd clamped down even tighter than before. He hadn't faked another failure in training, but he was still holding back and refusing specialized training.

Is he pulling away? Getting ready to leave?

Grabbing a chenille throw from her bed, she tossed it around her shoulders and stood gazing out the window at the dark street. Her mind couldn't process the idea of leaving. *Would you come with me . . . ?* She could never watch Simon walk away, never not go with him—the idea drove an icy chill through her heart. But neither could she imagine leaving the

Covenant. The decision to join had been difficult enough; its reversal seemed impossible.

In many ways it'd been easy to start fresh, become a witch, and join the covens; but in others, it'd been incredibly intimidating. Willa was accustomed to a simple life, a life that rarely changed. Being a homegrown Twelve Acres folk, raised by two parents who worked and lived in quiet ways, the greatest adventure she'd had before meeting Wynter in the basement had been the annual family road trip to nearby national parks. Her simple past made a future of greatness feel impossible, out of place.

But she'd taken a leap of faith, accepted Wynter and Rowan's offer, with Simon's support. Life in the Covenant was reality now, comfortable, although often unpredictable. She couldn't even fathom a life beyond what they had now. What was the alternative to life in the Covenant? What was Simon thinking?

Simon's words also brought up a whole new issue Willa had never considered. If Simon felt so out of place that he wanted to leave, did that mean they really were out of place? In her grimoire reading, a pattern had emerged of covens forming only where strong bonds and familial legacies already existed—not by accident, and not so suddenly. Witch circles formed carefully—*very* carefully. But here they were, members of True Covens and the Covenant, and all within a year of discovering their powers.

Maybe it wasn't fate, maybe it was just an accident. A mistake.

Now, in their room in Ruby's home, a place Willa loved more than anywhere else, she looked across the bed at Charlotte and questioned everything.

Charlotte had traded her token sweater for a cute lilac

top trimmed in lace, but her hair still hung in one long braid. Fiddling with the end of the plait and biting her lower lip, Char read her economics book. It occurred to Willa that she knew next to nothing about Charlotte, or any of the Covenant for that matter. Who were these people she'd turned her life over to?

Mentally exhausted from her night of worry and debate, Willa knew the only comfort was information. Answers.

"Hey, Char," Willa said, pushing her history book aside, "can I ask you something?"

"Sure," she answered, not looking up.

"How did you and Elliot meet?"

Char dropped her braid and looked up with a smile. "Actually, we grew up next door to each other. Our parents are in a coven together—just a regular one though, nothing fancy like us."

"So you always knew you'd be together?"

She shrugged. "Yeah. We were best friends as kids, and when we got older it just became more. We're soul mates like you and Simon."

Willa nodded, smiled. "What about the True Covens? How did that happen? How long have you been with Wynter and Rowan?"

Charlotte closed her book and drew her knees into her chest. She wore mint green skinny jeans, her feet bare. "Well, let's see. I met Wynter and Rowan when I was ten. Wynter and my mom knew each other when they were young—met during a family trip to Oregon or something. They reconnected later as adults. One night while they were visiting, Elliot and I snuck out of our beds and tried to eavesdrop on the conversation." She laughed. "'Course, it's kinda hard to spy on witches, but we did overhear them talking about Wynter and Rowan wanting to form two True Covens before they sent us back to bed." She paused to smile and shake her head at the childhood memory. "Anyway . . . Wynter wanted my mom and dad to join, but they are too loyal to their own coven. Elliot and I, however, couldn't let go of the idea."

"So you joined when you were only *ten?*" Willa raised her eyebrows.

"Not exactly. A couple weeks later, Elliot dreamed that we were standing with Wynter and Rowan on a high cliff, watching the sunrise. In the dream, she told us it was our destiny to join the True Covens." Char tossed her braid behind her. "I found Wynter's number in my mom's address book, and we called her. At first she laughed—politely, of course—and thanked us for our interest, but said they were looking for adults. We were devastated but resigned. Then, a year later, Wynter came to us, said she couldn't shake the feeling that we should be members of her covens." Char let her legs go and leaned forward. "I think it helped that we'd both recently completed our Elemental Challenge. The youngest successful challenges in our family histories, I might add."

"Impressive." *Wow! They were only eleven! Simon and I are so far behind.*

Char pursed her lips, looked at Willa with her piercing Mind-witch look. "So what's really on your mind? Why the sudden twenty questions?"

Willa shrugged. "I just realized I don't know much about you guys."

Charlotte narrowed her eyes and nodded. "Uh-huh. Is that it?"

Willa smiled as normally as possible. "Of course."

Charlotte leaned back on her elbows. "It's all pretty much the same old story: family connections and the guidance of the magic. Each of us demonstrated exceptional abilities with our Gift and were looking to do more with our skills."

"And everyone's been together for the last eight years?"

"Pretty much."

"What about . . ." Willa swallowed, looked at the quilt, "the two members that Archard killed? The ones Simon and I replaced?" She had wondered before, but never had the guts to ask.

Char looked away, suddenly fixated on the movement of the curtains. For a long moment she didn't speak, and Willa wondered if she ever would. Finally she said, "Their names were Levi and Bobbi. Levi was Cal's younger brother, Bobbi his sweet wife." She smiled sadly. "Cal was so protective of Levi. It nearly killed him when we . . . when we found Levi and Bobbi like that." Her voice clouded with emotion.

Willa couldn't help the question. "Like what?" she whispered.

Char sat up, crossed her legs and looked down at the quilt. When she spoke, her voice was barely audible, her face pinched in pain. "Archard flayed them piece by piece—probably had knife-happy Rachel do it." Both girls shuddered, having tasted the pain of Rachel's blade. "Then he strung them up from the trees at Cal and Darby's house."

Bile rushed up Willa's throat, her heart squeezed tightly. "Oh, Char. I'm so sorry."

A few tears trickled down Char's round, porcelain cheeks. She nodded. "Bobbi was so nice. She taught me how to make apple pie, and she had this laugh . . ."

A crow cawed loudly from the branches of the willow. Something in the bird's mournful screech sent chills down

Willa's back. Not only were she and Simon new, they'd taken the place of people who were meant to be there, people who were already True Witches, already family.

"We really are the misfits around here, huh?" She hadn't really meant to say the words out loud.

Charlotte pinned her with a look. "What do you mean?"

Willa exhaled, shook her head. "Nothing. Sorry."

"No, what is it?" Char reached out, taking Willa's hand. The gesture made Willa's throat tight.

"We're just so far behind and so . . . out of place. We're not family, and barely even friends—just strangers who were in the wrong place at the right time. And then there's Simon . . . I know everyone worries about him. Sometimes I just feel like we might be holding you all back."

"Hey, no," she squeezed Willa's hand. "No, you are *not*. We love you. You are right where you should be. Don't ever think otherwise. The magic brought you to us. That's as good as being actual family."

Willa appreciated the words, but she couldn't bring herself to fully believe them. She wanted to, but couldn't, push aside a shadow of doubt. Something she couldn't shake since remembering Simon's late night questions.

They both jerked in surprise when Elliot knocked on the open door. He wore his usual polo shirt and jeans. "Hey. Sorry! You two okay?"

Char smiled brilliantly at her soul mate. "Yeah, of course. Just startled us."

Elliot smiled back, his teeth extra white against his dark brown skin. "Good. Well, Simon just got home, so it's time for the next small challenge."

Willa nodded and slid off the bed. Char followed but

grabbed her shoulder before she could leave. "Hey, don't worry so much. Everything is fine," the Mind witch whispered. Then she hugged Willa hard and sure. Willa half smiled, doing her best to take her words to heart.

BLINDFOLDS AGAIN? REALLY?

Simon stood on the back porch, Willa at his side, a black silk blindfold on his face. They'd been blinded before coming out of the house, and Rowan had said nothing about this next test. Who knew what waited for them in the backyard.

Simon hadn't faked anything since Willa confronted him about it, but doing well in basic training was fine, acceptable. These preparatory tests were a different story. He was *expected* to fail or at least struggle. If he didn't . . .

Taking a slow breath, he tried to reach out and sense something from his coven-mates. An odd tremor answered his search. *What is that? What's going on?*

Someone pushed him forward, said nothing. He stumbled down the steps and moved over the grass. The willow rustled overhead, a few branches catching on his face. Willa was still next to him, her breathing loud. His own heart picked up speed. The yard smelled of wet earth.

Okay, not liking this.

Another push from behind, this one hard. Falling forward, Simon expected to hit the grass, but instead he kept falling until finally landing with a painful thud on what felt like wood. He rolled to his back with a grunt. Above him Willa screamed and then her body thudded too, but the sound was oddly distant.

The light changed, something blocking it from above. The air felt closed in, the sounds muted.

Simon ripped off his blindfold to total darkness. His hands lashed out and met smooth wood. *No. No way.*

Staccato thuds sounded from above him like a machine gun. His stomach turned over.

Buried alive.

The huff of his breath sounded as loud as waves in the narrow wooden box. His father had once locked him in a closet for a whole night for healing a neighborhood dog. The dark, musty air and sense of imprisonment of that night were *nothing* like this.

Hot anger rushed up his throat, made his hands hot with magic. Sweat broke out on his forehead and dampened the hair at the back of his neck. Blue lights began flashing behind his closed eyes. *What kind of a test is this?*

Or maybe the Covenant has finally decided to get rid of me.

He shook the stupid, paranoid thought aside.

Think. Think. What's the challenge here? What are we supposed to do?

Buried in the ground. Under the dirt. In the earth.

Is it an Earth challenge?

A ripple of emotion made its way through the dirt to his mind—heavy, black fear. *Willa! Oh, no. Willa is down here, too.*

Simon exhaled slowly and tried to reach out to her. *Willa?*

Simon? Came her trembling reply to his mind.

Are you okay?

He felt her hysteric, short laugh. *Oh, just great! You?* she said sarcastically.

He smiled to himself. *Okay, so what do we do? I'm thinking Earth challenge?*

Yeah, me too. But the most I've ever done with Earth is grow a sad little daisy out in the garden. How are we supposed to get unburied-alive?

He frowned and pressed his hands to the lid of the box above his chest. Could he push all that dirt up and away with magic? It would take a tremendous amount of power. He might be able to muster it, but he doubted Willa could, even though she'd become impressively powerful lately. He moved his hand to the side he thought Willa might be. He closed his eyes. *How far away is she?*

Slightly surprised, he got an answer, a diagram in his mind: she was only a foot away, buried as deep as he, about four feet down.

An odd, heavy slithering noise reached Simon's ears, breaking his focus. Goosebumps rose on his arms as he opened his eyes to the black *What is that?!* A moment later, the wood at his feet groaned in protest. A loud crack, the splintering of wood. Something hard, thick, and cold wrapped around his leg.

He jerked away as much as he could, but there was no escape. The intruder slithered up Simon's leg as visions of being swallowed by a giant snake flooded his mind. He reached down and grabbed at the thing. *Roots! Not a snake. Tree roots.*

Simon wasn't sure if that was better or worse.

Willa's screams broke through his panic, echoing in his head.

Willa?!

There's something in here with me. It has my leg. It's squeezing me. It hurts!

It's some kind of root. Can you pull it off or use magic?

The dirt outside the box shifted and more roots burst into his box—one on each side and one above. Dirt fell on his face, stuck to the sweat pouring off him. He turned, spit it out of his mouth, and tried to shake it off his eyes. Willa's screams pitched; he felt her coughing, panicking.

Simon, they're everywhere! The dirt is filling in. I can't breathe!

His box was also quickly filling in with dense dirt, making it even more impossible to move. Shoving his hands through it, he tore at the roots, pulling them from his legs and torso as best he could. His chest burned, air running low.

Think!

Simon!

Willa?!

He felt her coughing again, choking on the dirt, and then nothing.

WILLA? Then out loud, "WILLA?!"

Still no answer, in his mind or otherwise. Why wasn't anyone helping her? What kind of test was this?

Simon's anger blazed blue in his chest, hot and bitter. He lashed out to the side, using his elbow and then his fist to break through the box. Dirt sprayed into his face, but he didn't care. Magic poured out of his hands without command. The dirt between him and Willa's box moved aside lifted away by a bubble of energy.

Panic closing in around him, Simon scrambled toward Willa's box. The roots were still trying to pull at him. He sent a burst of magic at them, and they crumbled to dust. He punched his fist through the side of Willa's box, splinters of wood digging deep into his flesh. He groped for her, his eyes useless in the dark.

When his hand finally found her arm, a spark of heat flared

between their skin. He tugged her unconscious body toward him, wincing at the roughness it required to free her. Fumbling, he found her face. "Willa?" he choked out. There was no more air.

Simon pulled her against him and pressed his eyes closed. He let the magic inside him rise, like a river in flood. Then he let it explode. The impossibly heavy dirt above them erupted upwards. He blinked up at green willow leaves and fragments of dying sunlight.

Gulping down big breaths, he inspected Willa, her body limp and covered in dirt. He brushed the dirt from her eyes, nose, and mouth. "Willa? Come on, my Willa! Breathe!" He dug his hand into her hair, held her head, his lips pressed to her forehead, and sent a rush of his healing power into her body.

She responded with a horrid gasp, followed by a sputtering round of coughs. Simon sighed in relief and hugged her close. "It's okay. You're okay." He looked down her body and pulled away the roots wrapped around her legs and stomach.

She coughed more and then relaxed in his arms. "Simon?"

"Yeah, yeah. It's okay. We're out."

"You got us out?"

"Yeah."

"I couldn't breathe. The roots . . ."

"I know." Simon clenched his teeth, his anger still bubbling hot in his chest. He looked up to the lip of the pit he had blown in the earth. All ten other witches were looking over the side, staring down, covered in dirt. He resisted the urge to send another bolt of magic in their direction. Instead he let the magic dissipate out underneath him, shaking the ground for two protracted seconds.

WILLA SAT IN SIMON'S DUSTY arms at the bottom of the pit thinking, *I failed. I failed the test.* Though grateful to Simon for saving her, she still wished she'd been powerful enough to do something to help, instead of playing the damsel in distress.

Twisting her neck, she looked up at the faces of all her coven-mates staring down at them, trying but failing to read their expressions. Even Charlotte looked like she'd either seen a ghost or committed a heinous crime. *What is going on? Why did they do that to us?*

Anger came off Simon's body in turbulent waves of heat; she could hear his heart pounding a furious beat.

Beyond the heads of the Covenant were the delicate branches of the willow. *Maybe I can still do something to help us.* She lifted her hand, noticing with a frown that her skin was a dark shade of brown from all the dirt, and focused all her magical energy on the long, thin branches.

Simon looked down at her as the branches reached into the pit, the old trunk groaning as it flexed, and formed a swing of sorts under them. When the swing was woven and stable, the tree straightened up, lifting Simon and Willa out of the pit. The branches set them gently on solid ground, sitting as they were in the pit, then retreated to their normal places with what sounded like a contented whisper of leaves.

Simon stared down at her, his face as dirty as the rest of him, with dirt nearly as dark as his eyes. "I wouldn't call that failing." He hugged her tighter.

Rowan stepped closer, and Simon's face instantly darkened, the look he gave the Luminary as poisonous and threatening as a viper. "Just don't, Rowan," he said through clenched teeth. "How can you call almost killing us a test?!"

"Simon—" Rowan tried.

"No. No way. I'm done. This is ridiculous." Willa could see Simon's pulse racing in his throat and temples. She put her hand on his chest, but that didn't slow it down. "How long would you have waited to help Willa? Huh? She passed out, couldn't breathe. Did you even know that?"

"Of course!" Rowan said, kneeling down to get on equal ground. "Charlotte kept a very close watch. You were never in any real danger. We were just about to pull you both out when you . . . well, when you . . ."

"When I what? When I used my crazy powers that you all are so scared of? Yeah, I did. Willa was in trouble!"

Rowan exhaled, dropped his chin. "Please, Simon. Don't be upset. I had a theory about your powers, and I decided to test it."

Simon stiffened. "So we're lab rats to you now?"

"Simon," Willa said quietly. He looked down at her, eyes wild, jaw tense. "Let's just listen for a minute. Please?"

He looked at Rowan. "Why don't you just admit that you are afraid of me? That you don't know what I can or will do?"

Rowan's eyes narrowed, his lips pulling into a thin line. "I am not afraid of you, Simon. I'm trying to *understand* you."

"By putting Willa's life in danger? That's unacceptable. If you have a problem with me, come to me. Don't put her in the middle."

"You are missing the point," Rowan continued, his shoulders tense and his voice strained in a way Willa had never heard it.

"No, *you* are missing the point. If you want me gone just say it." Simon looked from Rowan to the others. No one spoke, most avoided his eyes. "Well, I guess that's my answer."

Rowan's blue eyes darkened. "You are out of line, Simon. No one is asking you to leave."

"I'm not your soldier!"

"Simon!" Willa broke in again. She pushed hard on his chest. "Stop it! Please give Rowan a chance to explain."

Simon's jaw clenched and then released, but he sat back, eyes square on Rowan.

Rowan nodded and passed Willa a grateful look, but she glared at him with equal venom. *I'm not on your side right now, Rowan.* She didn't understand why he would do that to them either.

"That night at the cave," the Luminary began, "everything was very intense, very emotional. You didn't have that burst of power until you realized Willa was there, until you saw her, yes?" Simon nodded stiffly. "Well, I started wondering if your loss of control was connected to your emotions, specifically concerning Willa."

"You think it's *my* fault he lost control?" Willa asked, horrified she might be a source of his problems.

Rowan shook his head. "No, not exactly. But, as we just witnessed, he used all his power to help you, to rescue you. I think the problem is an emotional problem, not necessarily a magical one. Does that make sense?"

Simon squinted in thought. "So, you're saying I can control my powers if I don't get too . . . *emotional?*" He shook his head forcefully. "What about the fact that I have more than one Gift? Don't you think that might have something to do with it? I feel this battle inside me all the time. I don't know what to do with it. What do I do with it?"

Rowan nodded thoughtfully. "I'm not trying to explain the *source* of your powers, just an idea about how to manage them. Acknowledging that there's a fight in you is good. If we can minimize that conflict inside you, manage your emotions and reactions, then things will get better."

"I'll never be able to manage my emotions if Willa's life is in danger." Simon shrugged, slightly defiant. "And you know what else? Her life was never in danger until we met you guys." With that Simon stood, lifting Willa to her feet. "Maybe this was a mistake."

Willa stared at him for a moment, panic popping in her veins. *He's gonna leave! My dream! Oh, no!* "Simon, take a breath. What Rowan said makes a lot of sense." Willa looked at Rowan. "I don't think he needed to bury us alive —" Rowan's eyes widened, and she gave him a look "—but you have to admit it proved a point."

Simon shook his head, looked toward the front of the house as if he were debating whether to stay or bolt. He folded his arms. "I guess. But I just . . . I need some time to think."

Rowan said, "Understandable. Go get cleaned up. Come back when you want to talk more."

Simon looked at Willa, the need to leave evident on his face. "Okay. Let's go." Without waiting, he turned and took off.

Willa blinked at him. Her mind suddenly felt the way her body had under the weight of all that earth.

She hurried after him. He yanked open the door to the Jeep.

Willa ran toward him. She wanted him to stop, to slow down.

"Stop. Just stop. Okay?" she said, breathless.

Simon released the door, his shoulders slumping forward. "Sorry," he muttered. "But, Willa, do you really want to stay after that? Aren't you mad? Nothing about this has gone well. I mean, Rowan just buried us alive to prove a theory!"

She shook her head. "I don't know. Of course, I'm mad, but . . . I can't think. I don't know what to think!"

He fell silent. After a moment, he stepped closer to her. She wanted to cry, to collapse into him, but fought it. This was not the time to break down; she had to *think*.

"Willa, I know you like being a part of this. But I'm not so sure it's the right place for us. Maybe we should move on."

"But we *are* witches. I can't go back to the way things were before. I can't! And I've never quit anything in my whole life." She sniffed, fighting the tightness in her throat. She laughed without humor. "In seventh grade I tried out for the volleyball team because one of my friends wanted to but was too nervous to go alone. We both made the team, and I played the *whole* season." She looked up. "I *hate* volleyball. But I couldn't let myself quit."

Simon gave a small smile, his eyes lightening for the first time. "You played volleyball?"

Willa scowled at him. "Yeah, and I was really good. I just hate team sports. I'm like you: I'd rather climb a mountain or take a yoga class. But that's not what we are talking about!"

Simon frowned. "Yeah. But this isn't junior high sports, this is our lives."

Willa sighed, her body heavy with exhaustion. "Exactly. We can't just run away from it. I don't think Rowan meant any real harm. You have to remember that we aren't used to how they do things, how they think. To them, burying us alive might be totally normal. We have to give this *time*. It's barely been six months."

"I know, but . . ."

"But you are used to being on your own, and I get that. And

I get that you feel like an outcast. I do, really. But I just . . . we can't leave, can't walk away because things get bad."

Simon sighed heavily, looking past her down the street with what looked disturbingly like longing for escape. "I'm not sure we belong here, Willa. I want to think we do, but . . ."

The echo of his words from her dream sent a wave of cold down her neck. "Maybe we have to earn the right to belong. We have to keep trying." She swallowed. "Rowan is trying to help, and you push him away. I try to help, and you push me away. We are getting desperate. Maybe that—" she pointed to the back yard, "—was Rowan getting desperate."

Simon blinked several times and looked away. Willa wondered if she'd gone too far, but she didn't regret her words. He needed to hear them.

He shoved his hands into his pockets, and after a silent moment said, "But what if another Dark witch comes after the Covenant? I don't want to spend my life fighting—I want to spend it helping, healing. When the quakes came, I thought about that a lot, and I'm not sure I can do it."

"But the quakes didn't come again. May's new moon passed without any quakes. Maybe that threat is gone."

"Maybe. But another will come. You can't wield this much power without others wanting to take it or destroy it. I should have seen that from the beginning."

Her anger flared again. "Simon, I'm not going to let you run away from this. You have unbelievable power. You need to embrace it, not hide from it. Let Rowan train you. Listen to him. Please, let him help! Let *me* help!"

Simon blinked at her again, shocked at her sudden fire. He turned away, jaw tense. "What if it doesn't work?" he whispered.

"What if it does?" she countered firmly. "And I'm going to find the answer to why you have multiple gifts. I promise. That's what I do—find answers. Okay? Can we at least try a little longer? Until the Elemental Challenge? If things are still bad or get worse, then," she swallowed hard, "we'll leave. Together. But you have to make more of an effort."

He held her eyes, and she tried not to let them get wet. *Did I just say that?*

"Okay," he agreed.

She exhaled, not realizing she'd been holding her breath. "Okay?"

He stepped forward, took her hands, lifted them to his lips, and kissed her dirty knuckles. "Thank you for yelling at me." He smiled. "For you, I'll stay, and I'll try to train with Rowan. We'll see how things go until the Challenge."

Willa studied his face. "Okay. Good."

Char came walking across the grass, head hung on her chest, hands in pockets. She stopped several feet away. "So sorry, guys. I know you need some time, but Wynter just got a call from a friend in England. Apparently, some baddie killed a bunch of monks. Will you come back?"

Willa looked up at Simon. "Not like this," he said stiffly, looking down at his filthy shirt and jeans. "We'll be back in a half hour."

Char frowned, her round face looking nearly childlike with the expression. "Yeah, of course." She turned away.

"Get in the Jeep," he said to Willa. "We'll clean up, and then we'll hear about what's going on in England." He opened her door. "I told you the bad guys would be back."

Willa nodded, a new knot of worry in her stomach.

CHAPTER 14
WANING HALF MOON

May—Present Day

For the last four weeks, Archard and Rachel had been scouring England. Digging and cutting into both land and flesh for answers. From references in the final pages of Bartholomew's grimoire, they guessed that the Dark witch's last days were spent somewhere in England, but the country had changed a lot over the last five hundred years.

And the legends were as varied as the landscape.

Some said Bartholomew died in Scotland, taken by the Celts and buried alive somewhere on the moors. Others affirmed that he and his Covenant had been hunted down by monks in southern England, their bodies dragged behind wild horses until there was nothing left. Still, others claimed the Dark witch had never died, but still roamed the earth, living in secret.

Archard believed none of it.

"What if he destroyed the boxes?" Rachel asked as she drove over yet another narrow, bumpy country road on their way to the port town of Bideford.

"Not a chance," Archard replied. "Bartholomew would never destroy those trapped souls. There is too much power in them."

Rachel slammed on the brakes of the rented Mini Cooper to wait for a flock of sheep to cross the road. "Still, they could be anywhere."

Archard shook his head and brushed at the thin lapels of his black suit. "No, he would have kept them close."

"How do you know that?" Rachel tapped her glossy black fingernails on the steering wheel.

"Because that is what I would do." Archard flicked a spot of lint off his pants.

Rachel cut a doubting glance in his direction and then laid on the horn, hurrying the sheep along. "Well, these monks better give us some real answers. The black moon is coming up fast."

"If rumor serves us right, these monks will know about every witch sighting, hunt, escape, and spell done in Southern England for the past thousand years. They were the ones responsible for the famous Bideford witch trial hangings. Three witches." Rachel shook her head. Archard glanced out at the lazy sheep. "They'll give us what we need."

Two hours later, they arrived at the ancient monastery, hidden in the hills outside Bideford. Rachel and Archard stood outside the squat stone building, glaring up at it in the brilliant morning sun. To the right, an apple orchard sloped away and around the monastery. To the left, a quiet field of grass rolled over the hills, soaking up the sunlight. The scent of garden soil and sea salt played on the air.

Rachel shielded her eyes as she squinted at the thick line of blue on the horizon. "This place has known magic."

"Yes, I feel it, too." He lifted a hopeful eyebrow at her as they made their way into the building. Heavy silence greeted them. The vestibule, ancient and unchanged since the day it was built, was lit only by an inadequately small candle chandelier. A yawning corridor spread out in front of them. From the darkness of the hall came the sound of shuffling, hurried footsteps.

Archard and Rachel waited impatiently for the owner of the footsteps to appear. Soon they saw a squat monk dressed in a traditional brown habit and sandals. At the sight of the two witches, he squared his shoulders, and crossed himself.

"You do not belong here," he said, his voice rough from disuse and heavily accented.

"No," Archard said, meeting the monk's tired eyes with his own steel gaze, "but we need information. Give us what we ask, and we will leave you in peace."

"And if we do not?"

Archard offered a wicked smile, all the answer the monk needed.

"State your request, witch; but know that we are accustomed to dealing with your kind," said the monk, his lips pursed in distaste.

Archard's grin grew. "I need to see your records from the 1500s. Anything to do with a man known as Bartholomew the Dark." Archard didn't miss the flash of recognition on the monk's face, although he tried to hide it.

"We know nothing of this man, and we do not allow outsiders to see our sacred records. You must go."

Archard had to admire the man's courage, the way he managed to keep his voice level as he said the words. He sighed. "I'm sure you can make an exception for us." Archard gestured to Rachel who glared, like a panther on the hunt.

The monk swallowed but didn't move. "Please go."

Archard stepped forward, his fine shoes clipping the stone floor. The monk stood his ground. Heat rose under the witch's skin as he locked his gaze on the man, who had the gall to stare back. Archard stepped around him, a predator's circle. When the monk began to protest, again demanding that they leave, Archard released his magic and the man's body burst into flames. His scream of pain and terror filled the stone room, echoing.

Rachel moved aside casually as the monk ran forward, flapping his arms, a chaotic streak of flames. She and Archard watched calmly as the monk dived out the door and then collapsed, a burning, shrieking heap.

The witches turned away. Rachel followed Archard down the hall, the monk's final cries echoing along the stone walls. They found the records housed in the basement, in a series of small rooms lined with boxy wooden shelves packed with scrolls, books, and papers. Oddly, no one else tried to bar their way.

"Where are the rest of the monks?" Rachel asked warily as they surveyed the shelves.

"It doesn't matter," Archard waved her off. "Do you see what we need?"

It took them only a few moments, searching with a bit of

magic, to find records that mentioned a Dark witch in the 1500s.

Archard gingerly pulled an ancient codex from its place and took it to a long wooden table in the center of the room. He waved his hand, morphing the Latin into English. The witches leaned in, head to head.

The satisfying triumph of discovery throbbed in Archard's veins. "These are the monks that killed Bartholomew," he whispered. "Holy moon! How do you think they managed *that?*"

Rachel leaned close to the writing. "It says they tracked down the Covenant not far from here. Bartholomew had an estate to the west, on the coast." She looked up. "Do you think he kept the boxes there?"

"Yes," Archard said with certainty. "The difficulty will be finding them. The estate may not exist anymore. And most likely, he kept them well hidden and guarded with impenetrable enchantments."

Rachel's eyes snapped wide. "The monks attacked, killing the Covenant members by trapping them in the house and setting it on fire. At first, they believed Bartholomew died with them. But it says that they found Bartholomew's body in an old church on his estate the next morning. No one was sure who killed him or how he died. That's strange." Rachel read on silently for a moment. "They burned the body, divided the ashes into six boxes. They sent each box with a different monk with instructions to bury the remains all over Europe in unmarked, twelve-foot-deep holes."

Archard stood up slowly, his eyes alight. "Let's go. We have to find that church."

THE MINI JOSTLED DOWN THE dirt road, which was abandoned and overgrown with tall grass. Archard held a map open on his lap, stolen from the monks, with the location of Bartholomew's estate marked in red.

"It should be around here somewhere," he said, squinting out the window.

"There's nothing here but trees and grass," Rachel snapped.

"Stop the car. We'll have to walk, search for ruins."

Rachel jerked the wheel, maneuvered the car off the road. Archard left the map in the car. For a moment they stood in the field, the grass reaching for their waists.

"Do you *feel* that?" Archard whispered, his hand held out in front of him. The air rippled with potent magical energy.

"Sun and moon!" Rachel whispered back.

"This way!"

The witches trooped off into the trees with hurried, eager steps, allowing the cold call of Darkness to guide them forward. Soon the trees parted, and the witches stepped out into a field of more tall grass. But this field wasn't empty.

Surrounding some barely visible stone ruins stood an army of monks—at least twenty—all standing in a line, elbow to elbow, faces set, brown robes flapping in the coastal wind. Archard glanced at Rachel. "Found the other monks," he said snidely.

One brave monk at the center of the line, called out. "Leave now, witches, and we will spare your lives!"

Archard stepped forward and collided with an invisible barrier. He put his hands out, pressed against the thin layer of magic. He laughed. "I see you've learned a few tricks from the witches you've hunted over the years."

The monk narrowed his wide-set eyes. His bald head and thin face dripped with sweat. "We learned to fight fire with fire."

Archard couldn't help the devious smile that spread on his face. With a short chuckle, he said, "Well, I highly doubt you've ever seen fire like mine." The witch pressed his hands harder into the barrier. A few sparks spurted from his fingers, then ripples of orange-blue flames crawled outward along the wall, spreading through the air, eating away at the monks' magic.

The monks watched, horrified, sweat-drenched.

As the flames finished their work, crackling down to the ground, Archard threaded his withering stare down each set of wide monk eyes, tasting the stink of their fear on the air. *Savoring it.* His mind groped for an elegant, devious way to end them, one that Bartholomew would approve. After all, the Dark magic in this place cried out, begging Archard to use it.

With the monks' meager wall devoured, nothing but ocean-scented breeze stood between them and the witches. The leader swallowed once and stepped forward. He opened his mouth to speak, but the words never left his throat.

Archard raised his hands to the sides, palms skyward. Twenty small stones levitated under his command, lined up, ready for battle. A second later they hissed, hot red, glowing, and heated by his fire. The monks froze and eyed the stones. Archard's lips twitched.

The witch let the moment linger, enough for the monks' fear to build, and then he thrust his hands forward, sending the stones to their targets—twenty red hot stones, twenty monk heads. The lead monk barely had time to lift his hand before the stone struck his forehead, dead center, the blazing stone melting flesh and charring bone. Twenty stones hit the ground with a collective hiss in the grass behind the monks a second before the bodies crumpled. A small curl of steam rose from each pierced forehead.

Rachel's laugh filled the humming air. "Very biblical, Archard."

He merely straightened his suit coat. They stepped through the maze of bodies to the ruins of the church, which consisted of a few piles of stones half buried in the grass.

"See anything?" Archard called to Rachel as she walked the perimeter of the site. He could *feel* it—the ground nearly vibrated with energy—but where was it; how could he get to it? "It's got to be underground. Look for some kind of opening."

"It's too overgrown." Rachel stopped and looked up. "We need to clear the site." Marching through the weeds, Rachel joined him, and together they lifted their hands to summon a whirlwind of magic to sweep over the sight. The air churned, spun, and then rocks, grass, dirt, and roots were ripped away, pushed back as easily as brushing crumbs off a table.

Left behind was a naked patch of dirt and one gaping hole in the center.

CHAPTER 15
WAXING GIBBOUS

July 1501

Bartholomew sat in a high backed chair, his long legs stretched out and his boots close to the crackling fire. His midnight eyes gazed intensely into the flames as his right hand rubbed absently at the leather cover of his grimoire. Resting in his lap, the tome was now more than a thousand years old, bursting at the seams with Dark spells and coveted secrets; yet it looked as pristine as the day the bookmaker finished it.

The witch found it easier to think with the book near him, and he currently faced a complicated decision—one that required delicate planning and the most intricate preparations of anything he had yet accomplished.

In his long life of one thousand and fifty four years, he'd been everywhere, seen everything, and shattered the boundaries of every type of magic imaginable. He was *tired*. Not physically tired—thanks to his healing abilities, which kept him eternally young and healthy, he still looked and felt like a fit thirty-year-old—but soul-tired, exhausted by the tedium of living. Food had lost its flavor, women their beauty, his bed its comfort; even magic had grown dull, boring.

Though he had always called England home, his great country was also becoming a bore. And with the wedding of Arthur to Catherine of Aragon only a few months away, things were only going to grow more tedious. He'd looked Arthur's brother, Henry, in the eyes and seen all the ridiculous trouble in his future.

The world currently had nothing to offer him.

It wasn't only a loss of interest in life and the world. Even after so much time, he felt the loss of his wife, Brigid, as keenly as that September day when they'd burned her. The vengeful burning of the entire town had done nothing to cool his rage, and neither had time or magic. He'd found brief moments of distraction while working his brilliantly Dark spells, stomping down his enemies, and ruling the night; but the pain always resurfaced, an inevitable grievous sunrise.

Recently, with all pleasures dulled, the only thing left was his pain, his hurt, magnified by the gaping mouth of so much time. Brigid's sweet voice haunted his dreams; her beautiful face plagued his thoughts. Several times in the last months, he'd woken in the middle of the night, sure he felt the heat of her body next to him, only to find an achingly empty bed. Though he'd searched diligently, no woman had been able to fill, or even lessen, the void she'd left in his heart. No one had been able to take her place, be his partner in magic and in life.

Loneliness was his only companion.

It was time for a change, a significant one.

Bartholomew sighed as he crossed one ankle over the other, the fire's heat not as soothing as it had been in times past. He narrowed his eyes, the thoughts in his head shifting, moving into place. Flicking a finger toward the fire, he sent a burst of magic into the flames. Mumbling his own brand of scrying spell, he asked the fire to show him the possibilities of the future he was contemplating. Having long ago mastered the skills of prying information out of the Otherworld, the flames quickly answered his request.

Slowly, a picture formed: faces and places shaped of orange-yellow flames. For several minutes, he studied the fire. When he had seen enough, the decision was cemented.

With another flick of his fingers, the flames returned to normal. He opened his grimoire, flipped to the back, and magically added another page. He placed his hand on the fresh page, closed his eyes, and with a whispered spell, inscribed his thoughts and plans into the paper. He would record it, but no one beside himself would ever be able to see it.

With the details down on paper, Bartholomew stood. He pulled his cloak around his shoulders. Then, with the book tucked under his arm, he strode out into the night. Shadows gathered around him, folding him into their camouflage so that he passed through the pre-dawn twilight unseen and unheard.

The small church on his estate hunched low to the ground, stone crumbling and thatched roof sagging. The Dark witch eased inside and marched past the empty, rotting pews. He stepped over the fallen cross and altar and bent down to lift a hidden hatch in the floor.

The hatch opened, creaking in protest, and thudded loudly when Bartholomew dropped it back. Gathering his cloak around his legs, he stepped sure-footed down the stone steps into the stale, sour air. At the bottom of the stairs, he held out his palm, and a small flame burst to life to light the way.

Cobwebs hung like silk curtains along the walls and from the stone overhead, moving aside magically to allow his passage. He followed a narrow hall deeper into the earth, twisting and curving like the body of a snake, the air growing ever colder.

Finally, Bartholomew came to a thick wooden door, adorned with iron hinges and a large curved handle. In the center of the door, a single symbol had been etched into the wood: a five pointed star. Bartholomew extinguished his flame by snapping his fist closed and placed his hand against the star. After closing his eyes, he muttered a spell. A loud *clack* echoed off the rock walls, and then the door swung open with a nasty breath of stagnant air. He sniffed at it and walked over the threshold.

The room beyond was lit by dozens of fat, drippy candles. On the wall opposite the door was a shelf carved into the stone; on the shelf were eleven iron boxes—containing the stolen souls of nearly an entire town. A smile twitched to life on Bartholomew's lips.

Seated in a simple, stiff wooden chair was an exquisite woman, a princess in a wasteland. Her body glowed strangely, emitting a supernatural light, like pearls in the moonlight. Curls of shiny, blue-black hair, like raven's feathers, hung down her back to the floor, her face like a painting: creamy, flawless skin, with black eyes and blood-red lips. A dress, a slip of black, with many layers of fabric, like wisps of shadows, enhanced her ethereal quality. The smile she flung at Bartholomew was colder than the arctic air around them.

"Are they safe?" he asked, answering her smile with a chilling stare.

She nodded once, continued to smile stiffly, unnaturally.

He moved around her to the shelf, inspecting the boxes. The air filled with mournful whispers. At the last one, he stopped, opened his book, and flipped to the last page. Cradling the tome in one arm, he used his other hand to pull a small muslin pouch from the pocket of his cloak. In the pouch was a tangle of brown moss soaked in his blood, a lump of coal, and a moonstone carved with a skull and crossbones. He laid the pouch on the box.

The ethereal woman floated over to stand behind him, hovering like a rain cloud. He ignored her and looked to his book. With a wave of his hand a spell appeared on the last page, the words burning bright blue.

Reaching into his shirt, Bartholomew produced a simple necklace: a long, tarnished silver chain and a crude triangular pendant that had once belonged to his wife. He clenched the pendant in his fist and shut his eyes. The words of the spell trickled out of his mouth, raining down over the box of trapped souls. The pouch ignited with blue-green flames, illuminating Bartholomew's hooded eyes. The flames burned bright for a few moments, consuming the offering. When there was nothing left to burn, the flames died, leaving behind a symbol scorched into the top of the box. The stacked and bisected ovals—the symbol of a True Healer and Bartholomew's chosen mark.

A throb of painful cold spread down his body, starting at his head and hovering in the space behind his heart. With a grunt, he reached out to grip the edge of the stone shelf, almost dumping his precious grimoire to the floor. The sensation continued to grow, the pain increasing until he had to clench his teeth together and squeeze his eyes shut. For a moment, it felt like the cold would ice over his heart and stop it right then. He held the stone shelf so tightly that a chunk broke off and crumbled in his hand.

Then the cold left him, like the shutting of a door, the spell completed.

He straightened up, took a breath, and closed his grimoire with a satisfied snap.

When he turned, the woman gave him a questioning look, her hair draped around her like a cloak. Her eyes moved from the box to the necklace in his hand. Bartholomew stepped within inches of her, trapping her onyx eyes with his.

"One day a witch will come for these boxes. Allow him to take just that one. Nothing else. Understand?"

She blinked once and smiled her ghoulish grin.

Bartholomew looked back over his shoulder at the box, an odd twist of excitement in his gut, a burst of real feeling that he hadn't experienced in ages. He spun away from the woman and made his way back up to the world.

Morning was just breaking in the eastern sky, cracking the night's facade. Bartholomew smiled as he walked away to meet his death.

CHAPTER 16
WANING HALF MOON

May—Present Day

Archard and Rachel stood over the black hole, looking down into the shadowy nothingness, the air unnaturally quiet in the field. The breath coming up from the hole smelled like Darkness. Rachel squatted down and squinted. "So, you think the boxed souls are down there?"

"I'm sure of it." Archard said, breathless and unable to slow the excited beat of his heart.

Rachel flicked her palm open, and a flame burst to life. She lowered it past the boundaries of the hole. "There are stairs. But who knows what kind of enchantments Bartholomew put in place to protect those boxes. It could be dangerous."

Archard frowned. "Rachel, it's not like you to hesitate."

She snapped her fist closed and scowled up at him, her

icy eyes hard. "This is Bartholomew we're talking about. You should show some respect, too."

A good point. "Then we need a revealing spell." He looked around the field. "Give me your ring, then get me some of that pine." Rachel slipped the antique, heirloom ring from her finger. It was made with one large, square blood-red garnet surrounded by tiny diamonds set in a thick gold band. She handed it to him and then went for the pine.

When Archard had the pine bough in hand—large, but not too big to carry—he stripped a small branch of its needles and slipped Rachel's ring onto it. He held out his hand. "Knife," he said without looking up. Rachel pulled the small knife from her boot, and handed it to him. Expertly, Archard carved a small, five-pointed star into the main branch.

"Ready?" he asked as he handed back the knife.

"Yes."

Archard held the bough in both hands and closed his eyes. *"Mighty Fire, power and dread, reveal the dangers now ahead."* Hot air swirled around them and the pine burst to life with brilliant white flames, pulsing and glowing.

"Follow me." Archard stepped down into the hole, descending the dusty stone steps with Rachel close behind. At the bottom, illuminated by the fiery pine, a narrow passage curved away to the right. Archard held the bough at arm's length, moving it back and forth through the air. "So far, no enchantments," he said. Rachel frowned, pursing her pink lips.

The witches walked in single file along the passage. The stone walls were dry and draped with cob webs. The air smelled of dirt and stale time and grew colder with every step. Archard led with slow, cautious steps, both of them constantly watching the burning pine bough, waiting for the flames to flair red in warning.

Soon, they stood at a heavy wooden door. The iron hinges shone flat black in the light of the white flames, with no signs of age. In the center of the door, carved into the wood, was the five-pointed star.

"This is it," Archard whispered. He moved the bough close to the door, leaning away, fully expecting it to flair red.

When the enchanted flames did not react, Rachel scoffed. "Not even the door is protected. I don't believe it."

Archard cocked his head, listening. The air grew even colder. "Is that . . . *singing*?" he asked, leaning his ear close to the door. A sound, deceptively faint, almost nonexistent, floated on the air. "I can't quite . . ."

Boldly, Rachel reached forward and tried the latch on the door. Unlocked. She pressed the heavy timbers aside and candlelight flooded the hall. Singing, soft and sublime, filled the hall.

Hearts racing and stomachs tight, the witches stepped into the chamber beyond. Hundreds of candles lit the cave-like room, and in the center was one simple wooden chair. Their jaws dropped at the sight of the creature sitting in the chair—was it a ghost, or something else? The pine bough flared blinding red and crumpled to ash in Archard's hand. Rachel's ring hit the stone floor with an ominous ping.

The mysterious woman turned two fathomless black eyes on them, her red lips moving as she sang her lilting song. Her black dress and raven feather hair floated around her like a cloud. The song stopped and she smiled a cold, unfriendly smile.

Archard looked at her, unblinking, and felt suddenly like a

scared child peering into the eyes of a cruel teacher. He knew immediately that whatever she commanded he would obey.

"So you've come," the woman said in a voice like diamonds—hard, but indescribably beautiful.

Rachel, not as impressed with the woman's beauty or power, stepped forward to retrieve her ring. With it safely back on her finger, she asked, "What do you mean?"

"*He* told me you would come."

Rachel widened her eyes. "Who told you?"

The creature ignored Rachel, focusing her eyes on Archard, smiling her horrid smile. "You came for them, did you not?"

Archard nodded submissively. Rachel narrowed her eyes at him. "Who are you?" she demanded of the woman.

The woman continued to look at Archard. "I am what I am," a cryptic, breathy reply.

Rachel moved her eyes past the creature to the stone wall into which was carved a single shelf. On the shelf, a row of iron boxes. "Archard! The boxes."

Finally, Archard was able to pull his eyes from the woman, the sight of the boxes and of so much power, deadening her enchanting hold on him. He took a step forward. The woman, seemingly without moving, stood, blocking his path.

"You may take only one."

"What? No. I mean to take them all." Archard found it difficult to look her directly in the eyes.

"Then you will die," she said airily.

Archard folded his arms. "Speak plainly, woman."

"When *he* left the boxes, it was on the condition that no one take them ever, *except* you." She waved a white hand in front of his face. "And you are allowed to take only one." She extended a slender, ghostly finger. "That one."

Her eyes and finger pointed to the box farthest to the right. Archard followed her eyes to the plain, unassuming box. Only one thing set it apart from the rest: the True Healer symbol burned into the lid.

"Why only that one?"

"Because *he* said."

"Do you mean Bartholomew?" She nodded once. Archard's heart thudded. "And if I try to take them all?"

Her grin spread. "Then I kill you. And quite plainly, *witch*, your powers are no match for mine. I did my best to prevent this, but here you are. So if you try to do more than he said, I will enjoy ending you in the most painful way possible."

Archard believed her. He did not know what she was, but he sensed enough to know that she was not a witch and not a mortal. "Do you know how many souls are in that box?"

She blinked once. "Not for me to know." She turned away and was instantly back in her small chair. "Now, go. I do not enjoy company."

Archard moved his eyes to Rachel. She narrowed her own and then crossed the room. Her hands hesitated a moment before lifting the box off the shelf. The room around them sighed. She tested the weight in her hands. "Feels empty. Archard, are you sure this isn't some trick, some . . . decoy?"

The woman answered, her wasted eyes still locked on Archard. "No trick. Souls have no earthly substance, you *fool*."

Rachel grimaced, bared her teeth. "If you are lying, *creature* . . ."

The woman's eyes flashed to Rachel, and with the full weight of that unearthly stare on her, Rachel shut her mouth. She moved sheepishly back toward Archard and the door.

"Did Bartholomew say anything else?" Archard asked,

intrigued beyond reason at the idea that the powerful witch had left a box just for him. *How did you see so far into the future, Bartholomew? How did you know I would come?*

The woman only blinked.

Archard looked at Rachel. "Well, let's go then."

"A warning," came that strange voice. "If you open it, you *will* regret it. Most grievously, I'm afraid."

The creature's enchanting nature could not deaden Archard's arrogance. "Oh, I doubt that," he shot back. Then, without a backwards glance, he led Rachel to the door and closed it hard behind them.

BACK AT THE HOTEL, ARCHARD and Rachel sat on the bed, the box between them, the sounds of mournful, muffled cries leaking from it. Archard could not pull his eyes away from the True Healer symbol burned into the top of the gray metal. Rachel trailed a finger along the lid of the box, over the etched lines of the Healer symbol, until her skin stung from the cold of it. "Will one box be enough?" she asked.

Archard frowned. "All of them would certainly be better; but yes, I believe one will work. Don't you feel it—how angry, how powerful they are?"

She nodded reverently. "So we wait until the black moon to raise the ghosts?"

Archard stroked his goatee. "No, I don't think so."

When he didn't continue, Rachel scooted closer and said, "But the power of the black moon—"

"The power in these souls is even more than I imagined," he interrupted. "We need the black moon for the Binding. The ghosts we can get anytime."

She shifted her eyes to the box. "But a Binding is supposed to take place under a blood moon."

"Traditionally, yes, but this is no ordinary Covenant—a rare moon, for a rare kind of Covenant. The black moon's power will ensure that the Binding holds the souls here in this world. Otherwise, I fear, the Otherworld might call them back."

"So why take the ghosts early? Are you thinking the full moon in a couple weeks?"

He shook his head slowly, brows pulled low in thought. "June's sun moon would be too soon. I need time to get all the spells right. We'll wait until July's, the blessing moon, just to be safe. We pull the ghosts from the Otherworld, with the help of these souls, and then two weeks later Bind them under the black moon." He patted the box. "That will give us enough time to be sure we can keep them here, and also allow them time to marinate in the box. Add their anger to this and increase the power. We will need that power."

Rachel widened her eyes in realization. "To break the Light Covenant."

"We can't bind our own until their bond is broken."

Moving closer, Rachel ran a cool fingertip over the rippled scar near Archard's right eye. "Who will you raise, Archard? What ghost-witches will you steal for your Covenant?"

Archard lifted his metal-gray eyes to her. "I know *exactly* who I will take." He eyed Rachel conspiratorially but didn't elaborate. He lifted the box and shoved it into a black velvet bag and tightened the strings. "Time to go. We need to get back to Denver. I have a lot to do to perfect the spells we'll need." He widened his eyes. "And I want you to find us a place in Twelve Acres. We're relocating."

CHAPTER 17
WAXING CRESCENT

June—Present Day

"Any more news from England about those poor monks?" Solace sat in her favorite rocking chair in the *Early Life of Twelve Acres* room, a book opened on her lap. Willa moved through the room, dusting the display cases.

"Nope. Nothing," Willa answered.

"So, that's it then? No one has any idea who did it, and now two new moons have passed without any more quakes?"

"Yeah, that's right." Willa swished the feather duster over a collection of chipped china and avoided Solace's waiting stare.

The ghost snapped her book shut. "Willa! Tell me what's going on! Is it over? Did the Dark witches just give up?"

Willa dropped her arm. "I don't know, Solace! *We* don't know. The whole thing is just . . ." Willa stabbed the duster at the front of a glass case, her frustration bubbling to the surface.

"Just what?" Solace prompted.

"Just insane," Willa snapped, throwing the duster onto a nearby table.

"Well, you don't have to yell at me about it!" Solace fumed, her face flickering.

Willa dropped into one of the chairs around an antique wooden kitchen table. "I'm sorry. I'm not yelling at you." She jabbed her elbows down on the table and then buried her face in her hands. "Ugh. I think my head is going to explode."

Solace moved to the chair opposite. "Why? What's wrong with you today?"

Shaking her head, face still shielded with her hands, Willa muttered, "A million things."

"Well, let's hear the list then."

Willa dropped her hands to look at her friend, Solace's face opaque in the dimly lit room. Willa exhaled a long breath. "It's not just this weird nebulous Dark threat looming over us. Ever since the buried-alive challenge, things have been . . . strained. Simon agreed to try training with Rowan, and it seems to be going well, but I can't shake the feeling that the tiniest thing might drive him off, for good this time."

"I highly doubt he'd actually do it. He's just trying to deal with the bizarre hand he's been dealt."

"I know. But he still hasn't opened up about the cave. It's been eight months, Solace. *Eight months!* I've read so many grimoires; I think I might now know as much about magic as the others in the Covenant, but I still don't have any answers for Simon. There doesn't seem to be *any* information on how he could have multiple gifts and be as powerful as he is. Maybe it's hopeless. Maybe we'll never know." Willa pressed the heels of her hands to her eyes. When Solace didn't say anything, she let the floodgate of her stress open. "And then there's the thing about me moving out. It was supposed to be right after the semester ended. Well, that was a week ago, and my mom keeps finding reasons to stall me. She also keeps asking me if I've talked to Simon about getting married, which I haven't—there is way too much going on to think about that. And now I don't know if moving in with the Covenant is still a good idea. I don't think Simon wants to. He's too used to living alone." She inhaled and went on. "And the Elemental Challenge is coming up soon. And I didn't do well on any of my finals. And . . . then . . ." Willa brought her thumb to her mouth and chewed on the already ragged nail.

"What?" Solace asked leaning forward, eyes wide with anticipation.

Shaking her head, Willa looked at Solace. "I still can't believe it really happened."

"What happened?!" Solace nearly lifted out of her seat.

"Simon's mom came to see me." A cold chill moved down Willa's neck at the memory.

"*WHAT?!*" Solace jerked back, blinking several times. "When?"

"A week and a half ago, just before school ended."

"A week?! Why didn't you tell me sooner? What did she say?" Her eyes grew even wider. "What did Simon say when you told him?" Solace scooted to the edge of her chair.

Willa hung her head.

"Sun and moon!" Solace gasped. "You didn't tell him?"

Willa shook her head. "I couldn't." She exhaled, the weight of the secret pressing on her. "I wanted to, but . . . he was so stressed out with finals, and his nightmares have come back and everything else. I've almost told him several times, but it just won't come out." She dropped her face into her hands and mumbled, "I feel terrible. I'm a terrible person."

"But what did she want? What did she *say?*"

Willa dropped her hands. "Solace, it was *so* bizarre. I mean, one of the weirdest moments of my life. She walked up to me on campus—"

"Willa!" Simon's voice echoed from the hall, startling them both, cutting off the story.

Solace jumped up from her seat. "No!" she whispered. "I can't sit here waiting to hear the rest of that story!"

Willa moved next to her. "I promise I'll tell you as soon as I can." Solace looked up at her with pleading eyes. "Sorry! Bad timing."

"The worst," Solace mumbled as Simon walked into the room. She scowled at him.

When he saw Willa his eyes lit up, and she couldn't help but smile back. He wore a white V-neck T-shirt, khaki shorts and flip flops, effortlessly sexy. "Hey!" he called out as he hurried over.

"Hey!" Willa said, slightly nervous considering what he'd nearly walked in on.

"Hello, Solace," he said looking around. "If you're here."

Solace's scowl deepened. Willa said, "She says hi."

"I certainly do not!" Solace stamped a translucent foot and vanished.

"Ready to go?" Simon pulled Willa into a hug and kissed her forehead.

"Of course, yeah. Let's go." Willa moved away from him to walk back to the office to get her bag but then stopped a few steps away. She turned back and opened her mouth. "Simon?"

"Yeah?" His smile fell, and he stepped forward. "You okay?"

"Of course, yes." Willa looked down at her wedge sandals and then back up, her heart pounding. "I just wanted to say . . ." *Do it! Tell him!*

He put a hand on her shoulder. "What is it?"

"I'm just frustrated with my parents—that's all. Solace and I were talking about it." It wasn't a complete lie.

Simon lowered his eyebrows but offered a smile. "I know. I'm sure they'll come around soon." He moved his hand to her neck and stroked the skin with his thumb. "You sure that's all you wanted to say?"

Willa smiled. *Coward!* Pushing down her emotions into a place she hoped he couldn't sense, she said, "Yeah. Let me go grab my purse." Then she turned and walked away, stomach knotting with guilt. *Why don't I just tell him?* As she approached the office, she had a terrible thought. *Am I keeping this from him because he's keeping something from me?*

She picked up her purse and looked around the small office. The clock on the wall ticked loudly. She stepped back into the hall, her stomach aching now, leaving the spiteful question unanswered.

Simon watched Willa closely as they drove out of town toward Denver for a night in the city. Tension and worry leaked from her every pore, but he couldn't get at the cause, with either his gift or his questions. The problem with her parents was bad, but not as bad as what he felt from her. Maybe lingering finals frustration? He felt guilty about that—it was his fault she'd spent so much time researching magic instead of studying. She wanted to help him, but he wished she'd just stop. It wasn't doing either of them any good. But how could he say that to her?

He'd begun the training with Rowan, which felt too much like therapy, but Simon didn't complain. He had to give it his best effort, for Willa's sake and his own. Maybe all of Rowan's emotional training actually *would* help; he had to stop being so skeptical about everything.

But his nightmares about the cave had recently come back, worse than before. It was hard not to attribute that to the training.

Simon flicked on the blinker and changed lanes. Willa stared out her window, body turned away from him. He suddenly wanted to pull the car off the road, gather her into his arms, and make everything better with a kiss.

If I just talk to her, open up, get this pain out, maybe everything would be better. I could fix it all if I just talked to her.

He opened his mouth. Shut it tight.

I am so broken. Why does she even stay with me?

He looked at the side of her face, her skin now tan, soaking up the summer sun, glowing like fresh caramel. Her dark hair fell over her back and shoulders like a shawl for her white halter top sun dress. Sensing his gaze, she turned and offered a small smile. The space behind his heart warmed.

He reached across and took her hand firmly in his. Maybe moving in with the Covenant wouldn't be so bad. Maybe giving up his independence to lie next to Willa each night would be completely worth it. Maybe it would help bring them back together and close the gap he'd driven between them.

"So, what do you think?" he said casually. "Indian, Italian, or Thai?"

Her smile grew. "I'm thinking a big greasy hamburger and fries."

He laughed. "I know just the place." He squeezed her hand. "And I say we forget about everything for tonight and just be two college kids on summer break. Okay?"

"Okay." She shifted closer to him, leaning over the center console. "Good idea. No magic, no parents, no challenges, no impending doom from a Dark threat."

"Exactly. Let's just be normal for one night. Eat greasy food and maybe some ice cream. Sit in a park, make out on the swings." He lifted an eyebrow at her. She laughed, and the sound was medicine for his soul.

CHAPTER 18
WAXING GIBBOUS

July—Present Day

Willa and Simon lay happily tangled in each other's arms on a soft flannel blanket under the canopy of the night sky and the spotlight of the nearly full moon. From the vantage point on top of the cliff, looking up, it felt like the chiffon sky might swallow them whole.

Willa closed her eyes as the cool mountain summer air trickled over her face. Below the cliff resided a sparkling clear lake, a jewel in the moonlight. Giant evergreens surrounded the lake, like favorite friends around a dinner table. Beyond the evergreens, a dense carpet of aspen trees spread out for miles. Even high above them, Willa could hear the rippling quake of the leaves as the breeze weaved through the aspens.

Simon had never brought her here before. When they'd rounded the last switchback and walked to the cliff's edge, her breath had caught in her chest at the beautiful view. "How did you know about this place?" she asked.

With a satisfied smile, he said, "I stumbled upon the lake on one of my solo hikes. Figured there had to be a hike to this cliff. Took me a while to find it, though."

"It's amazing!" Willa shook her head, kept her eyes wide to drink in the sight. "I can't believe I've lived near this all my life and never seen it." She turned to him, stepped close and held onto his arm, resting her head on his bicep. "Thank you for bringing me here."

Simon pulled her into a hug. "My pleasure. It's the perfect moonlight hike. Everything looks so different at night. Like it's not real, but a painting or a . . . dream."

He stiffened slightly at the word, and Willa lifted her head to look at the side of his face. A muscle in his jaw twitched. She opened her mouth to say something about his nightmares, but he pulled away, dropped his pack to the ground.

All tension vanished from his face, he smiled and said, "I brought some snacks. Help me spread out the blanket."

Now, nearly an hour later, the moon higher in the sky, Willa fought the urge to drift off to sleep. It was late, her body tired from the long hike, and she was warm tucked next to Simon. Her eyelids closed as she slipped under.

"One year," Simon whispered, pulling her back to the surface.

"What?" she whispered back.

"We've been together for over a year now."

Willa opened her eyes. "The best and craziest year of my life." She smiled. It was hard to imagine that everything they'd been through had all happened in just one year. Looking back, her life before Simon and the covens seemed unreal, like an imagined past or something she'd read in a book. "Do you ever think about what we'd be doing if we hadn't ever met or if we hadn't found Wynter in the basement?"

Simon's face grew serious. "Sometimes. I don't ever like to think about my life without you," he hugged her closer, "but I think about how things would be without the Covenant. Kind of hard not to, when everything is so crazy and . . . new. You know?"

"Yeah. I wonder how long it will take for it not to feel that way, for it just to be normal. I wonder when the questions will stop."

"What questions?" he asked, adjusting his head to look at her.

"All the whys and whats and hows." She met his gaze. "Does that make sense?"

He nodded. "Too much sense." He sighed.

She turned her head to the moon's white face. "At least we have these escapes to the mountains, right? Just us. No questions, no problems." She sighed. "It's a beautiful night."

"Yes, it is." Simon touched her face. "I love you, Willa. You know that, right?"

She lifted onto her elbow to look down at him, at the dark pools of his eyes and the fleeting worry there. "Of course, I do. I love you, too."

He put his hand behind her neck and held her eyes. "I don't want you to ever doubt that. I know things have been a little . . . weird lately, and I know it's my fault," she started to shake her head, but he kept going, "but you and me . . ." His words dropped off.

"I know," Willa said. She pressed a hand to his chest, lowered her lips to his. The meaning of his words, said and unsaid, were a flush of fresh water through her murky mind. At that moment, all was right.

The rustle of wings brought them out of the kiss. A large great horned owl landed on a rock only a few feet away. Regally, he tucked his wings back and blinked at the couple.

"Does he look hurt?" Willa asked. "Is he here for you to heal him?"

Animals still came to Simon on a regular basis. On the hike up, he'd healed a squirrel with a lame forepaw and a blue jay with a bleeding wing. Willa had seen him do it so many times now, but, still, each time the miracle of it warmed her heart in rarely felt places.

Simon lifted onto his elbows to study the owl. "No, I don't think so."

Willa smiled. "Should we go? It's getting pretty late, and don't you have the breakfast shift tomorrow?"

"Let's stay a little longer. I'll take a nap after my shift." He smiled and lay back down, opening his arm for her to slip down beside him.

She reached for her pack and pulled out her phone. "I better text my mom. Let her know I'll be later than I said." She typed, *Still on our hike. Be back late.* The reply came immediately. *Be safe!* Willa frowned at it.

"What's wrong?" Simon asked.

"I'm just sick of doing this," she lifted her phone. "It's worse than high school lately—having to check in all the time to avoid a fight." She put the phone away and snuggled next to him.

"Well, it's not much longer. Unless you give into them again."

"No way. This is getting ridiculous. Next week, as we

agreed last night—I'm out, no matter what. I've been patient long enough." She watched a sliver of cloud move across the moon and then added "I just hope I can make a clean break. I feel like they think I'm a two-year-old playing in the knife drawer, that every decision I make is going to get me hurt."

"I promise it's better than having them not care."

She nodded against his shoulder. "I know. I just . . . I'm ready to move forward, not go backward. I should have been out on my own by now, living as an adult. With you." Willa paused and then, before she lost her nerve, blurted out, "My mom thinks we should get married."

Simon shifted, and she sensed a hesitation or perhaps some shock. After a long pause, he said, "And what do you think?"

Willa sighed, "I'm not sure. My great-grandma Mabel told her that 'Marriage between soul mates is a perfect magical circle.' And last week, I stumbled across the witch wedding ceremony in one of those grimoires Wynter got from her friend back east." She rubbed her hand back and forth over his chest. "It's beautiful. Simple and perfect. It's called a Handfasting." She wanted to look at him, see his eyes, but was nervous about what she might find.

Simon put his hand on top of hers. His heart beat faster under her ear. "Willa, I . . ." The owl let out a high pitched, mournful hoot, cutting off Simon's words. They lifted their heads. The bird spread its wings and started to pace back and forth on the rock, continuing to hoot. Willa sat up. "What's he doing?"

"I don't know," Simon said as he sat up next to her. "It looks like something has spooked him."

The owl watched them, round golden eyes as bright and piercing as the moon. A chill lifted the hairs on Willa's neck

and arms. She scanned the dark landscape around them, searching for the source of the bird's anxiety. Suddenly, the air was
saturated with a heavy cold, so heavy it seemed to press down
on her. Then her necklace flared hot. "Simon!"

He gripped her arm and leaned forward, senses tuned outward. "Mine, too," he said in a hushed whisper. "I don't feel
anyone, but there is *something*."

"What is it?" Together they moved to their feet. Willa
braced, mind frantically going through all her training on
how to defend against a Dark threat. *No, no. Please not here,
not now.* The large bird continued to pace and hoot. Willa
watched its eyes, trying to follow the gaze, but it seemed to
only look at them.

The cold continued to press on her skin, and a pulse of
instinct made her turn. Behind Simon, curled near his shoulder, flashed a thin string of pearly white light. With a panicked
yelp, she reached out, grabbed his arm, and pulled him toward
her. He stumbled, reaching out to grip her shoulders.

"What?!" he said.

"There was something . . ." Breathing hard, she looked
around him, but found nothing. She spun, trying to find the
ribbon of light she was sure she'd seen. Pawing at his shirt as
if batting away a swarm of bees, she circled him once.

Simon grabbed her arms. "Willa? What is it?"

She blinked, focused on his face. "A light. I thought I saw
a light behind you, but . . ." Her eyes moved around the cliff
and over the trees. The only light was the moonlight, filtering
down through a few wispy clouds. *Was it a trick of the moonlight?*

Simon abruptly cried out, jerking away from Willa. He
stumbled back a few steps and then fell to his knees, gripping
his head. "Simon!" Willa screamed.

A STRANGE, PAINFULLY COLD PRESSURE sliced down through the top of Simon's skull, like a deadly icicle pushed into his head. Willa dropped next to him, her hands fluttering frantically from his arms to his chest.

"Simon?" she cried again.

He wobbled on his knees as the pain flared. Collapsing to the ground, he wanted to claw into his brain and stop whatever was happening. *Is someone breaking into my mind, like Archard did to Willa?*

Then it pulled away, so fast it left him gasping for air.

He sucked in a strangled gulp of air and flopped onto his back, his head throbbing madly. Willa leaned over him, her face pale, frightened. "Simon? Are you okay?"

He swallowed and took a few more breaths. His heart pummeled his ribs. "I . . . I think so."

"What happened?" She pushed the hair back from his forehead, her warm hands a sweet relief from the cold pain. "Oh, you're so cold. Your skin is like ice."

"There was this awful pain in my head." He put a hand on his chest, willing his heart to slow.

"Like someone breaking into your mind?" Her eyes widened. "Did you see anything? Any images? I thought your mind-lock was supposed to stop that sort of thing."

He started to shake his head, but the movement was jarring. "It is. It does." He exhaled and tried to think. "I didn't sense anyone trying to push in or see anything. Just a cold pain. Holy moon, what was it?"

Willa bit her bottom lip, stroked his forehead again. "I don't know, but I think we better get out of here fast. Can you stand?"

He closed his eyes and took another long breath. "Give

me a minute. I can feel my healing powers working." He took her hand, held it against his chest, and closed his eyes. "Just give me a minute." The heat of his unique magic swirled in his blood, quickly pulling away all remnants of the pain. He sat up.

"Better?" Willa asked, leaning over him, eyes still scanning up and down his body.

"Yeah, I think so." She stood and held out a hand. He took her small hand and dragged himself up to his feet. The pain was gone, but he still didn't feel right. He nodded, "I'm okay. Let's get our stuff."

Willa turned, took a step toward the blanket and their packs but stopped short. On the ground at her feet, yellow eyes wide and accusing, lay the owl.

Wings spread out to the side.

Dead.

Willa's scream sent a shivering ripple over the lake below.

CHAPTER 19
WAXING CRESCENT

September 1946

Chloe Winfred sat on the edge of her bed, gripping her new baby blue book bag to her chest. Her red plaid skirt, white blouse, and clunky Oxford shoes felt awkward on her tall, lanky frame. The blouse scratched her neck, and she knew the shoes would give her blisters if she walked more than a few feet, but at least she would blend into the crowd.

Just like her mother wanted.

Her mother meant well, but all her life she had tried—often with an alarming desperation—to make her daughter as normal as possible. And Chloe did her best to comply, meeting desperation with desperation, never knowing exactly who she was. There was a constant struggle inside her, a whirlwind of emotions and thoughts that never matched up with what her mother told her she ought to be. Something inside her was dying to get out into the light of day, but Chloe didn't know how to let it out.

First day of high school. Oh, goodie.

It would have been a thrilling day for her if she weren't so terrified about keeping her true self hidden and worried about doing everything her mother wanted her to do. Chloe took a deep breath and exhaled slowly. Her eyes drifted to the tall oak bookshelf on the other side of the room. She had all the respectable books that a girl her age should: a shiny set of encyclopedias, all the latest *Nancy Drews*, a collection of Shakespeare, a few Arthur Conan Doyle, and a spattering of pleasant novels. But the book that really mattered, the one that called to her in the dark of night, was tucked *behind* the bookcase, smashed against the wall, gathering dust.

Chloe set her book bag aside and crossed the room. She looked to see that her door was locked and then pressed her head against the wall next to the bookcase, squinting until she could just make out the dark form of the book on the floor behind the shelf. A familiar thrill fluttered in the space behind her heart and made her breath catch in her throat. Warmth grew around her.

Biting her bottom lip, she looked at the door again. There was enough time—her mother was busy cleaning up breakfast. Quickly, she dropped to her heels and then carefully slipped her hand into the small opening until her fingers brushed leather. Just that tiny touch sent tendrils of heat up her arm.

Awkwardly, she forced her smashed fingers to grasp the book and pulled it out.

Chloe held her breath, pressing the book to her chest, heart fluttering.

She pushed her feet out from under her and dropped to sit on the floor, her clunky shoes out in front of her, looking a bit too much like clown shoes. She rolled her eyes at the shoes and then looked down at the book in her hands. Her heart thumped more wildly, like a moth caught in a jar. Her eyes flicked once more to the door.

After a few seconds' hesitation, she laid the book on her lap, resting her right hand on the worn leather cover as soft as silk. Her hand grew hot as a faint light radiated from the edges of the pages. The light grew brighter and soon streamed out of the book in brilliant blue-white ribbons, swirling around her, just as the water used to under her command. It'd been years since she allowed herself to use her bizarre power over water. She missed it with a phantom ache, like a severed limb.

Eyes closed, Chloe lifted her chin to bask in the heat and energy of the light—something she had not done the first time she opened the book.

The book was odd from the first moment she laid eyes on it in Dusty Pages, the tiny antiquarian bookshop in town. Chloe liked to visit the store while her mother did the weekly grocery shopping at the market down the street. She loved the smell of the old books, the weight of them in her hands, and the quiet of the spaces between the shelves.

On that balmy June day, just a few months ago, she'd been lazily running her hands over the crusty spines of weather reference books from the early 1900s, when a blue-white light flickered in the corner of her eye. Blinking from the top shelf of a haphazard and dangerously tall stack of books on the back wall of the shop was a small brown book. Chloe stood unmoving for a moment, her mouth slightly agape, the *shush-shush* of the ceiling fan suddenly loud in her ears.

She walked forward, almost in a trance, the light growing brighter as she neared. Soon she stood just under the precarious stack, her head craned upward, her heart skipping off excitedly. Heat moved down from the book like a summer breeze rolling over a hill. She gasped, recognizing the feeling, the energy, and knowing she had to get away from it before something happened that would further anger and embarrass her mother.

Chloe turned on her heel and bolted from the store, ignoring the questioning call of the proprietor. She ran out into the street and didn't stop until she reached the far end of Main Street, next to the city park. She dropped onto a bench and covered her face with her hands, willing her body and mind to be still and forget.

But she couldn't. That curious space behind her heart throbbed, itching for her to go back. *No, no, no. I can't. I won't!* But the words were hollow even as she thought them. She knew that she would go back to get the book. The thing inside her, the thing her mother tried so hard to suppress, was waking up, taking over.

She fought with herself for another ten minutes, until the force inside her nearly lifted her to her feet. Shuffling and mumbling under her breath, Chloe stepped back into the bookshop, offering a shy smile and shrug to the shop owner, who only shook his head as he went back to work.

The second she turned down the aisle, the light burst out from the pages of the book, filling the room. Chloe put a hand over her beating heart as she stared in awe. She glanced back at the owner, bent over his desk. *How does he not see this?* Standing once again in front of the stack, Chloe marveled as the heat sparked along her skin.

She reached up her hand, lifting to her toes, but the book sat just out of reach. She glanced around for a step stool, but found none. So she tried again, straining up onto her very tiptoes, extending her arm as long as it would go. No luck. Chloe huffed, glared at the book. She didn't dare ask the shop owner to get it for her.

She continued to stare at the book, wondering if she could get away with standing on a stack of books without the owner noticing. The book shuddered, flew off the shelf, and nearly hit her in the head. Ducking out of the way, the book hit the shelf behind her, and *thunked* to the floor.

Chloe blinked at it. *Did I do that?*

"Everything all right back there, Chloe?" the owner called from his perch at the counter.

She flinched. "Yeah, yeah. Sorry, Lem. Just dropped a book."

She had to get out of there. She snatched the book off the floor and took it to the counter. "I'll take this one," Chloe said as casually as possible. She held her breath, waiting for Lem to notice the light pulsing off the exposed edges of the pages.

Lem looked over at her and raised an eyebrow. He picked up the book, flipped it open. "Hmm. Forgot I had this old blank journal. You keep journals, Chloe?"

Chloe blinked at him, looked down at the pages, most definitely *not* blank. Writing, lots of writing, words, symbols, and drawings filled every page. Maybe it had been a blank journal once, but someone had filled it. She swallowed, tried to smile. "Yeah, I like to write down random stuff. Nothing profound."

Lem nodded, punched a few buttons on the cash register. "That's twenty-five cents. Good deal, huh?"

Chloe nodded as she pulled the money from the pocket of

her blue skirt. She handed it to him in exchange for the book. "Thanks," she mumbled.

"See ya next week," Lem said, already turning back to his paperwork.

That afternoon Chloe had locked herself in her room to open the book in private. The light had burst out, causing her to panic and throw the small volume across the room. The ribbons of light moved around the space; she shrank away from their heated touch. When her mother called out, wondering about the noise, Chloe snatched the book and shoved it behind the bookcase.

Now, sitting on the floor, dressed for her first day of high school, Chloe opened the book for only the third time. The first page held a name and a strange symbol of an upside down triangle with waves of water inside it. She ran a finger over the name: *Amelia Plate—Gift of Water.* Her skin tingled, her heart raced. Something in that name snagged on her beating heart. Perhaps it was the reference to water. *Could this girl do things with water, like me?* The idea that she was not alone in her strangeness thrilled her.

She turned to the place she'd left off the last time. At the top of the page was another hand-drawn symbol of a pine tree, small and almost juvenile. Chloe ran her fingertip over the symbol and the word next to it: *courage.* Her heart squeezed. Hadn't she just been wishing for courage, for the strength to face a new school, new kids, new eyes looking at her as if she was somehow wrong no matter how hard she tried to be right?

"Courage," she whispered and then read the words written below it. "*Help me, all powerful sun and moon. Bring me courage, swift and soon.*" The words felt . . . *right* on her tongue. Heat stirred in the space behind her heart. She swallowed, repeated the words. *"Help me, all powerful sun and moon. Bring me courage, swift and soon."* The warmth flared again, spreading outward through her chest and into her arms, legs, and head. It felt amazing, like a hug, like a kiss, like liquid, delicious courage poured into her body.

Chloe smiled and closed her eyes.

"Chloe!" her mother yelled from behind the door as she rattled the doorknob. "You're going to be late. What are you doing in there?"

Chloe flinched, snapped the book closed, and shoved it behind the bookcase. "Nothing. I'm ready." She fumbled to her feet, grabbed her bag. Throwing open the door, she said, "I'm ready! Let's go."

Her mom looked at her with a raised eyebrow. "Why so excited all the sudden? I thought you were dreading this."

Chloe shrugged, still smiling. "Changed my mind. I just have a good feeling."

CHAPTER 20
WAXING GIBBOUS

July—Present Day

The box, in its black velvet bag, had not left Archard's side since he'd emerged from Bartholomew's underground keep. Since arriving back in Colorado he'd worked nearly nonstop on the spells for his grand plan, fueled by the constant hum of the ancient anger contained within the vessel.

Now, he and Rachel stood outside a rented house in Twelve Acres, only blocks from the Light Covenant. As careful as they had been to mask their presence, Archard was still surprised Rowan wasn't already charging up the driveway of this simple red brick rambler. Rachel fumbled with the key, opened the door, and stepped aside for Archard.

He started to move forward but stalled mid-step. "What is that?" he whispered. He spun around, expecting to see someone approaching, but found only the moonlit empty yard, with its neatly trimmed grass and box-shaped hedges. But the feeling he'd had . . . It felt like someone looking over his shoulder.

"What?" Rachel said with a yawn.

"I felt . . . something." He stepped down the porch stairs, gray eyes darting back and forth. The sensation remained, growing stronger: eyes digging into the back of his head. "Rachel, someone is watching us."

Rachel joined Archard on the lawn and lifted her hands. "I don't feel *anything*, Archard. There is no one here but us."

He scowled at her. The box in his hands shook, and he nearly dropped it.

"What's it doing?" Rachel asked, narrowing her suspecting eyes at the box.

Archard's heart started racing. He slipped his hand inside the velvet bag, fingers searching for the lock. He hissed when his skin met the metal. "Sun and moon, it's freezing!" Hurriedly, he lowered the box to the grass and ripped away the bag. The box looked the same, the lock secure, but pulses of ice-cold energy came off it.

"Are they trying to get out?" Rachel took a step back, voice revealing her fear.

Archard ignored her and lowered his ear to the box. Even from six inches away, he could feel the biting cold on his skin. For once the box was oddly silent. But why?

Ice crystals formed around the True Healer symbol. Archard watched in uneasy fascination as the lacy pattern crawled outward. Goosebumps rose on his skin. All at once, he felt drawn to the box, held in place by it, and also that he should run far away. His body grew rigid with fear.

Then, without warning, a rush of cold energy burst up into

Archard's face, throwing him backwards. Rachel screamed. It felt as if a glacier had fallen onto his forehead, the pressure unbearable. He cried out in pain, gripping the sides of his head.

Archard summoned his magic, using all the skill he could muster to push back the attack, vaguely aware of Rachel standing over him, chanting her own efforts. He couldn't breathe, his throat frozen. Death felt only moments away, and he panicked. He could not die now, not so close to triumph!

He called to his fire again and again, but the heat couldn't penetrate the cold, now starting to move down his body. *No! NO!*

The tremendous energy suddenly shifted, paused, and then retreated, freeing him. Gasping and coughing, he rolled away and managed to get to his feet. Bent forward, hands on his knees, he glared at the box, unchanged, unassuming on the grass.

He lifted his eyes to the orange-slice moon. For a split second he wondered if it was right to unleash the magic contained in the box, but then he stood up straight. *I beat it! I am in control.*

"Archard, what was that?" Rachel stepped cautiously to his side.

"Perhaps some delayed enchantment or protection." He shook his head. "But it's over." He walked forward, bent down, and scooped up the box. The moaning had returned, and he found a certain comfort in their awful cries. He slipped the box into its bag. "Come," he said to Rachel, "let's get settled and back to work."

THE TICK OF THE GRANDFATHER clock in the corner of the room grated on Simon's nerves. The icy pain from the cliff had been replaced with a jittery, electric energy that skittered along his nerves, heightening his senses and bringing to a boil a rush of power, the kind he hadn't felt since . . .

What happened up there? What's wrong with me?

He glared at the gold face of the antique clock, the second hand thudding past the numbers. *Has it always been that loud?* When Wynter pushed a mug of steaming peppermint and passion fruit tea in his face, he flinched.

"Sorry, Simon, I didn't mean to startle you," she said gently. "Here." She continued to hold out the mug. "Drink this. I dropped a calming potion in there too."

Simon took it stiffly, held it between his hands, the sweet smell filling his nose. Willa sat next to him on the leather couch, watching his every move. Wynter and Rowan sat opposite in another leather couch. The living room of Plate's Place still smelled like paint, but it was finally complete. The original wood floor shined with a high gloss, the old hearth now boasted a new granite fireplace and a dark wood mantel. The built-in bookshelves were full of books and grimoires, the wainscoting painted brilliant white in contrast to the slate blue walls.

And that clock.

Simon glared at it as he took a sip of tea, too annoyed to drink anymore. He set it on the coffee table, turning to Wynter and Rowan.

"So, what was it?" he asked in a tight voice, referring to his hike with Willa.

Rowan frowned. "I wish I could say for sure. It's very odd."

"Is it connected to the quakes in the spring? Or the monks in England? Rachel at the diner?" Willa asked, setting down her own cup of tea. "Did we stumble onto something?"

"Possibly," Rowan nodded. "I think we better go back tomorrow. Maybe we can discover what happened."

Simon sighed as he rubbed his forehead. "If there is something out there, why did it attack me? And why did the owl die? Are the two connected?"

"Maybe it didn't *attack* you. Maybe it just *affected* you in some way. The owl too. Maybe whatever hurt you, hurt it also," Wynter offered.

Simon grunted in frustration. *Maybe.* Why did everything turn into one big guessing game?

"I thought you guys were experts in witchcraft." Simon sat forward, elbows on knees. Willa's eyes went wide. "But it seems like all you do is shrug your shoulders and guess."

"Simon!" Willa said and put a hand on his back; but he didn't stop, *couldn't* stop, his fear and frustration bubbling over; and the strange power in his gut churning, seeking an outlet.

"You don't know why I have powers I'm not supposed to have, or how I killed three people without even trying. You don't know if Rachel was here, or what the earthquakes mean. And now something tried to tear my head apart, and you *still* don't know. Why—"

"Simon, stop," Willa begged, pushing harder into his back. Wynter and Rowan barely moved, listening silently.

"No. I want to understand," he flung back without looking at her. "We joined this Covenant so we could learn, so we could find answers when weird stuff happened, but so far we've had a whole lot of weird and *no answers.*" Simon's heart raced, and he found it hard to draw breath. His skin grew hot, tingly. His next words came out in a stiff yell. "WHAT IS GOING ON?"

The magic left his body involuntarily, and the gold face of

the grandfather clock exploded. Willa and Wynter screamed, ducking their heads, but Rowan didn't flinch. He watched Simon with a penetrating, inquisitive stare. Simon stared back as a shower of gears and glass hit the floor.

Simon rarely lost his temper. He'd learned from a young age to bottle up his anger. There was the time his father had slapped him across the face for healing his mother's finger after she cut it while making dinner. He'd wanted so badly to erupt there in the kitchen, a half cut onion on the counter and his mom's red blood on the white tile, but he didn't. He'd held it in, pushed out the front door and ran around the block until his ten-year-old legs crumpled beneath him.

Willa drew back her hand for a moment, turning to look at the remains of the clock, and then placed it back on Simon's back, applying slight pressure. "Simon?" she whispered. He blinked, breaking the stare-down with Rowan, surprised and suddenly ashamed and too shocked to say anything, even to apologize.

Rowan scooted to the edge of his seat and leaned toward Simon, his hands clasped loosely in front of him. Simon looked at the floor, his shoulders slumped forward. Rowan said, "Simon, you're right. We haven't had any answers lately, especially involving you. And for that, I'm sorry. There is much we know about magic and regular witchcraft, but being in the Covenant and dealing with Dark threats is almost as new to us as it is to you. We'll have to help each other along the way."

Looking at the white lip of his mug of cold tea, Simon nodded. Willa rubbed her hand up and down his back, a small comfort.

Wynter inhaled quietly and said, "First thing tomorrow,

we will go back to the cliff and try to find some answers. But I think now, Simon, you need some rest."

Simon nodded again. Willa spoke for him. "Can we stay here? In our room? I think we'd both feel safer."

"Of course," Wynter replied, her voice full of understanding and sympathy. "If you think your parents will be okay with it."

Willa sighed. "I'll think of something to say."

"All right. Rowan and I will check all the protections on the house before we go back to bed and . . . clean up the mess," Wynter said.

Simon flinched. *How did I let that happen?*

Wynter and Rowan stood. "Good night," Rowan said quietly.

Willa stood, tugged on Simon's arm. He rose to his feet robotically, followed her up the grand wooden staircase, a headache forming at the back of his skull.

THE HALL TO ALL THE bedrooms was quiet. Grateful no one had awakened with the noise of the clock exploding, Willa held tightly to Simon's hand, pulling him to the door of their room. If she hadn't been so worried about him, it would have been exciting to be spending another night there.

She turned the doorknob and pushed the door back. The lavender she'd hung above the small fireplace sent a puff of fragrance out into the hall. She was about to step in when Rain's door opened. She shuffled out into the hall, dressed in faded flannel pajamas, her hair squashed against her head. She blinked at them.

"I thought I heard something. What're you guys doing here?" she asked, moving forward. She looked at Simon. "What's wrong?"

"Long story," Willa said tiredly. "Can we tell you in the morning?"

Rain stopped next to Willa, still eyeing Simon, who stared blankly into the room through the open door. "Yeah. Let me know if I can do anything." She touched Willa's arm, and Willa noticed for the first time that all of Rain's tattoos were of water, in all different forms and colors.

"Thanks, Rain. Goodnight."

"Goodnight," she said with a small smile and then shuffled back to her room. Her door shut with a quiet click.

Willa turned back to Simon and pushed him into the room. He walked over to the deep armchair by the little fireplace, and collapsed. He held his head in his hands. Willa took a moment to look around the room, trying to calm herself.

The small room had turned out beautifully. She and Wynter had stripped the hideous wallpaper and replaced it with cream paint. The crack in the ceiling had been mended, the wood floor polished and refinished. Atop the new night-stands were two squat Tiffany lamps Willa had found in a vintage shop in Boulder. A small desk was pushed into the corner, near the two tall, narrow windows, and an empty bookshelf stood against the wall next to the door.

It felt like home. At least normally it did. Not tonight. Nothing felt right tonight.

She crossed to the windows and lifted them open. The warm night breeze pushed in, tossing the sheer curtains toward her. She caught a panel in her fingers and let the water-smooth fabric pull slowly away. Simon sat next to her, still and quiet.

"I've never heard you talk like that," she whispered. *Or be destructive like that.* A brief flare of anger rose inside her. *Except for the cave!* She hated that the whole thing had ever happened and hated what it had done to him. Maybe finding out they were witches hadn't helped after all.

He shifted and dropped his hands with a long sigh. "I know," he said weakly, avoiding her eyes.

She turned, sat on the edge of the bed, so soft and comfortable, much better than her bed at home. Her fingers trailed along the time-worn fabric of the blue, green, and cream quilt. "Are you *ever* going to talk to me?" She kept her eyes low.

Simon's head lifted, and she felt his eyes on her, but she couldn't find the strength to look at him. "Willa, I . . ." was as far as he got.

The words that she'd kept back for months pushed out of her like birds let out of a cage. They fluttered against her lips. "We are supposed to talk to each other. No matter what it is. That was always the deal—to be strange together. But ever since the cave, you've shut down." She inhaled. The cage wasn't empty yet. "I feel like a part of you is a stranger to me now, a stranger you keep hidden on purpose. I feel like every time we're together, we ignore what's wrong. We just pretend like it doesn't exist." She forced herself to look up. Simon's face broke into a hundred pieces; her heart tugged hard.

He swallowed and shook his head. "I can't believe I did that to the clock. I know you and Wynter were really excited about it. I'm sorry."

Willa gave him a small nod. "I don't care about the clock." She gripped the quilt. She kept one bird in the cage of her heart, one secret she wouldn't burden him with. Not tonight; he'd been through enough tonight.

After a long breath, he went on. "It's a stranger to me too." He leaned back in the chair and ran his hands through his curls. "I don't know what happened to me that day, but it *did* change me. There is this . . . undercurrent of power inside me, unleashed by whatever happened that night. And . . ." He dropped his head to the chair, rolled it to face the windows. "The guilt, Willa. The guilt of killing those people eats at me. I'm supposed to fix things, not *break* them." His voice caught, and he pressed his lips together until they drained of color.

Simon's eyes glistened in the weak moonlight passing through the curtains. Willa pushed away from the bed and knelt on the floor in front of him, her hands on his thighs. He turned to her; and she waited, knowing there was still more he needed to get out.

"What's wrong with me?" he mumbled, the words as broken as his face. "How do I fix it? My whole life I've been this . . . mystery. My parents wished I'd never been born, and then tried to neglect, yell, or beat my magic out of me. They called me a mistake, a freak of nature. *Evil*."

Willa's breath caught in her throat, she tightened her grip on his thighs. He shifted to lean forward and took her wrists in his hands, like he needed an anchor to get the rest out.

"They are the smartest people I know, and yet they couldn't accept what I am. But then," their eyes locked, "I found you, and things *finally* made sense. I felt whole, I felt *good*." He half smiled. "I was at peace with what I can do. You brought that peace. But then the cave." He shook his head. "I know what I did saved us, but I feel like I lost some of the peace that night. I couldn't bring myself to talk about it. Not even to you. Because . . ." He looked down at her hands.

"Because why?" she prompted.

"Because," his voice was as quiet as the breeze and as fractured as broken glass. "I finally thought my parents were right. That I am somehow . . . *evil*." He pulled in a ragged breath. "I didn't want to risk you looking at me like they did."

Tears rushed to Willa's eyes. "Simon," she choked and lifted up to put her arms around his neck. He pulled her tight against him, burying his face in her hair. The heat of a few tears touched her skin. She'd never seen him cry. "I'm so sorry that they treated you like that. It's . . . worse than awful. It's *wrong*." Pulling back, she took his face in her hands. "I've never met anyone as good as you. You are pure goodness. You have to banish your parents from your head. They don't deserve the space." He blinked his wet eyes. "And you *have* to talk to me. I will *never* look at you the way they did. I love you. To me, you are perfect. No matter what you do or what happens, I will still be here."

He laughed, a small, sad sound. Then his face turned serious again. "I'm sorry."

"Don't be sorry. You have nothing to be sorry for. Just be *here* with me. Don't retreat in *there*." She touched his forehead.

He closed his eyes briefly. "I get stuck in there sometimes."

"I know." She kissed the same spot that she had just touched. They were quiet for a moment. And then she asked, "So what happened downstairs?"

He shook his head. "I don't know. Ever since the cave, my powers have been building, and something about what happened on the cliff made it all spill over. Something about it made me lose control. The pain went away, but there's a weirdness lingering inside me."

Willa lowered her eyebrows. "Weird how?"

"I have a headache."

Her eyes popped. "But you don't get headaches."

"I know. And I felt irritated, antsy, while we were talking to Wynter and Rowan. I couldn't hold back the anger and . . . well, dead clock." He exhaled.

"What about now? Besides the headache, how do you feel?" she asked, touching his temple.

"Better. Still a little off; I'm not sure how to describe it."

Willa frowned, moving her fingers to run over his stubbly beard. She shook her head. "Sun and moon, what happened?" Her phone buzzed in the pocket of her hiking shorts and she flinched. With a grunt, she pulled it out. *Should have left it in my pack*, she thought as she frowned at the text from her mom.

"Your mom?" Simon asked. He stroked her hair.

"Yeah, of course." She sighed. "What do I tell her?"

"The truth."

She looked up at him, and he nodded. "Yeah, okay." She opened the message and typed a reply. *Something strange happened on our hike tonight—something magical. I need to stay at Wynter and Rowan's tonight so we can figure out what's wrong. Please don't worry.* She hit send and bit her bottom lip. Her mom didn't respond as quickly as normal. Willa looked up at Simon. "Uh-oh."

"Give her a minute to think."

The reply came. *Okay. I hope everything is all right. Luckily your dad is already asleep. Will you be back in the morning?*

No. We have to go back up to the cliff and do some spells.

Okay. Please text me. Let me know you are safe.

Of course. Willa's thumb hovered over the send button, but then she decided to add, *Love you.*

Love you too, came the response.

Willa exhaled. Simon said, "That actually went well."

She nodded. "Yeah, 'cause my dad wasn't involved." Turning slightly, she threw the phone onto the bed and then said, "Do you think you can sleep?" She touched his fore-head, wondering about the strange headache. A curl of worry unfurled in her gut. *What happened?!*

Simon half smiled. "With you next to me, yes, I think I'll sleep just fine." He kissed her.

Willa looked over to the small clock on the mantel of the fireplace. "It's already two. We better get to sleep if we're going back up there in the morning. And you better see if some-one can take your shift at the diner." She started to move off Simon's lap, but he held her in place. "What is it?" she asked as his face fell serious again.

"Thank you," he whispered softly.

Her heart squeezed. "You don't ever have to thank me."

CHAPTER 21
WAXING GIBBOUS

July—Present Day

Willa and Simon had fallen asleep quickly, exhausted but happy to be next to each other— even under the grim circumstances. Now, with dawn sluggishly moving into the sky, Willa was trapped inside a nightmare.

She stood on the cliff, looking down on the lake, its surface black and smooth as glass. The night hung about her like a brooding storm cloud. A whispering wind rushed past her, the words flying too fast to understand. Her head began to throb, a knocking of pain on the crown that radiated down through her whole body. Then, out of the night flew the owl, huge and threatening. It dove out of the clouds like a bullet, so close she ducked to escape its hungry talons.

The owl screeched a high-pitched noise of pain. Willa

turned to see it stop mid-flight as though it had hit a wall, then fall to the earth with an ominous thud. Willa held her breath as the prostrate bird haltingly turned its yellow eyes to her, beak spread open in a silent scream.

The dream changed, the cliff scene melting away.

She stood in a busy market, in another place and time, ancient and primitive. The smell hit her hard: body odor and human waste, mud, and animals. A horse-drawn cart rolled past her, slugging through the cold mud, the horse heaving forward with the effort. The man crouched on the cart in his filthy, homespun coat didn't even glance at her.

She was an invisible observer.

Squat timber buildings with crusty thatched roofs lined the muddy street, and people passed busily back and forth. Merchants called out to draw customers to their stores and wagons. A group of children ran past, oblivious to the terrible conditions in which they played. The air was crisp, hinting at fall; and Willa wished she had a coat, her T-shirt and nylon hiking shorts a poor hedge against the chill.

A bell tolled. Something in the deep *gong* rose gooseflesh on Willa's arms and neck and caused her head to throb. On the cue of the bell, the townspeople turned away from their duties and began to walk in a mass toward the sound.

Willa followed, pulled along by instinct.

The narrow street funneled the crowd into an open square, an unimpressive stone church at the head, its bell swinging in the tower. The square, now packed with stinking bodies, grew eerily quiet. Willa's stomach clenched nervously.

One sound cut through the unnatural stillness: a woman screaming, desperate, pleading. Willa's body and soul turned to ice. She followed the piercing cries, pushing past the crowd that couldn't see her. When she finally broke to the front of the throng, what she saw brought stinging bile to her throat.

A pyre.

A pole secured in the center.

And a young woman being dragged toward it.

The woman looked a few years older than Willa, more perhaps; it was hard to tell. Her dark brown hair was a rat's nest around her wild, dirt-smudged face. There were bruises around her golden-brown eyes and dried blood on her wrists and ankles. The rags she wore hung pitifully off her too-thin body. She fought against the armed guards that dragged her to the stake.

Willa stood transfixed, sickened and frozen with fright.

The crowd behind her suddenly burst to life, yelling, "witch! witch! witch!" Willa whirled around, for a moment thinking they were shouting at her, but then she saw the blood-lust and fear in their eyes, all aimed at the woman.

The guards threw the accused against the stake, and bound her with thick rope. She tossed her head back and forth, still pleading with her captors to have mercy. The crowd continued to taunt, and a few even threw food, chunks of bread sticking in her long, tangled hair.

Willa ran forward, desperate to help, even though she knew she was only an echo on the scene. In reality, the woman had died hundreds of years ago. Still, the need to lessen her pain and fear grew hot in Willa's chest.

"No!" Willa screamed. No one turned, no one heard. She climbed up the pyre, stumbling, and reached for the knots. Her hands went through them. "No," she whispered to herself.

Willa backed down the pyre and stood helpless and sick as they put torches to the wood. The fire caught slowly. The woman grew quiet, staring out at the crowd, her eyes desperately searching the faces. The crowd yelled for her death, like hungry dogs at a carcass.

Willa could sense that the woman was a witch, magic flowing in her veins. *Do something! Save yourself! Use the magic!* As Willa searched the woman's face, instinct told her something was wrong, that somehow the woman could not use her magic to save herself. *What did they do to you?*

The flames gained strength, crawling toward their victim, fumbling over each other, fighting for the first taste. Willa fought the panic racing in her veins. When the smell of burning flesh hit her nose, she turned and vomited.

The poor woman didn't scream or cry out, her face now strangely serene, making it all the more awful. Willa moved around in front of her and stared at her angelic features, memorizing her face. *I'm so sorry. So very sorry.*

The flames ate away at the witch's legs and climbed her torso, but she didn't flinch. Willa wondered if somehow she had already died. Terrified, she watched the flames skitter up the woman's hair, crowning her in fire for a moment before claiming her face.

Willa looked away.

From behind her a voice called out. At first, Willa didn't bother to turn, her body stiff with shock. Then the voice, deep and resonating, yelled again, "No!" Willa spun to see the crowd parting to let a man through. He ran forward, his black cloak billowing out behind him, and stopped before her.

After so much filth and ugliness, Willa's breath caught at the sight of this man's face, pristine and masculine, like a perfectly shaped stone statue. Though beautiful, the sharp cut of his jaw and the odd color of his eyes made him subtly sinister. His eyes were the color of stars: not white or black or gray, but each at once, and alive with light. His long hair was a deep yellow, neatly tied back from his bearded face. He towered over her, his broad chest and intense presence taking up so much space.

His fists curled at his sides. The guards approached cautiously, and the man raised his hand, hurling the guards through the air to crash onto the church steps. The crowd panicked. The man—the witch—threw another blast of magic at the peasants, and each of them collapsed to the ground, unconscious or dead—Willa couldn't tell, but feared the latter.

Only the crackling sound of the wood broke the silence, an icy chill in the air. Willa hugged her arms around her chest. The man moved his hand forward, swept it over the flames, extinguishing them instantly. Willa's stomach turned again at the sight of the blackened corpse of the woman. The man walked forward and pulled her body into his arms. He carried her like a child, tucked into his chest.

He dropped to his knees next to Willa, who watched as he adjusted the charred corpse and put one of his hands on her head. Pieces of her blackened clothing and skin flaked off under his touch. He closed his eyes, his face suddenly tense with concentration. The eerily familiar gesture sent another wave of cold down Willa's spine.

After a moment he opened his piercing eyes, now full of agony. The agony spilled out of his eyes and turned to anger on his chiseled face. Willa stepped back, frightened and fascinated all at once. Carefully, he removed a necklace from the burned body, placed it around his own neck and dropped it inside his shirt.

He stood, the woman's body falling apart in his arms. A ripple of cold moved off him and chilled Willa to her bones.

Then he turned and looked her directly in the eyes. Her heart stopped, breath deflated.

"You should not be here," he said darkly in a voice that burned her face. An icicle of pain stabbed through her head.

All went black.

"Willa!" Simon yelled, shaking her as firmly as he dared without hurting her. He'd been trying to wake her for ten minutes. "Willa, wake up!" His heart beat frantically. *Why won't you wake up?*

Willa's eyes snapped open, and she began to scream. She pushed away from him, moving toward the end of the bed. "Willa, it's me. It's Simon."

She stopped, crouched low on her hands and knees, ready to spring away, eyes wild and big as they darted around the room. "Simon?" she said in a weak voice.

"Yeah, it's me. I'm here. You're safe." Simon inched toward her.

She inhaled raggedly. "I thought it was him." Her eyes continued to move around the room, wary.

"Who, Willa? You were dreaming. A bad nightmare."

She finally focused on his face. "Yes. A nightmare." She fell into his arms, shaking.

"I'm so sorry," Simon said as he held her close against his chest, trying to calm her. "This one was bad. It took me ten minutes to wake you up. And you threw up."

She pushed back. "What?" Then she turned to look at

the mess down the side of the bed. She blinked several times. "That's never happened before. I'll have to take the quilt to be cleaned," she said absently and then buried her face in his shirt. "I'm so sorry."

"Hey," he put a hand under her chin and lifted her face, "Hey, no. You don't need to be sorry. Are you okay? What did you see?"

She looked at him with urgent eyes. "It was just . . . awful. First, it was the poor owl on the cliff, and then a woman burned at the stake. But the man . . ." She flinched, dug her fingernails into the skin of his arms. "Ugh. My head is killing me." She pressed a hand to her forehead.

"What man?"

"I don't know." She looked at Simon, eyes narrowing. "He was a witch—a powerful one. He loved the girl. He killed them all." She gasped. "Then he looked right at me, spoke to me." She shivered and again looked at him closely. "He kind of looked like you." She touched his hair.

A chill moved down Simon's spine. He hated the wild, fearful look in her eyes and how she rambled, not really making sense, her thoughts clipped short. She looked around the room again, checking the dark corners. Her body would not stop shaking. He hugged her again. "Okay, it's over. Come on, let's go downstairs. I'll make you some tea, and we can sit outside until you feel better."

When she didn't move, he lifted her into his arms. He'd never seen her look so small, so child-like, as though the dream had robbed her of something. He hoped she could get it back. "Come on, my Willa."

He stepped into the dark, quiet hall, her small body in his arms.

"He carried her," Willa whispered. "Just like this." She turned her face into his chest and started sobbing. "Her body fell apart in his arms."

A cold shadow moved over Simon's heart.

CHAPTER 22
WANING HALF MOON

September 475 A.D.

Bartholomew carried her torched body as carefully as he could. The foul, unbearable smell filled his nose, mouth, and lungs; his eyes watered. He marched out of town and over the hillside before collapsing under his grief. His knees hit the hard earth and more precious pieces of her body fell off, each one like a slice of his heart cut away, never to be repaired.

Moments, a few small moments, he thought. *If only I'd arrived sooner, then you, my love, would still be alive.* Time is the cruelest of masters, forever torturing the heart. He glanced down at her black and red face, deformed, melted, and bile rose in his throat. He gagged; it shamed him greatly to have to look away. Tenderly, he shifted her body to one arm and removed his long cloak. He cast it out before him and it settled to the earth. With aching reverence, he laid her body in the center and wrapped it slowly.

"Brigid," he whispered her name.

Kneeling before the bundle, Bartholomew gripped her necklace in his palm. It had survived the fire with only a slight scorching of the silver. He'd given it to her when they'd married. He'd given it to her for protection, enchanted it with a spell, a strong one—or so he thought.

Her death could only mean one thing: another witch had betrayed them, helped in her capture, bound her magic so she could not escape. Brigid was strong, incredibly powerful. This should never have been possible.

He lifted his eyes upward, to the half moon sharing the sky with the sun. "How could you fail me?" he whispered between clenched teeth. "How could you betray your most loyal subjects?"

A small sliver of light curled through the air to touch his cheek, to comfort and caress, but he turned away. The day grew cold around him.

"I should never have gone away," he whispered, both hands pressed gently to the bundle. "I stayed too long." He paused and began to cry. "I should have taken you with me."

A memory poured into his mind, both elixir and poison at once.

A week before he left, on his way back from pasturing the sheep, he saw Brigid swimming in the pond near their home—a favorite pastime of hers, but one he rarely witnessed. Quietly, he concealed himself behind a willow tree and watched. Her slim body, tiny yet strong, glided through the glassy water with ease. Sunlight pooled on the water's surface and followed behind her in long golden ribbons.

Bartholomew's breath caught in his chest as Brigid emerged from the pond, her body dripping, shedding water. Her skin, whiter than sheep's wool, glistened, and her long dark hair clung to her curves, flowing down her back and over her chest like a royal robe. Even after ten years of marriage, her body thrilled him, fascinated him, called to him.

The leaves above him rustled, and before he had time to look up, one of the long branches wrapped around his arm, holding him tight. Brigid's laugh rang out. He turned back to see her walking toward him, still with only her hair for cover. "Are you spying on me, husband?"

He smiled. "Perhaps." He held out his tree-bound arm. "Do you mean to trap me here?"

Her golden-brown eyes caught the sunlight, glinted with humor. "Perhaps." She stopped in front of him, put her wet hands on his chest. The tree released its grip, and he pulled her into his arms.

"I am forever under your spell," he whispered in her ear.

"And I will never release you."

Now, kneeling in front of her burned, blackened body, Bartholomew had never felt a more wretched pain. Never again would he touch her beautiful face, never kiss her lips, never watch her card wool near the fire with sure, strong hands. Her angelic voice would never float through the yard as she tended to her garden, and her magic would never spark in his blood.

The pain gripped his heart and soul with breaking force. He collapsed to the dirt alongside her body, a moan of pure agony escaping his mouth. The moan escalated into a scream, a yell of impotent anger, with all the power of his magic behind it. The ground shook beneath him, birds fled the nearby trees.

The magic again tried to reach out to him, to comfort with its Light, but Bartholomew only roared louder.

"Stay away from me," he growled. "I no longer want your warmth." Lying on his back, Bartholomew lifted his hands before his tear-wet face, the charred necklace hanging down near his mouth. "All this power, and she died. She *died!* Burned as a heretic, a *witch.*" He moaned again, this time a pathetic, beaten sound. A whimper.

After a deep breath, he rose to his feet, unsteady for a moment and then solid, a pillar of cold anger. He lowered her necklace around his own neck again and then scooped her body into his arms, headed for their home.

He'd bury her near the pond, under the willow.

Then he would exact a terrible vengeance upon those responsible.

CHAPTER 23
WAXING GIBBOUS

July—Present Day

Twenty minutes after awaking from her nightmare, Willa was still shaking. She and Simon sat on the back porch steps of Plate's Place, sipping tea and watching the sun inch slowly into the sky. The fresh, flower-scented air and growing light did nothing to improve her mood. Huddled next to Simon, his solid form an anchor to the present, she tried desperately to rid her mind of the gruesome image of the terrifying man holding the woman's charred corpse. A hopeless effort; that image would never leave her mind.

All her witch dreams were powerful, vibrant, and effecting, but there was something different about this one. Not only was it the first traumatic dream she'd had in months, it also felt *desperately* important. And she had no idea why. The events in the dream were so far in the past that she struggled to make any connection to the present.

What does it mean?!

The side door opened with a quiet squeak, and footsteps sounded on the wooden planks of the refurbished porch. Willa and Simon looked up as Wynter came around the corner. She smiled and sat next to Willa, putting an arm around her shoulders. "You're supposed to be sleeping," she said quietly. "Is something wrong?"

Willa leaned into her a little and sighed. "I had a dream."

"Bad?"

"Very bad."

Wynter hugged Willa a little tighter. "Tell me."

Willa launched into a recount of the dream, her voice hushed and quiet; it felt wrong to spoil the new day with such things. Having told the terrible tale, she said, "I don't know what it means. I can't find a connection to anything."

Looking out across the backyard, Wynter frowned. The willow began to sway. "Witches haven't been burned like that for hundreds of years. And despite the perception, it wasn't all that common. So yes . . . it is hard to see what that has to do with now."

"What about the other witch?" Simon asked. "The man. Have you ever heard any stories about someone like that?"

Wynter shook her head. "There are many witch legends, but it sounds like Bartholomew the Dark. He lived in the Dark Ages, and it's said he wielded unspeakable power. The stories I've heard also mentioned his strange eyes—that's what made me think of him. But who knows how much of his legend is actually true or if he existed at all. I can't imagine why you would dream of him."

"I threw up," Willa said weakly.

Wynter swiveled her head and raised her eyebrows. "After the dream?"

"No, *during*. I threw up in the dream, and when I woke up I'd also thrown up for real. That's never happened. I've had a few lingering pains and definitely panic after waking from a dream, but this was different. I know it's important." She inhaled unsteadily. "I just don't know how or why."

Wynter sighed and put her hand over her mouth for a moment. "I'm growing very tired of not having any answers. Who knew Covenant life would be so confusing?"

"Do you think it has something to do with what happened to me on the cliff?" Simon asked. He slipped his hand on top of Willa's, and she looked at the side of his face. The explosion of the grandfather clocked echoed in her head.

Wynter said, "They happened too close together not to be connected, I think." She pressed her lips together and then added, "How are you feeling now, Simon?"

"Fine," he mumbled, looking down at the steps. "Just a little leftover buzz. I'm really sorry about the clock, Wynter."

She waved her hand. "It's just a clock. Willa and I will happily shop for another one." Smiling, she added, "Now it's time to find out what happened. Let's go, huh?"

"Yes," Simon said as he stood. He held out his hand to Willa and then Wynter.

THE TWO-MILE HIKE UP TO the cliff was tedious and irritating. Simon couldn't help but compare it to the pleasant experience of yesterday—at least until the pain and the owl. Yesterday, he and Willa had walked side by side, sharing conversation or companionable silence. Today, no one talked and, while he walked at the head of the pack, Willa hovered at the back, distracted and distant.

He couldn't detect any remnants of the strange tension he'd felt last night, and only a tiny fraction remained of the rough, bubbling energy that had helped destroy the grandfather clock. Besides fending off the thick, confusing emotions coming from Willa, he felt mostly back to normal.

Simon couldn't decide if he should feel relieved or worried.

Finally, they turned the last corner and emerged on the cliff. A collection of scavenger birds were busy pouncing on and tugging at the owl carcass. The scene repulsed him, and bile stung his throat. Memories of the pain and of Willa's scream made it worse. He picked up a rock and threw it at the gorging birds, who instantly took flight, cawing in protest at having their free meal disturbed.

Rowan and Wynter stepped up next to him. Cal, Darby, Rain, Corbin, Hazel, and Toby hovered behind. Simon didn't see Willa. He craned his neck to look over the group, searching for her. *Where did she go?* A burst of panic punched his chest, and he flicked his head from side to side, looking for her. He could *feel* her . . .

"Willa?" he called out.

"Here," came the weak response. He whipped his head around to find her standing at the cliff's edge. Somehow she'd slipped past the group. He moved forward, avoiding the owl's mutilated remains.

"Are you okay?" Simon asked when he stopped next to her.

She looked up at him, her face round and vulnerable. "It's so sad; this beautiful place is ruined for us now." She reached out and touched his arm.

"Yeah," he nodded. Simon scanned her face, studying the echoes of the vulnerability and hurt that the dream had brought her. He wanted to wipe it all away with a touch or a kiss or a word but didn't think any of those could fix it.

"Willa. Simon. Come join us," Rowan called, waving them back to the group.

Willa moved to walk back, but Simon stopped her with a hand on her arm. The words came out before he considered them. "We can leave."

She blinked and then lowered her eyebrows. "Simon . . ."

"Leave the Covenant. Leave Twelve Acres. Whatever we need to do. I think this counts as things getting worse." Simon tightened the grip on her arm. He knew her answer before she spoke, but he held his breath hoping for something different.

"Simon," she whispered, flicking a quick look at the group. "This isn't something we can run away from."

"Willa, I didn't . . ."

"Come on," she cut him off. Disappointment and frustration flickered in her eyes. "They're waiting," she added, and he released her arm.

Simon pressed his teeth together. *Why did I ask that? Willa's not a runner . . . like me.* A catalog of all the times he'd run away pulsed through his thoughts: all the times he'd run from his parents' anger, only to come crawling back, too young to go anywhere else; then, at seventeen, running away for good to a hole of an apartment and working nearly full time to pay the rent while finishing his last year of high school. He'd spent one summer working in an orange grove in California because he wanted to be far away. And yet, he always ended up back close to home. He even decided to go to school at the same University where his parents taught.

I am so messed up.

Maybe running away wasn't the answer; it hadn't solved much in the past.

He shoved his hands deep into the pockets of his hiking shorts and followed Willa over to the group. He could feel their eyes on him, but he kept his own focused on the dusty earth.

"All right," Rowan began. "Simon and Willa, we are going to create a link between you and this place. I will help create the connection between you and the earth, working with your minds, while the others help focus the magic. The goal is to have the earth reveal to us what happened, replay the events of last night from the perspective of everything around here. Hopefully, we will get a clear and complete picture."

Willa shifted next to Simon, her arms folded tightly against her chest. The day had started off sunny and warm, but now black clouds gathered overhead, and a cold wind blew over the cliff. He wanted to step close to her and put his arms around her for warmth, but he hesitated and the moment passed.

Rowan said, "Stand here with me." He motioned Simon and Willa closer. "The rest of you form a circle around us." The other witches moved into place, and Willa stepped forward, Simon following a step behind. They faced each other in a small triangle. Rowan moved his eyes from one to the other, lingering on Simon. "Are you ready?"

"I guess so," Simon muttered.

Rowan frowned. "Simon, this spell requires that you open your mind to me and to the surrounding wilderness. For this to work, our three minds must be connected. It won't affect Willa or me very much; but, with your Mind gift sensitivity,

I'll need you to stay in control, to really focus. Pull out your emotions, like we've been practicing." He paused to study Simon's face and then said, "Can you do that?"

Simon swallowed nervously. There'd be no buffer, no barrier between him and everyone else's minds and emotions. And what about the spell? How would that amplify things? He looked over at Willa, and she nodded and took his hand. The gesture made his throat tight. *Even when she's mad at me . . .*

"I can do it," he said.

Rowan nodded. "Good. You'll have to push away the distractions that will come from our minds and focus only on the information coming from the wilderness. Does that make sense?"

"Yes, I think so." Simon shifted his feet, suddenly restless.

"Give me your hands," Rowan said solemnly. Simon lifted his free hand, placing it in Rowan's outstretched palm. Willa put her hand in Rowan's other hand, their small circle complete. Rowan took a deep breath as he closed his eyes.

Simon looked quickly over at Willa, who returned his apprehension. She closed her eyes, and so he did too. After a breath, he carefully opened the magical door protecting his mind. The downpour of emotions and thoughts weakened his knees. He had to grip Willa and Rowan's hands tighter to stay upright.

"Simon?" Rowan asked.

"Sorry. I opened my mind, and it's *really* intense." His heart began to race, and his chest felt a size too small.

"Are you okay?" Willa asked.

"I don't . . . just give me a minute." He kept his eyes pressed closed and worked to focus his Mind gift on just Rowan and Willa, shutting out the rest of the Covenant and the sensations he seemed to be getting from everything around him. Soon his hands were trembling with the effort.

"Simon," Rowan asked, "can I start? Can you do it?"

Simon ground his teeth together. Not only could he feel emotions, but whole thoughts and memories from *all* of them pounded into his brain. He'd only ever been able to hear Willa's thoughts—and then only occasionally—but now every mind cut open and bled into his. With so much coming at him, he couldn't even distinguish who the thoughts belonged to. "I'm trying. Why is it so much worse than ever before?"

"What do you mean?" Rowan asked, his voice heavy with concern. "How is it different?"

"I can hear *everyone's* thoughts and feel every emotion." Willa stiffened next to him. "It's . . . overwhelming."

There was a beat of stunned silence, and then Rowan said. "Try to filter it."

"I am! But there's so much . . ." his words broke off, finding it too hard to try to filter through everything and talk at the same time.

"We can't do the spell," Willa said.

"No!" Simon exploded. "No. We have to find out what happened. I can do it. Just give me another minute." Desperate, Simon pushed as hard as he could against the onslaught of thoughts.

Willa shook her hand in his. "Find me, Simon. Find Rowan. Stay with us."

Sweating through his T-shirt, the cold air chilling him instantly, Simon tried harder. About ready to give up, he suddenly found them. Just Willa and Rowan. The rest quieted. He exhaled. It was still a lot of work, but he thought he could survive the spell now. "Okay, do it."

Rowan didn't waste a second. "*Earth, solid and sure, open our eyes. Let us see, let us know, make us wise.*" The words came out in a rush. After a quick breath, he repeated the spell a second time, slower.

Energy ignited on the air, and for a moment Simon thought he would lose control of his mind, but the tenuous connection to Willa and Rowan held. He tried to ignore the actual thoughts, hanging on to the feeling of them standing next to him.

The magic grew fiery hot around them, pushing away the chill of the gray clouds. Then a picture formed in Simon's mind: the cliff in the moonlight and he and Willa lying together on the blanket.

Rowan spoke out loud, giving the rest of the Covenant the play-by-play. "We see the cliff top, dark, but flooded by moonlight. Willa and Simon are there by the trees." The scene shifted. "We are the owl, flying up from the lake. His nest is in one of the tall pines. He senses their magic. He sits on the large boulder opposite the trees."

Engrossed now in the vision, Simon almost forgot about the effort it required to keep his mind engaged. He watched from the eyes of the ill-fated owl, every detail sharp and clear.

Rowan continued, "The owl senses something coming over the mountain. It's not an animal or a person. It makes him nervous, frightened." Rowan inhaled. "It's getting closer. The trees see it too and pull their branches away from the chill of Darkness. It's so close . . ."

Simon leaned forward as if that could make things appear sooner. The bird's screeching hoots echoed in his ears. A light appeared behind a tree, glowing white.

Without warning, an excruciating flash of power surged from his mind, with no way to stop it.

The spell collapsed, and the vision ripped away. Simon opened his eyes with a gasp.

Power erupted from his body like a shockwave, sending Willa and Rowan hurtling backwards through the air, their hands ripped from his. Simon rocked back, staggered, staring for a drawn-out moment, unable to understand what had happened.

Rowan and Willa's bodies crashed to the hard ground, near the cliff edge.

Rowan groaned and rolled to his side.

Willa didn't move.

Horrified realization smacked Simon across his face. *I hurt Willa!* He dove forward, dropping beside her, lifting her limp body into his arms. *No! How could I do that?* Cradling her in his lap, he put a hand on her head and sent his healing magic into her body. Her eyes fluttered, and then she gasped, fully awake and looking up at him.

The first ridiculous thing that spilled out of his mouth was, "Why didn't you tell me my mom came to see you?"

CHAPTER 24
WANING HALF MOON

May—Six Weeks Ago

Willa had to stop herself from throwing the door open with magic. Instead she pushed with all her strength and sent the history building's front door swinging so hard it slammed against the bricks behind it, the loud *bang* partially satisfying.

She looked down at the paper in her hand, the red B+ at the top, and she ground her teeth together. When she'd turned in the research paper on underlying causes of the Salem Witch Trials, she was certain she'd earn an A+. Every fact was well supported, every theory solid, and the writing sharp. Willa ground her teeth harder.

The B+ smirked up at her, mocking. *I'm a witch! How could I not get an A? More importantly, I'm a really good historian.* Even with so little time to do the paper amid all her grimoire searching, she'd been sure this paper was good. But her professor, who probably knew less about Salem than anyone, assured her that the paper "lacked a solid foundation." *Whatever that means!*

With an exasperated sigh, she shoved the paper into her messenger bag and turned left down the sidewalk, toward the student union. It didn't help matters that she was starving.

The broad sidewalk, lined with trees, provided shade from the hot afternoon sun. Willa followed the path down a hill and around the English department building. As she approached the union building, a voice called out from behind her, "Willa Fairfield?"

Willa turned.

A tall, thin, severe-looking woman stared at her with large dark eyes. Her angular jaw line was made even harsher by her short blond hair, like some sort of warrior helmet. Obviously a serious professional, she wore an expertly fitted suit—neither flattering nor unflattering, just practical; low-heeled, but expensive shoes; and carried a Loius Vuitton laptop bag.

"Yes?" Willa said, scouring her mind to see if she knew this woman.

The stranger blinked once and stepped closer. "Willa Fairfield? From Twelve Acres?"

Willa frowned, took a tiny step back. Various scenarios rushed in her head of who this woman might be, the most unsettling of which included a witch sent by Rachel to kidnap her. She looked around, took her hands off her bag, and said, "Who are you?"

"I'm Cynthia Howard," she said evenly. "Simon's mother."

Willa's heart stopped and then raced off in shock, ready to beat out of her chest. Never in her wildest dreams would she have come up with *that* scenario—and she'd had some *wild* dreams. Simon rarely talked about his parents, and the few times he had he emphasized their non-existent relationship. Nothing but hurt and bitterness remained inside Simon for his parents; Willa had never expected to meet them. She was too surprised to think of an intelligent reply. "*You're* Simon's mom?" was all she managed.

Cynthia stepped closer. "Yes. Do you mind if we talk for a minute?"

Willa blinked, her surprise mounting by the second. "Umm . . . sure. Okay."

Simon's mom, who looked absolutely nothing like him, except maybe a little in the eyes, gestured to a bench under a large oak tree. Willa numbly sat. Cynthia sat on the opposite end, keeping her distance. She cradled her designer bag on her lap.

"Simon said you were very pretty," she began. It sounded more like a general statement of fact rather than a compliment. Willa could only half smile and gaze at the woman. "I'm sorry to catch you like this," Cynthia continued. "Are you on your way to class?" Willa shook her head. "Good," she said and then fell silent.

Willa looked at the side of her face, studying the jagged lines and angles that made up Cynthia Howard, no warmth in her person, no kindness. Everything about her was business-like, more machine than human being. How could she be any-one's mother, let alone sweet Simon's? Willa looked closer. *No, not even in the eyes.*

The silence became uncomfortable. Willa swallowed. "How did you know who I was?"

Cynthia nodded, flicked her eyes to Willa and then back

to her bag. "Simon showed me a picture once. The last time I saw him."

"When was that?"

Cynthia looked up. "Last September, I think. I also looked you up in the student directory."

Willa's mouth dropped open, but she quickly closed it. When Cynthia didn't continue, Willa tried to guess at what this meeting might be about. "Simon's doing really well. He's top of all his pre-med classes. A few medical schools have already contacted him, encouraging him to apply."

Cynthia frowned and looked away.

"We are moving in with some of our friends soon. Did he tell you that?"

Cynthia shook her head. Willa exhaled, suddenly frustrated with the strange woman. "Is there something you wanted, Cynthia?" It felt weird to use the woman's first name—too informal.

After a breath, she finally turned and looked at Willa. "I never told him about what happened before he was born."

Willa held her breath, her stomach twisting.

"The animals that would come." She scoffed. "At all hours of the day and night. They'd touch my belly, be healed of whatever ailment they had. They drove me insane." She looked down, remembering the swell of her son that had once been there. "Then the night he was born . . ." Her voice broke. Willa waited, leaning forward, her heart racing.

Cynthia made a face, repelled by her memories. "A woman came to my door in the middle of the night. I remember a full moon—the light made it hard to sleep. The woman—if you can call her that—was deformed, decaying and came scratching on my front door." She shuddered. "She came in the house. I fell backwards. She fell, too. She . . ." Cynthia's eyes had glazed over, and she lifted a trembling hand as if to touch a phantom in front of her. "She touched my belly, my baby. He . . . *reached* out for her. A rush of terrible heat came from inside me. It went out, and then another rush came back in." She swallowed, blinked. "I was terrified," she added in a whisper.

Cynthia paused again, inhaled a shaky breath. She turned her haunted eyes on Willa, wide and unsettling. Willa withdrew slightly.

"Then that old crone *died*," Cynthia spat out with venom. "Right there in front of me. On my floor!" She pulled back, took a long breath, and blinked her eyes back to normal. She adjusted her bag on her lap. "Simon was born a couple of hours later, but we didn't realize until he was a little older how strange he is; how wrong."

Willa's heart jumped, and she had to bite down to keep from snapping back in anger. She took a breath and then carefully said, "You are very wrong about Simon."

Cynthia looked up, her brow lowered. "I'm not often wrong, Willa." She bit down on the words, full of condescension.

Willa had no idea what to say next, her mind spinning. Cynthia looked at her as if she should say something, or understand or—worst of all—sympathize. The event with the old woman sounded like magic of some kind. The animals coming to be healed made sense. That still happened. But the woman dying? What did that mean?

Had Simon ever told his parents about what he'd discovered last fall? It certainly wouldn't be Willa's place to tell his mother that her son was an extraordinarily powerful witch. Willa looked at Cynthia and knew she wouldn't believe or accept it.

Finally, Cynthia decided to fill the silence. "I've never told anyone that, but, for some asinine reason, I felt I *must* tell you." She narrowed her eyes at Willa. "And I will never speak of it again." She lifted her bag into her hands. "Do with it what you will." With that, she stood and walked away, her sensible heels clicking rudely on the sidewalk.

Willa blinked after her. She shook her head, feeling dazed. Thoughts bounced around her mind, ricocheting. Two of those thoughts were desperately trying to come together, to form a connection, but there was too much interference from her amazement.

She sat back against the bench, and one question shoved its way to the front.

How do I tell Simon?

CHAPTER 25
Waxing Gibbous

July—Present Day

All the breath burst from Willa's lungs and the sides of her vision went gray and blurry. From the moment Rowan said they must connect minds, she knew she was in trouble. Now she had to come up with a legitimate excuse for keeping the meeting a secret. But what could she say?

Willa pulled her head away slightly so that Simon would take his hand off—she didn't like what that gesture reminded her of—and then said, "Simon, I . . ."

He shook his head. "No, I didn't mean to say that. I didn't mean to *see* that." His body slumped toward her. "Willa, I'm so sorry!" he said. "I don't know how . . . I never wanted . . ." Distress broke his face into pieces, and he looked away.

The pain and frustration in his eyes pushed aside her worry about how to explain her secret keeping. *What happened during that spell?* Everything had been fine. They were about to see what was coming over the tree, and then came a blinding flash in her head, the sensation of flying through the air, and hitting the ground—*hard*. She grabbed his sweat-soaked shirt. "Simon, I'm okay. What went wrong?"

He shook his head vigorously, still not meeting her gaze. "I have *no* idea. But I can't handle . . ."

His voice dropped off, and his eyes darted everywhere but her face. Willa tugged on his shirt, trying to get him to look at her. "Hey! What? *What* happened? Talk to me."

Simon opened his mouth but was interrupted by Rowan limping over and placing a hand on his shoulder. Simon looked up into the Luminary's pained face and then, with a grimace, lifted his hand and touched Rowan's. After a moment, Rowan sighed in relief and then sat in the dirt next to them.

"What happened, Simon?" Rowan asked quietly.

Simon let out a shaky breath; he wouldn't meet Rowan's eyes either. "I don't know. It came out of nowhere. Just like last night, and the clock."

His body began to tremble, and Willa moved her hand to his cheek. "Simon, look at me," she demanded. His eyes flittered around, like a hummingbird hungry for nectar, and then finally focused on her face. "I'm okay. Rowan is okay. Breathe. You have to calm down so we can figure out what happened."

He shook his head. "I'm dangerous. I hurt you." The pain in his eyes increased. "I *hurt* you, Willa. How do I live with that?"

Willa's heart missed a beat, clogged by the expression on his face and the tremor in his voice. "It was an accident," she offered weakly.

Locking eyes with her, he said, "I can't handle any more accidents."

A bird cawed loudly from overhead, and Willa looked up to see the underbelly of a large black crow. Chills slithered down her back.

Rowan cleared his throat. "Simon, tell me what happened."

Simon looked away from her and said to Rowan, "As we waited to see what would come from behind the trees, the thing that frightened the owl, this huge burst of power built inside me and then exploded before I even realized what was going on." He shook his head. "I have no idea where it came from or why."

Rowan nodded. "Was it like the cave?" He whispered gently.

Simon stiffened, and his jaw worked before he answered. "No, not quite. But it happened so fast . . ."

"We were so close. Do you think we could try the spell again?"

Simon jerked, and his jaw dropped. "Absolutely not! I just assaulted both your minds and nearly threw you off the cliff." He shook his head. "No. No way."

"Aye." Rowan dropped his chin to his chest and exhaled. "Well, at least we know it was some kind of presence, something that scared the owl, the trees. But I'm not sure how that helps us." Rowan shook his head.

Simon pulled Willa a little closer to him, and she put her hand on his arm for comfort. He said, "What's wrong with me, Rowan?"

Rowan rubbed at the back of his neck and took another long breath. He looked over at the group of their coven-mates, who had gathered under the trees, trying to stay out of the wind and the beginning of a frigid rain. After a long moment, he said, "Wynter and I couldn't have children."

Willa started, surprised by his seemingly random response. She and Simon exchanged a look and then focused on Rowan.

"We wanted them so badly, but it just wasn't meant to be." He looked over at Wynter, who smiled sadly in return. "It was hardest for Wynter. She's so nurturing and would have made an incredible mother." He folded his hands in his lap and looked down. "When you two came into our lives we . . . we felt like the magic had given us the children we'd never had."

He looked up, eyes misty. "I know you have your own parents, of course, and certainly aren't children anymore. All I'm saying is, we love you like our own. It's been our pleasure to teach and guide you—something we never got to do with our own children. I mean it when I say we will do all we can to help you." He placed a hand on Simon's knee. "I don't know why these things keep happening to you. My only guess is whatever made you the way you are has made it difficult to keep your powers in check. That the more you learn, the more powerful you get, and the harder it is to control."

Simon's eyes were glassy. Willa spoke, "We need to find out why he has two gifts. If we can, then maybe we can help him. Maybe even fix it."

Rowan nodded, and Simon looked down at her. "But how?"

Willa looked at her hand on Simon's forearm and rubbed absently at the cords of thick muscle. She inhaled. "I'm not sure exactly, but I think your mother gave me a clue."

Simon's eyes pulled wide. "What?" he breathed.

"I need to tell you what she said."

Thunder growled in the distance, echoing down the

mountain. Simon looked up at the sky briefly and then back at Willa with desperate eyes. "Tell me, then."

"I think we better get off the mountain first," Rowan cut in. Lightning flashed to validate his words.

Simon hesitated, "But . . ."

"Let's get to the cars," Willa said. "I'll tell you as soon as we're there." She touched his face and then moved herself off his lap.

"No!" he said through his teeth. "Everyone else can go, but I need to hear this *now*." The anger on his face melted into a plea. "I'll go crazy waiting as we hike back down." He looked up at Willa, dark eyes pleading, begging. "Please."

"Simon . . ." Rowan began and then stopped at the look on his face. He turned to the others and called out, "Get down the mountain! We'll be right behind you." They hesitated, passing looks of confusion, but Wynter pushed them toward the trailhead, and they soon disappeared around the rocks.

Willa sat in front of Simon, missing the warmth of his arms. The wind was freezing now, and she shivered. "Cynthia found me on campus just before school ended." She knew he needed to hear this, but it was still a herculean effort to push the words across the short distance between them. "I thought she might want me to tell her about you, about how you were doing in school and stuff like that, but *she* needed to tell *me* something."

Simon squinted in confusion. "She's never even met you. What was it about?"

"The night you were born." His brows lifted, and Willa took a quick, steadying breath. "When she was pregnant, animals came to her to be healed. They would touch her belly, and you'd somehow heal them. Then on the night you were born . . ." She swallowed and focused on Simon's hands, now balled into fists on his thighs.

"An old woman came to the door," she continued. "Your mom said she was hideous, crone-like, and that she was deformed and decaying." Willa shivered. "This woman came into the house and touched your mom's belly. Then she *died*. The old woman just dropped dead there on the floor in front of Cynthia. You were born a few hours after that."

Simon blinked, his face white. "What does that mean?"

"Your mom said she felt a powerful rush of heat when the woman touched her and then another right before she died."

"Magic," Simon whispered. "So does this crone have something to do with my powers?"

Willa shook her head. "Maybe."

Rowan spoke up. "I think it could." Willa and Simon turned to look at him. "Simon *healed* her and she died, which means she *needed* to die."

"I've done that before," Simon said in a small voice.

"Done what?" Willa asked.

"Healed someone and they died." He kept his eyes on the dirt. "My grandma had cancer. I was ten and wondered about the limits of my healing ability. So I tried to heal her." He exhaled shakily. "She died. I thought I had failed, or done something wrong. It took me a while to understand that she *needed* to die."

Willa's mouth hung open. She couldn't even imagine how that must have made Simon feel. "I'm sorry, Simon."

He shook his head, still not looking up. Rowan frowned and said, "The big rush of heat sounds like more than just the healing exchange. Perhaps some kind of power transfer occured."

"Can that happen?" Willa asked. Something in her mind was trying to form a connection, a buzz of instinct begging for her full attention.

Rowan shrugged. "Temporary transfers are possible, like when Ruby's ghost helped you rescue Wynter; and sometimes a bit of magic will leave a dying witch and go into a family member, but none of those cases result in power like Simon's. So, it's a working theory."

A snap of thunder overhead announced the storm's imminent arrival. A few drops of rain hit Willa's cheeks. She bit her bottom lip and tried to focus on the buzz in her mind. *What is it? What am I missing?*

"So, you think I might have that old woman's powers? That she was a witch?" Simon asked incredulously. Another snap went off, but this time in Willa's mind. *Holy moon!* Simon turned to her, "What is it?" he asked, sensing the change in her.

"Amelia! Amelia Plate." Willa's heart picked up speed. "The ghost who helped us find you and Wynter last fall. She's Ruby's granddaughter. Remember?" Simon and Rowan nodded. "She said something really strange to me that night when we talked in the room at Darby's house. It might mean something."

"What did she say?" Rowan asked, leaning closer.

Willa pressed a hand to her jittery stomach. "She said that Simon is a part of her and a part of a dear friend."

Simon's eyes grew wide. "So you think the old woman was *Amelia?*"

Willa shook her head and inhaled. "I don't know, but maybe. Why else would she say you were a part of her?" She looked from Simon to Rowan, whose faces were pinched in thought. "And the timeline fits. Amelia would have been an old woman when you were born."

"More guessing. Is there a way to find out for sure?" Simon asked. "Does Amelia have a grimoire somewhere?"

Willa narrowed her eyes. She didn't know of any grimoires, but there was one way to find out. The idea ran cold in her blood. "I know a way," she said quietly, looking at her hands, now cold from the wind and nascent rain.

"What?" Simon asked eagerly.

Willa brought her hands to her mouth and blew warm air into them. She looked up. "I have to go back to the cave and talk to Amelia."

CHAPTER 26
WAXING GIBBOUS

July—Present Day

Simon's mind ran at top speed. The hike down and drive home were a complete blur, the soggy, gray scenery whizzing past his eyes unnoticed. Willa watched him, and all her worry leaked out, spilling into his mind. He searched her feelings for fear or anger about what he'd done to her up on the cliff, but he couldn't find either. Which only made him feel more ashamed. It might make more sense if she were mad at him.

He turned and put a hand on her cheek. She smiled tenderly. *I don't deserve you,* he thought. "Are you sure you're okay?"

"Of course." She put a hand on top of his, leaning into his palm. "Don't worry about it anymore."

Simon pulled his lips tight, knowing he *would* worry about

it and would also never fully forgive himself for hurting her—even if it was an accident and even if he had healed her. Willa could not—*would not*—be his collateral damage. There was already too much of that.

"I'm sorry I didn't tell you about your mom sooner." She searched his face. "Are *you* okay?"

Simon smiled falsely in answer, unable to give her a straight answer. He didn't care that she hadn't told him sooner; he understood how strange that must have been for her. But her question . . . *Am I okay?* He felt broken, split in two. His mind turned to his mother's bizarre revelation and its heavy implications. He waited to be angry about what Cynthia had done, but he only felt reckless hope. This could lead to answers, to actual reasons for his powers. If finding out he was a witch had been a relief, this could be freedom. Because if he understood, he believed he could control it, reign it in, and not continually worry that something like today might happen again. It might also be possible that, if they knew how it had happened, there might be a way to fix it, to make him normal.

This was the first thing his mother had ever done to help him.

"I'm okay," he said. "And don't worry about the thing with my mom. I get it. It's so weird."

"Very weird, and now I understand a little more about why you are not close. She was . . ."

"I know." He exhaled and shook his head. "Are you sure you want to go back to the cave?"

"Absolutely." She pressed her lips together. "But I don't want you to come with me."

Simon blanched. "Why not?"

She looked down at his hands on top of hers. "Honestly . . .

because I think it will be too much for you." She looked up and hurried on to say, "Why relive it, Simon? You already do that in your dreams. It would just be torture."

Simon opened his mouth to protest and then snapped his jaw closed. The idea of going back there terrified him, as hard as that was to admit. He nodded. "You're right," he said quietly. "But I hate for you to go alone."

"I won't. Rowan will go with me." Willa looked to Rowan, driving the SUV. Rowan nodded into the rearview mirror.

"Okay," Simon said, but his stomach twisted with worry. *That place . . .*

He looked out the window. The rain beaded and raced off the window, the storm finally reaching its full potential. He turned his thoughts to a serious question that had been nagging at him almost from the instant he saw Willa soar through the air. *What do I do about my powers until we find answers? If we find them.* The cliff incident—actually both cliff incidents—had changed things, changed him. It wasn't safe—*he* wasn't safe anymore. He saw only one option.

Rowan pulled the SUV into the driveway of Plate's Place, killed the engine, and turned around. "I don't think we need to tell everyone about what your mother said, or the plans to go to the cave." He paused and Simon nodded.

"Thank you, Rowan. I'd rather not say anything until we know more." Simon swallowed a knot in his throat. He knew the looks he'd get from everyone once he got inside, the same looks he'd endured after the cave and after the buried-alive test—that questioning, almost fearful look. Keeping his mother's revelation from them would help, at least a little.

"Rowan?" Simon said when Rowan turned to get out of the car.

He turned back. "Yes?"

"I can't keep training. I have to stop using my magic." The words hurt like a punch to the gut.

Rowan blinked, Willa flinched. "What do you mean?" Rowan asked. "It's very important—"

"Not as important as not hurting anyone else," Simon said, cutting off Rowan's attempt to reason.

"But, Simon—" Willa tried.

"No, I'm serious about this," Simon said firmly. "We don't know what's going on, and it only seems to be getting worse. It's safer for everyone."

Rowan shook his head. "That's not a good idea, Simon."

He exhaled, frustration building inside him. This was the way it had to be, and he didn't want to fight about it. "Neither is more people dying." With that, Simon bolted from the car, leaving Willa and Rowan stunned.

WILLA STARED AT THE OPEN car door. "He's terrified," she whispered.

Rowan exhaled and rested his head on the seat. "He is capable of such greatness. I don't think there has ever been a witch as powerful as he. But this shutting down scares me. It might backfire, turn him into a ticking bomb instead of diffusing the problem."

"I agree. I just don't know how to change his mind." Willa sighed in exhaustion and frustration. "I think Amelia can help, *if* she will talk to me, *if* she is still at the cave. Simon needs answers, he needs facts—actual knowledge he can work with. We need to show him that his powers are a blessing and not a curse. I just worry . . ." she trailed off, her eyes moving to the side door that Simon had recently slammed shut behind him.

"What?" Rowan asked.

Tears filled her eyes, and she looked at him through the mist. "That it really *is* a curse."

As MUCH AS SHE WANTED to go in and talk to Simon, Willa knew she must take care of something else first. Rowan gave her the keys to his SUV, and she drove to her parents' house. Parked in the driveway, she leaned forward on the steering wheel and looked up at the small Tudor-style house, with its climbing ivy and smiling paned windows.

A new feeling bloomed inside her, the petals unfurling in an odd tingle of realization. *This is not my home anymore.* Of course, it would always be her childhood home and the place where her parents lived, but it was no longer the place she belonged. The realization felt both freeing and depressing, as most changes are.

After a deep breath, Willa got out of the car and bolted through the rain for the front door. Finding it unlocked, she opened it quietly. It was Sunday morning; her parents would be reading in bed. Slowly, she ascended the stairs, running her hand over the glossy wooden banister. She recalled the time she'd tied her mom's scarves to her stuffed animals, then tied one end to the banister, and sent them all bungee jumping over the edge. She smiled at the memory and then frowned. *Childhood knows nothing of what waits in adulthood.*

Her parents' door stood open; she stepped nervously into the doorway. At the sound of her footsteps, her mother looked up from her novel and gasped. "Willa, what happened to you?"

Willa sighed. "It's a long story."

Her mom's blue eyes widened, and she closed her book. She opened her mouth to speak, but Ethan spoke first. "Then you better sit down and tell us."

Willa and Sarah both looked at him in surprise. Willa said, "It involves the Covenant and magic, Dad."

He put down his Kindle and exhaled. "I know." He gestured to the armchair next to their bed. "Sit down. I want to hear; and, if I can, I will help."

Willa's chest grew tight with emotion. "Really?"

"Yes, good grief! Can we not make a big mushy deal out of it?" He smiled, the skin around his eyes crinkling into thick folds.

Willa crossed to the chair cautiously, not sure what to feel. "Wait!" Her mom said and climbed off the bed. "Umm . . ." she looked at Willa's wet, muddy clothes, "let me get a towel."

With the chair protected from her muddy clothes, Willa sat and told her parents about Simon and the cliff, about the owl and her nightmare, about Simon again. Her dad's face paled more than once, but he listened intently.

"So you're going back to that cave?" Ethan asked. "Is that safe?"

"Yeah, of course. The Dark witches aren't there anymore."

"Poor Simon," Sarah said. "What happens if Amelia isn't there anymore?"

Willa shook her head and brushed at a patch of dried mud on her knee. "I really don't know."

Ethan leaned forward. "Willa, I say this not to attack or argue but as a concerned father: Is it safe for you to be with Simon?"

Her first reaction was to be defensive, to jump up, and yell that he couldn't possibly understand, but she took a breath. "Dad, Simon didn't mean to hurt me. It was an accident, one he'll hate himself for. He needs my help."

"I understand that, I do," Ethan responded. "But it seems like maybe your relationship is a little unequal. You do a lot to help him, to keep him steady. It has always seemed things are more about him than you. Does he help you in equal measure?"

Willa narrowed her eyes, needing a moment to understand his question. "Wouldn't you help Mom if she found out she had cancer?"

He nodded, "Of course."

"Well, it's no different. Simon is going through a very difficult . . . magical illness right now. I'll help him, no matter what he gives back." She paused. "But he makes me happy, Dad. I feel at home with him, and he's my voice of reason. So yes, he helps me too. I know if the situation were reversed, he'd be there for me. He'll always be there for me."

"Good," Ethan said with a small smile. He looked over at his wife and then back to Willa. "I've always been a little skeptical of your relationship—it happened so fast—but I . . ." he exhaled, "may have judged him a little harshly. I'm sorry for that."

With a smile, Willa said, "Thanks, Dad." *Why the sudden change in heart?* she wondered. "I know this hasn't been easy for you and Mom, but thanks for trying to understand."

"I think I understand too well, and that is my problem," Ethan said, looking down at his Kindle.

"What do you mean, Dad?" Willa sat forward.

"Well, I don't understand the whole magic thing—that will always confuse me—but there was a thing with your Uncle Rod. You wouldn't know it now, but at your age he got mixed up with this bizarre group of people. They claimed to be a church, but really it was a cult. And it messed him up big time." He paused to take a long breath. "If he hadn't met Karen and she hadn't pulled him back, I don't know what would have happened." He lifted his eyes. "I know that you aren't doing what Rod did, but it felt too much like it. It scared me, and I'm sorry it took me so long to see passed that."

Willa could only nod, amazement and emotion locking down her voice. "I'm sorry, Dad. I didn't know."

"I know. I should have told you sooner."

Sarah hadn't said much during the discussion, but now she spoke up. "Are you really happy, Willa? Can you be happy in all that chaos?"

Willa looked over at the rain-spotted window. The storm had slowed, a few rays of sunlight breaking through the gray-ness. *Am I? Can I?* She tried to picture what her life would be like right now if she'd never met Wynter, never joined the Covenant. There would be college, a job, her parents. What would it be like if she'd never met Simon? A cold trickle moved down her neck. She turned back, the thoughts shifting in her mind like the storm clouds outside. "I am more me in this life. That's happy, isn't it?"

Sarah's eyes grew wet, and she nodded. "I think so."

Willa exhaled. "Why the sudden change?" she asked, look-ing to her dad.

He shifted uncomfortably. "I woke up in the middle of the night and went into your room to check on you—an old habit from when you were young. When you weren't there, I panicked. I had the phone in my hand to call the police when your mom woke up and explained." He shook his head. "I don't know why, but not seeing you there in your bed—something

clicked in my head. You're not little anymore. I can't check on
you in your sleep and keep you hidden away from the world,
real or magical." Looking down, he exhaled and then said. "I
still hate it. I hate this dangerous life you have, but it's not my
place to stand in the way—no more than if you'd joined the
military or something like that."

Willa blinked and sucked in a breath. She'd been comforted until that last part, but she was grateful for the honesty.
She nodded; unsure of a response, and so she said, shifting
forward in the chair, "I have to get back now. And . . ." she
swallowed and clasped her hands together, "I'm not coming
back. I'm going to pack a bag and stay at Plate's Place. I need
to be there."

"Are you sure?" her mom said, eyebrows pulled together.

"I'm sorry, but, yes. It's time."

"It's time," her dad said with a look of resigned understanding.
She nodded. "Yes. Thank you."

Ethan and Sarah exchanged a look. Willa wasn't sure what
to expect, imagining how hard it would be to let your only
daughter leave home, especially with her life a dangerous,
chaotic mess.

Abruptly, Sarah turned back, "There's something I want
to give you, Willa." She slipped out of the bed and went into
the closet. She came back with a small box. Gripping the sides,
she looked down at Willa. "I should have given these to you
sooner. But maybe there is something in them that will help
you, or Simon, or just be interesting for you." She held out
the box.

Willa stood to accept it. Inside were several books of different
colors, sizes and materials. "What are these?" she said, a strange
glimmer of emotion in her heart.

"My mother's and grandmother's grimoires." Sarah smiled. "I nearly threw them out so many times over the years, but could never bring myself to do it. I'm glad I didn't."

Willa's heart swelled, a few tears slipped down her face. All the grimoires she'd read over the last months, all those witches she didn't know, and now these. How wonderful would it be to read the words of her own family, to feel their magical echoes on the pages, and find a connection to the women she'd never known. Something about these grimoires gave her a grounded sense of identity. She was part of a legacy, not just a lonely anomaly. Her tears grew, and she found herself on the verge of sobbing.

"Thank you, Mom."

Sarah smiled, her own eyes wet. "Come on. I'll help you pack."

SIMON HADN'T MOVED FROM THE bed since he stormed into the house after bailing from the car. *Coward!* he thought for the fiftieth time—not only for running away from Willa and Rowan's shocked faces but also for choosing not to use his magic. It may be a logical course of action, but it felt wrong. It felt like running away. And, as he'd already decided today, running away never worked.

He exhaled forcibly as he rolled to his side. The storm final broke. Sunlight reflected through the raindrops on the window casting tiny rainbow prisms across the dark wood floor. Dazed from over-thinking, Simon watched the colors play against each other, a small headache pulsing in the back of his head.

The door creaked open, and he jerked toward the sound. *Willa!* She stepped in quietly, a loaded duffle bag on her shoulder and box in her hands. He'd never been so happy to see a duffle bag in all his life. He leaped off the bed and pulled her into his arms.

"Welcome home," he whispered. She laughed and then pulled back. A cocktail of emotions stirred in her eyes. "How did they take it?"

"Really well," she said quietly. "I guess." A frown pulled at her lips. "Simon, you can't give up your magic. I think that's more dangerous than using it."

Simon shook his head. "But what if—"

"Listen," she said sternly, and he pressed his lips together. "I know you're scared of hurting someone, but I had a thought. The cave, the clock, and today—they all involved your Mind gift, right?"

He nodded, "Yeah, I guess."

"Then you just have to stay away from anything that could aggravate *that* part of your magic. You can still use regular magic, train and do the Elemental Challenge. Right?" She dropped her bag, and it hit the floor with a loud thud. "That's the easy stuff. You can do that in your sleep."

Simon nodded, slowly, considering. *Can it work?* "It's still a risk . . ."

"Maybe, but probably less of a risk than suppressing everything." She grabbed his upper arms. "Do you really want to give up on the challenge? Give up the title of True Witch?" She gave him a small smile.

"I guess not," he pretended to debate. He'd been waiting months to see how well he could do in the Elemental Challenge.

Willa scoffed. "Just admit that I'm right."

He smiled. "Fine. We'll give it a try, but . . ." All joking and smiles drained from him. "But if anyone else gets hurt, even if it's just a scrape, I'm done, Willa."

Her face grew as solemn as his. "I know," she said quietly. "I know this is all kinds of messed up right now, and I'm sorry."

He hugged her. "For now, I'm trying to have faith that Amelia will save me once again."

"Me, too."

Simon thought of Willa going back to the cave, his trepidation increasing. A sudden thought formed in his mind, an urge he never expected to feel. The idea had been vague, awakened by something Willa said at the cliff, but now it expanded into an insatiable desire. "Marry me?" he blurted out.

Willa jerked back and blinked up at him. "What?"

He swallowed; the words shocked him more than her. All his life he'd expected to be alone, never daring to dream of such normal things as love and marriage. But suddenly, he wanted nothing more than to be tied to Willa in every way possible, legally as well as magically. He took her face in his hands. Of course, he knew he didn't deserve her after all he'd put her through the last months. He still hadn't fully opened up about the cave, but if he couldn't do that, he could do this. "I want to marry you. No one has ever loved me like you do, and I want to love you as completely as I can in return."

Willa stared for a moment, her face awash in shock. "Simon, I don't want you to feel obligated . . ." she exhaled slowly, "I know I brought it up on the cliff, but . . ."

"No, no, that's not it." He took her hands. "I *want* to. What did your grandma say? 'A perfect magical circle?'" He squeezed her hands.

She scoffed lightly. "But now? With everything turned upside down? It doesn't make sense."

"It does. Let's do something normal, something solid, something just for us; not for the Covenant, not for your parents—although I'm sure they'll be happy—but just because it's what we want." His heart raced, sweeping him away in his excitement. "Tonight! We'll do it tonight. Here, in the back-yard. Do you think Rowan counts as a minister or whatever?" His mind tumbled over the ideas, the images that followed. *Willa in a white dress.* His breath caught.

"What?!" Willa shook her head and looked at him as if he'd lost his mind. But behind her confusion he saw it: a glimmer of happiness.

He latched onto it. "Marry me, Willa. Be my best friend, my soul mate, my partner, my *wife.*"

Willa shook her head again, more slowly this time. She put a hand over her mouth. When she lowered it, her face transformed. A smile spread her lips, the kind he hadn't seen since the trouble with Archard first began—carefree, unre-strained happiness.

A laugh bubbled out of her, and the space behind his heart grew comfortably hot. Simon pulled her to him and kissed her until the candles on the mantel melted.

ARCHARD SAT IN THE SAME place he'd been sitting for the last twenty-four hours, the kitchen table spread with Bartholomew's and the Dreamer's grimoires and all his notes about the two most important spells of his life. He was so close to perfecting them. Now they only had to wait for the full moon in three days.

The front door slammed shut, and he looked up to see Rachel hurrying in out of the rain. She shook off her raincoat and dropped it lazily to the floor. He turned back to his work. "Anything?" he said.

She scoffed. "How long are you going to make me follow them around like some grimy P.I.?" She dropped dramatically into a chair.

Archard ignored her complaint. "Anything today?" he repeated.

She exhaled sharply and then said, "The girl Dreamer has officially moved into Plate's Place. I assume her big boyfriend will also. They spent the morning up in the mountains, doing some kind of spell. The Mind boy can't seem to control his powers." She laughed. "He threw his girl and Rowan thirty feet through the air."

"Any indication that they suspect us?" he said while scribbling another note on his papers.

"Of course, not. They are so clueless. So much for all-powerful Covenant magic."

Archard finally looked up again. "I've been thinking about that. I was sure they'd have been onto us by now, even with all the protection and blocking spells. I'm beginning to think that something is wrong with their Binding."

"What do you mean? How could the Binding work at all if it was flawed?" Rachel picked up the mug at his elbow and threw back the cold coffee.

Archard shook his head. "I'm not sure. It was just a thought. I have much more important things to worry about."

Rachel hummed an acknowledgment. "Well, at the very least, it will make it much easier for us to break the Binding."

"Exactly," Archard nodded, flipping a page in one of the grimoires.

CHAPTER 27
WAXING GIBBOUS

July—Present Day

Willa stood in the kitchen of Plate's Place, her chest tight with delicious anticipation. Wynter, Sarah, and Charlotte fluttered around her, fixing this and adjusting that. Willa waited to feel nervous, for her pulse to quicken or her stomach to twist; but instead, effulgent peace filled her from head to toe. She had never felt so calm, so content. None of the worries of the last weeks and months existed at this moment. All their problems pushed aside, saved for another day. Whatever might happen, now they faced it not only as soul mates, but husband and wife.

Dressed in her great-grandma Mabel's wedding dress, Willa had also never felt as beautiful. The satin dress, once white, but now turned winsome cream with age, gleamed in the lamp light. The glossy fabric was cool against her flushed skin, and the dress was nearly a perfect fit. There hadn't been time to properly clean it, so it smelled of dust and age, but Willa didn't mind; she adored that smell. The dress had a shallow, sweetheart neckline and cap sleeves made of delicate, flower-patterned lace—also yellowed with age, and paper-thin. The lace continued down from the sleeves to the high waist line, draping over the satin skirt in two A-line layers. Tiny silver beads lined the lace like droplets of dew. The skirt fell to Willa's bare feet, a small train flaring out in the back.

Wynter handed Sarah a simple, elegant crown she'd woven from willow branches and small white roses. Sarah took it with an emotional smile and stepped in front of her daughter. The mother of the bride wore a simple baby blue summer dress and sandals, her shoulder-length hair curled around her face. Willa answered her mom's smile with her own and dipped her head. Sarah nestled the crown into place and fluffed her daughter's long chestnut waves. She took Willa's hands and opened her mouth to speak but said nothing, her eyes brimming with motherly tears. Willa laughed and leaned forward to kiss her mom's cheek.

Charlotte lifted Sarah's camera from the counter and snapped a picture. Willa said, "It's not as grand as we imagined, but it feels perfect, right?"

Sarah nodded, a few tears slipping down her cheeks. "Absolutely."

Charlotte opened the backdoor. "Ready?" she said, beaming.

Willa took a slow breath, sparkling excitement in her blood. "Yes."

The women moved out into the backyard where the rest of the covens, Ethan, and Simon waited under the willow.

Willa gasped. Rowan had transformed the yard into a gorgeous wonderland. Garlands of roses and sunflowers were fastened to the porch and strung across the length of the grass to the willow, the smell blissfully intoxicating. Lanterns swung from the flower garlands, tea lights ablaze, throwing soft, glamorous light through the yard. Sprigs of rosemary and thyme lay out in lines, making a path from her to Simon. Along the path several ceramic urns stood proudly, overflowing with creamy peonies and lavender. The sun hung low in the sky, just about to slip behind the mountains. Nearly full, the snow-white moon rose opposite, adding its glistening light to the atmosphere. The willow shivered with joy, its leaves glistening in the candlelight.

Willa padded down the stairs, feeling suspended in a fantasy, a rare, mystical moment. Hazel handed her a bouquet of small sunflowers, mixed with rosemary and lavender sprigs. Tied to the stems of the flowers and herbs was a length of twine; from the end swung a rose quartz crystal. Willa caught her father's misty eyes and smiled warmly. The tension that had existed between them for so long melted away. Looking at him, she felt like she had as a kid, when he would take her into his arms.

Simon stood near the trunk of the tree, next to Rowan, dressed in the same fine black suit with its handsome frock coat that he'd worn for the Covenant Binding. He didn't wear a tie, leaving his crisp white shirt open at the neck. His blond curls glowed. His smile quickened the beat of her heart, and the look in his eyes made her stomach flutter in the best way.

Walking forward, the lush grass cool on her feet, Willa held Simon's eyes, aware only of him. He eagerly stepped forward to meet her, taking her hand and tucking it into the bend of his arm. The air hovered at the perfect temperature, that pleasant spot between hot and warm. The owl that lived in the willow hooted loudly.

Reluctantly, Willa pulled her eyes from Simon to look at Rowan, who smiled broadly. Also dressed in his black suit, shirt open, beard neatly trimmed, the Luminary looked very much his part as leader. He nodded and began the ceremony. "The poet David Whyte wrote, 'We are literally sparks struck from the creation of life itself.' If we are fortunate to find our soul mate, we instantly recognize that spark. It is not only magical, but essential. Mr. Whyte also wrote it is 'a human necessity to have an experience of the *timeless* in order to invigorate everything we must do in time.' The joining of two soul mates, a timeless, eternal ritual, allows us to go through our time, our lives, with the person who most perfectly helps us rise to the happiness and challenges that come." He paused to smile and give directions. "Simon and Willa, please join right hands."

Willa handed Charlotte her flowers and then held out her hand; Simon gripped it strongly. She smiled, feeling not only light and dizzy with happiness but also aware of a deep connection to the man in front of her. There had always been that powerful sense of joining, of being linked; but tonight it grew, matured.

Rowan stepped closer, four long silk ribbons in his hand: green, blue, red, yellow. He lifted the green ribbon first. "Will you stand together on a solid foundation of love, kindness, and forgiveness, as strong as the earth beneath your feet?"

First, Willa said, "Yes," and then Simon.

Rowan draped the green ribbon over their joined hands.

He lifted the blue. "Will you honor and respect one another, vowing to never break that honor, to be as faithful as the sea to the shore?"

Willa and Simon gave their yes, and Rowan draped the ribbon. Willa's pulse quickened as she continued to hold Simon's eyes. Marvelous warmth radiated from behind her heart.

With the red ribbon, Rowan said, "Will you share each other's pain and seek to erase it?"

"Yes."

"Finally, will you share each other's laughter and look for the brightness in life, to keep each other's spirits as light as air, carefree and unburdened?"

"Yes."

Rowan draped the final ribbon and then gently gathered the ends, tying all four ribbons together in a large knot on top of Willa and Simon's hands. "As your hands are bound together, so too are your hearts, your lives, your souls joined in a union of love and trust. Above you is the great moon . . ." Rowan lifted his head to the sky. A shimmering ribbon of moonlight serpentined down from the sky to wrap around the couple's hand, hot and electric. Willa gasped as the energy entered her body, filled her soul, and connected her to Simon.

Rowan continued, "Below you is the earth, around you, the air." A breeze shuffled through the weeping willow branches. "Inside you, the fire of your bond. This bond is yours forever to tend, to cherish, to savor. Cultivate it carefully, and your love will grow into the sturdiest tree, the most beautiful flower, the most enduring star in the firmament."

Rowan stepped back. The moonlight circling Willa and Simon's hands retreated quietly, leaving behind a glowing trail of opalescent white. "Simon, you may give Willa her ring now," Rowan instructed.

Simon reached into his pocket. Willa lifted her left hand. As Simon's hand came out to meet hers, it trembled, and his face shone with joy. "This ring belonged to Rowan's great-grandmother," he began. "It was passed down through several generations. When I saw it, I knew it would be perfect for you." He opened his hand, and Willa gasped.

An oval moonstone, not only milky white but also with flecks of blue and green, sat in a bed of silver, the setting designed with small loops along the base of the stone. The band, an intricate weaving of silver Celtic knots, was wide at the top to support the stone but thinned near the bottom. The metal had a beautiful patina, obviously old, but well cared for. The ring as a whole was poetic and lovely.

Simon slipped it onto Willa's finger, the metal warm from the magic. She beamed at Simon and then smiled her thanks at Rowan, who nodded proudly.

Willa also had a ring for Simon, this one a gift from her father. Charlotte reached forward and handed it to her. "This ring," Willa said, "comes from my family." She moved her eyes to her parents, standing together, holding hands. "This is my father's father, Grandpa William's, wedding band. Dad inherited it when William passed away a few years ago."

Willa slid the simple white-gold band onto Simon's finger. In the center of the band, a square of deep blue, beautifully veined turquoise sat regally. Simon gazed at the ring for a moment and then pulled Willa close for the softest, most tender of kisses he had ever given her.

When he pulled back, in his eyes she saw reflected all her

emotions and sentiments. Something inside her settled, as if it took a deep sigh and eased into a more comfortable position. She felt like she should say something to voice her joy, but words fell short, inadequate. Simon smiled knowingly, sensing her thoughts. He lifted her hand and kissed the knuckle above the ring he'd given her.

Rowan stepped forward to wave his hand over the knot of ribbons. Slowly, the slips of silk untied themselves and then floated through the air to Sarah. Her eyes wide, Willa's mother reached out to take the ribbons, a precious keepsake.

The group, their family, erupted in cheers and applause.

CHAPTER 28
BLESSING MOON

July—Present Day

Willa and Rowan rode in silence to the cave.
Willa had never thought she'd return to the place. It didn't feel like a real place anymore—she wasn't sure it ever had. Instead, it felt like somewhere she'd seen in a dream, intangible and elusive. It didn't feel like a location one could drive to on a sunny summer day, especially the day after a blissful wedding.

It felt like a haunting.

Unease wriggled in her stomach. What if it didn't work? What if Amelia wasn't there? Or worse, what if she was but wouldn't talk? But Amelia had helped once before, gone to great lengths to leave the place of her afterlife and come to Wyoming with news of Simon and Wynter. If not for Amelia . . . Willa shuddered at the thought.

The ghost was the only way Willa could think to get the whole story, if her theory proved right to begin with.

If Amelia wasn't the old crone . . . If this doesn't work . . .

Rowan turned off the main road, and the SUV bumped down the dirt lane that led into the forest and to the cave. Willa turned to him, and they exchanged a weighted look. She gripped the door handle, staring out the window, waiting to see the clearing where the cave resided.

When it came into view, Rowan stopped the SUV and turned off the engine. She felt like a wind-up toy, jittery and stiff. Her eyes scanned the landscape, heart beating uncomfortably.

"Look at this place," she said. "It's even more of a mess than when we left it." Half the trees were bent, broken, or stripped bare, and the ground had been chewed into a mangled mess. Goosebumps rose on her arms. "What happened here?"

Staring out the window, Rowan muttered, "Nothing good." He put his hand on the door handle. "Let's see if we can find out."

Willa squeezed her eyes shut, took a breath, and then got out of the car.

They crunched their way through the trees to the clearing. Neither of them stepped immediately out into the open area but instead hovered in the trees, staring at the black mouth of the cave, plagued by memories. Rowan's expression was pained; Wynter had almost died here too. Also, if Archard's fire hadn't erupted, she would have been the one to take his life, just as she had Holmes's. Wynter had killed to protect the covens, but she didn't seem affected by it like Simon. What was the difference?

"Rowan, is Wynter okay?" Willa asked quietly. He turned to her. "I mean, she killed Holmes and almost Archard. How does she deal with it?"

Rowan looked down at the ground and folded his arms. "Death is a natural part of life and magic. Sometimes killing to protect that which is good is necessary but never easy. Wynter understands that delicate balance, but it still hurts her. She has moments when she questions, when she cries over the life she took. Killing, even when necessary, is not easy for a Light witch because taking a human life for *any* reason touches Darkness." He looked up. "It's a fine line; one that is not easy to walk."

Willa nodded, understanding and also fearing. If killing always meant Darkness, what happened if a Light witch killed too much? She hugged herself, trying to fight the crawling feeling in her stomach and the chill inside the trees. Not only was the air cooler here near the cave but also heavy with something, like Marley's invisible chains: there, but untouchable; wrong, but unavoidable.

Rowan added, "It's easier for Wynter because she did it knowingly."

She nodded. *Exactly right.*

Rowan gave her a small smile and then looked back out at the mess of the clearing. She pushed her thoughts aside and turned back to the clearing too. Frowning, the Luminary dared a few steps forward. He knelt, placed a hand on the disturbed dirt, and closed his eyes. Willa watched, a trickle of nerves moving down her spine. Rowan flinched, stumbled back. "Rowan?" Willa gasped, reaching for him.

His normally rosy cheeks turned white under his beard. "Corpses," he whispered.

"What?" Willa gripped his arm.

He met her eyes. "The ground is full of dead bodies and soaked with blood."

Willa's limbs turned cold; her heart picked up speed. Looking with disgust at the dirt, she wanted to run far away. A wind raced through the trees, circling the clearing with the shushing sound of whispered words. She strained to hear, but the sounds fell off too soon, cut short. "Rowan?" she hissed.

He looked up into the canopy of leaves. "It's the trees." He listened. "They recognize us, and they speak of awful things. Sacrifices. All those bodies were *sacrificed!*"

The words felt like a slap. "The quakes? The missing people? The whole time it was here!" Willa inhaled sharply. "Who? Who did it, Rowan?"

Rowan pressed his eyes closed as he put his hand on the trunk of the closest aspen. "The trees cannot say." He exhaled in frustration. "Darkness has touched this place too many times." He turned to her, eyes wide. "Find Amelia. Quickly."

Willa glanced nervously at the ground, her stomach turning with thoughts of dead, rotting bodies. Her heart beat rapidly. She looked at the soot stains on the cave's entrance, the marks of the flames that had killed Archard. The thought of Rachel's menacing figure standing outside the diner flashed in her head. She spun back around. "Rowan, do you think . . . ? Sun and moon, was this Archard?! Who else would use this place to make sacrifices?"

Rowan's jaw clenched, he shook his head stiffly. "Find Amelia, Willa. We have work to do at home."

With a deep breath, she stepped out into the clearing, fists tight at her sides. Her head spun in several different directions, fear and worry fighting for her attention; but she wasn't here to worry about Archard being alive. She looked down at her wedding ring, thought of Simon and courage came in a small stream.

"Amelia?" she called, her voice weaker than she had hoped. She swallowed and tried again. "Amelia, are you here? I need to talk to you."

A few birds answered in reply. A quick scan of the surrounding trees revealed nothing.

"Amelia, please. Do you remember me? You helped us last year, just before the blood moon." Willa held her breath as long as she could, but still Amelia didn't answer.

She turned, shrugged at Rowan. He furrowed his brow. "Try one more time," he offered.

"Amelia, my name is Willa and this is Rowan, our Luminary. We live in your grandmother Ruby's house. Right now it's full of our Light Covenant. We are continuing your and Ruby's legacy. But I need some answers to help Simon. Remember Simon?"

"Simon. The boy who was trapped in the cave with the woman with pretty hair."

The voice came from the trees, drifting on the air to catch Willa's ears. She gasped and tried to find Amelia.

"Yes, that's right," Willa pressed on, eyes searching for the ghost. "Simon's powers are getting so strong that he has a hard time controlling them. I'm hoping you can help us understand how and why."

"You're the girl who loves him. True love, soul mates. Peter was my soul mate." A pause. "I helped you, traveled to see you." Amelia's voice still sounded far away, echoing, as if she were talking through a tube.

"Yes. Can I ask you some questions?" When Amelia didn't

answer, Willa added, "We really need your help one more time. Please!"

"What do you want to know?" Willa nearly screamed when the words came out right next to her ear. Amelia's shimmering form stood uncomfortably close, her tattered white nightgown billowing in an imaginary breeze. The ghost-witch's intense eyes were the color of moss: green and alive. Her hair was a dark shade of auburn, almost the same as Ruby's, and draped around her face.

Willa swallowed. "What did you mean when you said Simon was a part of you?"

Amelia looked away, and her face shifted out of focus. "I don't talk about it. I don't think about it."

Willa bit her lip. "I understand, but it will really help Simon."

It was the right thing to say. Amelia's eyes came back, narrowed but willing. "They took us from the house and brought us here. They broke our Binding, killed . . . my Peter . . . and the others. They wanted to form a Covenant." She looked at the cave.

"Who took you? Who is 'us?'"

"The Dark covens. They dragged me away from my baby, and Solace away from her mother."

The ground under Willa seemed to ripple, and she struggled to take in air.

"Solace?" she breathed.

"Yes. So young, so innocent." Amelia's attention wandered away again, her eyes fixed on some imaginary point.

Willa had to know everything now. "What happened to her? To you?"

Amelia looked at Willa and then flicked her eyes to the cave. "Nothing good happens in there."

When she said nothing more, Willa prompted. "Why did the Dark witches bring you here?"

Finally, Amelia brought her eyes to Willa's. "A spell. They tried to do a spell that would force me to join their covens. They needed one more. A Water."

Just like Archard. "Did it work?"

She shook her head, her hair floating up as if in water. "No. It all went horribly wrong." A shadow passed over Amelia's pale face. "*Horribly* wrong. They killed Solace. Slit her throat"—her fingers trembled near her own throat—"and her blood spilled onto my nightdress, my feet." Amelia looked down at the memory of the stain, moving her fingers along her body, fluttering, imitating the blood.

Willa pressed a hand to her heart and wished she could sit down. "No," she gasped.

"Yes. Her blood and death were to bind the spell, bind my possession by the Dark Luminary."

Willa blinked back tears. "I . . . know her. I know Solace. We are friends."

Amelia raised her eyebrows in question.

"Solace is a ghost at the Twelve Acres Museum. We've been friends for years."

Amelia smiled, both happy and sad at once. "I'm glad. I wondered what had happened to her soul. Poor Solace."

Willa exhaled. She knew she had to keep Amelia talking or risk losing her. She wanted to ask why Solace's ghost wasn't here with Amelia, but there were more important questions. Solemnly, she asked, "What did they do to you?"

Amelia's smile instantly faded. "The spell failed. They made the fatal mistake of thinking they could change my free will." She touched her neck, rubbing the skin. "Although the spell failed, it still ruined my life. It caged my magic, broke my soul. I spent the rest of my living days adrift. Not quite alive, not dead either."

"I'm so sorry," Willa whispered.

"My body never recovered from the effects of the spell, and I shriveled into a horrid, powerless mess. I spent years hiding here, avoiding people." She moved her eyes to the cave. "I couldn't go back to my family—what was left of them—and the Covenant witches all disappeared. I'm sure they thought me dead."

"How many of your Covenant did the Dark witches kill?"

Amelia's eyes dropped to the dirt. "Almost all of us. They killed my Peter and a few more before they came to Twelve Acres. I think Camille and Ronald got away. I have no idea what happened to my daughter, but Camille promised to look out for her, so I can hope."

Willa shook her head, her stomach sick. "Again, I'm so sorry. That's terrible." She had a snap of connection. "Wait, your daughter? What was her name?"

Amelia looked away, eyes wistful. "Lilly. The prettiest flower."

The ground seemed to shift again. Lilly was Amelia's daughter! Camille, Solace's mother, had protected her and hidden her after the horrible mess with the Dark covens. "Oh, Amelia. Camille kept her safe. I read it in her grimoires."

Amelia looked up at the sky. The briefest smile flitted on her mouth. "I failed them all."

"Amelia, how did you die?" Certain she knew the answer, Willa still had to hear it.

The ghost's mossy eyes looked at her. "Simon." She blinked. "For years I lived as the walking dead, my body long passed its ability to live; and yet, because of the curse, I couldn't die." She looked up at the trees. "Believe me, I tried everything."

Willa shuddered. "How did you find Simon if you didn't have magic?"

"I'm not sure, really. One night, a feeling grew inside me to walk. So I walked for three days until I came to the house. I could see the baby clearly in my mind, and I knew—*I knew*—that he could free me. Even before my Gift turned him into a True Healer, he had a powerful ability to heal. I needed to heal."

Willa took a quiet step forward. "*Your* Gift? What do you mean? Last time I saw you, you said that Simon is a part of you and someone else."

Amelia's form flickered, nearly disappearing. "He has our Gifts—a strange result of the curse. When they killed Solace, I absorbed her powers. So when the spell failed, both her and my gifts were locked away inside me. When I died, when Simon freed me, the curse was broken; and all those powers then transferred to him."

Willa's stomach knotted, the word *curse* slithering in her veins. She pressed her eyes closed for a second to steady herself. *Simon's powers are part of a curse!* She exhaled and tried to focus on what other information she needed. "You said you're a Water witch. What about Solace?"

"A Mind. A very sensitive one." Amelia flinched. "She was so scared." Amelia's body nearly faded away again. "I'm very tired. Isn't it strange that I get tired?" The ghost took a step away, her face already turned to the trees. "Did you see the dirt?" she said randomly, lifting a hand to wave it over the mess. "It's a bad sign."

Willa felt a curl of panic. "What do you mean?"

Amelia leveled her eyes on Willa. "Be careful, Willa. The Dark is coming." With that the ghost disappeared. Willa gasped in surprise and frustration. The clearing hummed oddly in Amelia's absence, and her words birthed a trembling dread in Willa's heart.

CHAPTER 29
NEW MOON

August 1948

Chloe looked up at so many stars and wondered how the heavens could hold them all. In a rare moment of clear sky on the Oregon coast, the universe dazzled onlookers with a sparkling display. She breathed in the cool ocean air, thick with salt and moisture. The rhythm of the waves crashing onto the sand and rocks matched her breathing. She felt the magic stir inside her and smiled at its warmth. Beneath the thick blanket, her bare skin flushed with the heat of it; she wiggled one leg out to feel the refreshing air and temper the magic's touch.

"What an incredible night," she said with a contented sigh.

The young man lying next to her rolled onto his side to gaze down at her, adoring and attentive. "I couldn't agree more." He brushed back her light auburn hair—the color of sunrise, he liked to say—and lowered his lips to hers.

A new wave of heat, one she was only beginning to understand, pulsed down her body. It felt strange, but exhilarating to lie next to Louis like this, her clothes tossed aside in the sand, the memories of their bodies moving together so fresh in her mind.

Chloe smiled as he pulled his lips away; she put a hand on his chest. "I wish it would never end," she whispered. "I wish I didn't have to sneak back into my room and sleep alone tonight. I wish tomorrow wasn't a normal, boring day. It doesn't feel like that should be possible after tonight."

Louis grinned, his small white teeth, straight and perfect. A breeze rolled off the ocean and ruffled the ends of his nut-brown hair. His hazel eyes, specked with green, brown, and gray, glistened as he stared at her. Chloe's breath caught in her chest, and she wondered if it would always do that when he looked at her that way.

"Just think," he said, trailing a finger down her cheek. "In a few weeks we'll be off to college, and you won't have to go home without me. We can spend as much time together as we want."

Chloe laughed, thrilled at the idea of so much freedom. She couldn't wait to move out and be on her own. She was tired of her mother watching her like a hawk, that constant glint of worry that her daughter might do something . . . *unnatural.* "I can't wait. I'm so glad we decided to go to the same school. It's going to be perfect." She slipped a hand behind his neck and pulled his lips to hers.

After a moment, Louis pulled back, fixing his deep gaze on her. "I love you, Chloe. I think I've loved you since that first day of senior chem. I never thought I'd fall for a lab partner." He smiled warmly.

She blinked, surprised. The words hit her heart, sparking off into a million tiny pieces of excitement. After a moment to soak in the feeling, she returned the sentiment with passion. "Oh, Louis. I love you. I have for so long."

He laughed and kissed her again. Then he lay back down next to her, gathered her into his arms. "I should have said that a long time ago," he whispered in her ear. "I love you," he repeated.

Chloe smiled as she pressed her body closer to his. Every part of her felt light and delicious, like spun sugar. Nothing had ever tasted as sweet as those words. She wanted to lie there and savor it forever.

But after a few moments, a thought soured her sweetness. How could Louis love her if he didn't even know who she really was? If he didn't know what she could do? Chloe had spent her life hiding her gift. For the last three years, she'd faithfully studied the spell book she found in the bookstore but always in secret. All her experiments with magic were done in extreme secrecy.

Right now, she could feel the weight and joy of all the water around her, the ocean calling out to the power inside her. She'd known she had to hide her magic from her mother, but was it right to hide it from the man who loved her? What if he asked her to marry him someday? She couldn't hide her whole life, and certainly didn't want to. Not from Louis. She'd already spent much too long doing that.

Chloe's stomach knotted; her hands grew cold.

Do I tell him?

Louis hugged her tight and kissed her hair. "Hey, you okay?"

Chloe ran her finger over his chest. If he could sense such

a subtle shift in her emotions, why shouldn't she tell him? He loved her and knew her better than anyone else. It was time. "Yeah, I'm fine. There's just something I want to tell you."

Louis closed his eyes, content with her touch. "Oh no, you got another fella on the side?" he joked. Chloe smiled weakly, but didn't laugh. Louis opened his eyes. "Hey, what is it? Is it serious? Come on, you know you can talk to me about anything."

She nodded, exhaling to ease the tension in her stomach. *How do I start?* "There's something about me you should know. Something no one else knows." Chloe craned her neck to try to see his face. She needed to see his face when she said this. With a hand still on his chest, she pushed up into a seated position, keeping the blanket wrapped around her. Louis followed her lead and sat up too.

Chloe tried to smile. "This is hard to say."

He took her hand. "Just say it, baby."

"You know how you like to tell me there is a glow inside me, a spark you've never seen in other girls?" He nodded, smiling. "Well, there's a reason for that." Chloe swallowed, not sure how to explain. "I suppose it might actually be easier to show you than to tell you." Chloe studied his face for a moment, open and receptive, then turned her eyes away from him, lifting her free hand toward the ocean. Her palm flared hot as she called to the magic, and within seconds a huge globe of water lifted from the sea, floating toward them under her command. She guided it closer and then swept her hand in an arc to form the water into a dome over them, completely encasing them in a cool, salty bubble.

Finally, she looked back at Louis, her body full of anticipation; she had never shown anyone her ability before. But what she saw on his face was not the wonder and awe she had hoped for. All the color had drained from his skin, now white as the sand beneath them. His body shrank away from the water, eyeing it with malice. Something cold formed in Chloe's gut. "I've been able to do things with water since I was a little girl," she rushed to say, hoping further explanation would help ease the shock. She regretted not saying something to prepare him first. "Don't be scared," she added; and he flinched, finally looking at her. Everything in his face changed, foreign and wrong.

"What the hell are you? Some kind of . . . *witch*?" he spat at her.

Something in that word on his tongue sliced a hole in her heart. "Louis, I . . . it's just . . . You don't need to get angry."

"Angry? I'm not angry. I'm *disgusted*." He looked up at the water. "Get this away from me. *Now!*" The harsh cut of his words made her flinch and the water dropped all around them, soaking them both. Louis immediately leaped to his feet, brushing vigorously at the water on his skin as if it might infect him. He snatched his clothes off the sand.

"Louis, wait. I'm sorry! Please don't go," Chloe begged, still sitting in the sand, the blanket pulled tight around her body, her wet hair plastered to her face. Panic turned her stomach. "Please! Let me explain."

Louis turned cold eyes on her. "Don't ever talk to me again, you . . ." he looked around where the water dome had been and then hissed, "*freak!*" With that, he was gone.

Chloe blinked after him, the surface of her eyes hot, stinging. She pulled the blanket even tighter and higher up her neck, trying to rid herself of the creeping feeling of raw exposure, of a nakedness she'd never felt before. Her body grew cold. Tears streamed down her face.

Mom was right to make me hide it.

Sitting in the wet sand, the ocean pulsing behind her, Chloe felt something inside her crumble and begin to die, a painful death that would linger and grow worse when the word *witch*, spray painted in red, appeared on her house's fence two days later; a pain that turned to acid when a group of guys from school, Louis in the lead, cornered her in an alley, threatened horrible things, pushed her around and then left her shaking and alone; a bitterness that would sour when she was forced to change colleges and disappear from everything she had known.

A terrible secret that would fester inside her her entire life, flaring red hot on the day she watched her own two-year-old daughter grow a tulip from the ground, clapping when the bloom burst to life.

CHAPTER 30
BLESSING MOON

July—Present Day

The minutes didn't drag—they sat down in the mud and threw rocks at him. Nothing could distract Simon while he waited for Willa and Rowan to get back from the cave. He'd tried talking to Charlotte and Elliot, but he couldn't focus on the conversation. Reading was hopeless; TV a lost cause. Finally, he fled to the backyard.

Wynter and Rowan had used their gifts to turn the once wasteland into a lush haven; it looked nothing like it had the night they rescued Wynter. Where there had been dead grass, there was the softest, most vibrant green lawn. Where there'd been dead bushes and dusty earth, there were now overflowing flowerbeds, rose hedges, and a huge garden that produced fresh produce overnight.

And, of course, the gigantic willow lording over it all.

Simon walked under the weeping branches, which reached

out to brush his arms in greeting. Images of the wedding moved pleasantly through his mind. Though impulsive, the decision had been right. He had never felt as stable, as at-home as he had last night. Though he had always considered Willa family, now it was official in every way, and that eased his lifetime ache more than anything else had.

If only all the contented emotions could take away the dull ache at the back of his head.

He passed the pumpkin patch and continued out into the open land behind the yard. The house had several acres around it, most left to their own devices, trees and field grasses growing wild. He stepped off the manicured lawn into the tall grass and kept going until he was lost in the privacy of the land.

Simon stopped, took a long, loud inhale and then pushed the air out. It did nothing to quell his frazzled nerves. His mind flopped back and forth between two questions, afraid to confront either one. *What if Amelia was the old woman? What if she wasn't?*

He didn't want to wonder; he just wanted Willa to get back and tell him.

Taking out his phone, he checked the time and his text messages for the hundredth time. He slipped it back into his pocket and paced in a circle. He picked up a stick and hurled it out into the grass. He paced more.

Finally, *finally*, Simon's phone buzzed. Willa texted, *We're back. Where are you?*

He quickly responded and then started to walk back to the house. Another message came. *Stay there. We will come to you.*

Simon exhaled, lightheaded from the sudden racing thump of his heart. He sat down on the trunk of an old fallen tree.

His right foot bounced, jittering, but he forced himself to stay seated.

Two long minutes later, Willa, Rowan, and Wynter appeared, the swish of the grass announcing their arrival. Willa hurried forward, almost running, and threw her arms around his neck. He closed his eyes as he pulled her tight against him, wincing slightly at the wave of emotions coming off her. "So, it's that bad?" he asked, trying and failing to sound nonchalant.

Willa sat next to Simon, took his hand and looked up into his face. "It's good and bad."

Rowan magically pulled another log from its resting place several yards away, floating it to sit in front of Simon's log. He and Wynter sat, facing Simon and Willa.

"Did you find Amelia?" Simon asked, impatient.

Willa nodded. "Yes, and she answered all my questions. She was the woman who came to your mother."

A whoosh of air left Simon's lungs. "And did she somehow give me her gift? Was she a Mind or a Water?"

Willa frowned. "It's more complicated than that." Simon listened closely as Willa related the story about the cave and the curse and Solace, his heart beating faster with every twist of the story.

"Solace, too?" Simon asked, shaking his head and clasping his hands together. "Holy moon! So I have Solace's Mind gift and Amelia's Water? But I don't manipulate water any more than a regular witch."

Rowan stepped in. "Simon, I think you actually have *three* gifts. Your own, which I believe is Water—not Mind—and then Solace and Amelia's. I think you were originally gifted with a powerful ability to heal, a talent reserved for Water witches. That's why you could heal animals in utero. When your own gift merged with Amelia's, it turned you into a True Healer, someone who can heal animal *and* human, any injury large or small. The healing pushed aside the normal water abilities, and Solace's strong Mind gift further masked them." Rowan stroked his beard and then added, "If we worked on it, I think we'd unearth yet another great talent with water."

Simon flinched at the word *talent. More like another problem, another thing I don't know how to control.* He exhaled, trying to keep his emotions in check. *Three gifts!* He turned to his logic. "Okay, so now that we know *what* I am, how does it help me control it? Witches are supposed to have one gift; how do I control three fighting for attention? Is there a way to fix it?"

"Lots and *lots* of training will aid in controlling it," Wynter offered. "You'll need to get to know, understand, and perfect all three, together and separately. It won't be easy, but I think doable." She frowned briefly. "As far as fixing it—we don't know of any way to do that."

"You will need to be careful—all the time," Rowan added.

Something in his tone hinted at more information. "Why? I mean, besides the obvious."

"How do you think you controlled that witch with your voice at the cave? How you threw those others without any effort?" Wynter asked.

Simon frowned at the question but answered. "I've always assumed it had something to do with my Mind powers. I used my Mind to control them. Is that right?"

Rowan shook his head. "We don't know much about True Healers, but Wynter and I received a call from an old friend in Scotland just yesterday. He called to talk to us about that weird business with the monks, but we also got into True Healer lore." He shifted on the log and hesitated.

"What is it?" Simon asked, stomach cold with anticipation.

"You didn't do what you did at the cave because of your Mind gift, you did it because you are a Healer," Rowan said slowly. He met Simon's eyes and held them. "True Healers have the power to heal, to change a body, but that means they also have the power to *control it*."

Simon blinked several times. "As in *control the person? Manipulate them? Take away free will?*"

Rowan and Wynter nodded. Willa tightened her grip on his arm. He looked over at her, her eyes glassy with unshed tears. She whispered, "Yes, that's exactly what it means."

"But . . . but," he stammered, mind a blur of confusion. "You guys always said that the magic couldn't affect free will, couldn't force."

"It appears there is one exception," Wynter said delicately.

So, not only was he a three-gift-freak, but also capable of the most terrible thing he could think of. Simon continued to look at Willa, her understanding face a steadying force, but something inside him was spinning, teetering on an edge.

What do I do with this?!

Simon's fear of his own powers suddenly changed to disgust. His mind flooded with pictures of his small, childhood self: at five, cowering under the boisterous yell of his father, forced to turn away from a dying cat and leave the poor animal unhealed; later, finding the cold, stiff body and crying as he buried it, terrified his father might discover him; at twelve, locked in his room for a whole day because his mother had heard from another mother that Simon had fallen during a pick-up soccer game and broken his arm, and the woman had seen the unnatural angle of his arm, and then watched as he straightened out the bone, held the arm for a moment, and then ran off to rejoin the game; at sixteen being locked out of the house on several occasions, mostly in the winter, because of an argument about his *horrible habits that he refused to give up*; kicked out at seventeen; forced to survive on his own.

Control.

Control.

Control.

Reality hit him hard enough to take his breath away. Amelia hadn't given him a gift; she'd passed on a curse. *My powers are the result of a Dark curse gone wrong, and my healing powers have the ability to hurt, to force.* Simon pulled his arm from Willa and ran his hands back through his hair. The open field suddenly felt like a small box.

"Simon?" Willa asked, quietly, her voice tense.

He jerked, pulled his mind out of his memories, out of the truth. *My parents were right—I'm an evil freak.* His head suddenly throbbed, the dull headache surging to a roar in his ears. Another burst of unexpected, unexplained power ricocheted inside him and then exploded out of his body. The grass around the logs burst into a perfect circle of flames. Willa gasped, flinching away from the fire. Simon lifted a hand, rested it on her hot cheek. He opened his mouth to say something, but he could find no words. The pain in his head made it hard to think clearly.

Instead of apologizing, he pulled his hand back and stood up. He walked away, the flames parting to let him pass. Then he ran, ran fast through the field, despite Willa's calls for him to stay. The late afternoon sun poured down mercilessly, the first day of summer that felt truly hot. Simon ran in the orange heat, oblivious to the temperature. He wasn't sure what he was doing, why the urge to leave was so strong. He should turn around and go back to Willa, his wife whom he had promised to stay with always; but he suddenly felt trapped, all good feelings from last night turned putrid and rotting, his body achy, antsy.

Simon got into his Jeep, his stomach sick and his head too full. He peeled out of the driveway and took off down the street.

He'd struggled with control his whole life: fighting it, having it, not having it. *Needing it.* Now he had to face the odd juxtaposition that the same power that helped him keep people alive, that healed, could forcibly control people; and that was *out of control.* His healing powers were sacred to him, as much as his heart and soul. As strange as it had always been, it was still an essential part of him, a part he clung to—often desperately—because each time he healed someone else, his own pain lessened, disappeared for a few glorious moments. Each healing justified the pain he'd endured as a child. If it hadn't meant so much to him, he would never have endured his parents all those years. He'd have given up.

Until now he had considered his gift a blessing, a calling.

Simon had always assumed the *incident* at the cave happened as a result of his Mind powers, that he had somehow reached into the witches' minds. That made a broken kind of sense to him.

But now, with Amelia's revelation and the Healer lore . . .

My ability to heal . . .

How could that gift be two-faced?

It's not right.

Before he realized it, Simon had driven out of town and up the canyon. He rolled down the windows and turned the music all the way up to try to drown out his own thoughts, but it didn't help. After several miles, he pulled off to the side of the road and got out. He walked blindly, not following a path.

The crunch of foliage and the crisp mountain air helped cool his emotions, and soon he could think clearly. *So what are my options? What do I do?* Simon sat down on a log, elbows on knees, and looked thoughtfully out through the trees.

Option one: training: listen to Wynter and Rowan's advice, train his powers so as to use them effectively and minimize the risk of hurting anyone. But what if he hurt someone *while* training, like he had Willa? And what if learning to use his gift—*gifts*—more effectively actually made him more dangerous? He had no desire to perfect the ability to force others to do what he wanted.

Option two: suppress—smother his healing gift, push aside his most powerful ability, and never use it. But would it even be possible? He hadn't done very well at controlling any of his magic lately. Ever since the cliff, everything had been heightened, intensified. He could feel the energy growing inside him, trying to get out, begging to be used. Could he actually manage to suppress part of his powers while trying to be a normal witch? Could he isolate one gift while pushing down the others? And what would he do if someone got hurt and needed help? What if it was Willa? Would he turn his back, not use his ability to heal?

Option three: walk away.

A shiver moved through him. *Walk away.* Leave the Covenant; leave witchcraft and never use magic again. Run away for real, somewhere far away, and not come back. Maybe the time had come to stop pretending. His powers had never brought anything but trouble and pain. Why should he persist? It sounded like the safest option, but it would also be the most painful.

How could he walk away from Rowan, Wynter, and the Covenant? And worse, how could he ask Willa to leave? He couldn't go without her, and he knew she wouldn't let him leave alone.

Another thought hit him, and his stomach turned cold with nausea. *If I give up magic, should I give up Willa too?* The space behind his heart throbbed so painfully that he had to lean forward and concentrate on his breathing. *No. I could never give her up. That's not an option.*

The wind teased the leaves of the trees over his head.

A bird called out to the forest.

Simon stared off into the trees, his heart ice, his hands twisting around each other.

Something rustled in the foliage to his right. Simon turned his head. Limping badly, a gray wolf moved out of the trees toward him. Simon inhaled sharply. *Wolves don't live in Colorado.* There had been rumors of sightings for years, but the closest known population lived in Yellowstone.

What are you doing here?

The wolf, whose head had been hanging down in pain, looked up and met Simon's eyes. The creature whimpered softly. The animal was ragged and dirty, skin stretched tightly over its ribs.

Simon remained seated, watching the crippled wolf make its way forward. The options churned inside him, unprepared to face the choice so soon. The animal stopped and held up its foreleg, bloody and deformed, most likely crushed. It would never heal on its own, and soon the animal would starve to death. Simon sighed heavily and rolled his eyes skyward.

The wolf hopped closer.

Dull golden eyes were locked on Simon's, silently begging for help. Simon stayed still, staring back. He balled his hands into fists, so hard they started to tremble. All he had to do was reach out one of his hands, place it on the wolf's head, and heal it.

It was as simple and as complicated as that.

For the first time, Simon wondered if he had the right to heal. Was it his place to step in and change the course of a life? What gave him the right? It was all the result of Dark magic anyway. Every animal, every person he'd ever healed moved across his mind, each a flash of regret. Each action had been rooted in a mistake, a curse.

The wolf whimpered again, nudged Simon fists with its dry muzzle.

Simon met its eyes once more, swallowed, and pulled his lips into a thin, tight line.

He stood up and walked away for the second time that day.

CHAPTER 31
BLESSING MOON

July—Present Day

Willa sat in the shade on the front porch, staring out at the road, waiting. *Waiting.* One of her grandmother's grimoires rested on her lap, but even the allure of ancestral knowledge couldn't keep Willa's mind focused. She rubbed her hand on the cover, fiddling with the leather tie. Pulling her eyes from the road, she opened the book. On the first page, in a compact script, she found, *Tara Algood. Gift of Air.* Willa inhaled. *Proof.* She held in her hands real evidence that her grandmother had been a witch, that she had inherited the magic.

Tara Algood had died in a car accident when Sarah was only seventeen. Sarah never spoke of her mother. Willa had never thought much about her grandma. Tara Algood had always been just a name and a single battered photograph of a dark-haired smiling woman holding a newborn version of

Sarah. Willa wondered what had happened between them to make her mom so bitter.

Willa wished she'd known Tara, seen the true color of her eyes, heard her laugh, sat in her lap, seen her work the magic of her Air gift. At least the grimoires could be a window into her life and her magic.

At the sound of a car, Willa stiffened and looked up. But it wasn't Simon.

With a sigh, she sat back in the porch swing and rubbed at the ache of worry just inside her skull. The truth had not been as comforting as she hoped. Could he handle it, reconcile it? Willa bit her lower lip and looked down the street.

It was just the shock. *Right?* He just needed time to process, to logic everything into place. *Like he always does.* But this was so big and so complicated. Willa wondered if maybe she should have left well enough alone. Maybe this time answers were not a cure but an infection.

The look in Simon's dark eyes when Rowan told him the awful truth about his healing powers filled her head. Even now it made her heart drop. Simon had never vocalized it, but Willa knew how important that gift was to him. Could he recover from this?

The sound of voices drifted from the house, the Covenant deep in conversation about the bodies in the ground at the cave and Amelia's revelations. The skin on Willa's neck prickled. Something big was going to happen. It'd been building for months, many strange little incidents, like drops of poison in a cup of water. Now she felt the cup was about to spill over. Right down their throats.

At exactly the same time as Simon's mental breakdown.

Rocking slowly, smoothing her hand over the grimoire,

Willa couldn't forget the look on Simon's face as the fire had erupted around them in the field. His surprise had been equal to hers, but there was something else, something . . . resigned, a look of realization, the realization that his worst fear had been confirmed. His powers were the product of a Dark curse. She knew the words must be thundering in his brain: *My parents were right.*

Willa exhaled; anger at the Howards was heating her blood.

But there had been something else in Simon's eyes in that moment, something angry and dark. A look so foreign she didn't know what to think of it.

Another image plowed through her thoughts, one she'd been trying her best to keep buried over the last few days—the witch with moonlight eyes. Since that first horrible nightmare right after Simon was attacked on the cliff, she'd dreamed only of him. All night, she'd watched his life play out. Horrible things she had never imagined were possible. At the end of each event, she'd stand face to face with him, just staring, her body growing colder and colder until, finally, she woke shivering. As soon as she managed to fall asleep again, it started all over.

Willa yawned and checked the street again, then her phone, and her unanswered texts and calls.

"Any sign?" Charlotte pushed opened the screen door and sat next to her on the swing.

"No," Willa signed. "I hope he's okay."

Charlotte handed her a tall glass of ice water. "I'm sure he is. Knowing Simon, he's up there," Char nodded toward the mountains in the distance, "thinking everything out."

Willa sipped the water and nodded. "I know." She exhaled. "So how are things inside? Any progress?"

Char scoffed. "Not really. No one can even comprehend the idea that Archard might still be alive, so they are thinking about every other reason in the world why all those bodies are buried in the clearing." Charlotte put a hand on Willa's arm. "I'm sorry about this whole deal with Simon. I can't believe the poor guy is stuck with *three* gifts. That's total overload. No wonder he's been a little nuts. Sometimes I go crazy with just my one."

Willa nodded absently as she watched another car drive down the road—still not Simon. "I know. I thought I was helping. I thought . . ." She shook her head and dragged a hand down her face.

"What?" Char said quietly, leaning forward.

Willa sighed. "I don't know. I thought knowing would be better, even if it was bad news. Then we had our beautiful wedding, and everything seemed better, like it would work out no matter what. I thought, somehow, that would soften the blow." She shook her head again and stared blankly at the road. "Did it make it worse?"

"Oh, Willa, no," Char comforted sincerely. "I don't think anything would have helped Simon hear what you had to tell him today. But at least he knows he has you here, waiting, wanting to help. That will bring him back."

Willa nodded, fighting a rise of emotion in her throat.

Charlotte touched Willa's arm again. "Well, I promised Darby I'd help her 'wrangle up some supper.' Her words, not mine." She smiled and stood. She watched the road for a moment and then added, "I'll bring some out to you."

Willa nodded her thanks, her eyes already moving back to the empty road.

Finally, as the sun set, Simon pulled into the driveway. Willa stopped rocking and sat on the edge of the swing, her heart beating wildly. She was relieved to see him, but too much worry remained to let the relief sink in.

Simon got out of the Jeep and walked to the porch, his eyes on the ground and his shoulders bent with his burden. He sat next to her and, without looking at her face, pulled her hands into his, kissing them several times. Willa held her breath but answered his grip with strength. Shifting, he dropped his head into her lap. She cradled it, running fingers through his blond curls, still *waiting*. He wouldn't have come back unless he'd decided what to do.

Somewhere down the street, children yelled to each other, playing, carefree.

Simon inhaled a shaky breath and finally spoke. "There was a wolf in the woods." Willa didn't say anything. "For the first time in my life, I hesitated. I wondered if it was right to heal." He turned his face further into her legs; his next words were slightly muffled. "I walked away thinking my gifts are a Dark curse."

Willa stifled a gasp and felt something inside her grow cold, an avalanche of panic. "Simon . . ." she began but stopped when she realized he was crying. It tore at her. At first, she hesitated, unsettled by such raw emotion, but then she wrapped her arms around him to hold the pieces together.

After a few aching moments, Simon sniffled and sat up, his face blotchy, eyes large and watery, mouth twisted in pain. She took his face in her hands and lightly kissed his trembling lips. "Tell me," she whispered.

He hung his head. "I got halfway back to the car before I realized I couldn't live with myself if I walked away."

The coldness in Willa thawed instantly, and her heart beat with warmth. "You went back." It wasn't a question.

He nodded and sniffled. "Yes. All I could think about were the times my father forced me to leave animals behind, to walk away." He held her eyes. "I never told you that." Willa shook her head, her own eyes filling with tears. "*That* felt Dark—walking away. But turning back . . ."

"You made the right choice. There's nothing Dark about you, Simon."

He shook his head. "Yes, there is, but . . ." He pulled her delicate hands from his face and held them. "But it's a choice, the same choice I have made every day of my life." He smiled weakly. "Why would I stop now?"

Willa laughed, tears tracking down her cheeks. She threw her arms around him and held tight. "I was worried I'd made a mistake," she whispered.

"No, you didn't. It's hard to accept, but now I know what's really inside me. I'll train it, control it. Maybe one day we'll find a way to fix it." He drew back, wiped the tears off her cheeks, and she the ones off his. "I can do it if you're with me."

A spark of heat flashed behind Willa's heart. "I'll always be here."

"I know." Simon dropped his forehead to hers. "I'm sorry about before, about running off. That was stupid. But I just . . ."

"I get it." She pulled back and met his eyes. "I would have run off too. That was a lot to take in." She smiled. "But you never have to run away. Even if it gets really bad, stay with me. I hate worrying about you like that."

He nodded. "Sorry about that too. I would have been back sooner, but I had a little complication."

She frowned. "What do you mean?"

Simon looked over at the Jeep and whistled, high and short.

A large wolf leaped out of the open window of the car and trotted over on his long, slender legs. Willa's jaw dropped. The animal sat in front of her, so big, with eyes like gold coins, glistening in the evening light. She shrank away, nervous.

"It's okay, Willa. This is not a normal wolf; he's safe." Simon reached out to pat the wolf's head. The animal walked forward, rested his chin on Simon's leg. "I tried to get him to leave, but he wouldn't. He kept following me."

Willa stared at the wolf. "Seriously?"

Simon laughed. "Yeah, it was really weird. I sensed a . . . connection when I healed him. Never felt anything like it." He shrugged. "He wasn't just there to help himself; he was there to help me." He smiled. "We kind of bonded."

Willa looked from Simon to the wolf. "I read about this in one of those grimoires. Some witches have a connection to an animal, a magical bond. Almost like a soul mate, only with an animal. The animals are called Familiars." Slowly, she reached out a hand and rested it on the wolf's head. The wolf looked up, meeting her eyes, and she could see a kind of human-like understanding and depth. She laughed and rubbed behind his ears. "He's beautiful. Familiars are pretty rare, though."

Simon shrugged. "Rare, huh? Sort of my calling card, I guess."

She smiled. "What are you gonna call him?"

"I don't know. I hoped you could help me with that." Simon ran his hand down the wolf's back.

"Hmm . . ." Willa put her hands under the wolf's face and looked at him. "What's your name? It has to be something strong and majestic, right?" The wolf licked her hand, and she laughed. Willa searched her mind for a minute. "How about Koda? It means 'friend' in Sioux." The wolf stood up and wagged his tail, licking her hand again in agreement.

"I think he likes it," Simon said. "How did you know that name?"

Willa shrugged. "I did a service trip to an Indian reservation in junior high. For some reason that word stuck in my head."

Simon smiled and looked down at the wolf. "Well, Koda, welcome to the family."

Koda looked back and forth between Willa and Simon.

Simon patted Koda's head as his face fell solemn again. "Willa, I want to go with you to tell Solace."

Willa blinked. Her mind hadn't gotten to that through everything else, but there would certainly have to be that moment, the moment of walking into the museum to tell Solace how she had died. The ghost was already mad at Willa for not being able to go to her and Simon's wedding, not that Willa could have done anything about it. But this . . . It wasn't a conversation Willa looked forward to. "That's a nice idea," she said.

"I know I won't be able to see or hear her, but I think I should be there."

Willa nodded and took his hand. "She'll be happy to have you there. We can go tomorrow." Her stomach tightened. *Oh, poor Solace. How will she take it?*

Simon exhaled and offered a small smile. "Okay, sounds good." He sighed. Willa settled into Simon, his arm comfortably around her shoulders. Koda lay down at their feet as if that had always been his spot.

The sun slipped under the horizon, and twilight turned the mountains to indigo shadows. The full moon winked above the mountains, taking over the sky for the night. Finally, Simon said, "What was it like going back to the cave?"

In a whisper, Willa answered, "Terrible. That place is so . . ."

"Yeah, I know." Simon pulled her a little closer.

"No, but there's something else we didn't get to tell you." Willa shifted her head to look up at him. "We found bodies buried in the ground outside the cave."

Simon flinched, pulling his chin in to see her face better. "What?"

"I know. The ground was all torn up, and Rowan saw the bodies. The trees told him that they were sacrifices. *Sacrifices,* Simon, of human bodies. The quakes in the spring, all those people missing."

Simon shuddered and Koda lifted his head as if to listen more intently. Willa looked at the wolf as Simon said, "It all happened at the cave? That's really . . . Holy moon! Does that mean it was Rachel? Who else knows about that place?"

"We don't know. Some of us are starting to wonder if Archard really did die."

Simon's jaw dropped. "But Rowan checked."

"Yeah, but it's Archard."

Simon exhaled. "Oh, man. How messed up would that be?"

She nodded. "And there was one more thing we learned up there. Remember the Lilly in Camille's grimoire?"

"Yeah, of course. It's your and Solace's new mystery." He smiled.

"Well—get this—Lilly was Amelia's daughter." Willa's

heart beat a little quicker. She couldn't wait to tell Solace. Her friend had had a memory of Amelia having a baby a couple months ago; Solace had known Lilly. At least Willa would have some good news to go with the bad.

"Whoa. That's crazy."

"It's possible she's still alive. Amelia said Camille promised to get her to safety when the Dark covens came here. She'd be in her eighties, I think, but *if* she's alive, that means the Plate bloodline still exists."

"That'd be amazing."

Willa nodded, her mind turning, working in historian mode. "How cool would it be to find her, talk to her?" She sighed, "But there are no clues in the grimoires as to where Camille took her. Maybe she took her to Italy. So it's nearly impossible to find her."

"Too bad," Simon said. Thunder cracked in the distance, and both of them—and Koda—flinched.

Willa leaned forward. Angry clouds had gathered in the last few minutes, clogging up the sky and swallowing the mountains. "Where did those come from?"

Simon leaned forward too, eyes narrowed at the clouds. He shook his head. "No idea. It's been clear and hot all day."

A sudden wind plowed through the yard, yanking leaves off the trees, and throwing Willa's hair in her face. She pulled it away in time to see several skeletal arms of lightning pulse across the sky. "Sun and moon!" she whispered.

Simon grunted in agreement, and Koda growled at the sky. "We better get in. I got a lot to talk about with Rowan anyway." He looked over at Willa, eyes heavy with meaning. "If I'm going to learn to control all the mess inside me, we need to get started right away."

Her heart squeezed tight. "Good idea." Her smile was inter-rupted by a tremendous burst of thunder.

Koda stepped to the edge of the porch and howled at the darkening sky.

CHAPTER 32
BLESSING MOON

July—Present Day

July's full moon, the blessing moon, climbed the sky, steady
and bright. Its bone-white light gave objects below a sub-
limely spectral quality, as if the world were something
viewed through an ancient mirror.

Archard was ready, any margin for error eliminated. The
time had come to test his skills. Dressed in his finest black
suit with matching shirt, and shoes polished to a high sheen,
he stood like a vogue wraith at the gates of the Twelve Acres
cemetery. In his hands, he held the iron box.

Rachel, also in black, tight and sleek as a machine, stood
next to him. Behind them, a passenger van. Inside the van,
ten random strangers lay unconscious.

Rachel said to Archard, "I'll go and set up the barrier." As
she trotted off, she pulled a vial of blood from her pocket. The

spell—pulled from Bartholomew's book, of course—would keep them hidden from the town and prevent any interruptions as they pulled the ghosts from the Otherworld.

When she returned, the spell in place, Archard nodded to the van, "Let's get them into place." Rachel stepped up to the van and threw back the door. She took a pouch from her jacket pocket. Carefully, she sprinkled a powdered potion on each face and then backed out of the van.

"Move!" she commanded. Soon the ten people stumbled from the van, reeling like drunkards, to follow her into the cemetery. Their eyes stared vacantly ahead, unaware of the danger.

Archard took a large bag from the van and followed. Anticipation was alcohol in his veins, making his head spin giddily. No one in history had ever attempted this. It was ingenious, revolutionary. *Legendary.* He imagined the stories to future generations. *Archard the Dark created a Covenant of ghosts. He pulled the souls from the Otherworld as easily as pulling apples from a tree.* Eyes would widen following such statements, and listeners would gasp in wonder, envy, and—best of all—fear.

Archard the Dark: the only witch worthy of the same title as Bartholomew.

His stomach fluttered, his smile grew.

Rachel organized the drones into a line behind the headstones of Ruby Plate and several members of her Covenant. Archard knelt and placed the iron box on top of her grave, the moans growing in pitch, floating out of the metal.

"I'm coming for you, Ruby," he hissed to her grave.

The brilliant Light Luminary had escaped the clutches of his grandfather several times. Archard's grandfather, Horace, had tried and failed to form a Dark Covenant. He had been able to break Ruby's but nothing more. Tonight, Archard began the long-awaited process of erasing his ancestral shame. No one would remember Horace's mistakes after Archard's triumph.

While Rachel corralled their ten victims—randomly kidnapped from Denver for the occasion—Archard opened his bag of supplies. He placed white pillar candles all around the graves, a large flickering circle, yellow flames contrasting the white moonlight.

Finished with the victims, Rachel handed a moonstone marked with a black skull and crossbones to Archard. "Is it time?" she asked, smiling, but unable to hide a flicker of fear in her cool blue eyes.

Archard dismissed it; he couldn't expect anyone, not even Rachel, to be as open to the Darkness as he. No one was like him. He bent and pulled Bartholomew's grimoire from the bag, reverently running a hand over the round silver medallion on the cover. *At least not anyone living . . .*

He placed the book next to the box of souls but didn't open it. Archard had all the elements of the spell memorized, etched into his brain. The grimoire was there for symbolic reasons only.

"Yes, it is time." Shivers of pleasure moved down his spine as he thumbed the glass-smooth moonstone. *It's time!*

Rachel nodded and went back to their victims, forcing each one to his or her knees. Their bodies bent easily but stiffly, their heads wobbling as she pushed them down. Brushing her hands off, Rachel then joined Archard at Ruby's grave.

They knelt together in front of the boxed souls. Archard must open the box to release the power of the souls but must keep them contained. The instant the box opened the souls would try to flee to the Otherworld, but he had to harness them, ground them, or he'd lose their power. From the bag Archard pulled the needed ingredients.

First, he unscrewed the lid of a mason jar and carefully sprinkled crushed shells on Ruby's grave to form a square. Next, inside the shell-square, the blood of a crow formed two intersecting arrows pointing in the four cardinal directions. Lastly, he placed the iron box in the middle of the square and folded several strands of dried seaweed over the lid.

Archard put his hands on top of the box—his fingers instantly growing cold—and mumbled the words that would keep the souls from escaping. Then he turned to Rachel. "Remember, it's your job to make sure none of the souls escape. Keep close watch. If they start to break the barrier, we must close the box at once. I'd rather start over than lose them."

She nodded solemnly, her eyes fixed on the box. "We won't lose any."

"Good." He inhaled. "Here we go." With another spell, Archard pried open the iron box. The metal groaned in protest before the lid snapped open. In an icy rush, the souls flooded out of the box, only to be stopped by a dome of magic. The invisible dome filled with the ethereal white ghosts, their bodies without real form, mixing together like a cloudy, milky liquid. Faces, screaming in protest or pain, swirled inside the trap, mouths stretched wide, eyes elongated in frightened, angry grimaces.

Archard leered back, drinking in the potent power.

Pleased that the trap was solid, he stood and moved to his living victims. He paced, scanning their empty, unfocused eyes. Ten ignoramuses' lives in exchange for ten ghosts pulled from the Otherworld. He swiveled his head. "Rachel, bring me the stones."

She dug in the bag and produced ten moonstones, each strung on a length of twine and etched with a sinister death's head. Archard hung one around each victim's neck. They hung heavily at each chest, the small ovals nearly the same color as the trapped souls a few feet away.

The night, still and silent until a moment ago, now filled with the sounds of tossed leaves and rustling grass as the wind raged against the dark magic. Somewhere down the road, a screen door creaked open and shut again and again. Thick gray clouds gathered, swelling and crackling with lightning. The full moon soon vanished behind their thunderous walls.

Only half of the witches Archard wanted were actually buried in the graveyard. Their souls would be easy to pull, their graves acting as a magnet. It would require the exchange of one soul for the other, a sacrifice, to pull the five remaining ghosts whose graves were elsewhere in the world. He'd decided to use a sacrifice for all ten anyway as an extra precaution.

Archard moved back to the first of the kneeling victims. He held his hand to the man's high, dry forehead and called to his fire. His palm flared red-hot. Numb to the pain, the victim only blinked as the witch branded a name into his head, the letters burned there for the Otherworld to identify.

The first name: *Charles Plate.*

Archard moved down the line, burning a name into each forehead, wiping off bits of charred, red-black skin from his hand with a handkerchief.

Ruby Plate
Amelia Plate Moore
Peter Moore
Jennifer Plate Garrett
Carson Garrett

Camille Krance
Ronald Krance
Solace Krance
Rupert Holmes

Nine Light witches and one Dark, the Light witches in honor of his ancestors who tormented them and almost destroyed them completely. And the one Dark witch, Holmes, as punishment for the epic failure of letting Wynter escape, which directly resulted in Archard's own failure at the cave. Five women and five men to complete the two True Covens, with himself and Rachel at their heads.

The temperature dropped steadily, but the power of the spell kept Archard hot, feeding his fire. Sweat poured down the back of his neck and trickled along his spine. Sniffing lightly at the smell of burnt flesh, the witch moved back to the trapped souls. He slipped his own moonstone from his pocket.

Archard glanced at Rachel, who shivered in the cold. She nodded in encouragement. He dropped to his knees in front of the trapped souls, still swirling in the magical dome, their moans now loud and haunting the air.

A deep breath.

A look at Bartholomew's grimoire.

He thrust the hand holding the moonstone into the dome. Instantly, the ghosts started gnashing and biting at his flesh. He pushed his teeth together, ignoring the pain, sending heat to the limb to try to protect it from the ghosts and the glacial cold inside the trap. Eyes closed, heart jumping in his chest, Archard began his chant, a slow slur of words so Dark that the earth shuddered beneath him.

The air temperature plummeted fiercely, the clouds roiling overhead. The smell of snow filled the air. Archard continued his chant, over and over, his voice rising in volume with each repetition. Rachel joined in, throwing her power into the words.

A visceral crack snapped in the air, and then a flood of moonlight broke through the clouds, pulled to the moonstones. The stones around the sacrifices' necks glowed bright, sucking in the light and then throwing it back out in tremulous lines that all connected to Archard's stone.

He'd breached the Otherworld, thanks to the power of the trapped souls, whose cries and screams opened the door. The Otherworld would try to pull them in, take them back, but he'd keep them there as he pulled the witches' souls from the embrace of the world beyond death. The trapped souls were the key, and he would use them to rob the Otherworld.

Sudden screams rent the snow-scented air, sounds so terrible even Archard winced.

The first ghost floated into view. *The great Ruby Plate.* Archard sneered as her flickering form rose from the grave. He guided her toward the dome and her white body slithered inside, trapped with the others. Archard took strength and satisfaction from the horror and shock on her face.

The sacrificial victim with the Light witch's name burned in her forehead collapsed, dead, eyes now clear with fear and realization.

The next few ghosts came quickly, easily, snagged from their graves and shoved into the trap. More bodies thudded to the ground. The power of the souls grew with each addition. So much that Archard's grin became a permanent addition to his devilish face.

So much power!
More!

The snow started to fall in thick white curtains. Soon it covered Archard's head and shoulders. His hand in the dome was now a tattered, bloody mess, and the flesh had grown unbearably cold. Frostbite would be unavoidable.

He ground his teeth hard. Now he must pull the grave-less ghosts.

Archard's chant changed, the words specific to pulling ghosts without graves. He had no doubt that the power behind him would be more than sufficient.

Give them to me!

The Otherworld fought hard, but in the end, it had no choice but to bow to Archard's terrible might. The screams continued to fill the air, but the thick snow now deadened the sounds. Rachel, teeth chattering and skin blue, put her hands to her ears and collapsed to the ground, moaning.

Archard ignored it all, singularly focused. Not even the pain of his dying hand could stop him now.

A few more.

Soon the remaining souls slithered out of the slate-gray sky and into the dome. The trap was no longer sufficient to hold so much power and anger. Archard had only seconds before he lost them all. Quickly, he moved his hand downward, screaming in pain as he pushed the box closed, pulling the white fog of souls inside it.

The ground quaked under him, outraged at the savage betrayal it had endured. Archard collapsed next to Rachel, cradling his hand to his chest, shaking violently. He blinked up at the snow, the feathery flakes landing on his face like whispers.

His triumphant laugh echoed through the night.

CHAPTER 33
Blessing Moon

July—Present Day

Cold. Bone numbing, soul freezing cold. Willa had never felt cold like this. It snapped along her skin like a vengeful bird and dove deep inside her, burrowing into the inner most parts of her body within seconds.

A light appeared, a gauzy ripple moving before her eyes. She couldn't be sure, but it felt like the thread of light radiated the cold. But how could it be? It was barely there.

The light curled through the air, moving closer to her. Closer and closer. She watched with dreadful awe, wondering what it would do, what it *could* do. Then, in a blink, it vanished, and Simon stood in front of her, his face flat, almost sad, but more emotionless than she'd ever seen it. A faint glow emanated from him.

He reached out to her; but when she reached back, he

disappeared, leaving her alone in darkness. Only the cold remained. Willa stood painfully still, waiting for what would come next, what would break out of the heavy blackness.

A voice floated on the air, far away, the words lost in the distance. Willa strained to hear.

"Hello?" she called stupidly.

"Help me . . ." came a response. Were those the words? The black air sucked them away before they fully formed in her ears. "Help . . . me . . . Willa."

"Where are you? Who are you?"

"WILLA!" Her name came as a scream, awful and exploding with fear. Then another figure flashed before her, not the one she expected, and one that had not haunted her dreams in months. *Archard.* His cold eyes tore into her out of the surrounding blackness, their colorless hue adding to the cold inside her body. Then, ever so slowly, like a taunt, he smiled.

Willa woke with a start and found herself in her and Simon's bedroom in the breathy blue light of the full moon. Panic lingered inside her, an urgent need to act, to help. But who? The cry for help hadn't had a distinguishable voice. She couldn't even say if it'd been male or female. All she knew was the thick, icy fear behind the words.

And the evil in Archard's smile. *No, no, no! It's not possible.*

She pushed out of bed, instantly hissing at the cold. Assuming that feeling, too, was an echo of the dream, Willa thought little of it as she grabbed the fleece blanket from the end of the bed and wrapped it around herself. Aimlessly, she wandered over to the window, comforted by the sound of Simon's even breathing. Bright blue-white light filtered in through the sheer curtains. *Is that the moon?* The light felt too bright, too white.

Releasing a hand from the blanket, she parted the curtains. She blinked, stared hard, and then looked back at Simon. *Am I still dreaming?* She let the curtain fall, released the blanket, and turned to run. She bolted down the stairs two at a time, not caring how loud her footfalls were. She leaped down to the first floor and crashed into the front door. Scrambling with the lock, she threw it open.

I'm awake. I know I'm awake.

Standing on the porch, Willa gaped at the thick cover of snow, glowing in the light of the full moon, covering the green grass and burying the flowers. It sparkled innocently, beautifully, but oh-so wrongly. She stepped stiffly down the porch steps, too shocked to even notice the cold bite of snow on her feet. She needed to touch it with her hands. She bent, scooped a mound of powdered-sugar snow into her hand and let it fall with a whisper of unnaturalness.

It's July. This is wrong. Something is so wrong!

Quickly, Willa reached farther out over the untouched snow blanket and drew a five-pointed star. "Powers of the Earth, protect us," she whispered. The star glowed bright for a moment and then Willa dashed into the house to wake the rest of the Covenant.

TWELVE POUNDING HEARTS. TWENTY-FOUR NERVOUS eyes. A snowy winter-wonderland in summer.

The Covenant stood in uneasy silence, gathered in front of the living room windows, staring. All they could do was stare at the whiteness. Someone had turned on the heater, and the air hummed with forced heat, smelling of hot dust. No one had thought to turn on a light.

Simon had his arms around Willa; she shivered. Koda stood at his side, nose pressed to the glass of the window. Simon felt like he might drown in the flood of worry pouring out of his coven-mates. It thrashed at his mind-door, making his head ache.

"Sun and moon," Rowan finally whispered, breaking the silence.

"What could throw the Powers off so greatly as to bring . . . *this?*" Charlotte asked, also in a whisper. It was not a night for regular voices. "Earthquakes are one thing, but this . . ."

Wynter touched the window glass. "I don't dare imagine."

"It has *never* snowed here in July before," Elliot said, looking down at his phone.

"It's only around Twelve Acres," Hazel added. "It didn't snow in Denver. It didn't start snowing until we got close."

Rowan shook his head but kept his eyes at the windows. "This isn't freak weather. This is *magic*."

More silence. Simon's head was pounding now, getting worse instead of better. Willa stirred in his arms, and then in a small voice she said, "I saw Archard in a dream, just before I woke up to find the snow."

Every eye immediately moved away from the windows, turning their shock and confusion on Willa and her words. Wynter stepped closer. "What did you say?"

"Archard," Willa breathed. "I saw him. It was so cold and then so dark. Someone called for help. Then he stood there, *smiling*." Her shivering increased, and Simon tightened his arms around her.

Wynter and Rowan exchanged a look. Wynter hugged herself and said, "Please, no. Holy moon, please *no!*"

Rain stepped closer, "So all that's been happening—the quakes, the bodies in the clearing, those poor monks in England, and now this—it was all *Archard?*"

Rowan ran a hand back through his long hair, loose and messy from sleep. "I just don't see how. I checked. There is a body buried in his grave. I . . ."

"It's him," Willa said stiffly. "I wouldn't dream of him if it wasn't."

Darby scoffed. "How could anyone survive what we saw?"

Simon narrowed his eyes in thought. It all seemed impossible, but . . . "Holy moon!" he said in realization. Everyone looked to him. "Rachel. She must have waited until we left and then saved him. But he still would have been badly burned." Another idea hit him. "Do you think the sacrifices at the cave were used to heal him? Is that possible?"

Rowan's face paled. "Yes. I think it is." He looked out the window. "That's why the quakes came on the new moons—new moons are best for healing spells."

A smothering silence filled the room.

"Archard is back," Rowan said, the words dropping into the room like the blade of a guillotine.

Simon winced as a new punch of emotion hit him: worry morphed into fear and terror. "What do we do?" he asked quietly.

"A spell," Darby answered. "A powerful one to show us what caused this. We've got a full moon; let's use its power to find him. And this time, we make sure he stays good and dead."

Rowan sighed. "Everyone find a coat and some shoes and then meet out back."

In a mismatch of coats, sweaters, and any other winter clothes that could be scrounged up, the Covenant gathered on the back porch, gazing suspiciously at the snow, now six inches deep.

Rowan pushed through the pack and moved down the stairs. "Let's circle, covens together." Once in a circle, men as one half, women as the other, shoes buried in snow and cold reddening their cheeks, Rowan said, "Join your pendants."

Simon reached into the neck of his hoodie and pulled out his pendant. He lifted it over his head and held the pendant out. The other five men held theirs out to meet his. Heat sparked in the cold night. The magic flared, forming the silver pendants into a circle of six parts, triangles pieced together, chains dangling underneath.

The women did the same. Soon the two spinning circles hovered in the middle of the witches, heat and energy spilling off of them. The circle stood ready to perform full moon Covenant magic.

"Join hands," Rowan instructed. More heat flared, and the willow behind them shook off the snow, eager to witness the magic. Rowan lifted his head to the full moon. All faces turned upward, skin bathed in milky light.

Simon's pulse quickened, pushed up by the magic flowing around and through him. He caught Willa's eyes across the circle; nervousness darkened her face.

Rowan closed his eyes and chanted the spell in a commanding voice. *"Powers of the Earth, show the plight that now plagues your shining Light. Show your Covenant the Dark that has brought this unnatural mark."*

The Covenant then joined with him to repeat the spell two more times. The air shifted; the willow stilled. Furtive, nervous glances moved around the circle, flicking around the yard. Simon *felt* the voices before they started.

Eerily quiet and then swelling loud, the whispers filled the yard.

Help. Help us. Stop it. Must stop it. Please, help.

Willa gasped loudly and then started to cry. Simon wanted to move to her, but couldn't break the circle. With the voices came a chilling feeling worse than fear, more like anguish, like heart-ripping loss. He dared to open his mind-door a crack, reaching out to the sound of the voices.

HelpusHelpusStopitStopItStopItNOOOOOOOO

Everyone in the circle winced at the words pressing hard into their heads, the emotions too thick to bear. Simon couldn't find anything to hold on to, no single person or mind to grip; there was just that feeling, like falling down a dark pit. He slammed his mind-door shut, unable to take it anymore.

His head pounded.

Willa screamed as she collapsed to the ground, breaking the circle. The voices immediately stopped. Simon rushed to her side. Her hands cradled her head, pushing hard against her hair. "Willa!"

"We have to help them. He's hurting them."

"Who? Who is it? Is it Archard? Who's he hurting?"

She moaned. "I . . . I'm not sure. I saw them in my head. They looked like ghosts, but it was hard to see through the pain." She looked up, her eyes watery. "Did anyone else feel that? Or see that?"

Wynter bent down. "No, just you."

Rowan said, "You think Archard is hurting ghosts?"

Willa reached out her hand. Simon helped her to her feet. "I think so." She looked at the snow.

"How on earth could Archard hurt ghosts? And—more importantly—why would he? What's the advantage to him?" Wynter asked.

Willa shook her head. "I don't know."

Simon looked over at Rowan. "What do we do now?"

Rowan set his jaw; his eyes flashed with anger. "We find Archard. Whatever it takes."

By dawn the Light witches had found nothing. After the spell, the Covenant split up and searched Twelve Acres. Walking the snow-quiet streets, Willa and Simon had kept their eyes open and flinched at every sound. No one was out; not a single car passed by. Willa started to feel as if the whole town had been deserted.

Worried and slightly paranoid, she'd stopped at her parents' house. When she saw they were safe and asleep in their bed, Willa left a note telling them to stay inside and text her if they saw or heard of anything unusual—besides the snow, of course.

Now, back at Plate's Place, the Covenant huddled around the kitchen table, nursing steaming mugs of coffee or tea. Willa leaned on Simon's shoulder, too tired to keep her own head balanced on her neck. No one had spoken for nearly five minutes, an undercurrent of tension pulling at their feet.

Willa lifted her bleary eyes to the window. The snow had stopped hours ago and was already beginning to melt. When the sun came up in an hour, all evidence of the Dark magic would evaporate. Willa knew they were all thinking the same things: where was Archard, and why hadn't he come for them? Because, whatever he had planned, it would most definitely involve them.

Willa had other questions. Why ghosts? The echo of the pleas for help brought chills to her arms. Her mind searched for reasons, possibilities. What would he do with ghosts? Ghosts didn't affect anything, didn't do anything—as far as she knew. They were just there, echoes of a life lived. What advantage would ghosts be to a Dark witch bent on revenge and power?

She thought of Solace, sitting primly in her rocking chair, reading a book, and nearly smiled at the idea that she could be any use to a Dark witch. But then a ripple of fear washed over Willa's heart and she sat up with a jerk. Her cup of tea tipped over, spilling across the smooth surface of the table.

Simon turned to her. "What's wrong?"

She popped out of her chair, already headed for the door. "Solace! I have to see if Solace is all right." Chairs scrapped on the floor as others stood, alert to her panic.

Simon snatched his keys off the table and followed her. "I'll drive."

Willa plunged out the side door and ran to the Jeep, Simon only a step behind, their feet slapping in the puddles of melted snow. Wynter called from the door, but Willa ignored her. She had to get to the museum; suddenly the whole world seemed to depend on it.

With her nerves tied in fiery knots, the one-minute drive up the road felt like an eternity. Finally, Simon parked out front. Willa ran to the door, fumbling with her keys. She unlocked it, and the big wooden door flew open with a squeal of protest. She stepped inside the dusty foyer.

Instantly, she knew something was wrong. "Solace!" she

squeaked. Then louder, clearer. "Solace, are you here?" Willa took off running, racing through the museum, frantic. After one unsuccessful lap, Willa stopped in the main exhibit hall, panting. Simon hovered behind her, unsure how to help. She closed her eyes and tried to *feel* the ghost's presence, a feeling she knew as well as the sound of her own breath.

Come on, Solace! Be here!

"Willa?" Simon asked tentatively, breaking her concentration.

A defeating crack of understanding broke her heart in two and turned her bones cold. Her hands started to shake. "She's not here," she breathed, the words fumbling on her lips.

Simon blinked and shook his head. "But I thought she couldn't ever leave."

"She can't!" Willa heart palpated furiously. She spun around to face him, her eyes big and wild, like uncut gems. "Holy moon, Simon! Solace is *NOT* here!"

CHAPTER 34
WANING CRESCENT

July—Present Day

"Willa, you can't keep sitting here, just *waiting*."

"Yes, I can."

"But it's been almost a week!" Simon rubbed at the back of his neck and took a breath to calm his voice. "I miss you. You've barely been home. You haven't been training. Have you even slept a full night?"

Willa only moaned in response; her head pillowed on her arms on the cluttered desk in the back office of the museum. Beneath her face lay Solace's favorite book, an 1813 edition of *Sense & Sensibility*. Simon sighed quietly, more from worry than frustration. He'd been trying to convince her for the last half hour that sleeping alone in the storeroom and wandering the exhibits all day would not bring her friend back. But she mulishly clung to the idea that Solace would somehow reappear, that she was only hiding or playing a trick, instead of . . . whatever had happened.

Simon stepped closer and put a hand on her back. "Come on, my Willa. You're going to drive yourself crazy. Plus, Bertie keeps calling me wondering if you're having some kind of psychotic break."

Willa scoffed but didn't say anything.

"Come home. Sleep in your own bed, with me, work with your magic, and help us figure out what happened." He rubbed her back. "That is all you can do."

She flinched away from him, sat up. The dark circles under her eyes gave her a haggard, beaten look that he hated. "No! I'm the only one who can see her. I have to be here if she gets back. If she needs help. . . I can't accept that"—her bottom lip trembled—"that *he* took her from me." Her eyes glassed over and the tears slipped down her cheeks. "*I can't! I won't!*"

Lifting her chin, she set her jaw, trying to fight the hiccup of sobs in her chest. Simon reached out a tentative hand, touched her shoulder. To his surprise, she collapsed into him, burrowing her face into his stomach, her hands clenching his belt. Simon cradled her head in his hands, his heart breaking, aching to make it better.

After a moment, he knelt down in front of her. "Listen: Elliot had a dream last night about Archard's house in Denver. Rowan and Cal went to check it out. This could be our break in finding him and figuring out what happened. Don't you want to be at home when they get back?" He said the words as gently as he could find.

She sniffled, nodded. "I do, I just . . . It's Solace, Simon."

"I know." He wiped her hot tears away and pushed back her hair. "But you can't do anything for her sitting here torturing yourself. You know she'd want you out there, solving the mystery. Right?"

"Yeah." She exhaled her frustration. "I *should* be able to do something. What good is this Power of Spirits if I can't help her and the others?" Her eyes dropped away. "I hear their voices all night long. And last night I dreamed that Solace stood between Archard and that other witch, the creepy one with the crazy eyes." A shiver shook down her torso.

Simon gripped her upper arms. "I know exactly how you feel." When she looked at him, he gave her a small smile.

Her own lips twitched into an attempt at a smile. It broke his heart to see her trying to be happy when he knew she was so devastated. The smile faded away, and her eyes turned desperate. She said meekly, "Maybe she crossed over. Do you think she crossed over and those voices I heard have nothing to do with Solace?"

Simon frowned. It would be too amazing of a coincidence, and Willa knew it; but he hated to pick apart her fragile hope. "It's possible."

Willa's tired eyes wandered away again; she knew he was placating, knew that's what she wanted him to do. "I never got to tell her how she died. Never got to tell her that you carry her magic." She pressed a finger to his chest. "Maybe that's a good thing."

He couldn't take the haunted look on her face any longer. He stood, pulling her with him. "Come on. You need some real sleep."

"But what if . . . ?" she began half-heartedly and then gave up the argument, allowing Simon to pick up her bag and guide her out of the museum.

Solace's copy of *Sense & Sensibility* sat heavily on Willa's lap. She shouldn't have removed it from the museum—it was a precious artifact and worth a lot of money—but Willa couldn't leave it behind. She caressed the soft leather cover, fingering Jane Austen's embossed name.

Her mind moved to one of the last conversations she'd had with her ghost-friend. They'd sat in the hot, poorly lit office in the back of the museum, Willa polishing some of the silver artifacts, Solace lounging on top of a bookcase. "I wonder if I had a beau?" the ghost mused, a favorite question.

Willa had smiled. "Oh, of course you did." Always her answer.

"Do you think he was like Willoughby or Colonel Brandon?"

With a roll of her eyes, Willa said, "Hopefully neither one. Jane Austen's men are too perfect for my taste. Too . . . dashing, not enough . . . manliness."

Solace sat up, hand on her heart, feigning offense. "How can you say that?"

"Because it's true." Willa smiled as she dotted more polish onto a large platter.

"Willa Fairfield, you take that back! I'll not hear you insult Jane Austen in my presence." Solace liked to play the dramatic.

"Oh, come on, Solace. Wouldn't you rather have a man with depth, with complications, with . . . realness?"

"I don't think that's a word."

Willa rolled her eyes again. "How about a man like Mr. Rochester, in *Jane Eyre*? Much more interesting."

"That cranky old man? Sun and moon! I suppose next you'll suggest that horrid Heathcliff from *Wuthering Heights*." Solace shook her head.

"Well, at least Heathcliff loved with fiery, eternal passion instead of—what's that phrase from your book?—'polite affection.'"

Solace rolled her eyes. "You're crazy. Isn't Simon perfect, like a Jane Austen man?"

Willa scoffed. "Most definitely not, and that is why I love him."

Solace sighed and fluttered back into her lounging position. "Oh, to be in love."

As the memory faded away, Willa smiled sadly and turned to look at Simon's profile. He'd let his hair grow out a little in the last weeks, and the yellow curls had softened around his face, covering the tops of his ears and draping his forehead. She liked the wild effect. Her eyes traveled down his stone-cut jaw to the bulk of the muscles in his arms as he held the steering wheel. There was certainly a little of both Rochester and Heathcliff in him: a complicated mix of passion, intelligence, and tortured past.

His nightmares had stopped. She hadn't realized it before, but his bad dreams had stopped at the same time hers began. Did that mean he had finally come to terms with the cave, or was he too distracted by the recent events to worry about three dead witches?

Sensing her stare, Simon turned. "You okay?"

"Yeah, just . . . tired." A smile twitched at her lips and then fell away. "What about you?"

He looked at her briefly, turned back to the road. "I'm fine."

"That doesn't sound too convincing."

He sighed. "I know." He brushed at the curls on his forehead. "It's hard to be convincing when I don't know how to feel from one minute to the next."

"Yeah," she nodded. "Do you think our lives will always be like this? This crazy up-and-down chaos?"

Simon turned to her with concern. "It's all *my* fault."

She blinked. "What do you mean?"

He bit his lower lip, looked out the windshield. "I'm a mess, and I've dragged you into the middle of all of it. And I really am sorry for that."

"Simon . . ."

"I think the training is helping though. Rowan is a task-master." He smiled. "I *have* felt more in control." Simon kept one hand on the wheel and with the other fiddled with the top of the gearshift.

Willa forced a smile. "That's good." She looked down at her hands. "What about . . . I mean, if Archard comes . . ." She felt Simon's eyes rest on her, and she exhaled. "What about in a fight?" He didn't answer right away, and Willa could sense his struggle.

Finally, he said, "I guess we'll find out." He huffed out a breath and added, "I can still feel it growing. The training helps, but my powers are still increasing. I don't know what's fueling it, or if I can slow it down. The thing that really scares me though . . ." He gripped the gearshift knob until his hand was white.

"Tell me," Willa whispered.

He didn't look at her as he pulled the car to a stop outside Plate's Place. "That deep down . . ." He paused again and licked his lips slowly. "I like the power." The words barely left his mouth; Willa wasn't even sure if she'd heard him correctly.

A chill brushed her neck, causing the hairs there to stand on end. Unsure how to respond or even what to think, she rested her head against the window and gazed out, her eyelids like heavy drapes. Maybe Simon enjoying his powers was a good thing. Maybe it meant his acceptance of them, his willingness to work with them. But ripples of worry moved off her heart. Yet, could she complain that he was talking to her, telling her something like that? She wanted that, had asked for it.

A streak of movement came around the side of the house. Willa sat up. "Was that Koda?"

Simon turned. "What?"

Spinning in her seat, Willa looked out the back of the open Jeep. "There!" She pointed. Simon swiveled his neck. The wolf ran down the street, away from the house.

"Where is he going?" Simon said, eyes narrowed at the retreating form of his Familiar. The wolf suddenly stopped, looked back at them, and then gave a short howl. "He wants us to follow him."

Willa frowned; she was still trying to figure out the witch-Familiar relationship. She was used to animals coming to be healed, but not to having one around all the time—especially a wolf that acted more human than canine. "Okay. Go," she said.

Simon flipped the Jeep around. The wolf loped through the streets, his spindly legs propelling him effortlessly. Willa noticed the confused looks of bystanders as the wolf raced by.

A few minutes later, Koda turned down a road Willa knew well. She held her breath, her heart jumping, senses alert. Koda stopped at the iron gate of the Twelve Acres Cemetery. The town cemetery was small, clean, and peaceful. The gate, designed in the shape of intertwining ivy vines, stood squarely in a squat stone wall.

Simon parked the Jeep. He and Willa exchanged a look and then followed the wolf through the gate. Koda padded ahead, looking confident of his destination. Willa visited the cemetery often. Part of her town historian training included knowing the graves of all the important people who had lived in Twelve Acres. Plus, it offered a serene place to walk and think.

Koda cut sharply off the path and onto the grass. He weaved through the newer headstones to a group of much older ones. Willa felt dizzy, her head a bobbing balloon. Simon gripped her arm. "What's wrong?"

"That's Ruby's grave," she stuttered.

Simon's head snapped back. Koda whined, pawing at the foot of the tall stone. The late afternoon sun pooled in the etched names of Ruby and Charles Plate. Simon left Willa, dropped next to his wolf. "What is it, Koda?" he said.

Willa closed her eyes, trying to push down the wave of fear rising in her throat.

"Willa! Look at this," Simon called, looking up at her from the grass.

Willa swallowed and dropped to her knees. Near the bottom of the stone was a mark, black, eerie, and wrong: a small skull and cross bones. The sight of it brought stars to Willa's vision. She teetered and Simon caught her.

"No, no. That can't be here," she mumbled. Koda pushed his nose forward to meet Willa's eyes. He lifted a paw and put it on her knee. In the sun-yellow circles of the wolf's eyes, she saw her fear confirmed. She shook her head quickly.

"What is it, Willa?" Simon tightened his grip on her.

"Check the other headstones!" Koda moved closer so Willa could lean into his body. Simon crawled over to check the stones for Amelia, Peter, and Amelia's parents.

Willa watched him closely, her hand buried deep in Koda's bristle-brush fur. When Simon's face fell, she knew.

"They all have that mark," he said quietly.

She closed her eyes and tried to pull in a steady breath. *Is it possible? Did Archard really . . . ? Why?* To Simon, she said, "Call the Covenant, and tell them to come as soon as possible."

WHILE THEY WAITED FOR THE Covenant, Simon left Willa sitting in the grass with Koda and checked several more headstones, but found nothing. He knew he wouldn't, but he still had to look.

As unsettling as this discovery was and how strangely Willa reacted, he was relieved to have something to think about other than his tongue-in-cheek revelation to Willa about enjoying his power. *She must think I'm some kind of psycho.* He stopped to stare out over the field of headstones. *Maybe I am.* Yes, training helped a little. Yes, Rowan's guidance was surprisingly astute; but while part of Simon felt relieved by the effects of training, the other only worried more. If he learned to control his powers, he could use them more efficiently. And if he learned to enjoy instead of fear, it would be easy. He didn't know if he'd be able to hold back in a fight, to resist the urge to use everything in his arsenal. What if the next time he used it on purpose?

"Simon!"

He looked up to see the other witches at the gate. He waved them over. Charlotte trotted past him to sit with Willa and put a comforting arm around her. Rowan stopped next to Simon, his face pale and drawn.

"Any luck at Archard's house?" Simon asked in a hushed tone.

Rowan heaved a sigh. "Nothing. The house was empty and looked like it hadn't been lived in for months."

Simon shook his head. "Well, I'm afraid we found something here, and it has Willa really freaked out."

"Show me."

Simon led the group over to the headstones of the deceased witches, knelt, and pushed aside the grass. The symbol, the size of a quarter, glared back from the gray surface of the stone of Ruby and Charles' grave. At the sight of it, Wynter gasped.

"What does it mean?" Simon asked.

Stroking his beard, Rowan said, "Well, the obvious: it means death. Necromancers—Dark witches known for trying to raise the dead—used that symbol." He squinted at the mark. "But that was centuries ago. Necromancers no longer exist because the spells were all wiped out by Light witches. Too many terrible accidents."

"That mark looks fresh," Wynter said.

"It is." Willa spoke up from her spot on the grass. Koda sat panting beside her, refusing to leave her side. "I've been here a hundred times and *that*"—she pointed to the mark—"is definitely new." She patted Koda's head, her eyes trained on the headstones. "Archard took them, like he took Solace," she said quietly.

Next to her, Charlotte started and leaned forward to look at Willa's face. "What are you talking about?"

Willa's jaw tensed for a moment as if the words would be painful to say. "I think Archard took Solace and the ghosts of these witches. He did it on the full moon—it's what caused the snow." She inhaled a shaky breath. "The voices we heard— it was them. Asking for my help." Her face screwed up with emotion.

Rowan squatted in front of Willa and nodded to Koda; the wolf nodded back. "Willa, why would you think that?"

Willa looked past Rowan, up to Simon. He had figured her sensitivity to the marks was just her instincts, but the look on her face said there was more to it than that. "I only told you a small part of that dream I had about Solace with Archard and the other witch."

Simon narrowed his eyes, sensing the awful tremor of fear in her. "What else happened?" he asked.

She wetted her lips and exhaled. "I'll show you." She turned to Rowan. "All of you." Then to Simon again, "Can you get my dream cradle out of my bag? It's in the Jeep."

WILLA CUPPED THE VELVETY BLUE pouch in her hands, staring down at the black side-ways looking eye symbol on the outside. The scents of lavender and sage drifted up to her nose. The weight of the moonstone inside pressed into her palm.

Only once before had she shown her coven-mates one of her dreams. Last time, they were desperate to find Simon and Wynter, and her dream about Simon standing in a cave had done nothing to help. What she would show them probably couldn't help either, but they needed to see it.

Koda nudged her with his snout, and she stood up. Simon put himself next to her and briefly brushed his hand along her hip. "Do you need help?"

"No," she shook her head. Loosening the purse strings, she pulled out the moonstone, milky white and as big as her palm.

Wynter moved to her other side. "I put up a blocking spell, so no one walking by will see us. You can start now."

Willa inhaled, long and slow, closing her eyes for a moment. She didn't want to relive this dream, to see the ancient witch cross over from the mist of sleep to the sunshine of this place.

After a roll of her shoulders, she lifted the stone out in front of her and said the spell that would bring her dream to life. *"Dream cradle, reveal your nighttime keep. Moonstone, show what you hold deep."*

The stone grew warm, then hot, bursting to life with a blinding flash of light. The light flickered a few times, like an old movie projector. The Twelve Acres Cemetery fell to the background, and an ancient graveyard, black and foggy, materialized as if from a thick fog.

The dream progressed in silvery shadows. The Dark witch crested a hill, a moonstone in his hand, this one etched with the death's head. Willa shivered as he pulled the ghosts from their graves, hooking them like fish on a line with his twisted magic. When he ravaged the townspeople of their souls, she wished Simon would step closer and put his arms around her. She dared to turn her head and look at him. A strange expression contorted his face, a mixture of emotions and thoughts she couldn't identify. His eyes darted back and forth, following the movements of the witch.

Finally, the witch boxed up his plundered souls and the dream switched to a new scene: this, the one Willa had mentioned: Archard and the Dark witch flanking Solace. Solace, in her purple dress and curls, hung her head, slumped forward as if asleep standing up. The Dark witches stared forward with looks of triumph and satisfaction.

Willa's bones grew stiff with cold. She looked away.

She was surprised to find Simon standing right next to her, gazing at the ancient witch with a curious expression. The moonstone flickered off, the light retreating. She lowered her arm, continuing to look at Simon.

"That's the witch you've been dreaming about?" he

whispered, his eyes focused on the spot where the dream had appeared.

"Yes," she whispered.

Simon turned to look at her, his eyes pinched, forehead wrinkled. He took her hand. "I'm so sorry."

Rowan interrupted by saying, "I didn't know that was possible—pulling souls from the grave." He reached out to steady himself on a tall headstone.

"It shouldn't be," Darby hissed.

"Who is that?" Rain asked, her arms hugged tight around her torso.

"I don't know," Willa answered. "Wynter mentioned legends about a witch named Bartholomew the Dark, but I have no way to know for sure." She slipped the moonstone back into the dream cradle. "I started seeing him in my dreams the night Simon was attacked on the cliff."

Rowan nodded. "I see why you believe Archard has taken ghosts. If he somehow discovered that other witch's magic . . ." A chilled wind moved through the cemetery. Koda gave a low growl.

"But why?" Wynter said. "What's the point of taking Solace, Ruby, and the others?" She touched Ruby's tombstone tenderly. "It can't just be revenge."

Another wind blew across the cemetery, and a thick cloud moved over the late July sun. Willa sat down in the grass, too tired to stand anymore. Koda trotted over to sit next to her. Then, one by one, all her coven-mates sat in the grass.

After several long moments of restless silence, Rowan said, "It's time to go to Oregon."

Willa's head jerked up. "What?" she and several others said together.

"There's one more spell we can try to find Archard." Rowan looked from face to face and reached into his pocket. He pulled out a fountain pen, black and sleek as a dagger. "I found this at Archard's old house. It'd fallen among the rocks in the driveway. I'm going to assume it belonged to him, or at least that he used it. If so, we can use it to find him."

Rowan turned the pen over in his hand, and Wynter added, "We know one very powerful locator spell, but it must be performed by the ocean." She looked at Rowan. "We know the perfect place on the Oregon coast. We'll do it on the black moon, to reinforce the spell."

Rowan leaned closer to Wynter. "We could stay with her. I mean, if you are all right with that."

Wynter frowned and then exhaled. "Yes, it's fine. I'll call her when we get back."

"Who are you talking about?" Willa asked.

"My mother," Wynter said, looking at Willa. "She has a big house near the cove. We will stay with her for the night, after the spell is done." There was an edge to Wynter's voice; and when she looked away, Willa wondered what had passed between Wynter and her mother.

"But before we go," Rowan said, "We should finish Simon and Willa's Elemental Challenge."

Willa's jaw dropped, immediately forgetting about Wynter and her mother. Simon scoffed. "Are you sure, Rowan?" he asked. "It seems . . . insignificant right now."

"On the contrary, having the strength of a True Witch will greatly aid you both when we find Archard. Because if we find him, there *will* be a fight—one far worse than last time." Rowan let his gaze rest on Simon for a moment. Then he looked over at Willa. "The challenge is far more than a rite of passage.

It solidifies, balances, and enhances your powers. You both need that."

Willa nodded tentatively. "Okay. But is there time? The black moon is two days away. When do we do it?"

Rowan slid Archard's pen into his pocket. "Tomorrow. Dawn."

RACHEL WAITED UNTIL THE COVENANT left the cemetery and then hurried back to the house. Seeing through the blocking spell Wynter set had been easy; Bartholomew's divination spell cut through the Light witches' concealment like a wind through the fog. And his cloaking spell let her observe the light witches undetected.

Archard sat at the kitchen table poring over Bartholomew's book, making notes on the spell they would use to Bind the ghost Covenant. He wrote slowly, awkwardly, his right hand wrapped in bandages.

Without looking up, he asked, "Have you seen my black fountain pen? It would be easier to hold with these damn bandages."

Rachel's jaw dropped in surprise. Archard looked up at her. "What is it?"

"The pen—I just saw Rowan with it. Apparently, one of their Dreamers saw the house in Denver. They went to check it out. Rowan found your pen."

Archard huffed and adjusted the ballpoint in his awkward hand. "Sun and moon! So they *do* suspect I'm alive; and now they're going to do a locator spell. Well, it's about time they did *something*."

"Yes, and they plan to do it on the night of the black moon." Rachel leaned back in her chair and propped her feet up on another. "In Oregon."

Archard narrowed his eyes and then sighed. "Ocean magic. Hmmm."

"They also found the marks on the graves."

Archard threw down his pen. Absently, he scratched at his healing sores through his bandages. "Do they know what it means?"

"Not really, but the other Dreamer—the girl—she's having dreams about Bartholomew."

He raised his eyebrows. "Really? Now that *is* interesting. Anything that could hurt us?"

Rachel took a long drink of water from Archard's glass. "She saw you, too. They know there is a connection, but are clueless beyond that."

Archard pursed his lips as if he smelled something foul. "Interesting."

Rachel nodded, took another drink.

"Make the arrangements for us to go to Oregon," he said.

"Why?" she set down the empty glass.

"Because we are going to crash their little spell, and then make them watch as I Bind a Dark Covenant made of Light witch ghosts." The pleasure of the idea filled his body, his skin flushing red. "That will be much more satisfying than killing them now and Binding the ghosts later. This event deserves an audience."

Rachel nodded in approval. "I'll get everything ready."

"Be sure we have something strong to pack the box in. The power has grown exponentially since the full moon, and

I'm worried about the integrity of that old iron." He looked down at his notes. *It's almost time!* Archard's confidence and arrogance had also grown since the full moon.

"I have a feeling we are going to need every ounce of that power if we are going to pull this off." Rachel dropped her feet to the floor with a loud slap.

Archard furrowed his brows and looked back up. "Do not doubt me, dear. This will be one of the greatest successes in the history of Dark magic, next to my accomplishment on the full moon. I will sit beside Bartholomew as a lord of Darkness."

"Of course, Archard," Rachel said blandly and then left the room.

CHAPTER 35
WANING CRESCENT

July—Present Day

For a moment, there was only the promise of light, a glow behind the mountain peaks as dawn grew in the east. Then, suddenly, ripples of pink flowed over the sky. This morning the weather was pleasant, the temperature hovering between warm and hot. Willa whispered a morning chant to herself, *"Hail fair sun, ruler of day, burn clear and bright to light my way."* An extra whisper of warmth touched her cheek.

A hum under her skin announced Simon's approach. He stopped just behind her, stood silent for a moment as he too watched the sun rise. Then he said, "They're ready for us."

Willa turned and smiled at him nervously.

"You ready?" he asked as he stepped forward and took her hands. Dressed in T-shirts and shorts, they looked ready for a day at the gym.

Willa exhaled. "Ready as I'll ever be. Right now, I'm just looking forward to it being over."

Simon nodded. "Yeah, me too."

"It's hard to focus on this with . . . everything else going on." She closed her eyes, fresh fear rising in her gut. *What's going to happen? Can we save Solace, Ruby, and the others?*

"I know, but I'm sure, once the challenge starts, we won't be able to think about all that stuff." He frowned.

Willa nodded, folding her arms over her chest, suddenly feeling chilled.

The couple turned and walked down the hill to the field chosen for the challenge. Rowan had picked an abandoned farm field with a spattering of old cottonwood trees, overgrown and wild, and just far enough out of town to be private.

The Luminary met them at a fallen rail fence, the boundary of the field. None of the other Covenant members were in sight. He folded his arms and smiled soberly. "Well, here we are. Everything is prepared. I know the circumstances aren't ideal, but I have every confidence in both of you. Try to put aside everything else." He blinked his blue eyes and then added, "Willa, you'll go first."

Willa's stomach dropped. "Okay," she managed to say, despite the sudden tightness in her jaw and throat. She hadn't practiced for a week, and she still had an exhaustion hangover from her vigil at the museum. Simon turned to her and took her face in his hands. His dark brown eyes focused on hers. "You will be amazing." After a smile, he brushed a kiss onto her lips.

His words helped in a tiny way, enough to steady her nerves so she could follow Rowan out into the field without shaking knees. Touched by the bright light of dawn, the dry grass glowed gold and the trees' leaves shimmered green. As Willa followed, she listened to the sound of a running irrigation line, doing her best to clear her mind.

Rowan stopped in the middle of the field and turned to her. "Now, remember, you may only use the element I call out to defend the attack. It doesn't matter how you use it, but it must be *that* element. And we will not go easy on you. Everyone will push hard."

Willa nodded and chewed her bottom lip. "Okay, I'm ready." *Am I?*

Rowan smiled with empathy. "I know you are. I'm sorry we have to do this now, but know you can still triumph." He put a reassuring hand on her shoulder, and she nodded. "Best of luck, Willa." And then he was gone, moving away to place himself behind her, leaving her alone in the middle of the field.

Just a test. Just a test. I'm good at tests.

Her heart tripled its speed; her pulse throbbed annoyingly at her neck and wrists. Two long breaths did little to help. Fists at her sides, Willa closed her eyes.

Breathe.

"Ready!" Rowan yelled from behind her. Willa braced her whole body, ready to act, trying to ignore the shaky sensation in her core. "AIR!"

Rain appeared out of nowhere and threw a wall of water at Willa. It hit her full force, knocking her off her feet. Soaking and sputtering, Willa scrambled to her feet. Instantly, another blast of water hit her in the face, the liquid pushing into her eyes, nose and mouth. For a moment, she was drowning standing up. Then with a forceful cough she steadied herself.

Air. Use the power of air.

With a quickness that surprised her, Willa rolled out of the way of the next water wall and sprang to her feet. She called to the magic. Another wall came at her; she ducked under it. Then two walls, one from either side, raced down upon her. Just in time, Willa dove out of the way but was again soaked when the two collided midair in a dramatic splash.

Focus.

She hurried to her feet. *Swift and effectual power of air . . . !* Immediately, her hands grew hot, she lifted them in front of her. The next wave rolled only a few feet away, glistening in the sun, churning over the grass. Her hands grew hotter. A small cyclone of air appeared before her. She gasped, but kept her focus. She pushed more magic and energy into the cyclone until it grew as tall and wide as she.

Unleashing it, the air pummeled through the wall of water, sent it spattering backwards in a million scattered drops.

"Ready!" came Rowan's call. She didn't even have time to smile at her first success. "FIRE!"

Oh, no!

Fire was her weakest skill. Her failure at the candle test haunted her.

Willa dropped to the ground in a crouch, eyes and ears attuned, waiting for the next attack. The field was eerily quiet except for the huff of her breath.

The ground around her trembled furiously, and the heads of plants erupted in a circle around her, growing faster than she could escape, encasing her in a ring of hawthorn bushes.

Pale pink flowers burst to life on the branches all around her, deceptively hiding five-inch-long thorns. She moved to push the branches aside, but they struck back as quick as snakes, leaving wicked slices on her forearms and hands. Jerking back, she hissed at the pain.

Fire. Find the fire.

Closing her eyes, ignoring the throbbing of the cuts on her arms, Willa focused. *Mighty fire . . .* The heat answered, and, when she held out her hand, a burst of flame shot outward into the bushes. It surprised her—never had so much fire come when she called.

More.

Soon her palms were torches, spewing out jets of flame that burned a large channel though the bushes. Sweat-soaked and breathless, Willa crawled out. The thorns grew back so quickly that her legs suffered a few more nasty cuts. Collapsing free of the bushes, Willa sucked in fresh air. Her body cried out for a rest, but immediately Rowan's call came up.

"WATER!"

Willa clamored to her feet and spun, just in time to dive out of the path of a huge fireball. It crashed and erupted in the remains of the hawthorns next to her.

Great. More fire.

Focus. Use the water.

She pushed up and took off, the whizzing sound of another fireball close behind.

I need water.

Whipping her head side to side as she ran, she tried to orient herself. She had to find that irrigation ditch. For a few seconds, she held her breath, listening, waiting to hear the laugh of the water. She turned to the right.

There it is!

She moved toward the sound and soon saw the small ditch, overflowing with cool, clear water. Unfortunately, Darby stood just beyond it, a fresh fireball balancing on her hand. Willa pushed her legs harder.

Get there.

Darby launched the ball. Willa tensed to dodge it, but the ball fell short, hit the ground in front of the ditch and erupted into a ten-foot wall, blocking her way. The heat scorched her skin, Willa put a hand up to shield her eyes.

No! Now what?

An idea came.

Am I strong enough?

Willa squeezed her eyes shut and summoned the water. It responded quickly, easily, rising from the ditch in a tall pillar. She held it in place with her outstretched hand. The magic tingled along her arm, put energy in her blood. For the first time during the challenge, Willa marveled at how amazing it felt to have so much magic churning inside her.

She lifted her other hand, brought the two together and then slowly separated them. The pillar split into two. She pulled her right hand back, and the water fell on the wall of flame, extinguishing it with a loud hiss and a rush of steam; left hand thrust out, and the second pillar spiraled its way to Darby.

When the Fire witch cried out, her voice garbled by the water, Willa grinned, all nervousness gone, forgotten. The euphoria of her powers pulsed inside her.

More.

Rowan called the last challenge. "EARTH!"

Willa took a breath and scanned the field, waiting. The air around her began to churn, her hair whipping into her eyes. When she turned, she stood face to face with a towering, ugly tornado. It curled down from the sky, growling and twisting.

Willa bit her tongue to keep from screaming out,

backpedaling away. Her mind desperately grabbed for an idea. The power-high she'd felt a moment ago puttered out.

Too much! How do I stop a monster?

The gray cyclone, now as wide as a car and towering to the clouds, surged forward; and Willa continued to back away. She tripped on a large rock and went down hard on her back. The funnel cloud took the advantage and scooped her up into its spinning embrace.

This time she did scream.

Upside down, disoriented and incredibly dizzy, Willa wanted to call out defeat, but gave one last ditch effort.

Focus. One more time. Find the power. Just like with the water.

In the chaos of the funnel, she managed to see the branches of a large tree not too far away. She reached out, but the tree was just beyond her fingers. With everything left inside her, she called to the Earth, to the tree.

Hear me. Help me!

Her hand trembled as she reached, her body continuing to spin.

The tree . . .

Heat leaped from her palm, arcing over to the branches. The tree shuddered in answer to her call, and, with a wooden grunt, leaned itself to the side, extending its branches into the tornado. Limbs and leaves tore at her face, but she managed to get a solid grip before the tornado moved away.

The tree snapped back into place, pulling her with it, free of the cyclone.

"Thank you," she whispered to the tree, just before her arms gave out and she tumbled the long fall to the ground. She hit with a painful thud, knocking the breath out of her lungs. Her vision went black around the edges and bile rose in her throat. Her chest stuttered, trying to pull in air; and for a terrifying second she wondered if it would. Then, with a strangled gasp, the air rushed in. Choking on it, she rolled to her side, coughing and sputtering.

Then the pain hit. Her body felt like a piece of paper, crushed, wadded up, and set on fire. Tears welled in the corners of her eyes.

Simon arrived, his hurried footsteps crunching the grass. His strong arms caught and held her, one hand resting gently on her head.

In a wave of heat, all the pain pulled away. She blinked up at him. He had her cradled in his arms, his hand still on her head. The position brought a flash of the nightmare of the girl being burned, the witch holding her. She flinched at its sudden, powerful invasion.

"Are you still in pain?"

She shook her head, tried to smile, but was too exhausted. She pushed the image from her mind. "I fell out of the tree."

Simon laughed and hugged her tight. "I knew you were tough, my Willa, but that ... amazing doesn't even come close." He kissed her forehead.

Then Rowan was there, kneeling in front of her, his face alive with a smile. "Willa, lass, well done. So well done." He leaned in, kissed her cheek. "Can you give me your hand?"

She raised it weakly, and he cupped it in his own. *"Powers of the Earth, mighty above all. Earth, Air, Fire, and Water now we call. A True Witch at your command, against the Dark she will stand."*

Willa's pendant, tucked inside her shirt, flared hot, and where it touched her skin a glorious rush of power and energy moved outward until it had filled her. She gasped and sat up, no longer exhausted. The cheers of the rest of the Covenant made her smile.

THE COVENANT GATHERED AROUND WILLA, offering congratulations and praise. Rain stepped forward, her black hair tipped with fushia, and held out her fist. "Wicked-good job, Willa."

Willa bumped her fist into Rain's. "Thanks. Those were some serious water walls. I thought I was gonna drown." Rain smiled and moved aside for Darby.

Darby kissed Willa's head. "I don't appreciate being all wet, but I'll give you credit." She grinned. "So proud of ya, ya little peach."

"Thanks, Darby."

Wynter pushed through and took Willa into her arms, giving her a crushing hug. She pulled back, and the two exchanged a tender look.

Willa turned to Hazel and Toby. "So whose handy work was that tornado?"

Hazel smiled, her gray hair bright in the morning sun. "Both of us, actually." She gestured to Toby who also smiled and adjusted his glasses. "We had to give you something hard." The group laughed. Hazel hugged Willa.

Finally, Charlotte threw herself at Willa. "That. Was. *Incredible!*"

Willa laughed. "Thanks, Char."

"Really incredible," Elliot added. "I'm pretty sure none of the rest of us did that well."

Willa blushed. "Oh, I doubt that. And anyway, Simon still has to go. He'll show us all up."

"I doubt *that*," Simon said, embarrassed and more worried

than he let on. If all he did was show everyone up, then it'd be a good day. He took Willa's hand and kissed it.

Watching her fight had been thrilling and awful all at once. Each time she got in trouble, every part of him screamed to run out and help. But seeing her triumph—that made him warm with pride and a comfort he didn't quite understand.

Rowan cleared his throat. "Okay, now. It's Simon's turn. Charlotte and Elliot, please take Simon and Willa back to the fence while we reset. I'll meet you when we're ready."

The four walked back to the outskirts of the field, talking excitedly about Willa's challenge. Simon only half-heard the chatter, his mind drifting through a maze of worry, anticipation, and fear. After seeing the extreme tests they'd thrown at Willa, he couldn't help but wonder if he'd be able to control his powers or the urge to experiment with them; because there could be no pretending, no taking it easy this round. He needed to keep his healing gift suppressed while he used the elemental magic—they had to be separate.

"Simon?"

He turned to see all three staring at him. "Huh? What?"

Willa put a hand on his arm. "You okay?" Her ocean eyes communicated sympathy and understanding, touched with concern.

He smiled weakly. "Just nervous."

She nodded.

Simon looked passed her; Elliot and Charlotte offered sympathetic smiles. He appreciated their encouragement, but the first thought that came to mind was *they don't understand*.

Rowan came running from the field. "Okay, we are ready. Are *you*, Simon?"

Simon swallowed. "I think so." Willa squeezed his hand

as she lifted to her toes to kiss his cheek. She caught his eyes, held them. He felt her warmth move into him. She released his hand, and he joined Rowan to walk out into the field.

Rowan cut him a glance. "What are you thinking?"

He scoffed. "Too many things."

His mentor nodded. "I wish I could tell you that it'll be fine, it'll be easy, but that would be lying."

"Thank you. I appreciate that."

They stopped in the middle of the field. Rowan faced him. "We're not going to make it easy on you. This is a test of control for you, as well as the elements. We know your magic skills are superior; now you must prove yourself master of them." Rowan stepped a little closer and held Simon's eyes. "I do not expect you to be perfect at it yet. Don't put too much pressure on yourself. You need to be calm first, before you can be in control. We are prepared. Don't worry about us."

Simon swallowed a sudden knot in his throat; his heart thudded hard against his ribs. He nodded. Rowan clapped him on the back and then moved away.

Calm. Stay calm. This is just about the elements; no Mind games; no healing.

"Ready!" Rowan yelled. Simon clenched his fists. The first trickles of sweat popped on his forehead. "EARTH!"

Corbin walked out from behind a tree, his hands spewing water, directing it at the ground. The flood raced toward Simon at neck-breaking speed. He turned to run, dodge the current, but the water already grabbed at his ankles. He went down, the flood rolling over him, carrying him along.

Focus. Call to the earth. Calm.

He turned his body against the current and spotted a large rock to his right. He swam for it and maneuvered himself in front of it to brace himself. Legs out, wedged into the ground, body pressed against the rock, Simon lifted his hand. The water beat against him, a thousand angry punches.

Earth . . .

Heat flared on his palm. A moment later the grass around Corbin's legs grew tall, wrapping around his legs. Corbin flicked his eyes to the slithering fingers of grass, but kept the water coming strong. Simon tugged his hand backwards, like pulling a rope, and the grass jerked Corbin off his feet. The Water witch fell flat on his back, stopping the flow of water.

Simon exhaled. *One down.*

"FIRE!"

He braced himself, face and clothes dripping. Before he could take a full breath, a whistling sound came from behind. Simon spun to see the sky full of logs, branches, and sticks of every size. The first few hit his body. He grunted with their impact, putting his arms up to save his head. The wood battered him to the ground. A large, heavy log fell on top of his legs. The *crunch* of one of his lower leg bones filled the air. He cried out in pain.

Fire! Find the fire. NOW!

Simon pushed his hands out, summoned mighty fire. Flowers of flame burst out from his palms, spreading wide in front of him like a shield. The logs and sticks hit the fire, instantly hissing to ash. Simon's leg roared, and his body ached, but only for a moment. By the time the last log hit his flames, his leg and bruises were healed.

He dropped his arms, sucking air, exhausted; but there would be no rest.

"AIR!"

With a grunt, Simon rolled to his side and pushed himself

to his feet, his leg a little tender, but sturdy. A sound like rushing water came at him from all directions. He expected another
flood, but instead, four powerful blasts of icy air hit him at
once: front, back, right, left. He stumbled under the force, his
cheeks instantly red from the cold, and his hair flying in all
directions as if the wind might pull it from his head.

He dropped to his knees, trying to keep air in his lungs,
but every breath was ripped away before he could pull it in.
Panic erupted inside him, and with it the terrible feeling of
his powers boiling up to take control.

No, no, no. Calm it. Push it down. Just find the air.

His thoughts reached outward, searching for the source
of his struggle. In his mind, he could clearly see Hazel and
Toby standing on the other side of the assault. And then he
felt it. How easy it would be to push his powers outward and
command them to stop. One little word with the force of his
odd skill behind it. *Easy.*

I won't. I can't.

Simon had been without a full breath for a couple minutes
now, and the edges of his vision faded, his body slumped in
weakness. But he lifted a hand. *Swift and effectual power of
air* . . . A fierce tingle and then his own air exploded from his
hand, pushing back the opposing winds. Simon leaned into
his hand, forcing the air out, while trying with all his might
to suppress the desire to use his other powers, the strength of
the temptation nearly as debilitating as the air assault.

With one final push, a surge of hot magic flew out of his
hand and completely dispersed the four winds. He collapsed
to the ground once again, pulling in long drags of steady, warm
air. Rowan didn't wait.

"WATER!"

The call of the water sparked energy in his blood. Somewhere deep down, his Water gift, the one he'd actually been born with, responded. He'd only felt it a few times recently, a weak tremor of this long hidden blue spark inside him; but now it was unmistakable, powerful. He jumped to his feet, snapped his head from side to side, ready. The water flowing in the irrigation ditch sang out to him, as did the water in the ground, inside the grass and trees. He could feel every drop of water in the field.

Use it!

The ground under his feet rumbled and fell away. He went with it, tumbling with the dirt and rocks into a deep pit, too deep to climb back out of, and too much like another pit from a few months ago. But he didn't have time to think about it. Fire came in a torrential downpour of white flame, hotter than anything he'd ever felt. He barely had time to lift his hands to draw the water out of the soil around him to fight it.

Steam filled the pit as he continued to pull water from all around to fight the extra-hot flames. The fire didn't stop. Soon the irrigation ditch ran dry, the dirt dust, and the grass as brittle as spun glass.

Simon fell to his knees, fighting, but losing. White, painful blisters bubbled up on his hands and arms. The never-ending flames were too much, too strong; and he was running out of energy and water. The urge came again, that raging hot desire to reach out and control. Cal and Darby appeared in his mind, standing at the edge of the pit, supplying the fire, propelling it down on him.

I can't . . .

He rolled his eyes around the pit. There was no way out, as long as the fire rained down.

Just use it. Use the power.

The flames came hotter, harder; and Simon struggled to push them away.

More water . . . All I need is more water.

His Water instincts reached out, but his head was foggy; his body near collapse.

There! There's some more.

He pulled hard. The fire sputtered. He pulled even harder.

Screams echoed down into the pit. Something scratched at his mind. Was someone calling his name?

He kept pulling, and the fire stopped.

Who's screaming?

SIMON!

"Willa?" Lowering his hands, Simon listened. Moans drifted down into the hole. "Willa?!" Simon struggled to his feet and stared at the edges of the pit, the blue sky above. No one came to the lip of the pit. "Rowan? Wynter? *What's going on?*"

Panic raced in his veins. Using his quickly recovering strength, he summoned the power of Earth. The edges of the pit rumbled and then shifted to form a few ledges. He climbed from ledge to ledge, scrambling over the top of the pit.

The field was a dry, barren wasteland.

Simon gasped, frozen in terror.

The entire Covenant lay on the ground like broken dolls, sprawled out, faces pale, ashen.

Willa's unmoving body lay crumpled at the edge of the pit, her hand fallen over the side as if she had been reaching down.

CHAPTER 36
WANING CRESCENT

July—Present Day

"Willa!" Simon dropped to the ground and lifted her limp body into his arms. Her skin was pale and drawn, her lips cracked. "What the hell?" He lifted her hand into his, sending a wave of healing energy into her body. A few seconds later her eyes fluttered.

"Simon?" she said hoarsely.

"Yeah. Are you okay? What happened?"

Willa sat bolt up, her eyes frantic. "Go help them!" She moved away from him. He hurried over to each member of the Covenant, taking their hands and healing them as fast as he could. Everyone out of danger, Simon stopped near the pit, arms limp at his sides.

Holy mother moon! Did I do this to them? How?!

All around him the field had been sucked dry of moisture: the leaves on the trees shriveled and brown, the grass gray and the ditch empty. Simon ran all the details of the fight in the pit back through his mind, but he couldn't find where he'd gone wrong. He'd fought so hard to make sure he didn't cross the line into powers he couldn't control.

Did I do ALL of this?

His body began to tremble; his heart couldn't find a steady rhythm. His head pounded, and the earth was spinning.

A hand on his arm. "Simon?"

He focused in on Willa's face. Things steadied slightly. He grabbed her shoulders. "What happened? Did I do this?"

Her brows furrowed in sympathy, with her lips pressed thin. "Oh, Simon. Yes, you did."

"But . . ." his eyes flashed to the wretched scene around him. The other Covenant members had gathered together, hanging back. "But I don't understand. *How?*"

Willa put her hands on his chest and bit her lip. "When you were fighting the fire, you pulled water from everywhere, everything. At the end . . ." She moved her palms to his cheeks and held his face, "you even pulled it from *us.*"

Simon's heart went cold. "What?!" He jerked away from her hold. "No, I didn't. I *didn't* do that."

Willa's face broke and her shoulders slumped forward. "Simon . . ."

"No!" Simon stepped back, haltingly, stiffly. "No, I didn't want to hurt anybody. *I tried so hard not to,*" he yelled.

"I know," she whispered. "But look—we are fine. We're fine." She pointed to herself and the group. Simon turned to them but then flinched away from their fearful stares. Rowan stepped forward.

"No." Simon said, holding up a hand to him. Rowan stopped. "This is why I didn't want to train. It made me drop my guard. I thought I was in control! I shouldn't have listened. I should have just stopped! There is no way to keep my gifts separate. This proves it!"

"Simon, please . . ." Rowan asked, taking one more step forward before stopping, the look on Simon's face enough to stop the fall of rain.

Simon's chest heaved and his head pounded. *How could this happen? I didn't even know I'd hurt them.*

Willa was there again, a warm hand on his arm, her pretty eyes pleading. "Simon."

He pulled back, looked at her in desperation. Both hands at his head, he pulled at his hair, pushed against the pounding at his temples. His stomach grew sour.

How could he stand here, knowing he'd almost killed all the people in the world that mattered to him? How could he live, knowing he'd done it without even realizing—again? These weren't Dark witches ready to kill him. This was his family.

Bile crept up his throat, stung his tongue. There was so much noise in his head.

So he ran.

SIMON HAD NEVER RUN so far before.

His legs pumped out mile after mile, barely noticing the strain. His feet pounded the ground until they were numb. Heart pumping, lungs sucking air, muscles flexing. But no matter how long he ran, his head remained a mess of noise. It wouldn't stop.

Simon didn't see the scenery he passed; didn't notice the turned heads of the people he passed. He cut through two towns before it occurred to him to stop.

Where are you going?!

He stopped, looked around, and found himself on a dirt road. The overgrown grass along each side told him it was a forgotten dirt road, rarely traveled. Nothing offered any stable orientation; the slumped roof of an old house a little way down the road was the only thing he could see to ground him.

He walked, his body heavy, and his spirit in the dirt. The road curved, and soon the little house stood before him. More a shack than a house, almost too small to be called a proper dwelling, the sight of it somehow fit his mood. The steeply pitched roof sagged, and the porch cover drooped in a kind of sad smile above the weathered front door and single window. It reminded Simon of a childhood story he couldn't quite recall.

The threadbare porch steps called to his aching body. Simon sat carefully, the wood groaning under his weight but holding. He exhaled, resting elbows on knees. A hot summer wind tossed the high grasses around him, teasing the weeds to his left in what once must have been a nice little kitchen garden.

Willa asked me not to run.

Simon looked back over his shoulder at the unhinged screen door, hanging to the side like a dead limb, and wallowed in his guilt. The sound of Willa's desperate, angry cries for him to stop, to come back, echoed in his head. Below the window was a child's scooter, constructed of wood and what looked like roller skate wheels, obviously homemade. Seeing it there, rotten and forgotten, made him suddenly sad. *How could I do that to her? I need to go back.*

But how do I face them all? I nearly killed them without even knowing.

I almost killed them.

I almost killed Willa.

He hung his head, thinking of the epic and dangerous failure of his challenge, wondering how things had escalated to that. A rustle in the grasses around the house made him lift his head. Koda emerged, tongue lolling out, panting.

"Koda! How on earth did you find me?"

The wolf trotted over and stood in front of him, nuzzling Simon's hands with his nose. Simon rubbed at the wolf's ears and marveled. He had no idea the Familiar bond was *that* strong. "What am I supposed to do?" Simon dropped his hand and again hung his head. "None of them will trust me, or feel safe around me again. There's no coming back from this one." He looked at his hands. "I want to fix it, but is there a way?"

The wolf sat, his golden eyes attentive, receptive.

"I should leave the Covenant. That's the only way to fix it."

Koda whined in protest.

"What else is there? I'm an unstable element. I put everyone at risk. And every time I try to do better, someone gets hurt ... or worse" Simon turned his hands over, looked at the creases in his palms and the band of his wedding ring, and then added quietly, "If I don't leave now, one day they will ask me to. If this keeps up, I may even lose Willa."

Koda whimpered and licked his hands.

Simon scoffed. "I was so stupid to think I could learn to control this ... this *mistake*." He inhaled. Then added quietly, "This curse." A crow landed in the dead garden to pick at the weeds. Simon watched its head bob up and down. The all too familiar headache returned, pulsing at the base of his skull. He rubbed at it and, with a groan, said, "I didn't even know what I was doing. *I didn't even know!*" He lashed out a fist, ramming it into the porch railing, knocking through two spindles. Instantly, he felt bad for it.

My childhood. My parents. The cave. The clock. The cliff. The challenge. The porch spindles.

Maybe my life has never been about healing. Maybe it's always been about breaking things.

Simon didn't want to let circumstances control him as they had for most of his life. He needed to learn to handle his powers—there had to be a way. But he couldn't do it while in the Covenant. The risks were too great. This was something he had to do on his own. He'd told Willa after finding Koda that he had a choice, but he'd made the wrong one before.

The wolf blinked, stepped closer, and rested his chin on Simon's knee. The witch put his hand on the wolf's head. "Maybe leaving doesn't have to be permanent, but I have to go. I have to get away from everyone so that I can't hurt them anymore. Once they are all safe, I'll train; I'll learn. I'll get this under control if it kills me." Rowan, Wynter, and Willa would say that he couldn't do it on his own, that he needed the support of the covens, but that had yet to work. His powers had been fine until joining the covens.

A new idea formed in his head. Maybe the Covenant was the problem. Maybe something about the high concentration of magic created a recipe for disaster for him. Maybe his tangle of powers would never be able to handle being around so many other witches. The logic of it was grim, depressing, but made perfect sense. He didn't just have to leave the Covenant for their good, but his own.

So maybe I can't come back?

But what about Willa? She'd always been a grounding

influence, always able to pull him from the edge; but was it selfish to take her with him? If she came, she would be in danger. If she came, she had to leave everything she loved. The space behind his heart flared with burning pain. The image of her lying over the side of the pit—her skin gray, her lips cracked—made him feel like his legs had been swept out from under him. He flinched. He'd hurt her twice now. He couldn't stand the possibility of hurting her any more.

But walking away would also hurt her, deeply, and far worse than any physical injury. Because now he wasn't just a boyfriend and soul mate walking away, now he was a husband and soul mate. If he left without her, he severed the knot, he broke the promises.

Simon fingered his wedding ring.

One of the promises he'd made was to protect her, to always do what was best for her. But what was best? She'd proved today during the challenge that she was fully capable of protecting herself.

If the Covenant magic created problems with his magic, did their soul mate bond do the same thing? Most of his freakish displays of power involved his love for her, his concern for her safety. Did his powers make it impossible for him to safely be with her as well as the covens? Did his misfit powers doom him to be alone, truly alone? The idea cut him deep.

How did he know? How did he decide?

Koda lifted his head and whined quietly. Simon's whole body filled with a crackling, broken pain. "I have to leave her," he whispered as tears filled his eyes.

The crow cawed and lifted into the air.

No one said a word for several minutes after Simon ran from the field. They huddled together, wrapped in silence. Willa stood apart looking at the trail he'd made in the dry grass, her heart breaking, her throat raw from calling after him. She didn't want to look back and see the worry in her coven-mates' faces, didn't want to wonder what they were thinking or what they might say.

Oh, Simon.

Footsteps crunched behind her; and she braced, not ready to talk to anyone. Wynter stepped next to her, took her hand. For many long moments, she said nothing. Then, "Willa, we love Simon so much."

Willa looked over, her eyes instantly wet with tears. "Aren't they afraid of him? We've never talked about it, but they worry. I know they do."

"This is a Covenant, Willa, a *Light* Covenant, we are bound to each other even beyond death. Yes, everyone is shaken, worried, but not *about* Simon—*for* Simon. The thing that hurts us the most is not being able to help him."

Willa's face fell into tears. "I gave him answers. And it only made things worse!" She sobbed for a moment. "What will we do? He'll want to leave; he'll think he has to. He's been on the edge of it for months. This will push him over that edge, and I have no way to pull him back." She looked at his trodden trail. "What if he won't come back?"

Wynter wiped a tear from her own cheek. "Then we'll go get him."

"And then what? More training? We have nothing to offer him to make it better."

"We have a stable support system. Something he's never had and never expects. You are his wife now and we his family. If there is a way for him to gain control of his powers, then we will find it together."

"And what if there isn't?" Willa swallowed, her fear tightening her throat. "What if there isn't a way to make it better? I thought knowing why would help, but look what happened. What if every turn he takes ends in hurt? Eventually, it will break him. It will ruin him."

Wynter blinked. "Willa, I . . . oh, my dear, then we will do our best to pick up the pieces."

Willa collapsed to the ground, sobbing freely, sucking in dry air.

HE's NOT COMING.

Sun and moon, what happens if he doesn't come?

Simon, where are you?!

Willa stood on the sidewalk in front of the Plate's Place, arms crossed, eyes roaming up and down the street. They'd waited at the field as long as they could, but Simon didn't come back. She'd have called him, but his phone sat on the desk in their room.

A nauseating sense of panic twisted in the bottom of her stomach; and, no matter how much she rubbed them, her hands remained ice cold. She'd tried to reach out through their connection, but she only got empty silence. He was either too far away or blocking her.

Koda was nowhere to be found either. Willa hoped the wolf had gone to find Simon, that at least he wouldn't be completely alone. And that maybe the Familiar could bring him home.

Bring him home, Koda. If he doesn't come back soon, I'll lose him.

Willa's mind filled with the scenes of the unbelievable things he'd done. She, Charlotte, and Elliot had watched from the edge of the field, not speaking as they marveled at Simon's abilities. Even when his leg had been crushed by the log, he wasn't beaten.

Then the pit.

Darby and Cal with their unrelenting white flames.

"He'll never beat those flames," Elliot had whispered, his face pinched in concern. "They are too strong."

When the irrigation ditch had run dry and the grass under their feet turned to dust, Willa's worry became its own flame in her chest. That's when she'd ran to the edge of the pit. Soon everyone gathered close, watching, like horrified spectators at a carnival freak show. Willa turned to Rowan, standing behind her, his eyes wide and body stiff. "You have to stop it, Rowan!"

He didn't answer. Instead, he turned away from her and watched as a tree was sucked dry of all its moisture.

"Darby, Cal—*stop!*" They ignored her too, the same transfixed, fascinated look on their faces. She knew they'd keep pushing. Just like when they'd buried her and Simon alive— they had to see how far Simon could go.

She dropped to her knees at the edge of the pit. "Simon!" Charlotte ran up behind her, grabbed her shoulders.

"Willa, get back before you get hurt!"

"No!" she yelled, shrugging her off. Before Charlotte could try again, all of them were suddenly doubled over in pain. Willa collapsed to her side, her throat burning with thirst. Inside her body, it felt like small hooks had caught onto her tissues, dragging them forward. When she opened her eyes, she watched in horror as tiny droplets of water beaded up on her skin and then flitted away through the air toward the pit.

"Simon," she gasped, realization taking her breath away. Then, because her throat was sand paper, she used her mind in one last effort. *Simon!*

Standing now, on the sidewalk, Willa shivered. She looked down at her arms, the memory of the water being pulled from her body a loud echo on her emotions. *Poor Simon.* His face when she'd told him what he'd done, the heart-breaking realization, and the overwhelming shock. How could he not have known? What did that mean about his powers?

Willa exhaled.

The street was still empty, and Willa's body ached to have a task, something to take her mind off the wait and wonder. She spun around and hurried toward the house. She still needed to pack their things for the early morning flight to Oregon. As she climbed the front steps, she gave herself a weak pep talk. *He'll make it. Get things ready, and he'll be here.*

By nightfall, Willa had everything packed, but Simon had not returned. Mad with worry, sitting on the curb, huddled over her knees, her nerves became a jittery mess.

"Willa, it's late," Char said from behind her. "Come inside; eat something. I'm sure he'll be here soon."

Willa rounded on her friend. "How do you know, Char? You don't know anything about it!" Anger heating her cheeks, Willa turned away, feeling only a slight amount of remorse for lashing out at innocent Charlotte. "Leave me alone!"

Charlotte stood for a moment, and then retreated to the house without a word. Willa was both sad and grateful. She didn't need anyone hovering over her, trying to make it better.

Better didn't exist. But, oh, how she wanted some comfort! Some solid way to know that it *would* be okay, that Simon would be back, and that they'd find a way to fix everything.

But Simon wasn't back, and with each hour that passed the likelihood of him returning decreased.

Willa looked down the dark, empty street. Silent tears slipped down her cold cheeks and fell into the gutter.

MIDNIGHT. WILLA'S HOPE WASTED AWAY, sitting heavy in her gut, a shriveled chunk of garbage.

1:15 a.m. I'll never see him again!

2:24 a.m. Eyes like sandpaper, she allowed herself to lie down on the park strip grass, fighting the urge to let sleep erase the pain. *Stay awake! Stay awake!* The night was warm, but she shivered.

3:02 a.m. Willa blinked up at the pattern of white stars, bright and mocking in their peaceful beauty. Then she rolled over and fell asleep, Simon's name on her lips.

4:30 a.m. Arms lifting her from the dewy grass. "Simon?" she said, starting to wake, her heart pounding. "No, lass," Rowan answered. "Go back to sleep. I've got you." She passed out again, partly from exhaustion and partly from disappointment.

6:50 a.m. Willa woke suddenly, confused, disoriented. Instead of the park strip grass, she lay in their cozy bed, the quilt tucked up to her chin. She flopped over, hoping to find Simon lying next to her, but found only a lonely pillow.

Voices came from downstairs, and foolish hope churned in her gut. *Is that Simon?* She threw back the covers and ran from the room. Half way down the stairs, a flicker of instinct made her stop: something in the sound of the words being said, the frantic, almost whispered tone of the voices. She froze, ears straining.

"It's too dangerous," Darby said to mumbles of agreement. The whole Covenant sat together in the living room.

"We have to help him," Wynter said. "We can't just turn him away."

Willa's heart squeezed shut. She gripped the banister so hard her joints hurt.

"But we don't know what we're dealing with," Rain added. "His powers are wicked scary and obviously dangerous. What happened today was not some small accident, like being able to explode dirt or light candles."

"He puts us all at risk," Cal agreed. "Perhaps we jumped the gun, Binding the Covenant before we knew more about his powers."

"I'm training him. I'm working with him," Rowan defended. "He just needs time."

"How can you train something you don't understand, Rowan?" Darby asked softly. "His abilities are the result of a Dark spell gone wrong. Who knows what that might mean?"

"He's not even a true Mind. He's a Water, a Mind, *and* a Healer," Cal said. "That throws off the balance of our circles. Maybe that's why none of our spells work as well as they should. And why the Covenant magic is not as strong as it's supposed to be. Maybe his condition has crippled the bond."

Hot tears slipped down Willa's cheeks as she silently lowered herself to the stairs, hugging her knees to her chest. She closed her burning eyes, dropped her forehead to her knees. *Are they right?*

Wynter said in a strained voice, "There is nothing Dark about poor Simon. He's as much a victim as Amelia and Solace."

A tense, silent pause. A pause of doubt.

Willa held in a sob, her chest aching.

Finally, Charlotte said, "Even if his strange gifts are affecting the magic, he deserves our help."

"But we are about to go after resurrected Archard," Cal said. "It's going to be bad, *really* bad. We barely survived the last fight. Is it worth keeping the Covenant together, knowing Simon may lose control in a fight and kill us all?" He scoffed. "Hell, he may do Archard's job for him."

Wynter gasped. "Cal! That's not fair. How—"

Another voice cut in, and Willa's head jerked up.

"It's okay, Wynter," Simon said, his voice low and dangerous. Before she knew it, Willa flew down the stairs and into the living room, ready to throw herself at Simon. But the sight that greeted her brought her to a jarring halt. Simon stood in the doorway from the kitchen, face pale, hair a mess, shoes dusty and fists tight at his sides. Koda flanked him, wolf eyes bearing down on Cal. "Cal is right. This is all my fault. I'm making everything harder. So I'm leaving after we do this spell in Oregon."

CHAPTER 37
Black Moon

July—Present Day

Simon's hands trembled, his mind a hurricane of the words he'd overheard. *Holy moon! What if they're right?* It made sense. Cal's logic was sound. His unnatural gifts were a mess. Of course they messed up the Covenant Bond, as much as the Covenant magic messed up his powers. The problems ran both ways. *All this time it was me.*

The assault of negative emotions all centered on *him* turned his stomach. He'd been expecting it, but the reality of it almost knocked him over. He wanted to say something; he'd planned his apology, but now the words were lodged in his throat. *I shouldn't have come back.*

Willa stumbled around the sofas and grabbed his arm. Cal started to fumble out an apology. She jerked her head to him. "No, stop! No more. We will meet you all at the airport."

Without waiting for a response, she tugged Simon after her, up the stairs and into their room.

She slammed the door shut behind them with magic, rattling the objects on the mantel. She pressed her hands flat to Simon's chest and then shoved him as hard as she could. "Don't *ever* do that to me again!" she yelled, fresh angry tears running down her face. "Not ever! How could you be so selfish?!"

Simon stumbled backwards, met with the bed, and nearly fell. Startled but not surprised by her anger, he dropped his head. "I know. I'm so sorry. I just . . ."

She threw herself at him, pounding her fists into his chest. Simon let her, knowing he deserved it. "All night! All night I sat in the gutter waiting, wondering." She punched harder. "How could you do that to me?" Her anger gave way to fitful sobs, and Simon hated himself more than ever before.

He trapped her wrists. "Willa, I'm so sorry . . ." Before he could complete his thought she pulled her hands free and threw her arms around his neck. Simon pulled her tight, burying his face in her hair. "I'm sorry," he repeated. "I needed time to think. What I did . . ."

Willa sighed and drew in a wavering breath. "I know."

Simon blinked and drew back. "You're right though." More guilt swelled in his gut. "It was selfish to stay away, and even more to come back like this."

She inhaled sharply and pulled back, holding his eyes. "What do you mean?"

Simon couldn't meet the intensity in her blue eyes. He looked away and said, "Cal is right. I'm messing up the Covenant bond, and I think the magic of the Covenant is messing with my powers. It's all so wrong and screwed up."

Willa sat silent for a moment. She moved off him and sat

next to him on the bed. "You weren't going to come back. You were going to leave us. Leave *me*." Her body trembled.

Simon faced her. He reached for her hand, but she pulled it away. Emotions knotted in his chest. "Willa, I almost killed you."

She slid off the bed and went to the window, her back to him. Koda had followed them upstairs and trotted over to sit as sentinel at her side. Her silence cut Simon's heart in two. "Willa?" he said slowly.

"I didn't know it was possible to hate and love someone at the same time." Her voice was ice.

Simon's whole body tensed. "I don't want to take you away from everything you know and love. *That* would be selfish. I can't stay. Don't you see that? I don't work in the Covenant, for so many reasons. I tried, Willa, but we can't keep pretending it's okay. I thought it would be best if I just disappeared. No one wants me here. I scare them, confuse them. I only came back to . . . well, I thought I could apologize before leaving. I thought . . ." He sighed and ran a hand back through his hair. "And I was scared of what I did, how I did it, and how it felt. Coming back was . . ."

"Then I'll go with you." Willa said, her voice firm. Her words surprised him.

Simon winced. "Willa, you can stay. I don't want to—"

"No!" she snapped with surprising bite, spinning around to face him. "Don't you dare! Nothing breaks us apart. *Nothing!* I will not let you pull away from me." Her tears returned and each one broke Simon's already-mangled heart. "If you go, I go. You are more important." Her tears clouded her speech again.

Simon reached out for her. She reached back, and he pulled her into his lap. Gripping her hips, he dropped his forehead to hers and deeply inhaled her lavender scent.

"*Nothing*." He whispered and then kissed her passionately, pouring all his love and all his hurt into his lips. She returned his fevered kiss, and he prayed that she felt his love, felt his devotion to her. He didn't want her to ever doubt that. "Willa, I came back for you. I thought it would be better to leave, to remove myself from your life, but I couldn't do it. I *can't* do it, even if it might be the safest, smartest thing to do. And I don't know if that makes me even more selfish, or sad, or happy, or . . . a lunatic. The last thing I want is to ruin your life. More than I already have."

When she drew back, her eyes were clear. She sniffed and inhaled. "I don't forgive you for last night. Not yet anyway—or anytime soon. But I understand your fear, your logic of thinking you had to leave. But it was wrong," she held his eyes, "a mistake. And if you *ever* treat me that way again it will be me walking away. Clear?"

"Absolutely," Simon said meekly. "I'm so sorry."

Willa nodded, took a deep breath, and then rubbed at the dust cemented in the creases around his eyes. "No one ever said you ruined my life. I don't have a life without you, you jerk," she whispered.

Simon gave a sad laugh. "When I started to go, to actually walk away, having made the decision, the pain was unbearable." He caught her eyes and touched her face. "I could walk away from anything in this world, but not you."

Willa half smiled and nodded. "Maybe this isn't our

path after all. Maybe we aren't supposed to be a part of the Covenant. We've kind of been forcing it all along; I guess. We could go now, if you want. We don't have to go to Oregon."

He sighed and shook his head. "I feel like I have to go. It's the only thing I can do to apologize for the awful thing I did to them all at the challenge. I can't ever make up for it, so I've got to at least help them find Archard." He looked away from her, over to the window and the clear blue sky beyond. A fresh surge of bile burned his throat. *How could I do that to them?* "But, after that, I have to leave the Covenant." He swallowed his sadness. "It's just too dangerous. I can't risk being in the fight with Archard. Who knows what could happen?"

"Okay, I understand," she whispered sadly. Tugging on one of his curls, she pulled his attention back to her. "We better get ready to go. The flight leaves in an hour."

Simon nodded. "Okay."

They fell into silence as they listened to the group moving around downstairs and then hearing the front door shutting as their coven-mates left the house. The cars rumbled to life and pulled away. The sudden quiet hummed with tension, and the air grew humid with the hot, sticky words that were not being said about what happened during the challenge, and about what would happen next. Willa bit her bottom lip, obviously wanting to say something more. Simon desperately hoped she wouldn't; he didn't know what else to say to her. She leaned over and kissed his cheek.

"You take a shower," she said.

Simon exhaled, opened his mouth as if to say something, but then quickly shut it tight. Finally, he said, "I really am sorry it took me so long to come back. I promise I won't ever hurt you like that again."

Willa exhaled, nodded and then moved aside. Simon wanted to pull her back to him and kiss her again, but instead he left to the bathroom, guilt and cowardice following him.

THE GRAND FORESTS OF COLORADO were reserved and economical. Every bit of growth eked out in a careful, steady manner, and toughness was paramount to survive the harsh mountain winters. But the forests of Oregon were wild, uninhibited. With an endless supply of moisture and nutrients, the trees, foliage, and moss grew out of control, tripping over each other to reach for the sky. Every inch of ground and tree burst with vicious beauty.

Simon stood on the dirt trail inside the towering Douglas Firs and breathed in the unconstrained energy of the place. The thick air smelled of wet dirt, salt water, and life, as sweet as ice water on a hot day. He'd never felt anything so intoxicating. He wondered, if he laid down on the side of the trail, if the lush foliage would immediately grow over him.

Gingerly, he reached out and fingered the dripping feathers of moss hanging from the trees, as soft as Willa's hair. His fingertips warmed at the touch, magic bleeding from the surface of every plant. Any space left between the trees filled with incandescent mist, somehow glowing bright despite the dying sunset light. Willa stood next to him, her head lifted to the sky, eyes big with wonder, searching for the distant tops of the giant trees.

It wasn't just the forest. Simon could also feel the extra energy of the black moon sizzling on the air. The rare event of a second new moon in one month boosted the magic of everything around and inside him; it sharpened every edge and whispered of possibilities.

And thirdly, something about *him* made everything feel different. Once the emotion of what he'd done during the challenge wore off, he felt the energy of it. Similar to how he felt after the cave, the power still hummed just under his skin. But this time it was different, more intense. The pleasure of it had kept him away from Willa all night. It scared him; it thrilled him. It begged him to accept it, to open up to the possibilities of it. Like a small voice in his head, it tempted him to ignore the wrongness of what he'd done, and instead marvel in the brilliance of it.

Something had changed when he pulled the water from his coven-mates' bodies; and it wasn't just their opinions of him.

Willa reached out, took his hand; and sparks of energy moved between their palms. All her thoughts poured into his head. He gasped at how vivid they were, how dangerously intimate, even for him.

Willa lowered her chin and looked at him. "What is it?" she whispered.

Simon stiffly shook his head, his throat dry, as her memories of his challenge played in his head. When he saw the drops of water leaving her body, and felt the desert-dry panic she'd felt, he dropped her hand and stumbled away.

"Simon!" she hissed, reaching for him.

He held up a hand. "I just . . . There's something about this place and the moon. Can you feel that?" Gripping the sides of his head, he inhaled the enchanting air, trying to clear away her memories. "I'm so sorry, Willa."

She stepped closer but didn't touch him. "For what?"

He looked up, eyes pained. "For what I did in the challenge. When you touched my hand I felt . . . I saw . . ." He wanted to be disgusted with himself; he *tried* to be, but fascination dominated his feelings.

She cut him off. "I know, Simon, but we can't do this now. We have to catch up to everyone else."

Something in her tone stopped any further apology. Nothing he could say would be adequate anyway. "Yeah, okay. Let's go."

Willa took off at a jog, hurrying down the winding path. Simon followed, dreading what was to come. He wanted to help, but things with the Covenant were an awkward mess. He and Willa had sat alone near the back of Darby and Cal's private jet. Not even Charlotte and Elliot had spoken to them. And no one had looked him in the eye. His big mistake had excised them from the group, a swift cut. Now he had to stand in a circle with them and perform the spell, knowing that none of them were sure he should be there, and that all of them feared him. His attempt to apologize was turning out to be torture—for everyone.

After seeing and feeling Willa's memories of what happened, he couldn't blame them.

Dangerous freak.

They followed the trail downward, crossed a wooden bridge, and then the trees thinned. The sound of the ocean pulsing into the shore filled the air. Simon could feel the pull of the ocean in his stomach. The call of the water. He grimaced.

Sun and moon, what a mess! I've made such a mess of our lives.

Willa hurried down a set of stairs built with railroad ties, Simon behind her, and then they were standing on the beach. The cove curved away, a crescent of dust-colored sand, tucked in between the tree-covered cliffs. At the far north end, a waterfall cascaded down the rocks, out of the trees and into the ocean, water meeting water.

Simon thought that he had never seen a more mystical place. He stopped to gaze out at the gray ocean, ever moving and singing its constant song. As he stared at the white, foaming curl of a wave hurrying forward to kiss the sand, a thought hit him, one his frazzled mind hadn't thought of yet.

Where will we go?

Simon blinked in shock. He had decided to leave; but, beyond that, he hadn't considered.

What will we do? Leave town, enroll in another school? Train on his own, alone in the mountains? Go back to not using the magic?

"Simon," Willa called. He turned his head; she stood in front of him, the frigid sea breeze tossing her long hair. She held out a hand. "Come on."

He swallowed and took her hand.

The Covenant gathered around a large pile of driftwood at the edge of the surf. Wynter held an old grimoire tight against her chest, and she smiled weakly at Simon and Willa. Rowan nodded solemnly. No one else acknowledged them, deliberately keeping their eyes on the sand or out at the ocean. Simon wouldn't admit it out loud, but he *was* shocked at how cold they all were to him, despite what he had done. His sense of self-preservation hoped for better. An opposing thought answered his disappointment. *You don't need them. You have always been better off alone.*

Rowan cleared his throat. "Let's go over how the spell works." He turned to Wynter.

Wynter opened the book. "This spell draws heavily on ocean and mirror magic. We will light the fire, and then one of us will need to levitate this mirror," she gestured to a large flat mirror resting in the sand.

"I can do that," Elliot offered.

"Thank you, Elliot. It needs to hang above the flames, facing down so that we can see the reflection." Elliot nodded. Wynter went on, "We then call to the Water and Powers with the spell written here. Using the pen Rowan found as a guide, the magic will locate Archard. If it's successful, we will see him and his location reflected in the mirror." Wynter lowered the book and looked around the circle.

Rowan said, "It's powerful magic, and it will take all our focused efforts to make it work. Yes, we have the added power of the black moon, which will greatly aid us, but our focus object is so impersonal. Normally, we'd use a hair or piece of clothing, but all we have is this." He pulled the pen from his pocket and frowned at it. "We need to set aside our problems and be one. Can we do that?"

Simon lowered his head. No one spoke. Willa tightened her grip on his hand.

Rowan repeated, louder. "Can we do that?"

There were grumbles of consent around the circle. Simon's stomach twisted.

"I'm very disappointed in all of you," Wynter said quietly, bringing all eyes immediately to her. "This betrays our sacred bond. To turn our backs on one of our own is to turn our backs on the Powers."

Awkward, thoughtful silence filled the cove; even the ocean seemed to quiet and listen. Yet no one said a word.

Rowan shared a look with Wynter and then said, sadly, "Let's begin. Pray this works. But know that we will revisit this problem later tonight at Chloe's house. No one will sleep until we hash through this. Understood?"

Quiet nods.

Willa's head suddenly jerked up. "What name did you say, Rowan?"

Rowan blinked in confusion. "Chloe. Wynter's mother. Her name is Chloe. Why?"

Willa frowned. "Umm, nothing I guess. I thought you said something else."

"Are you okay?" Rowan asked.

Willa nodded. Simon caught her eye, and she shrugged.

"Then light the fire, Darby," Rowan said.

WILLA WATCHED THE FLAMES CRACKLE to life, rising higher and higher into the air. The heat of it washed over her, pushing aside the cold ocean breeze. She clung to Simon's clammy hand. Simon's hands were *never* clammy. Stealing a glance, she could see the tension in his jaw, the fatigue around his eyes. Simon *never* looked tired.

What's happening to you?

She pulled her mind back to Wynter's mother. Why did her name sound so familiar? Why did it stir something in her heart? She didn't know anyone named Chloe. Should she? Her instincts itched, and she couldn't scratch deep enough to soothe them. Willa hoped the spell wouldn't take long—she needed to meet this woman.

Now that the flames were as tall as a man, Rowan asked everyone to remove their shoes and circle around it. With Simon close, Willa moved forward, bare feet sinking in the cold, grainy sand, and the heat of the fire stinging her eyes.

The fire smelled different than fires at home, salty, airy, and somehow . . . *blue*, despite the orange-yellow flames.

Wynter and Rowan moved around the circle to stand on either side of Willa and Simon, clearly demonstrating their place. It helped to close the sudden separation she and Simon faced. But only a little. The rest of the witches fell into place around the fire. Wynter signaled to Elliot. He lifted his hand out toward the square mirror, as big as a sheet of plywood. It lifted easily into the air. He guided it up and over the fire. It hovered there, mirror-side facing down, throwing the flames back at them.

Willa looked up to see her own orange face reflected in the mirror, with Simon next to her, eyes staring blankly out at the ocean. His reflection only amplified the change in him, the strangeness. If killing three strangers had damaged him, the fall-out of nearly killing everyone he loved might actually destroy him. She looked away.

Wynter opened the grimoire again, its dark blue cover deepened in the firelight. Rowan threw the pen into the mouth of the flames. Wynter began the spell. *"Glorious ocean, the life of the world, guide us, direct us, Darkness unfurled. Show us the witch that threatens the Earth. And we will fight to prove our worth."*

Heat separate from the fire stirred in the air. Together the twelve witches lifted their hands toward the ocean to call to the power of Water, summoning the strength of the ocean to give energy to their words.

The surf rose instantly, rushing forward to gather around their ankles. Willa hissed at its icy touch and marveled that the fire did not go out. In fact, with the water around it, the flames grew higher, stronger and soon took on a blue tint.

The Covenant repeated the spell together. "*Glorious ocean, the life of the world, guide us, direct us, Darkness unfurled. Show us the witch that threatens the Earth. And we will fight to prove our worth.*"

A strong wind rolled in off the ocean, blew past them and into the forest beyond. In answer, the cove filled with the rustling, creaking sound of trees. Willa thought she heard whispers mixed in with the sounds. She shivered at the memory of what the trees had said when she and Rowan had gone to the cave.

What are they saying now?

The wind circled back to swirl around them, the whispers growing, but so muddled that it was impossible to tell what they said. The water around their feet grew higher, and soon Willa's jeans were soaked up to the thighs. Freezing, she wished she'd brought more than a sweatshirt.

The wind died, and all eyes turned up to the mirror. Willa held her breath. The flames disappeared from the glassy surface; instead she saw black smoked curling in on itself. She stared hard, her heart racing and breath catching in her lungs. Slowly, an image appeared. Trees—aspens. And then a clearing with mangled dirt. Willa gasped. *The cave!*

The mirror zoomed in on a man lying on the dirt, the earth all around him dug up and disturbed. His body writhed in pain, and his mouth hung open in a silent scream. Willa didn't even hear the flames eating the wood or hear the ocean's waves anymore.

The man in the mirror sat up, another scream on his lips. His body was covered in the rippled, folded scars of burns, dripping with blood; but in a blink they were gone, and Archard stared down on them. Moans of fear split the silence. Willa closed her eyes, ripples of cold moving down her body. She groped to her side until her hand met Simon's.

She'd been right, her dream true. She *hated* that she was right.

Archard—alive.

Willa opened her eyes. Clear now of the dismal images, the mirror reflected only the flames and their terrified faces. She caught sight of Simon's reflection. He looked at her in the mirror, reflection to reflection, but it wasn't his face. A sharp icicle of pain hit her head. She collapsed to the wet sand, the water quickly retreating back to its proper place, rolling over her, splattering into her face. She heard Simon drop next to her.

The pain raged, pulsing cold against the back of her eyes. Despite it, she forced her lids open into slits to look at him. But it still wasn't her Simon. She screamed and crawled away, kicking up sand into his face.

"Willa!" Simon yelled.

That face. She knew it. She feared it. But why was it here? *How?* Had anyone else seen it? And why was it masking Simon's?

Wynter pulled Willa into her arms, and the pain ebbed away. Simon moved cautiously forward. "Willa?"

She didn't dare look at him again, so she buried her face in Wynter's shoulder.

"What's wrong, Willa?" Wynter asked.

Willa shook her head, her hot tears wetting Wynter's white dress.

"Willa—" Rowan started, but his words were cut short by the sudden uproar of the trees. All eyes turned to the forest, shaking and swaying of its own accord.

"What's going on?" Simon asked, tense.

Rowan's face drained of color. "They say . . . 'He's coming.'"

ARCHARD STOOD IN THE SHELTER of the trees, his heart thrumming a wild song of anticipation. His graphite eyes peered down to the beach below, where the twelve Light witches gathered around their fire. He watched eagerly as their mirror burst to life with his own image, and savored the candy-sweet taste of their reaction.

He'd expected the spell to reveal his current location, but thankfully the Dreams girl had broken the circle before it could.

Turning to Rachel, standing behind him in the trees, holding Bartholomew's grimoire and the black bag with the boxed souls carefully in her hands, he said, "It's time. Let's open it."

Something inside him had changed after the ghost spell on the blessing moon. He felt a new strength, a depth to his magic that pulsed inside him with indomitable energy. A new intuition had awakened, and he could sense the Dark magic all around him, he could control it without the aid of as many spells. He'd truly broken the will of the Powers, and now they cowered to his every desire.

This is what Bartholomew felt.

Rachel pulled the box from the sack with a velvet whisper. Archard took it from her, placed one hand on the lid, and muttered the names of the souls he wanted: the ten imprisoned ghost-witches. Then he handed the box back to Rachel. He pulled his marked moonstone from his pocket, held it aloft, directly in front of the box.

"Open it," he commanded. The lid creaked back. His moonstone burst to life, a thread of milky silver snaking out from the stone into the box. The ribbon of light gathered the souls Archard requested and brought them out, leaving all the others trapped. Ten misty spirits dropped like liquid to the ground and then rose to their full heights, a line of ghosts, eerie-white in the black night. A moonlight tether circled each neck, connecting them to Archard's stone. Leashed, silent, and controlled.

Archard grinned, met the poisonous stare of each ghost-witch, and then turned his face back to the beach.

The Light witches were all gathered around the pretty Dreamer, anxious eyes flicking between her and the True Healer. The mirror had been lowered to the sand, forgotten. Archard tasted savory revenge on his tongue. How he hated these witches and their self-righteous piety! They may have bested him once, but not this time. Bartholomew's magic was his alone to command, and not even their Covenant power could stand up to its force. Before, he had only had a taste of that strength; but now that he had consumed Bartholomew's whole book, digested it, and been reborn in a kind of Darkness, they could not even fathom—nor escape.

He would enjoy every second of their agony this night.

"Let's go," he threw back to Rachel. He tugged on the stone, testing the strength of his ten, tenuous leashes. They held nicely, each of the ghosts jerking forward to follow him to the beach. He took a few steps forward, and suddenly the trees erupted in upset chatter, their branches swaying and leaves rustling fiercely. He glanced around, smiled again, and then stepped down into the sand.

TIME SLOWED. EVERYTHING, INCLUDING THE ocean, held its breath. Willa, still wrapped in Wynter's embrace, lifted her head and looked over her shoulder. *Am I dreaming?* What she saw felt so unreal, so unnatural that it could only be the twisted illusion of a dream.

In the dark night of the black moon, the Light Covenant watched as Archard, as alive as they'd ever seen him, strolled down the sand. In his hand a stone that radiated ten strands of white light, each one attached to the neck of a ghost. The apparitions were still too far away to recognize, but cold dread pricked Willa's heart.

"Wynter, do you—"

"Yes, *yes*. Holy moon, I see them all."

A dreadful scream cut through the air and brought time snapping back. Willa and Wynter turned to see Rain hit the sand, her shirt soaked with blood. Next came the screams of all the Covenant members as their bond dissolved in the acid of Rain's murder. Willa clutched at her chest, gasping for breath through the searing pain behind her heart. Her symbol necklace grew freezing cold against her skin. The pain tasted of grief, sour and potent. Until that moment, she hadn't realized just how deeply she was attached to her coven-mates. Seeing Rain dead in the sand felt like her own death, and the sudden ripping sensation behind her heart felt like eternal damnation.

Through the sting of the broken bond, Willa looked over at Simon, also clutching at his chest. His eyes met hers, and his face said the same things she felt. *I didn't know.* Willa wondered if they would have felt this same pain walking away, leaving.

"Rain!" Wynter screamed as she scrambled to get to the girl, but she was too late. Rain's black eyes glared up at the moon-less sky, unblinking, empty. Willa looked down the beach. Archard's free hand hovered in the air, lifted out toward Rain's lifeless form.

Simon moved up behind Willa, pulled her to her feet, placing her protectively behind him. The rest of the Covenant, finally shocked into action, moved close to them, forming into a tight group. Rowan and Wynter cast out a protective shield of magic, enclosing the group inside it.

Archard, closer now, brought with him a freezing wind. It lashed at the Light witches faces and arms. Willa blinked at its fierceness and moved closer to Simon, the vision in the mirror of another face over his forgotten.

Narrowing her eyes, she tried to see the faces of the ten ghosts that Archard pulled behind him. There was something different about them—their bodies more liquid than the sheer, fluttery ghosts she knew. Another tug of dread, and then the icy fear of recognition.

She pushed away from Simon, moving to plunge forward. Rowan caught her arm and held her. "Willa! What are you doing?"

"Solace! *Holy moon!* That's Solace!" she pointed a trembling finger at the spirit of her best friend. "No! And . . . Ruby! Oh, Ruby! Amelia, too! Charles and Solace's parents. Ruby's Covenant." Willa felt her mind slip into hysterics. She pulled against Rowan's hold, every part of her desperate to help.

But Rowan held her tight, and Simon stepped forward to take her other arm. "Willa, stop!" Simon begged.

"No, no, I can't. I have to help them. It was them. I knew it! They asked for help, and I didn't do anything, and now look . . ." Cold tears poured down Willa's face.

The Covenant looked intently at the line of ghosts. Wynter let out her own shriek of terror and dropped to her knees, cradling her right arm. "Holmes!" was all she said. Rowan let go of Willa to crouch next to his wife, throwing his arms around her, his eyes alight with anger and fear as he recognized the ghost of his wife's torturer.

Archard was only a few feet away now. Ice had formed on the wet sand, and Willa shivered in Simon's arms. She didn't look at the Dark witch, instead her eyes moved from her friend to the other Light witches she knew so well, despite having never met them when they were alive. The *eyes*—it hurt to look directly at their eyes. All the sorrow and fear in the world seemed caught up in their hollow eyes.

The reality of what Archard had been able to do turned her stomach. If he could do that . . .

"Good evening," Archard called out over the sound of the surf. "So sorry to interrupt your little spell." He smiled a dagger-sharp smile. Pleasure, bright and potent, shone in his eyes. He glanced down at Rain's dead body at his feet, nudged her with his shoe. Willa clenched her teeth together.

Rowan transferred Wynter to Darby's care and turned to face his opponent. In a rough voice, his accent thick, he said, "What have you done, Archard?"

Archard's smile flashed again. "I have become the most powerful Dark witch since Bartholomew walked the earth."

Rowan blinked. "Bartholomew is a myth."

A loud laugh rose into the air. "You are such a fool, Rowan. I did *all* this"—he gestured to his own face and then tugged on the leashes—"with Bartholomew's grimoire." Archard gestured to Rachel and the large black book in her hands. Just looking at the book made Willa's stomach turn; she'd seen it before in some of her dreams about the mysterious witch. *Bartholomew. His name is Bartholomew.*

Archard inhaled loudly. "Unbelievable power, Rowan." To

prove his point, the witch jabbed a hand forward, and Hazel cried out, clutching her chest. Willa spun around just in time to catch Hazel as she fell dead, her chest ripped open, a mangled mess of blood. Willa's stomach turned violently, and she backed away from her coven-mate's body. Simon helped her to her feet and held her close.

Rowan's jaw fell open, and he stood silent for a few seconds. Then he swallowed. "What do you intend to do with this power?"

Archard laughed again, and then narrowed his cold stare at the Light luminary. "I intend to make you watch while I Bind a Dark Covenant using these ghosts." He tugged on the leashes again, causing the ghosts to stumble forward. Willa winced, aching to reach out to them. Archard continued, "And then I will kill each one of you." He lifted a finger, dragging it through the air, marking each of them. "You last, of course, Rowan, so that you can watch the rest of your coven-mates die slow, painful deaths. Then you can die knowing you've left the Powers in *my* hands."

SIMON'S HEAD POUNDED, THE PAIN like sledge hammers against the interior of his skull, demolition from the inside out. The breaking of the Covenant bond had rattled him, but something else was happening inside him, something set free. His blood boiled with the want—no, *need*—to strike out at Archard. A voice in his head whispered, *Use your power. End this with only a few words. Save them now or more will die.*

He shook his head and moaned quietly at the pain and overwhelming desire.

No! I can't use it.

The pounding only increased until he trembled from the effort of resisting. Willa, locked tight in his arms, didn't look up, didn't notice, all her attention given to the ghosts quivering behind Archard.

Rowan was talking to the Dark witch, but Simon couldn't focus on the words. At least not until Archard said, "And then I will kill each one of you . . ." Simon's attention snapped onto the Dark witch. He found no doubt in the statement, no hesitation, and Simon's Mind gift told him that the witch had more than enough power to do it. This wasn't like before, when the covens had been evenly matched and Archard had been desperately out of control. Simon knew without a doubt that Archard could—and *would*—defeat them. His heart sank with the knowledge.

The pounding in his head flared, and the voice urged him on again. *You are the only one who can stop it.*

Rowan swiftly lifted his hands, throwing sand at Archard, a cue for attack. Simon released Willa, and they used their fresh, strong elemental skills to throw anything and everything they could think of at Archard. All their coven-mates using their strongest skills, an all-out assault.

The air filled with sand, water, fire, wind, rocks, drift wood, even large tree trunks—a hurricane of magic.

But after a few minutes they realized that there was no retaliation. Together, the Light witches stopped their assault, lowering their hot hands. When the air cleared, Archard stood unharmed exactly where he'd been before. The debris of their attack strewn in a perfect circle around him, the ghosts, and Rachel.

Willa gasped, put a hand over her mouth, but Simon did not feel surprise, only irritating trepidation.

Satisfied that he had their attention, Archard lifted his free hand, throwing a handful of stones at them. Simon lifted his hand to deflect the marble-sized stones; but, instead of falling on top of them, the stones fell in a circle around them, *thunking* into the sand, red and round. Before any of the Light witches could react, a thin column of red flame surged upwards from each stone, fiery prison bars.

The covens backed away, bumping into each other, jostling for space out of the reach of the red flames. Simon's stomach turned with the fear pulsing off of his coven-mates. *Trapped!*

"Water!" Rowan yelled. The covens responded by summoning a wave of water that rushed forward and lifted into the air, crashing down on top of the trap—and on all of them inside. Simon closed his eyes against the water and curved his body over Willa to protect her from the brunt of its cold weight. Sputtering, he wiped his face and blinked at the unaffected bars. Now he and his coven-mates were soaking wet and freezing, as well as trapped.

Archard laughed. "Those flames cannot be put out by anyone or anything but me. Your pathetic little elemental tricks will have no effect. So I suggest you settle in."

Willa reached for Simon, looked up into his eyes. The frantic fear darkening her beautiful face pulled at his desire to use the power inside him. *If you're going to save her, you know what you must do. Would you rather watch that witch murder her?*

Simon flinched. Willa grabbed his hands. "What's wrong?" she whispered. Simon shook his head, unable to explain. Then Charlotte and Elliot were beside them, fear wafting off them like a putrid stench.

"What are we gonna do?" Charlotte asked.

"We have to help them," Willa said desperately, moving

her eyes to the ghosts. "We can't let him do this to Solace and Ruby and the others. It's too terrible." Glassy tears rimmed her eyes. Simon pulled her close.

"But how?" Elliot said as he turned his eyes to Rowan. Rowan, Wynter, Toby, Corbin, Darby and Cal were huddled together mumbling a spell, hands held out toward the bars.

"They can't break it," Simon said matter-of-factly. The three turned to look at him with curious eyes. He looked down. "Don't you feel it, Char? Something is seriously different about Archard. His magic . . ."

They all turned to look through the bars. Archard moved the ghosts into a circle, making his preparation. In the shadows lay Rain and Hazel's bodies, now forgotten, half-covered in debris from their attempt to get at Archard. Willa sniffled and said, "Poor Rain and Hazel."

Simon couldn't help the thought that maybe Rain and Hazel had been the luckiest of them all.

RACHEL HANDED BARTHOLOMEW'S BOOK TO Archard. He took it into his arms and moved to the center of his circle. The ghosts, still tethered to his moonstone, swayed and moaned around him, but it only gave potency to his purpose. Carefully and respectfully, he laid the book in the sand and opened to the page where Bartholomew had recorded the spell he'd used to Bind his Covenant. With a few minor adjustments, Archard knew the spell would work to Bind his own, untraditional Covenant.

Archard closed his eyes and took a moment to savor the racing of his heart and the pulse of the magic rushing in his veins, eager to be released. This moment would be even greater than the spell on the blessing moon. *A thing of legends!*

Deep breath and then Archard's eyes flashed open.

From the pages of the book, he pulled a single piece of parchment. On the page he'd written the names of all his ghost witches, as well as Rachel's and his own—marked down in his own blood. Next to his name was the Luminary sun symbol. He ran a finger over the symbol and smiled.

Then he stood.

Next to the book he conjured a small flame, burning from nothing and hovering above the sand, red and brilliantly fractured like rubies in the sun. He held the paper above the flame, out of reach, and left it to flutter there, suspended by magic.

Turning his face to the obsidian sky, with the darkness cut by the jagged stars, Archard inhaled the crackling power of the black moon, more than strong enough for his Binding spell. It was, after all, a night known for Dark magic. Fate had brought him to this moment to make magical history.

Rachel joined him in the gap of the circle, surrounded by the ghosts. Archard glanced over at the Light witches cowering in their cell and met Rowan's eye. Archard held his opponent's stare and then turned back to his covens. Lifting a hand, he summoned the moonstone; it rushed through the air to his grip. The ten strands of light still held the ghosts, and now Archard sent a separate thread to wrap around the whole circle, its icy touch pulling them together. Rachel's eyes widened, but she looked at him with eagerness.

With his witches enclosed in the moonstone's hold, Archard closed his eyes and snarled out the Binding spell.

"Beneath the shadow of the supreme Black Moon,

I summon the Powers, no longer immune,
To the foulest of wrong, the blackest of black.
These souls I Bind, though bodies they lack,
And form a Covenant, rare and Dark;
To rule the Powers, I make my mark."

Archard, with merely a blink of his eyes, sent the piece of parchment with all their names written on it into the hungry mouth of the flame. The fire snatched the paper, devouring it in one ravenous gulp. Then, in a flash, the flame snuffed out.

A tremendous rush of power, cold as the dead of winter, blew through him, settled into his bones. Archard gasped, Rachel cried out in surprise, and the ghosts moaned loudly, their voices pitching into screeches of protest. For a brief and terrifying moment, Archard could feel the minds of all the ghosts in the circle, he could *feel* their anger and grief. He feasted on it, savored it as it gave potency to the power now solidifying inside him.

Then the connection settled, normalized.

The air hissed in disgust.

The Binding completed.

CHAPTER 38
BLACK MOON

July—Present Day

First, there was silence, a slimy, thick silence that saturated the air and smothered all sound.

Then cold, a biting, vengeful sting of wind that brought with it the most horrible feeling of hopelessness and loss.

The ocean turned to ice, the curls of the waves frozen in grim white snarls. The echoes of the groans and cracks of the flash-frozen ice cut through the silence, sounding like the cries of wounded on a battlefield.

The earth suddenly jerked under Willa's feet, and then there were too many sounds to hear at once. The trees screamed out in protest, and the ground shook, disgusted at the betrayal. The tortured ghosts wailed. The Light witches all fell to the sand, unable to stand with the continuous tremors and quakes.

Yet Archard and his newborn Covenant stood strong, untouched by the aftermath of their Binding.

Birds fell from the sky, frozen to death. They hit the sand all around the Light covens, eyes staring wide in shock. Willa buried her face in Simon's chest, wanting to wail in agony, run away.

Rowan mumbled that they must move closer together to protect themselves from the cold and the quakes. Whole sections of the beach had split into great chasms, swallowing everything on top. Rocks and boulders fell from the surrounding cliffs, some rolling dangerously close to where the Light witches huddled in their prison.

There is nothing we can do, Willa thought. *Our magic is completely useless.*

Through nature's chaos, Archard's triumphant cry rang loud, more chilling than any noise that came before. Willa's chest still ached with an empty throb at the loss of their Covenant bond.

What will we do?

She peered through the fiery bars, trying to pick out Solace's face. Willa could think of nothing more terrible than her sweet friend and all the other great witches locked into a perverse Dark Covenant, some pulled from their comfortable after-life, now puppets in Archard's twisted scheme. Bile burned her throat. All Solace wanted was peace, and now this . . .

The earth grew quiet once again, retreating from the beating it had sustained, crawling away to mourn. Archard turned and sauntered toward them. Everyone around her stiffened. Charlotte moaned in fear; Willa took her hand.

As Archard drew closer, Rowan stood, instructing everyone else to stay where they were. Archard stopped directly in front of him, his slick black hair and trimmed goatee frosted with ice, but his face flushed red. One scar, an echo of what he'd endured in the cave, curled at the edge of his right eye like a warning. Something had changed in his eyes, something Willa wouldn't have thought possible. They'd grown colder, with a chilling depth, almost impossible to look at straight on.

"It is done," Archard said proudly, his voice rippling with triumphant pleasure. He held out his hands, sparking with black pops of his new magic. "You would not believe this power!"

Rowan said nothing.

Archard smirked. "And so now, Rowan," he twisted the name, drawing it out in mockery, "it is time to be rid of you and all your coven-mates." He waved his right hand, twisted and red with more recent scars, at the covens. "And I think I'll start with . . ." Those penetrating eyes moved around the circle and stopped at Willa. "The pretty Dreamer."

BEFORE SIMON COULD BLINK, WILLA's body was ripped from his hold. The flaming bars parted for a split second to let her out and then returned to trap him behind. Her startled, terrified scream cut open his heart. He jumped to his feet and moved to the bars, wrapping his hands around them despite the searing pain of his flesh burning.

"Willa!"

Archard chuckled as he set his fathomless eyes on Simon. With his arms around Willa, pulling her back against him, the Dark witch dropped his lips close to her ear. "Willa, is it? Remember me? I once had a wonderful time breaking into this beautiful head." He trailed a finger down her cheek; she pressed her eyes closed tight.

Simon pulled on the bars with all his strength, crying out

as the flames reached down to the bones of his hands. The voice in his head escalated to a yell, *End it! Do it now!*

Simon preferred the pain of his hands burning to the struggle of pushing aside the now too alluring urge to use his healing powers to end another life. But, looking at Willa, feeling her pure terror and Archard's unwavering intent to kill her slowly and painfully, there was no question as to what his decision would be.

Rowan's voice cut through Simon's thoughts. "Archard, take me instead. Take me as a prisoner. You can torture me for a lifetime, just let my covens go unharmed."

Simon dropped his hands from the bars, ignoring the throbbing flesh as it quickly repaired itself. "Rowan, no—" Simon started, but Rowan held up a hand. Wynter gripped her soul mate's arm, weeping silent tears, shaking her head.

Archard laughed loudly, throwing his head back. He took a chunk of Willa's hair in his hand, pulling her head, forcing her to look at him. Simon pressed his teeth together, marveling at how Willa managed to meet the witch's eyes without making a sound. "Do you hear that, Willa? Your Luminary is ready to valiantly (and predictably) give up his life to endless pain for you. Should I let him do it?"

"No," was all Willa answered, her voice thin, but steady.

Archard nodded. "Well, I agree with you. As fun as it might be, killing you while he, your hulk of a soul mate, and all your coven-mates watch will be a far sweeter pleasure. And then, I think I'll take Wynter next. Do you think Rowan will survive it, Willa?"

Willa did not give him the pleasure of an answer. Archard sneered at her defiance. "Simon," he called. "It is Simon, if I remember correctly from our little rendezvous in the cave last fall. Is her flesh as sweet as it looks?" Archard put his face to Willa's neck, inhaled dramatically and then kissed the vulnerable skin over her racing pulse. For the first time a whimper escaped Willa's mouth as Archard's lips left behind a round, angry burn mark.

Simon's boiling anger overtook his senses, and he threw himself against the bars. His clothes and skin hissed on contact, but the prison held. Archard laughed and then, pushing Willa with him, stepped close to the bars.

"Shall I kiss her again, Simon? Her skin tastes sweet like . . ." he licked his lips, "lavender. I think I'll taste every inch of it." Archard dropped his mouth close to his previous mark. Willa squirmed and whimpered again.

"NO!" Simon yelled.

Archard drew back slightly. "Willa, my dear, say goodbye to Simon."

Willa's bright blue eyes, spilling over with terrified tears, met Simon's. His soul screamed. She should never have that look in her eyes, and he knew it would haunt him forever. *Save her!* Something inside Simon snapped. The fight over, all hesitation gone. He had given Rowan a chance to stop it, he'd tried to break free, but now there was only one thing to do.

Simon gave in.

The relief of it ran through his blood like a narcotic, sweet and intoxicating. He exhaled, steady now. The pounding in his head stopped.

Archard moved to hurt Willa again, dropping his thin lips to her neck.

"Archard," Simon said quietly, standing behind the bars,

fists at his sides. The Dark witch lifted his head, eyes narrowed with surprise. "Let her go." Archard immediately let Willa go, but looked completely confused as to why.

Willa dropped to the sand, blinking up at Simon.

"Simon . . ." she whispered, but he did not hear.

"Drop the bars," Simon commanded next, and the bars fell. The rest of his coven-mates stared as wide-eyed as Archard, even took a step away from Simon. Not even Rowan tried to stop him.

Simon calmly stepped forward to face Archard, who cowered slightly, looking up at the witch towering over him. "What is this?" Archard hissed.

"This is your death," Simon answered calmly. "One you cannot come back from."

Archard looked as if he would say something more, but instead his face drained of color; his eyes locked with Simon's. Simon placed a hand on the witch's chest. Beneath his palm he felt the frightened flutter of Archard's heart, the easy push and suck of his black blood. A ripple of warmth moved from Simon's hand to Archard's heart, and the chambers seized shut. Archard managed a pathetic moan before collapsing to the sand, eyes frozen wide in disbelief.

Mildly shocked at how easy it'd been, Simon stared unemotionally down at Archard's dead body.

A shrill yell rose up from the circle of ghosts as the bands of white light shattered, releasing them. Rachel stood as still as a statue, too shocked to move or flee. Simon lifted a hand and swept it through the air. Rachel's neck snapped violently to the side, and she too fell to the sand.

Lifting both arms out to his sides, Simon levitated the bodies of the two Dark witches and, with a swift thrust of his hands, he sent the corpses sailing far out to sea, until they were out of sight.

Simon then turned and scooped Willa up into his arms. She tightly hugged him back but whispered in his ear, "What have you done?"

CHAPTER 39
BLACK MOON

July—Present Day

Oh, Simon what have you done?! Willa warred between feeling immensely relieved and sick to her stomach. Simon had used the power he feared and hated most. He'd saved her—saved them all—but how would it change him? How would he handle having taken life on purpose? Even if it was Archard, dead and cast out to sea.

Simon pulled back and took her face in his hands. "Are you all right? Let me see your neck." He placed a hand over the burn mark. When he withdrew, the redness was gone, but a round scar remained. He tried again, but still the circle of white skin stayed. He frowned. "There's a scar," he said solemnly. "I can't fix it."

Willa lifted her hand and felt the raised ridge of skin. *As if the memory of this night weren't damaging enough . . .* "At least you stopped him."

Simon still frowned at the scar. "I'm sorry I let him hurt you. I should have acted sooner. Are you sure you're okay?"

"I'm fine." Willa dropped her hand from the scar, too disgusted to touch it anymore. She looked up at him, searching his face.

Simon lowered his mouth to hers and kissed her urgently. Willa wanted to savor the kiss, but her worry got in the way. When Simon pulled back, she said, "Are *you* okay?"

He gave a small smile. "I think so. I feel . . . normal. Better than I have in months. Is that weird?"

"I don't know." *Yes.* She studied his eyes. Was there something different or was it just the shadows?

The ghosts appeared at their sides, no longer looking like hollow threads of liquid, but instead just as Willa always saw them. "Solace!" Willa yelled. "Are you okay? Are any of you hurt?" Willa moved her eyes to Ruby, Amelia, and the rest of the group. Holmes was not among them. Where had he gone? *Back to hell, I hope.*

"Sweet Willa," Solace said. "We are fine now. Thanks to Simon." She paused to smile at him. "But it was so unbelievably awful. I was sitting in my chair reading, and then this fiery pain in my chest started. For a split second I thought that I was crossing over. Next thing I knew I stood in a cemetery, looking at that Dark witch." She looked out to the ocean.

"I'm so sorry. I didn't know what had happened. I had no idea. If I had . . ."

"Don't blame yourself," Ruby said. She looked exactly as she had in the fall with her old-fashioned red dress, regal face, and long auburn hair. "We are free now and can return home. All of us."

Solace smiled, radiating joy. "Willa, as terrible as it was, there is one good thing that comes of this."

"You can cross over," Willa said, forcing a smile.

"Yes, isn't it marvelous?" Solace put a hand on her heart. "Both Amelia and I, we've been trapped, but you know that. And look, I'm with my parents again, and I have *all* my memories. Of course, they are not all good." She turned to Simon. "I'm so glad you are the one who has my powers. I can't think of anyone else I'd rather carry my magic."

Simon nodded respectfully. "Thank you, Solace. It's nice to finally meet you face to face." He smiled, and the ghost smiled back.

Willa sighed, a sense of relief daring to set in. "Oh, Solace. I'm so happy for you. But can I ask a question?" Her friend nodded. "If you died at the cave, why have you been at the museum all these years?"

Camille stepped forward, tall and graceful with dark blonde hair and blue eyes, the same happy round face as her daughter. "That was me. I tried to call Solace's soul away from the cave, but the spell was interrupted."

"You did the spell at the Museum?" Willa asked, intrigued.

"Yes. Our Covenant's meeting room was once there." Camille looked at her daughter and smiled. "It was wrong of me to use Otherworld magic, but I am glad it brought Solace to you."

Willa smiled, her eyes filling with tears. "Me, too."

Amelia moved closer and looked up at Simon. "Thank you, Simon. That wretched man deserved to die, *had* to die, to end what he started. I shudder to think what would have happened had he been left to rule his Covenant. But I must say . . ." She paused and studied his face as if looking deep inside him.

"What is it, Amelia?" Willa prompted. Simon stared at the ghost expectantly.

"There is a shadow . . ." was all the ghost said and then turned to Willa. "Find my Lilly, Willa. She's lost her way, pushed aside the magic. Help her come back."

Willa blinked in surprise. "I'll try, Amelia, but I don't know if I can find her."

"I promise that you will know her when you see her. Listen to your instincts."

"We must go now," Ruby said, taking Amelia's hand. "The Otherworld is eager to correct this heinous mistake. We are not the only ones who've been trapped in that box." Ruby gestured to another group of ghosts who hovered above an iron box sitting in the sand. Even from far away, Willa could see that they smiled and talked excitedly to each other.

Willa leaned close to Ruby. "Are those the souls that were trapped by Bartholomew? The witch I saw in my dreams?"

Ruby nodded, her hair floating up with the movement. "Yes. Poor things. Trapped in that box for hundreds of years." She shook her head. "Such terrible magic."

Willa shuddered with the memory of the dream and a flash of Bartholomew's face.

Ruby turned back to her. "It was good to see you again, Willa."

"Thank you, Ruby." Willa turned to her best friend, her tears spilling over and heart aching. "I'll never see you again."

Solace smiled. "Not never, Willa. Thank you for being so wonderful and keeping me company. I owe you so much."

"You owe me nothing. I couldn't have asked for a better friend."

Then, in a blink of an eye, they vanished, Ruby's group and the others—all gone. Willa turned her face into Simon's chest, and he held her as she cried. Behind them, the ocean broke through the ice, the air now warming, and rushed back to the shore, eager to recommence its eternal rhythm.

After a moment, Simon tensed, and she pulled back. "What's wrong?" she sniffed. Staring off down the beach, an odd mixture of emotions played on his face. "Simon?"

He blinked and looked back at her. "The book," he whispered.

"What?" Willa sniffed, wiping the tears from her cheeks.

"The grimoire Archard used—it's still there on the beach."

Willa turned. The book lay open in the sand, the breeze coming off the sea rustling the pages. "Holy moon! Bartholomew's grimoire. Simon, he is the witch I've been seeing in my dreams."

Simon's eyes widened in understanding. "We certainly can't leave *that* behind."

"No. We better tell Rowan—"

"No," Simon interrupted. Willa narrowed her eyes at him. "I just mean—look—he's got Rain and Hazel to look after." Simon shifted his eyes to Rowan and Wynter standing over Rain's body. "I'll take care of it."

Willa bit her lower lip. She hated the idea of having that book anywhere near them, but even more of Simon being the one to take care of it. "Umm, okay."

Immediately, Simon ran over and scooped the book up into his arms. Willa watched uneasily as he carefully closed the tome and slipped the thick metal clasps into place. With only the stars to light the black night, Willa wasn't sure, but it looked like he smiled as he did it.

ROWAN LIFTED RAIN'S COLD, BLOOD-STAINED body from the sand and cradled her tenderly in his arms. Toby did the same with Hazel's. "Time to go," Rowan said and then started toward the forest. The group fell silently into step behind him. Willa and Simon hurried to find their shoes, left in the sand before the mirror spell, and then followed the group up into the trees..

The feeling of separation was worse than before. In turn, each of the Light witches glanced back at Simon with fearful, wondering eyes. Although each look stung her heart, Willa couldn't blame them. What Simon had done didn't even make sense to her.

Walking hand in hand with Simon through the dark trees, Willa stole her own questioning looks at him. The weariness and tension had left his eyes, and his hand was dry and warm in hers. And that black, abominable book was tucked securely under his arm. She opened her mouth several times to say something, but always snapped her jaw shut again, unsure of what exactly to say or ask. Simon too seemed lost in his own head, quietly looking around at the gigantic trees, occasionally glancing at her when he thought she couldn't see.

Back at the rented SUVs, the bodies were placed carefully in the back of the one Rowan was driving. He covered them in a blanket and then moved his hand over, casting a spell of preservation that would hold until they could return the witches to their families. Willa wanted to cry again but held back the tears.

What just happened? Two hours ago, the worst thing to worry about was Simon almost accidentally killing us all, and now . . .

She and Simon got into the car with Rowan and Wynter. The rest crowded into the other vehicles, not even hiding their avoidance. Simon didn't seem to notice, but Willa felt a sharp stab of hurt. Any hope of finding a way to stay with the covens evaporated.

They drove in silence. Simon kept the grimoire on his lap, a hand securely on top of it. Willa couldn't help looking over at it every few minutes, its presence so unsettling. The scenes from her dreams, especially the poor bookmaker who had crafted the ancient tome, replayed in her mind, potent and draining. She tried to distract herself with the scenery outside the window but failed.

Soon Rowan turned off the main road onto a long wooded driveway. At the head of the drive sat a long, low-profile house, all glass and wood beams, windows glowing yellow in the black night. The house was tucked inside the trees, bending around them, cradled by them, cozy and inviting; Willa sighed at the sight of it.

Rowan parked and turned off the car. He paused, turned slightly as if to say something, but then got out of the car. *Not even Rowan knows what to say.* Simon had saved them all, saved the magic and the Powers of the Earth from imprisonment in Archard's twisted grip. They should be celebrating, but there was nothing joyous in this triumph.

Willa suddenly felt unbelievably tired and wished for her own warm bed back in Twelve Acres, Koda's calming presence standing watch at the window, with a long night of dreamless sleep. She wished they'd brought the wolf with them instead of leaving him behind. Her attachment to the animal had grown, surprising her. Koda may have been Simon's Familiar, but Willa needed him, too.

She followed Simon out of the car and up the steps of the house. A woman stood in the open door, backlit by more warm light, her features hidden in shadow. Wynter approached her first. "I'm sorry to show up like this, Mom, but we've . . ."

Chloe held up her hand to stop Wynter's apology and then dove forward to wrap her daughter in a tight embrace. Wynter blinked in surprise but returned the hug, her eyes pressed tightly shut. Chloe released her daughter and turned to the ragged group of witches waiting on her steps. "Please come in. You are all welcome. I have hot soup, bread, tea, and warm beds."

She greeted them each personally as they passed through her door. When Willa stepped close enough to see her face, her heart burst into an excited pace. The auburn hair streaked with gray, green eyes, regal face. The older woman looked just like her daughter, but there was something more, something the space behind Willa's heart begged her to see.

"What's your name?" Chloe asked.

"Willa."

"Well, welcome, Willa. Come in and get comfortable."

Willa could only nod and walk past as Chloe turned to Simon. After more pleasantries, Willa and Simon stood inside the foyer as Chloe shut the door. Willa turned to ask her a question but realized she didn't have one to ask. She knew she'd never seen the woman before, rarely heard Wynter speak of her and yet . . . A feeling of strong recognition coursed through her, as if she *should* know her.

"This way," Chloe said. She wore a set of blue flannel pajamas and slippers, her short hair slightly mussed, like she'd been sleeping or lying down, but there was pink in her cheeks and the same vibrancy in her eyes that Wynter had. She had to be in her eighties, but showed few signs of age, only a few wrinkles and gray hairs to give her away.

Willa and Simon followed her into the kitchen, a welcoming room of white cabinets and marble counters. Simon looked down at Willa and then leaned close to her ear. "Is something wrong?"

Willa looked up at his dark brown eyes. "I'm not really sure. This whole night is . . ."

He nodded, understanding the words she couldn't put into place.

The kitchen smelled of onions, fresh parsley, and baking bread. Wynter was already dishing out bowls of soup. She handed one to Willa, but nearly dropped the bowl she held out to Simon when she saw the book under his arm. "Simon! What is that?"

"Bartholomew's grimoire," Simon said evenly. "It was sitting there in the sand, and I didn't think it was a good idea to leave it."

Rowan joined Wynter at the stove, frowning at the book. "Should I have left it?" Simon asked.

"No, no," Rowan said shaking his head. "Of cours, not. I think we all just forgot about it. The question is what to do with it? It should be destroyed."

Simon frowned and said, unconvincingly, "Yes, it probably should."

There was an odd moment of stand-off: Rowan wanted to take the book, but Simon's posture suggested that he wouldn't give it up. "Simon," Willa said. "Maybe Rowan should take it."

Simon looked down at her and nodded. "Yeah, yeah. Of course." Simon held the large black book out to Rowan. "But I don't think we should destroy it until we study it."

"What?" Rowan said with surprise.

"Well, everyone thought that Bartholomew was a myth, and now we have the only evidence that he actually existed. And Willa has been dreaming about him. Wouldn't it be wise to see what's in the book, who he *really* was?" Simon turned to Willa. "Don't you agree? I mean, from a purely historical point of view, that book is priceless."

Willa nodded reluctantly. "That is true. But I don't really know how it would help us. We won't ever use any of his magic." The idea of studying the grimoire repulsed her; she'd learned enough about Bartholomew in her dreams. Not even the historian in her wanted to know more.

Rowan shook his head. "It may not be safe. This is no ordinary grimoire. But you do have a point."

Wynter said, "Let's not decide right now. We can discuss it at a better time. Okay?"

"Okay," Willa said, an undercurrent of foreboding moving inside her at the idea of keeping that book around.

Simon nodded. "Okay. Good."

"Until then," Rowan said. "I'll keep it safe." Rowan tucked the book under his own arm and left the room. Simon watched him for a moment and then calmly accepted a bowl of soup from Wynter.

Willa and Simon took their bowls to a couch in the family room and ate greedily. Willa thought it felt both amazing and wrong to sit and eat soup after what had happened, almost ashamed by her hunger when Rain and Hazel's corpses lay out in the trunk of the SUV.

No one spoke. Chloe attempted some small talk but soon realized the group was past amiable discourse.

Bellies full, Chloe walked Simon and Willa to one of her many bedrooms. This one was small, painted melon orange and had a double bed dressed in white linens. "Get some rest. There is a bathroom with a shower just through there." She pointed to a small door to the right. She moved to leave the room, stopped, and then turned to Willa. With a serious expression, she said, "I'm so sorry about what happened tonight. I know what it's like to lose a friend."

"Thank you, Chloe," Willa whispered.

Chloe smiled somberly. "Good night."

"Good night."

Willa stood by the bed, too exhausted to move, her arms heavy weights at her sides. She desperately wanted a shower to wash away the salt, sand, and memories, but the effort seemed monumental. Simon, already in the bathroom, the water running, poked his head back out and, seeing Willa just standing there, crossed to her. "I'll help you," he whispered

She looked up at him and suddenly wanted to cry. A flash of what she'd seen in the mirror during the spell invaded her mind. She'd almost forgotten about it in all the chaos that followed, and she still had no idea what it meant. "Simon, I . . ."

"Shh," he soothed. "Save it for tomorrow." He stepped in front of her, kissed her forehead and helped her undress. Simon lifted her like a child and carried her into the bathroom. He set her inside the small glass-enclosed shower, the water steaming hot and instantly relaxing. She closed her eyes, dipped her face into the pulsing stream, and exhaled. Steam rose in clouds all around her.

With the salt and sand washed away, Simon shut off the

water, wrapped Willa in a fluffy white towel, and carried her to the bed. Tucking her into the covers, he kissed her once on the lips.

Physically drained, mentally wounded, but warm, her eyes soon fell closed.

The last thing Willa saw was Simon standing at the window, gazing out at the trees in the night with a curious expression.

EPILOGUE
Black Moon

July—Present Day

Bartholomew stood by the window, gazing out at the layered shadows of the trees. Memories of his long-ago home, once also tucked into the privacy of big oaks, floated through his mind. Not a sad kind of reminiscing, instead he felt only wonder and elation at how perfectly things had worked out.

There was so much to experience and savor after the long years of having his soul trapped in a suffocating lead box with no feeling, no senses—nothing but fuzzy grayness. This modern world offered many pleasures, new things.

He'd planned it all, known he would return to a new time, but the reality of it was wonderfully intoxicating. Of course, things hadn't gone exactly as planned. No, they'd gone much better.

The plan had been to inhabit the Dark witch that found the box. Bartholomew had almost done just that, been easily pushing inside Archard's mind and body several weeks ago when a strange twist of fate had taken his soul elsewhere. A tremor in the air had stopped him, a call of instinct. He turned to it, traveling through the air to the mountains. And there— holy moon!—he'd found the young man, Simon. The young man's soul had called out to Bartholomew because they were one and the same: True Healers and gift misfits.

However, entering the young man wasn't as easy as it would have been with Archard, who was already open to Dark magic. Simon's Lightness repelled Bartholomew's soul, but the witch knew his way around such things. A simple sacrifice of the owl that had sat conveniently nearby created enough disturbance in the magic to open a crack to slip through. The girl, Willa, had felt his presence, sensed the magic of it because of her unique gift, but once Bartholomew settled himself in a corner of Simon's mind all was well.

The possession incomplete, the Light still forming a barrier between Bartholomew and Simon, Bartholomew waited patiently. Those weeks in Simon's mind had not been a waste. That time had been essential. It'd given him the knowledge and skills to act proficiently as Simon, to slip into his life with ease.

Bartholomew knew *everything*.

So, slowly he worked at breaking down the barrier, cutting back the vines of Simon's defense. All it took was one moment of giving in to his incredible powers, one crack in the door to Darkness. Bartholomew pushed Simon's powers, awakening them much quicker than natural. The boy had amazing skill—so like himself. And Bartholomew had almost had him in the pit during the challenge, had helped push Simon's powers so far, but it wasn't until that moment on the beach that Bartholomew had been *invited* in.

Now the reincarnated witch held out the thick, muscular arms of his new body, turned them over, flexed the fingers. This was what he'd been missing at the end of his other life: vigor and *newness*. A million ideas raced through his mind, with potential as an elixir in his blood. He had a specific plan, one he'd sharpened the details of before his death, but felt no hurry. He had plenty of time to enjoy himself while he made preparations.

What should he do? Where should he go? And most importantly, how did he get his book back without causing a big scene with these Light witches?

How incredible it had been to hold it once again!

After a while, Bartholomew grew dizzy with the thrill of it all. He crossed to the bed and climbed in next to beautiful Willa. Softly, he moved her nearly dry hair aside and gazed at the round scar on her neck. A strange thing—with his powers, there should never be a scar. Perhaps he had underestimated Archard's control over the Darkness.

He kissed the spot, and she sighed divinely in her sleep. Putting his arm around her, he pulled her warm body against his own, inhaling the floral scent of her hair.

One decision was easily made. He would not leave this pleasant creature's side. He wondered if she would still dream of his life as she had while he'd been trapped in Simon's mind. That had surprised him, her Power of Spirits gift extraordinarily powerful, more than she realized. But that strength pleased him as well. Brigid had been unique, unusual in her abilities. So much about Willa reminded him of Brigid.

Bartholomew closed his eyes and settled into the bed. This

girl alone was worth coming back for. Perhaps—finally—he had found a woman worthy to take his wife's place.

In the warm dark, he whispered, "Good night, my Willa."

ACKNOWLEDGEMENTS

The following people deserve endless thanks and a lifetime supply of homemade cinnamon rolls dripping with maple icing.

My husband, Matt, earns the most praise. There will never be enough thank you's for a man like my man. You are the best! To my three sweet and crazy kids—you are each amazing. To all of my family members, Harman and Bills, thank you for being patient with my weirdness and encouraging at each step.

To my fabulous agents, Fran Black and Jenn Mishler, thank you for always being there to give encouragement and to fight the battles.

Beta readers saved this book. Thank you so much, Carol Higginson, Matt Harman, Michelle Parker, and Brook Mann.

To the good people at Jolly Fish, thank you for believing in my work and for all that you do. Special and copious thanks to my editor, Reece Hanzon, who gets as excited about bad guys as I do and worked many hours to help make this book better.

Thanks to all who read my KSL column, watch my Studio 5 segments, follow on social networks and read my blog. I appreciate your support!

And to you, dear reader, thank you for giving your time to my book! You matter more than you know.

TERI HARMAN has believed in all things wondrous and haunting since her childhood days of sitting in the highest tree branches reading Roald Dahl and running through the rain, imagining stories of danger and romance. Currently, her bookshelf is overflowing, her laundry unfolded, and her three small children running mad while she pens bewitching novels. She also writes a book column for ksl.com, Utah's number one news site, and contributes regular book segments to Studio 5, Utah's number one lifestyle show.

Join in the magic and chaos at teriharman.com.